Also by Neil Howard and available
from The Lighthouse Press, LLC

Hunter's Prey
Student Body

For more about the author and his
literature please visit the web site
www.Neil-Howard.com

Bloody Mama Blues

a novel by

Neil Howard

The Lighthouse Press, LLC
Mobile, Alabama

The Lighthouse Press, LLC
Publishing books since 1998

The Lighthouse "L" icon is a registered trademark of The Lighthouse Press Limited Liability Corporation, formerly, The Lighthouse Press, Incorporated.

The Lighthouse Press, LLC is an independent, publisher previously out of Lighthouse Point Florida (after which the corporate name is derived) that has relocated to Alabama. We publish titles in fiction and nonfiction across all genres and represent established as well as debut authors. Our titles are available at or through local bookstores and on the World Wide Web. Please visit our web site for more information.

www.TheLighthousePress.com
P.O. Box 9612, Mobile, AL 36609

The Cataloging-in-Publication Data
is on file at the Library of Congress

ISBN: 978-1-932211-20-7

Printed in the United States of America
Book cover/Dust jacket design by Mythic Studios

Dedicated to my fellow Vietnam veterans
who were forever changed by a futile war
waged by an ungrateful nation.

Bloody Mama Blues

Based on actual events...

The deluge pelted the corrugated steel roof with a staccato beat. The hours dragged on, driving the damp cold deep into the bone. Lieutenant Mike Hardy checked his watch: 0320 hours. He wrapped a musty army blanket tighter around his body, but the scratchy wool provided little insulation. Despite his attempts to block out the monotonous rhythm, the *thump, thump, thump* continued its persistent intrusion.

God, how much longer? The rain had forced him to forfeit another night of sleep—*shit!*

Gingerly maneuvering himself into a sitting position, he avoided head contact with the empty bunk above. One lump from a recent encounter prompted this precautionary measure. Rather than traveling barefoot across the room, he groped for his jungle boots. His hands ached with the cold as the preliminary search proved ineffective. Where in the hell had he left them?

Ah-ha! Still wet, he pulled them on reluctant feet.

Shrouded in the blanket, he hobbled across the moldy grass mat before stumbling into his improvised desk made from ammo boxes.

Shit, he silently cursed, fumbling in space until finding the light cord. Yanking hard on the cord he flooded the room with illumination. Blinking eyes refused to adjust at first, but he eventually found the chair in near blindness.

Hardy considered writing a letter home. As all personal letters mailed from Vietnam required no postage, he addressed the envelope and wrote *FREE* in the top right corner. He then changed his mind and set it aside for later.

Four hours from now the truck convoy would make its daily trek south.

Oh God, he groaned silently. With a few more hours of sleep he could almost stomach the smell of diesel fuel and the noise from forty roaring engines. Hell, he could even endure the rain and mud.

Thump, thump, thump.

Hardy's aching bladder prompted a move to the front door. Rain assaulted him when he stepped outside. Rather than face the long walk to the latrine, he aimed his urgent stream from the doorstep.

Hell, the rain will wash the urine stink away.

Returning indoors, he grabbed a towel to dry off.

Damn—he smelled mold in the fiber. *Everything in this country either molds, rots, burns or blows up!* He flung the towel away in disgust before turning off the light.

Two more hours left to go. Flopping back on his bunk, he kicked off the soggy boots. If he could only sleep for an hour—he waited. Thoughts and images thwarted his efforts to drop off. Ginny, a former girlfriend from college came into focus. Blonde and smiling, she extended her arms to him. As she faded away, he found himself surrounded by little Vietnamese kids begging for candy. With a toothless smile, an old Papa San chased the kids away. Ginny returned to wave a sad goodbye. Another kid came back for a treat, but when he reached up for the gift blood spurted from his hand. Hardy pulled the blanket over his head in an attempt to shut out everything. He felt reluctant to conjure up the most innocent of scenes. If he could only close his eyes for a moment...

Thump, thump, thump!

You will report to Travis AFB at 1400 hours on 24 November 1970 for transport to Long Binh, Republic of Vietnam. Today was November 21st. Lieutenant Mike Hardy had three days to explore the city on the bay.

Three days in San Francisco!

Having just left Panama after two weeks of intensive jungle school training, he now lounged on a Boeing 707, flying cross-country with an old buddy from Officer Candidate School, Harry Clay. After graduating from OCS, the two men had struggled to survive Panama. Now, they laughed about the heat, snakes, rain and rugged training. It's always easy to laugh about adversity once it's behind you. Hardy still carried scars on his hand from an encounter with a black palm thorn tree. And to his dismay, he never completed the night land navigation course. Although the army presented him with a certificate of completion, he never attained the lofty status of *Jungle Expert*. Somehow, this shortcoming did nothing to keep him from his appointed tour of duty in Vietnam.

Harry had attended jump school at Ft. Benning after OCS. Later, they assigned the new lieutenant to the job of Basic Training Officer at Ft. Dix, New Jersey. Mike had skipped parachute training due to a severe dislike of falling long distances from moving aircraft. Preferring firm ground, he resigned himself to the life of an infantry officer. Recognizing this inclination, the US Army assigned him as an Advanced Infantry Training Officer at Ft. Polk, in the middle of Louisiana, in the middle of no-where. He recalled swamps, armadillos, an infatuation with the company commander's wife, and scared kids preparing for war. This was their last stop on the journey to hell.

"You pay attention to me, young man, or you're gonna die in Vietnam," screamed the training NCO.

The threat had turned into a cliché, but it always captured their attention. With a sense of foreboding, most of them assumed they were going to die anyway—no matter how much they learned. Hardy could see the resignation on their faces. He hated his involvement in the conspiracy, but he kept his mouth shut, trained the troops, drank gin, and tried to contain his lust for the captain's wife. Unfortunately, she did nothing to help put out the fire. He fought an endless battle to fend off her suggestions of secret trysts, late night swims and country picnics. Relief came after he received orders for Vietnam. Leaving her behind on the arm of her husband, his sexual frustration teetered on the verge of overload.

Harry brought him up-to-date on his experiences during the past year. He thrilled Mike with stories about New York City, parties, willing ladies, and numerous conquests. Unable to match Harry's totals, Mike intentionally neglected to mention the captain's wife; that chapter would remain closed forever. Ft. Polk was history, and now San Francisco beckoned ahead.

"Hey, you guys! Want a ride in a limo—same price as a taxi? I'll take you into the city in style." A seedy looking driver smiled, revealing stained chipped teeth. His clothes had a wrinkled, unwashed look and his 'limo' was a 1959 black Cadillac. The doors featured an array of angry dents, and the tires looked like they might never survive the trip.

"C'mon guys, I'll tell you all about the city—no extra charge."

After handing over their bags, they climbed into the chariot to paradise rather than endure more of his sales pitch.

"You guys soldiers?" The uniforms must have tipped him off.

"Yeah," Mike replied.

"Are you on your way to Vietnam?"

"That's right," answered Harry.

"Going to spend a few days in Frisco?" The driver exhibited uncanny intuition. Many others must have passed this way before.

"Yeah, three days and we're off to Travis," Mike replied.

"Got a place to stay?"

Harry and Mike looked at each other. Here it comes.

"No," Harry said. "We'll find something."

"Oh yeah, sure," said the driver. "There're lots of

places in Frisco—expensive places."

They drove on in silence for almost ten minutes. It seemed to take forever to reach the city.

Finally, the limo driver pounced. "Hey, listen. I've got a great deal for you two. My uncle owns a nice little hotel downtown right in the middle of the action. You know what I mean, ha-ha."

They had a pretty good idea.

"Ten bucks a night—each, and at the end of three days I'll take you to Travis for ten bucks—each. Now, how's that for a deal?"

Mike did some quick mathematics. He had $140. 00 in his wallet with no idea when he'd see his next payday. What the hell, all he needed was a bed. They agreed to the offer with some trepidation.

True to his word, their guide did his best to give them a quick course on surviving San Francisco. "Hold onto your money and don't give your heart to no girl," he advised. "These broads will rip you off in a heartbeat. Love 'em and leave 'em. There'll be more waiting here for you when you get back."

His positive outlook about their safe return sounded encouraging, but from the back seat of a 1959 Caddy, heading God knows where, their enthusiasm started to wane.

"Well, here we are."They'd arrived in the middle of the city, but nothing resembling a hotel emerged from the concrete. This part of town didn't look like the tourist district. They followed limo man as he guided them into a dilapidated brick building and introduced them to 'Uncle' Jerry. Jerry just happened to have two rooms for $10 bucks a night—towels included. For a mere $30 bucks in advance, they could each have keys.

The driver observed the whole process with interest, "You guys all set? Great—stupid me, I never told you my name. I'm Bill. When do you want me to pick you up?"

"I guess we need to leave at noon on Wednesday," Hardy replied.

"Great. I'll be here, no problem. Have fun." Bill waved while ambling out the door.

The two friends trudged up four flights of stairs to rooms 403 and 409. Surveying their temporary quarters, they observed that each room contained a single bed, a chair, a towel, no TV, and the bathroom was located at the end of the hallway. Welcome to San Francisco!

"Hell, we've stayed in worse places," Harry said.

"Yeah, right," Mike said. "Let's get out of these uniforms so we can check out the action."

Jerry proved himself helpful by suggesting several places of interest within walking distance—all strip joints. San Francisco had earned a reputation for promoting nude dance clubs.

Walking two blocks, they stumbled onto a club called Moe's. *Absolutely Nude Dancers* and *Girls, Girls, Girls* beckoned the lighted marquee. After they handed over the $3 entry fee, the doorman promised nothing would be left to the imagination.

"You'll see every wrinkle and dimple," he said.

With little hesitation, they paid admission to cross into the land of flesh—naked female flesh.

It took a minute for them to adjust to the low light, but their eyes soon focused on the stage. A beautiful young lady danced before them wearing nothing but a smile. Transfixed by the sight of the fully exposed dancer, the two men bumped their way toward the bar.

"College girls," shouted the bartender over the loud music. "They love doin' this shit. What'll you have to drink?"

Mike and Harry ordered draft beer without noticing they each paid $3 for the brew. Their eyes fixed on the alleged college girl who had committed herself to expanding their education. Mike had never watched a girl dance naked before. He marveled at her lack of modesty and her total abandon. His previous experience consisted of several visits to topless joints.

Out of the corner of his eye, he noticed a blonde woman walking toward them. Moving with deliberation, she slid onto the stool next to him. Mike hated to tear his eyes away from the stage, but he managed a quick glance at his new friend. She looked young and attractive, but her features seemed a little frayed around the edges.

"Hi," she smiled.

"Hi," he replied.

Mike turned his attention back to the stage hoping she'd go away, but then again—he really wanted her to stay. They passed the next few minutes in silence, until his neighbor yelled at the girl on the stage.

"Hey, Dorothy, you're being real naughty tonight!"

The featured attraction had just offered a highly revealing pose leaving Mike gaping at the sight. Dorothy smiled with glee before repeating the view for her audience.

"You really liked that, didn't you?" the blonde said.

"Yeah, I…Yeah, sure," he babbled.

"I used to dance up there but gave it up. Would you like to see me dance like that?"

He almost choked on his beer. "Sure. I bet you'd be great."

She offered him a warm hand. "I'm Clara."

"I'm Mike." Smiling, he held onto her hand too long. She seemed to enjoy the contact.

"Listen, Mike, I'd like to stay here with you, but you'll need to buy me something to drink. The bartender's a real bastard, but he makes the rules."

"Okay," he said.

"Thanks. I really want to stay here with you."

Squeezing his arm, she ordered a champagne cocktail. The bartender promptly delivered it for $10. During this transaction, Mike noticed another girl sitting down next to Harry. She promptly went to work on him, but Harry wanted nothing to do with her.

Finishing his beer, he turned to Mike. "Hey, I'm going to get something to eat, want to come?"

Clara looked into Mike's eyes; he knew the response immediately. "No thanks. You go ahead, and I'll catch up with you at the hotel."

With a smile of resignation, Harry walked away from the club leaving Mike to deal with his fate.

"Do you have a hotel room near here?" Clara asked.

Temporarily caught off balance, Hardy hoped that she had greater delights in mind outside the confines of Moe's. Then it hit him: *She's a whore!* He couldn't afford a hooker.

He winced. "Yeah, two blocks away."

Sensing his discomfort, she attempted to put him at ease. "Hey, relax. I really like you. Let's just talk and see what happens."

Reassured, he ordered another beer. They shared their life stories for about thirty minutes. Mike hardly noticed that a new girl had moved on stage to take Dorothy's place. He told Clara about his home in New England, his short experience in the army and his orders to Vietnam.

She nodded. "I knew you were a GI."

Sharing little about herself, she offered snippets about her background as a dancer, and her life as a part-time student. She majored in accounting and finance. Somehow, he couldn't see her pouring over financial statements, but he let it pass. His mind remained fixed on more earthy ventures.

"Mike, this is really great. I'm getting to like you a lot, but I can't sit here any longer. Damn rules! I hate to ask, but if you buy a bottle of champagne we can sit on the other side of the room and talk for as long as we want."

"How much?" he groaned. He felt his resources quickly

dwindling.

"Twenty-five dollars, but no one will bother us."

Too late, she had him hooked. It's difficult to make rational decisions when you're young, horny and on the way to Vietnam. "Let's go."

He handed over the price of admission for solitude with Clara. The champagne was a cheap brand of California swill, but they sat in a dark corner with no interference from anyone. Clara rested her hand on his leg, stroking it gently as they continued their conversation.

The hours passed. Mike's passion for the girl continued to intensify. At some point during their time together, she permitted him to put his hand between her legs. She opened her thighs as he moved higher up the scale. The invitation left little doubt about her intentions.

"Listen, you're a nice guy, and I don't want you to spend all your money in here. I'd like to meet you later. Do you want to get together tonight?"

God, yes! He almost screamed before composing himself. "Sure, when?"

"I get off at 1 a. m. Meet me out front. We'll go to your place, okay?"

"Sounds good; I'll be here."

"Do you mind if two of my friends join us? I already have plans to meet Phil and Dorothy. You remember Dorothy, don't you?"

Oh boy, did he!

"We can double-date and have a little party at your

place. We'll bring the beer," she said.

"Sounds great, Clara." The possibilities seemed endless. "I've got three days to party."

"Good, now get out of here before you're broke. But, before you go, give me a kiss."

Her kiss tasted warm, wet, and full of promise. Completely enthralled, he barely glanced at the naked girl dancing on stage on his way out. Humming, he strolled out of the bar into the cool night air.

Hardy walked the streets, drank a cup of coffee, and promptly returned to Moe's at 1 a.m. He found Clara waiting with her two friends. She introduced Mike to Phil and they shook hands. Clara laughed as she introduced Dorothy.

"You two have already met."

Mike mumbled something stupid. His three companions looked amused at his discomfort.

"Great, let's go," Clara said. "Mike will lead the way."

She grabbed his arm as they hurried off. Phil followed behind, carrying a paper bag with Dorothy at his side.

The short walk to the hotel passed quickly. In good spirits, the four revelers laughed along the way. Clara and Dorothy seemed to delight in their freedom from Moe's. Arriving at Uncle Jerry's hotel, Clara expressed her displeasure. "What a dump! But, what the hell, let's have a party!"

Mike felt like melting into the sidewalk.

After tromping up four flights of stairs, he ushered his

new friends into his frugal room.

"Only a single bed, wow, you must be on a tight budget?" Clara teased. Sensing his discomfort, she gave him a big hug. "Hey, it's okay. We'll make do. Let's have some beer!"

They drank for about an hour until Clara took charge. "Look, there's only one bed. Mike and I will take a walk for an hour. After that, we'll come back for our turn. Is that okay with everybody?"

Phil and Dorothy agreed with the plan. With reluctance, Mike nodded his assent. Glumly, he followed Clara out the door.

On the way down the stairs, Clara noticed his disappointment. "I wanted to be alone with you, and this seemed like the best way to make it happen for us," she explained.

They walked in no particular direction before discovering an all-night coffee shop. Mike felt an urgent need to make love to this girl, but time conspired to delay their intimacy. Was it really going to happen? His pulse throbbed as they drank coffee and made small talk.

After an eternity, Clara looked at her watch. "Let's get back. I really want you, Mike."

Returning to the room, they found Phil and Dorothy pulling their clothes back on. The bed sheets lay in a twisted shambles. The confined space gave off an odor of sweat mingled with sex. The two couples chattered aimlessly while Clara's friends completed their preparations to leave. After offering perfunctory good-byes, the two lovers found themselves alone.

Wasting no time, Clara moved quickly into Mike's arms. They kissed and groped in desperation. She seemed pliant and experienced. He felt himself being swept along on a wave of passion. Serving as a sexual tour guide, the girl from Moe's directed him to the bed.

After settling him down, she slipped away from his grasp. "Mike, I'm going to dance for you. This is only for you."

Humming a tune he didn't recognize, she began a slow, sensuous dance. Nimbly, she unbuttoned her blouse removing it without missing a beat. Deftly, she slid tight pants down over smooth hips.

Mike felt ready to explode.

Expertly, she unbuttoned the clasps of her bra, revealing two perfect globes. He sighed with anticipation. For the grand finale, she moved toward him clad only in transparent panties.

"The rest is up to you. Do you think you can handle it?" she said.

Eagerly, he grasped the elastic waistband with both hands, pulling the nylon barrier down to her ankles. Mike drank in her nakedness while burying his face in her warmth. Clinging to her, not sure of his next move, he soaked in the pungent aroma of her sex. Impatient with the delay, Clara urged him to proceed to the main event.

Guiding him back onto the bed, she began to remove each article of his clothing. She nibbled him during the entire process. Allowing her to control the moment, Mike felt like putty in her hands. Naked and vulnerable, he began to explore the mysteries of her body. He stroked and tasted each part of her. She boldly returned the favor. Nothing was off limits. The erotic possibilities seemed endless.

He floated along on a wave of ecstasy until his mind began to wander. *Vietnam! Stop it! Block it out! The girl, think only about the girl. Think only about this moment. Make love to her. Don't think about—feel her, taste her. She wants you now!*

"What is it?" she asked.

"Vietnam. It won't go away. I thought I could forget going for a while. It came back. I'm sorry."

She stroked his face. "It's all right. I understand. Relax and hold onto me. We'll make it go away."

As she held him, he concentrated on the total comfort of her body. Slowly, he began to explore her again as if for the first time. Clara's prediction came true. The unwelcome distractions evaporated in her embrace. With his dilemma resolved, they made love with desperate intensity. Each climax carried them deeper into the throes of passion until, drained and exhausted, the two lovers collapsed.

They awoke to sunlight pouring into the room. Clara said little as she retrieved her clothing scattered about the floor. After she finished dressing, Mike pointed her to the bathroom down the hall. She returned smelling of soap and toothpaste.

Sitting on the bed, she ran her fingers through his hair. "You're a great lover," she said.

"Yeah right, if I get a second chance." He had a premonition that he'd never see her again.

"Well, you're going to get another chance tonight. Meet me again at the same time. I'm taking you to dinner." Without waiting for a response, she kissed him before skipping out the door.

Languishing in bed for an hour, Mike relived each moment he'd shared with Clara. No, they hadn't experienced genuine love. Maybe vanity made him assume that she needed him. Her passionate lovemaking couldn't have been an act. On the other hand, the entire episode seemed unreal.

Pulling himself together, he hurried down to Harry's room. He still felt flashes of guilt for separating from his friend the night before, but he found Harry filled with good cheer. Having met some fraternity brothers from the local chapter, Harry and his cohorts had spent the night in unabated debauchery. Now, they had plans to indulge in reckless abandon for the next two days. Mike, in turn, revealed selected excerpts from his experiences with Clara. In the end, they agreed to continue on their separate paths. After sharing lunch, they walked away from the restaurant in opposite directions.

The hours crawled by while Mike waited to meet Clara. Dwindling funds had lightened his wallet, so he settled for a hot dog and a Vincent Price movie to kill time. No one could rival Price in his mastery of the horror film genre. Returning to the hotel, Mike napped and read half a novel. He considered leaving the hotel early, but waited until the appointed time to meet Clara. At 1 a.m. he found her standing outside the club with Phil and Dorothy. Groaning, he expected to share his room again.

Clara made a point of reassuring him. "Phil is going to drive us to Chinatown for dinner," she said. "He'll drop us off at your hotel after we eat, okay?"

"Sure, I'm starved."

After arriving in Chinatown, Phil guided them to a late-night restaurant. Generous portions of exquisite oriental food soon filled their plates. Clara insisted on paying for the meal before they returned to the hotel. Saying goodnight to Phil and Dorothy, Mike thanked them for a wonderful evening. At last, the couple found themselves alone.

After running upstairs, full of Chinese food and lust for each other, they ripped off their clothes. The two lovers fell on the bed in a tangle of body parts.

Completing their physical exertions, Mike attempted to learn more about Clara. But, in the end, she still remained a mystery. He contented himself with hearing selected portions of her life history. At one point, he made the mistake of asking if she'd sold any more bottles of champagne at Moe's.

"That's my job," she bristled. "I get a cut on all the

drinks I sell."

Passing some time in silence, Mike feared that she might leave. "I'm sorry. I just can't stand the thought of you sitting in a dark corner with someone else," he explained.

"Listen, I'm with you now. Let's enjoy the moment."

They made the most of the moment by making love three times before the final collapse. Clara left in the same fashion as the morning before. Kissing him goodbye, she promised to spend more time with him later that evening.

They met at the appointed hour for the last time. Mike hated farewells. Once he left San Francisco he didn't expect to see Clara again. She gave him an address and told him he could write…if he wanted. She would try to write too…if she had time. Mike asked if he could take a photo of her before leaving. Still naked, she stretched out on the bed flushed in the afterglow of sex.

"Take it like this," she laughed. "Give the boys in Nam a thrill." Modestly covering strategic parts of her body, she said, "Fire away!"

Taking full advantage of her erotic poses, he snapped photographs from several angles. He hoped to have them developed by someone who appreciated fine art. Once he retrieved the finished prints, he would never share them with anyone.

Mike wanted to stall their last farewell. When the time of departure arrived, she touched his face and whispered, "Please take care of yourself. You're very special to me."

With unexpected tenderness, she kissed him goodbye. With a sad smile, the girl from Moe's walked out of his life.

Bill and his 1959 Cadillac met them at the designated hour. Mike and Harry looked impressive dressed in their uniforms: two more young officers leaving for duty in Vietnam. All the way to Travis Air Force Base, Bill chattered about sports, politics, women, and the economy. The two friends would have time to share their San Francisco adventures later. From experience, Bill knew where to find their destination. He deposited the two officers and their baggage in front of the departure building. Thanking him, Mike and Harry left a $5 dollar tip—not enough for a down payment on a new limo.

The two young officers would spend the next eight hours completing paperwork and waiting. The base terminal had filled to capacity with soldiers appearing anxious and depressed. None of the replacements looked forward to this journey—20 hours on a Boeing 707, via Alaska and Japan, into an unknown inferno. Mike prepared himself for the ride of his life. San Francisco would soon fade into a distant memory, but thoughts of Clara would linger. Having shared only a brief time with her, he knew he would never forget the girl from Moe's.

CHAPTER 3
Travis Air Force Base

Time passed with agonizing monotony; seconds, minutes, and hours all merged into a mass of tedium. Mike and Harry had spent the last five hours in a customs holding area at Travis Air Force Base. In spite of the usual bureaucratic turmoil, the two friends had managed to stay together during the flight processing. Earlier, they had approached a weary customs agent as he attempted to pass them through his station. The dazed man seemed preoccupied with counting off the days left until his retirement. Feeling the need to declare something, Harry announced he was carrying, "A case of the ass."

Unfazed, the agent ignored the remark. He must have suffered through a host of indignities at this station. Mike assumed that all the agents had probably received instructions to tolerate GI humor. After clearing customs, another lethargic agent directed them to the holding area. Upon entering the room, a sign warned that no one could leave the area until directed to board the airplane. At that point, the interminable waiting had begun.

The waiting room offered cold drinks and snacks, but these provided only a temporary diversion. Bathrooms stood close at hand, but they afforded little entertainment except for graffiti on the walls. After scanning all the hand etched notices, Mike felt relieved not to find Clara's name and telephone number listed with the others. A television playing "I Love Lucy" reruns blared from a distant corner of the waiting room. Card games evolved out of a desperate need for recreation. Officers segregated themselves from enlisted men. No one spoke about Vietnam.

Mike and Harry passed the time recalling their adventures in San Francisco. Mike shared some of his experiences with Clara. He related the encounter without any graphic detail or embellishment. Later, realizing he had described the girl in reverent tones, he wondered why. She was only a bar girl. She would do it with anyone. There was nothing special about her. He tried to swallow this fabrication for a while, but he knew it wasn't true. Three days with Clara had left an indelible mark on him that would last forever.

Harry had no trouble sharing the intimate details of all his adventures. His fraternity existed to debauch and corrupt college maidens. Young ladies flocked to the frat house in order to lose themselves in the revelry. They defied all warnings by willingly placing themselves on the altar. Harry had freely indulged in the virgin sacrifice.

Mike's college sexual experiences fell way short of Harry's recent exploits. New England colleges in the 1960's lacked the free expression of their west coast counterparts. East coast students had heard about the sexual revolution, but the desperate men encountered resistance when they tried to convince their female partners to join the ranks of the enlightened. Catholic dogma still maintained a solid hold on student morality. Frustrated male students settled for 'reading' *Playboy* and hoping for better days ahead.

Mike left Harry's company after they had exhausted all conversation. Over three hundred male soldiers waited in the holding area along with a sprinkling of females in uniform. These women looked like administrative types, or nurses and kept to themselves. Mike felt sure he'd find at least one familiar face in the crowd. Most of the young captives looked detached from reality. Discovering no one recognizable from his past, he returned to his seat.

Mike was dozing when they announced his flight. Harry jabbed him in the ribs, "Let's go. We're off to paradise."

The weary lieutenant nodded without offering a witty retort. Unknown forces propelled him forward with all the other bodies in uniform. He had no control. He had no free will. He had no fear or regret. He experienced something else—fatigue, confusion and anticipation. In spite of everything, he felt anxious to embark on this journey into the unknown.

Approaching the Pan Am 707 on the tarmac, Mike felt an overwhelming sense of finality. Mentally preparing for the long flight to Vietnam reminded him of strapping into a roller coaster at the carnival. It didn't matter how much he dreaded the dangerous ride ahead. Once the attendant locked him into the seat, there was no turning back. He braced himself to take the ride of his life.

At first, Harry had little to say after taking his seat on the plane. He only broke his silence to ask the stewardess what time the bar opened.

Smiling, she patted him on the shoulder like an overly tolerant aunt. "No booze on this flight, GI. This is a soda pop run." Without waiting for a response, she wandered off to greet her other charges.

Harry stretched within the limits of his assigned seat. "Hey, this isn't so bad: pretty stewardesses, comfortable seats, and free food. Who needs beer?"

Mike had always admired Harry's ability to project good cheer in the face of adversity. He felt compelled to bring him back to reality. "Yeah, tell me how great you feel after twenty hours on this plane. You're going to need more than optimism after they drop us into the jungle."

"Relax, Mike. Things are going to be great. That stewardess loves me. I'm going to enjoy flying twenty hours with her."

So it went. Mike could never poke holes in his friend's logic. Harry seemed convinced that he'd score on this flight.

Who knows, Mike mused, *the cocky bastard might actually succeed where thousands of others had failed.* While Mike sighed in resignation, Harry waited patiently for the object of his lust to return.

They departed Travis after midnight. The lights of San Francisco faded to a distant memory as they headed west out to sea. The long journey had begun.

First stop—Anchorage, Alaska. The temperature hovered at 15 degrees above zero. After arrival, the pilot announced a short delay for minor repairs and he directed everyone to disembark. Exhausted passengers welcomed a temporary reprieve from the flight. Inside the terminal, Mike expected to encounter local Eskimos, but he only discovered people like himself in plush fur parkas. Winter had arrived in Anchorage.

Mike attempted to cajole Harry into taking an excursion outside the terminal. He wanted to romp in the snow, but Harry felt compelled to find his stewardess. Mike left alone for a trip into the Alaskan wilderness. Once outside, he felt the bite of frozen air in his lungs. It reminded him of winters in New England. His thoughts turned to skiing and warm nights by the fire. He missed the dancing and parties inside the ski lodge. He missed Anne, Becky, Diane, Amanda and the others. Skiing and girlfriends existed in another life—a part of his life now closed. Shivering from the cold, he put these memories away for recall at another time. He returned to the warmth of the terminal.

After a two-hour delay in Anchorage, the airplane took off on a direct course to Japan. During the flight, Harry still tried to make time with the stewardess named Sherry. She applied some cute moves to rebuff his advances, but lingered long enough to enjoy the game. She had professional experience handling horny GIs, but seemed to welcome the diversion during the long flight.

Mike tried sleeping to fill the time, but all attempts proved useless. He managed to doze off once or twice while listening to the drone of the engines. Something always seemed to interrupt his sleep.

At one point the pilot announced, "Good morning, ladies and gentlemen. We have just crossed the International Date Line and have lost an entire day; unfortunately, that day was Thanksgiving. Don't worry we've planned a little celebration on board. The flight crew tells me that we have chicken for lunch. I'm sure they'll try their best to dress things up. I'll talk to you again soon."

Mike had never missed a Thanksgiving celebration with his family. He sensed a mutual sadness emanating from all those around him. The lonely soldiers ate chicken on plastic trays, while remembering turkey dinners with all the trimmings. They resented being separated from loved ones during the holidays. Each passenger begrudged traveling on an airliner so far away from home. They reflected on their final destination, while praying for a safe return from the war—so much for Thanksgiving.

Seven hours later the pilot's voice barked over the PA system. "Good evening again, ladies and gentlemen. If you look below, you can see the coast of Japan ahead. We'll be landing in Yokota to take on fuel in about forty-five minutes. You can get off for a short while to stretch your legs."

Feeling exhausted, Mike tried to remember the last time

he'd enjoyed a good night's sleep. It must have been in San Francisco while Clara slept beside him in bed, but lovemaking had interrupted their slumber. Heck, he'd give up a whole month of sleep to return to her side. He could always find time to sleep later.

The stopover in Yokota proved uneventful. Local authorities forced all the passengers to remain in the waiting area while the plane took on fuel. The few Japanese in the terminal largely ignored the soldiers suffering from jet lag; just more GIs being led to the slaughter. Some concessionaires displayed a minimal interest in potential customers, but the interest vanished once the sale concluded. The short respite in Yokota offered Mike no opportunity to experience true Japanese hospitality.

Mike, Harry, and the other passengers boarded the Pan Am 707 for the last leg of the trip. The schedule called for them to land in some place called Bien Hoa, outside of Saigon. The flight would take another five hours. After landing, the army would transport them to the 341st Replacement Company in Long Binh. Mike settled in for the remainder of the long ride.

As the sun broke the horizon, an amplified voice broke through the fog of sleep. "This is the Captain. If, you look below, you can see the country of Vietnam. We'll be landing in Bien Hoa in about thirty minutes. I wish you all the very best for a safe return. Good luck!"

They had arrived.

CHAPTER 4
Long Bien, Vietnam

The 707 touched down on the Bien Hoa runway in early morning. As the airliner rolled toward the terminal, Mike watched with interest as ground crews serviced helicopters and military planes. Fuel trucks moved with deliberate haste among the warplanes. Smoke from far-off fires drifted over the air base. Outside the security fence, Vietnamese civilians rode with reckless abandon on bicycles and motor scooters. American soldiers, dressed in faded jungle fatigues, lounged around the terminal building. The passengers peered through the plane windows as the 707 came to a full stop.

The doors opened. A blast of heat and the acrid smell of burning garbage greeted the new arrivals. Mike grabbed his carry-on bag before descending down the mobile stairs. He experienced a rush of anxiety as he stepped onto the steaming asphalt. All of the passengers had read media reports about the enemy firing rockets at air bases. From this moment on their lives stood in jeopardy. Mike could tell that Harry had grasped the same harsh reality.

The ground crew herded them in single file toward the terminal building. Lounging outside the terminal, a group of seasoned veterans welcomed the rookies with words of encouragement.

"Welcome to Nam, you cherries!"

"You're gonna die, mothah fuckers!"

"Charlie's gonna chew your ass!"

"Momma can't save you now!"

"Welcome to hell!"

They looked like a rag-tag bunch with bandannas tied around their heads, assorted jewelry slung around their necks and bracelets wrapped on their wrists. All had sunburned bodies and dirty faces, and several of them carried walking sticks. Mike learned later that these were called *Short-Timers'* sticks. Each notch represented one day less in Nam. All in all, the veterans seemed like a good-humored bunch so the newcomers endured their taunts without comment.

No customs agents greeted them at this end of the trip. Reception personnel wearing armbands led them to army buses driven by Vietnamese. The new arrivals loaded their duffel bags onto $2^{1/2}$ ton trucks. After shuffling onto the bus, the men plopped down on bench seats and opened the windows hoping to find a cooling breeze. They found none. These buses were not designed for comfort. Unaccustomed to suffering from the heat, the passengers turned their attention to the escort NCO making an announcement.

"Gentlemen, welcome to Bien Hoa Air Base. You are outside the city of Saigon, but do not expect to visit *Sin City* anytime soon. No gook pussy for you, yet. We have work to do. I am Staff Sergeant Foster, and I will accompany you to the 341st Replacement Company. You will notice I carry a side arm. VC are reported in the area, but don't worry. If attacked, I will protect you."

Hair bristled on the back of Mike's neck as nervous laughter erupted. He suppressed an urgent need to check out all the Vietnamese in close proximity to the bus.

Sgt. Foster continued. "You'll be safe with me. I've never lost a cherry yet. You won't be issued weapons until you reach your assigned units. Until then, you'll be under my care. I'm not going to ask for questions, because you'll have more than I want to answer. Everything will be explained in due time. I'll leave you with three pieces of advice. Always keep your weapons clean, your boots dry, and never fuck anything over here unless you wear a rubber. Have a nice day."

So far, Mike had not enjoyed anything close to a nice day. He kept looking out the window for VC. He expected to see a grenade thrown into the bus at any moment. Would he hurl himself on the grenade or would he yell at another soldier to do it for him? He had no idea. He wanted to think of himself as heroic, but he wasn't sure how he'd react under fire.

Mike had endured agonizing leadership drills during his entire six months at Officer Candidate School at Fort Benning, Georgia. Every day at the "Benning School for Boys" his decision-making ability faced new challenges. The instructors loved to see their officer candidates wilt under pressure.

"Okay lieutenant, you're in charge. Do you attack that fortified position up ahead before the enemy gets away, or do you wait for reinforcements? Quick, you have to decide now! Men's lives depend on you making the right decision. You have to decide now! What are you going to do, lieutenant?"

Hardy never forgot that phrase: "What are you going to do, lieutenant?" At this moment, he had no idea.

Harry had focused his thoughts in other directions. "Hey, it's not so bad. Let's look on the positive side. Some of the women look good. I like those long white dresses and the black shiny hair. I wonder why they don't smile or look at us? Maybe, they're just shy or afraid of GIs. I bet with a little effort we could get them to warm-up."

"Sure we could. We'd let them get warm enough to put a knife in our guts," Mike said.

"You have no trust my friend. Look at them. They're harmless." Harry waved to everyone in sight, but only the children waved back.

"It's not a matter of trust. I think they hate having us here."

"You're wrong, Mike. They love us. We're going to make Viet Nam safe for democracy and corruption. How could anyone hate a country that introduced them to *Coca-Cola* and *The Beatles?*"

"I think *The Beatles* are of British extraction."

"Yeah, okay. There's lots of other stuff I could mention. Look at that girl on the bicycle; she's beautiful!" So it went.

Mike left Harry to continue his study of the natives. He wanted to take in as much of the culture as possible during the bus ride. Signs of poverty existed everywhere. Babies played in mud puddles. Two haggard women sat in front of a hut picking lice out of each other's hair. When one of them captured a critter, she squeezed it between her fingers before popping it into her mouth. Mike nearly gagged.

Thirty minutes later they reached Long Binh and the 341st Replacement Company. The military compound had installed sandbags and barbed wire for security purposes. Mike observed a telephone pole covered with signs pointing in different directions.

> *Los Angeles, 9,380 Miles*
> *New York, 12,462 Miles*
> *Pittsburgh, 11,981 Miles*
> *Atlanta, 11,236 Miles*
> *Yuma, 10,266 Miles*
> *HELL, 2 Miles*

The sign to *Hell* pointed in the opposite direction. You really had to appreciate GI humor. Graffiti was everywhere. One witty dogface had carved his predicament on another pole.

> *Short-timer - Only 364 days to go!*

Normal tours of duty lasted 365 days in Vietnam. At

this point, Hardy had no intention of counting off the days remaining in his tour.

Exhausted after the long trip from Travis, Mike needed to collapse on a bed. The army had other plans for him. Someone directed him to an in-processing station where he was handed a stack of forms to complete. After an hour of writing, they sent him to the medical hut. Following a quick check-up, the medic handed him a bottle of large orange malaria pills with orders to take one daily.

One GI sneered when he received his bottle. "It's a trick. These ain't for malaria. You start takin' these fuckin' things and your dick will never get hard again."

Immediately after the medical check, the new arrivals attended a cultural orientation. The instructor gave them some *DO'S AND DON'TS:*

Do learn and respect Vietnamese customs.

Don't forget you are the foreigner.

Do be as helpful as you can.

Don't get overly familiar with the Vietnamese.

"I'm goin' to get real familiar with some of 'em," a voice drawled from the back of the room.

Do learn what the South Vietnamese have to teach. It's their country, and they can help you survive.

Don't think Americans know everything.

And so it went. The lecture continued with a few more interruptions from the gallery.

The last stop was the supply room. The clerks issued them jungle fatigues, boots, mosquito nets, canteens and other useful pieces of equipment. Mike struggled under the weight of it all as he stumbled into the transient barracks. Dropping everything on the wooden floor, he collapsed onto the bed. He would have gladly remained there for days, but Harry had other plans.

"Come on, Hardy, get up. We're going to the club for a beer. I'll buy."

"No, you go ahead. I'm going to stay right here. If I don't move in three days, box me up and send me home. What club?"

"There's an officer's club next door. The beer is cold, the bar girls are hot, and the club has slot machines. Just don't get the girls and slot machines mixed up. The slots are the ones that take quarters. C'mon, I've already checked it out."

Harry never had any trouble finding the action. Numbly, Mike lifted his tired body off the bed to follow his friend out of the barracks.

The club must have served as an old warehouse before someone added a bar and a few beer signs. Slot machines lined the back wall and an old jukebox played fairly recent hits. The management had scattered a few tables and chairs around the room for those not inclined to sit on bar stools. Vietnamese girls in short, slit dresses hustled drinks to customers. *Hey Jude* by *The Beatles* boomed from the jukebox. Mike and Harry moved to the bar.

A name tag identified the husky bartender as *Hank*. Hank wore a faded Hawaiian shirt. Known as the resident expert on replacement procedures and assignments, he could judge anyone's potential for survival simply by reading his orders. Hank's prognostication skills were in great demand, but he usually chose to evade the issue. He preferred the safer role of serving as a tour guide for the transients.

"These guys are always asking me all types of weird shit," he said to Harry.

"One guy asked me the best way to get killed. Do you believe that? He figured he was goin' to die anyway so he wanted to make it quick and painless. Another grunt wanted to know the best route to go AWOL. The dumb fucker was ready to walk home and wanted directions. This place seems to make people crazy. The best thing is, do your twelve months and keep your mouth shut."

"How long have you been here?" Mike asked.

"Who knows? I lost track. This is my third tour and I've got about four months to go this time. I don't believe in all that short-timers shit. Counting off days is for losers. Every time the army sends me home they turn around and send me right back. I guess there's a shortage of good bartenders over here. I must be good. These crazy grunt assholes shoot all the bad ones."

Hank moved down the bar to wait on his other customers. Mick Jagger and *The Rolling Stones* worked hard inside the jukebox. Harry began to review all the options.

"Okay, three days and we get orders, right?"

"Right," Mike replied.

"We're infantry officers, going to the bush, right?"

"99% chance of that. What's your point?"

Harry fell quiet for a moment. "I think I'd rather be a bartender."

"Come on knock it off, Harry. Twelve months and you'll be right back home at the frat house telling war stories. College girls love war heroes."

Neither of them believed this, but they accepted the fiction rather than having to deal with the reality. A popular study predicted that new lieutenants only lived for about twenty-four hours after hitting the bush. The novices usually ended up iced by the gooks, or killed by their own men.

Hank returned as they wrapped up their contemplations. Refilling their glasses, he offered some suggestions. "There's a movie in the Mess Hall at 1900. John Wayne, I think. We've got a *Steam and Cream* on the other side of the compound. But there's no action there, except a steam bath and massage. They've got better places outside. You could always stay here to take advantage of my charm and wit. Just don't ask me no war questions. I've got no answers, and I'd probably lie anyway. The war's not here, it's outside this bar. Have a great time in Long Binh, but don't leave the compound. We're afraid you might try to hump your sorry asses back home."

Mike and Harry discussed the options, but in the end

Mike left the bar to collapse in bed. Exhaustion and beer ended any need for more social activity. Harry remained behind to work his magic on the bar girls. Mike would hear all about the conquests in the morning. Weaving with fatigue toward his bunk, he landed heavily on the mattress. Sleep came quickly. He remained comatose on his bed throughout the night.

Surprisingly, Harry had little to say the next morning. He mumbled something about a girl named Lily, but refused to elaborate. Mike joked that *Mighty Casey* must have struck out at the plate. Uttering an obscenity, Harry walked away. Mike later found out the lady in question belonged to Hank.

The second day proved uneventful. Mike endured a haircut from an old Vietnamese man with shaking hands. His ears survived intact. After marking all his new equipment with his name, he repacked his duffel bag. Later that morning, the new replacements sat through more mind-numbing briefings. Someone on the staff announced that they'd receive their orders the next day.

Harry still felt compelled to explore, so he and Mike traveled to the steam bath. They undressed, wrapped themselves in towels, and entered the steam room. After fifteen minutes of hot steam, they showered their sweating bodies before moving to the massage tables. Girls in short, white uniforms waited to complete the process. They oiled, pounded, and whacked the two men for thirty minutes. Hardy tried to converse with his assailant on several occasions, but she ignored his attempts. The young woman seemed bent on completing her routine without interruption. He remained silent until she finished her ministrations.

They spent more time with Hank during their second night in Long Binh. The bartender regaled them with more stories about nut cases who had entertained the replacement company.

"One guy wanted to go home so bad, he ran naked through the compound screaming. I guess he wanted everyone to think he was crazy. The Vietnamese thought it was a real hoot. They laughed for weeks after it happened. Never saw them so happy. Anyway, the MPs locked him up and sent him home in chains—never a dull moment around here."

Looking sheepish during Hank's monologue, Harry still suffered from Lily's rejection the night before.

Hank didn't believe in holding a grudge. "Hey, don't worry about it. Lily's been around. I'm just not ready to share her with anyone. You'll find your own girl. They're all looking for GI boyfriends. It's their only chance to live the American dream. C'mon and relax; I'll buy you a beer."

After that, they ended-up best friends. Hank made it a point to educate Harry on how to succeed with Vietnamese women. Harry hung onto every word. Mike digested several bits of wisdom before wandering over to the slot machines. He'd found out long ago that some mysteries are best solved alone. He wanted the satisfaction of making his own discoveries. Expecting to gain more experience after each contact with the opposite sex, Mike hoped to live long enough to complete his education.

The big day arrived. At 0900, the replacements headed for company headquarters to receive their orders. Mike had not slept much during the previous night. He anticipated the worse, but at the same time expected to feel disappointment if he didn't receive an assignment to an infantry unit. The army had trained him to fight and lead men into battle. Now, he faced the moment of truth.

"Clay!"

Harry walked up to claim his envelope. He didn't tear it open at once, but walked off to face the moment in private.

"Hardy!"

Mike's arm felt heavy as he reached for his envelope. Most of the GIs tore open their envelopes immediately. Mike could hear cheers and groans behind him as he walked away. He regarded his envelope for some time as he considered all the possibilities. Unable to wait any longer, he ripped open the envelope to determine his future.

You will report to the Da Nang Support Command for assignment to the 73d Transportation Company, Chu Lai.

What? Support Command? Transportation Company? Where the hell was Da Nang or Chu Lai? How could this happen? For some reason, the army had not assigned him to an infantry unit. Although he'd trained as an infantry officer, the army had plans to send him to a truck company. Unless the powers above changed their minds, Mike could look forward to a future as a REMF! REMF was an acronym for *Rear Echelon Mother Fucker*. He rushed to find Harry.

He located Harry leaning against the barracks building holding his orders by his side. "What did you get?" Mike asked.

Harry handed over his orders without saying a word.

You will report to the Saigon Support Command for assignment to the 44th Military Intelligence Group.

"What's going on here? There must be some mistake," Mike croaked. He handed his orders to Harry. "I can't drive a truck, and you haven't been trained in MI."

"Somebody must have screwed up," Harry said. "Our names and service numbers are right. I'm going to find out what's going on."

Mike followed him back to company headquarters.

The replacement NCO could offer no insight. "These things happen. They must not need infantry officers right now."

"What?" Harry replied in shock. "I hear they're dropping like flies. Replacements are needed all the time."

"Listen, take my advice. Don't fight it. You lucked out! You might just get to go home alive," he said.

Harry stared at the NCO in total disbelief and said, "I don't believe this shit."

He sounded like someone who had just received bad

news. Sharing his disappointment, Mike knew how he felt. At the same time, he experienced a surge of relief. Comforting words like *survive, alive,* and *home* filled him with great satisfaction. What the hell, he'd learn how to drive a truck.

Mike and Harry said their good-byes the next day. Harry climbed aboard a bus for Saigon, while Mike headed for a flight north to Da Nang. Mike didn't expect to see his friend again anytime soon, and knew that he'd miss his company. The army had determined that they go in different directions to lead separate lives. Friendships in the military always ended-up as transitory. Hopefully, he'd make new friends during this time in Vietnam.

Mike climbed aboard the old Air Force C-123 with several other replacements heading north. They all looked young, and they all had assignments to the bush. He felt a twinge of guilt traveling in their company, but he had no control over his circumstances—the die had been cast. No matter what the assignment, each soldier had a responsibility to do his duty.

The C-123 shook and rattled as it left the ground. The pilot pointed the plane north. More questions formed in Mike's mind, but the answers would come soon enough. Da Nang and Chu Lai waited.

"Gentlemen, welcome to the Da Nang Support Command. I am Col. Alfred E. King, Chief of Staff. Brigadier General Robert Lancaster is the Commander of the Support Command. He sends you his regards and hopes you all have successful tours of duty. The Da Nang Support Command exists to provide logistical support to the entire northern region of South Vietnam. We provide the bullets and chow to keep our troops in the field. You are now part of that team. The war in Vietnam can't be won without us. You all come from different backgrounds and have different areas of expertise. You will use your skills to contribute to the team. Each of you has an important role to play to help us bring home a victory." So it went.

Col. Alfred E. King must have worked as a high school football coach in his past life. During the entire presentation, he puffed and paced as he whipped his troops into shape before the big game. Unimpressed, Hardy had observed this technique too often in the past. To shut out the posturing, he let his mind drift away.

During an earlier briefing, Mike learned that Da Nang was the largest city in South Vietnam north of Saigon. The city supported a major US Air Force Base, and a large contingent of US Army personnel. As a result of this strong US presence, the local economy thrived and vice ran rampant. Everyone competed for GI dollars. Everything was available for sale.

The army kept Hardy confined to the processing center during his short stay at the Support Command. Da Nang seemed like an unnecessary stop on the way to his final destination, but no one ever deviated from established procedure. He accepted this inconvenience as part of the process. With little time to enjoy the sights, he hoped to return for another visit. During his initial glimpse of the city, he observed that French influence surfaced everywhere: restaurants, wine shops, bakeries, and clothing stores. Entire sections of Da Nang looked distinctly European, or at least what he perceived as European. This assignment counted as his first excursion away from American soil. Arriving in Vietnam, he experienced the pressure of traveling into a foreign country for the first time in his life. Unfortunately, this trip had carried him deep into a war zone. He viewed the war not as a conflict between different ideologies, but rather as a staged political event. Could he die for a cause without fully understanding the motives of the key players? The magnitude of this predicament left him with the added burdens of anxiety and confusion.

The others in his party seemed just as confused and anxious. He had little opportunity to learn about them, although they shared the common experience of transients thrown together at the behest of the army. The army's purposes had nothing in common with their own, but the new arrivals departed for their assignments without protest. Leaving protest to others back in the States, these soldiers performed their duty for reasons uniquely personal to each man.

Hardy hated a number of things about the army. He hated those who used their power for the mere purpose of manipulating others. He hated the bureaucracy and the confusion it caused. He hated the paperwork, the waiting, and the long lines. He hated the fallacy of unquestioned leadership and the theory of blind obedience. But, in spite of everything, he felt proud of his involvement in the war effort. Somehow, he wanted to make an impact.

Mike thought about Hank the bartender's simple formula for survival. The bartender lived in his own world, never counted off the days remaining in his tour of duty, and never attempted to shape opinion. Hank had found the perfect compromise. He did his job and kept the beer cold. Mike knew he had to find his own answers, but the path to enlightenment seemed fraught with obstacles. At this moment, his biggest obstacle was finding transportation to his new assignment—the 73d Transportation Company in Chu Lai. Consulting a map, he found Chu Lai located 60 miles south of Da Nang.

Everyone at the Support Command seemed too busy to offer much help or advice. One member of the staff muttered something about a chopper hop to Chu Lai. Another pencil pusher advised him to travel during daylight, because the MPs closed the roads at night. Although Mike had received his assignment, no one could tell him how to get there. This tour of duty looked like a blind date with destiny. The army had left him to his own devices.

Good fortune came his way in the form of Staff Sergeant Buddy Wallace. He met Buddy outside the headquarters building loading mailbags into the back of a jeep. Mike stopped to ask him directions to Chu Lai.

"I could tell you how to get there, but you're shit out of luck. Chopper left over an hour ago—last one out today," Buddy said.

Buddy had the rumpled, faded look of a veteran. Unmilitary hair hung over his ears, and his face featured a three-day stubble. He seemed unimpressed to address a lieutenant in the US Army. Hardy let the breach of military courtesy go without comment. He'd learned to accept this new form of relaxed discipline.

"Shit, you'd think someone would help me get out of here."

"You're new in-country," Buddy said. "You might as well get used to the fact the army doesn't give a fuck about you. The only way to survive over here is for GIs to help each other out."

"Yeah, well thanks. I think I'll try to find a bunk for the night."Mike started to walk away.

"Hey, relax. I'll take you to your new home. I'm heading that way right now. It's a two-hour drive, and I could use the company. As I said before, I'm Buddy Wallace. If you want to act like a military asshole call me Sergeant Wallace. My friends call me Buddy." Smiling, he offered his hand.

Experiencing some awkwardness, Hardy felt temporarily unnerved by this informality. However, he quickly warmed to Buddy's friendly demeanor. Right now, he needed a friend.

"Thanks a lot. . . ah, Buddy," he said.

"Good, you're learning fast. You'll do okay. I've seen a whole bunch of shit birds with shiny bars go down in flames because of bad attitudes. Life's too short over here to make enemies."

"I've got a lot to learn," Mike said.

Mike accepted Buddy's offbeat philosophy, knowing a number of fellow officers who rated as shit birds. He made a vow not to join their company.

"Come on, let's go. I'll give you the scenic tour."

Mike threw his bags into the back seat. Trying not to act like a tourist, he still felt curious about his surroundings. He pounded Buddy with questions during the entire trip.

After answering Mike's questions, Buddy shared his personal view of the war. He also explained the futility of trying to stop the North Vietnamese. "Gooks don't give a shit who rules the country. They just want to be left alone to farm and fuck Mama San. They only join the VC to protect their families. Otherwise, Charlie would blow them all away. Fear makes them join up. All that other propaganda is bullshit."

"What do you do?" Mike asked.

"I run mail and dispatches between Chu Lai and Da Nang several times a week. The old man hates my sorry ass so he tries to keep me out of the way. Since I perform little favors for him on the side, he doesn't want to lose me completely. He likes old booze and young pussy. He hates the fact that he owes me for supplying his vices."

"Sounds like you've got it made," Mike said.

Buddy laughed at this assessment. "Hey, you do what you can to survive. Most everyone has a little side-action over here. You'll find out for yourself. Believe it or not, I used to have a real addiction to doing things by the book. This place changed all that. It's real easy to cross the line —you'll cross it, too. The only thing to remember is: don't get in so deep that you can't dig your way out. I've seen lots of losers crash and burn over here. After you've been around for a while you'll know what I mean. I'll look you up in six months to check up on you."

Mike had heard about the availability of sex and drugs in Vietnam. However, he couldn't see himself working as a pimp or a drug lord. He planned to survive by doing his job well enough to return home in one piece. Opportunities might arise to sample the available pleasures, but he had no intention of participating in the corruption.

Hardy turned the discussion to other topics. "Tell me about Chu Lai."

"It's a great place! Best assignment in Nam. It's right on the South China Sea—beautiful beaches, clubs, and recreation areas. 'Course, it's surrounded by barbed wire, and Charlie shoots rockets at us every night. Otherwise, it's a little piece of heaven."

"Sounds like a dream vacation," Hardy said.

"You'll like it," Buddy said. "Great place to do business."

Buddy could never stray too far away from his adventures in free enterprise. Hardy made it a point not to ask about his business dealings. He tried to focus on the *true* nature of their mission in this country. No matter how much he tried, Mike couldn't sway Buddy from discussing his forays into the world of vice. As they drove on, Hardy listened in silence for the rest of the trip.

"Okay, you're home. Welcome to Chu Lai."

As they turned off the highway, two large gates opened wide for them. The MP on duty waved them in.

"73d Transportation, right?" Buddy asked. "I know where you guys hang out. You're going to live on top of Chu Lai Mountain. The VC just love the place. It makes a great target for their rockets!"

In reality, Chu Lai Mountain was a large sand hill at the far end of the compound. Buddy said you could see the ocean from the top. A sign greeted them at the entrance:

WELCOME TO
THE 73D TRANSPORTATION COMPANY
"WE DELIVER ANYTHING, ANYWHERE, ANYTIME!"

Hardy liked the slogan, but he didn't care much for the surroundings. Roaring trucks spewed noxious diesel fumes throughout the company area. Mechanics walked around the compound covered with grease. Dogs barked at Vietnamese civilians squatting in front of metal buildings. Finding nothing that resembled a headquarters building, he ended-up having to ask directions.

Buddy unloaded his passenger in front of a primitive hut made of plywood and tin. Shaking hands, Buddy left him with one last piece of advice. "Keep your ass covered!"

With a booming laugh, he drove off in his jeep. Hardy felt certain their paths would cross again.

The hut felt like a furnace inside. A clanking metal fan struggled to move the sweltering air around. Flies buzzed overhead, while a solitary GI tapped at an ancient typewriter.

"I'm reporting for duty," Hardy said.

After he stopped his pecking, the clerk turned to face him. He seemed irritated by the interruption. "You got orders?"

"Yeah, right here." Hardy reached into his briefcase.

"You're an infantry lieutenant. What are you doing here?" The clerk appeared less than thrilled to address an infantry officer.

"I have no fucking idea. The army sent me. Where's the C.O?"

"Captain Adams. He's around here somewhere. Boy is he goin' to be pissed off!"

So far, the introductions had not gone well. Hardy had to tough it out. He fired off his best imitation of John Wayne. "Listen!Keep your damn opinions to yourself. Go find him right now, and tell him I'm here."

"All right, it's your funeral. The old man's in a rotten mood." He shuffled off muttering.

Hardy waited for his first meeting with Captain Phillip Adams. He mumbled to himself. "I don't give a shit. I'm in a rotten mood too."

Adams arrived five minutes later. As he proceeded toward his office, he shot the new lieutenant a look of contempt. "Come in here," he snapped.

The clerk smiled with smug satisfaction as Hardy passed by his desk. After entering Capt. Adams office, Mike offered a crisp salute. He almost gave the company commander the 'Lieutenant Hardy reporting for duty, sir' routine, but thought better of it. Adams sank into his chair ignoring the salute. The captain's eyes glared icy blue; his face looked like a pale, pockmarked battlefield. Hardy thought it odd that Adams had no suntan after spending months in Vietnam.

The company commander viewed the new lieutenant with something akin to discovering fresh dog turds on his desk. "What the hell are you doing here? I didn't request any lieutenants. I've got more than enough already. The ones I have are qualified transportation officers. I've got no use for a grunt in my truck company!"

Welcome to Chu Lai.

Hardy considered a number of different responses. He wanted to spit in the irate man's eye, but opted for a less drastic reply. "I'm sorry you're disappointed, but I didn't request this assignment. I expected to receive orders for an infantry unit. Somehow, the army decided to send me here."

"Bullshit! I'm not disappointed... I'm... I'm pissed off," he snorted. His attitude conveyed innate meanness. "Go wait outside. I'm going to call battalion to straighten this crap out."

Hardy retreated from the office. The clerk shook his head as the newcomer entered the orderly room. The gesture wasn't intended as a show of sympathy; it merely confirmed a prediction come true. Returning to his typing, he left Hardy largely ignored. Mike heard fragments of the telephone conversation coming from the next room.

Adams alternated between whispering and yelling into the mouthpiece. "Who sent the asshole here? Bullshit, I refuse... What am I supposed to do with... I need drivers, not... Great! Fucking, great! Is that the final...? Thanks a lot!" He slammed down the phone before storming out of his office.

"Okay, I'm stuck with you. Just stay out of my way. Find your own place to bunk down—useless grunt!" Pushing past Hardy, he stomped outside.

After Adams moved safely out of range, Mike said, "Nice to meet you, too."

"The old man hates the infantry," the clerk said.

"Well, this looks like my lucky day. I'm stuck in a truck company with a C.O. who hates grunts."

"The other guys are okay. It's just that the old man gets a bug up his ass sometimes."

"Great. Where do I sleep?" Hardy asked.

"The officers all live in the hooch on the hill, but there's no room. The rest of us live down here. There's an old storage hut next to the officers' hooch, but it's in real rough shape. You could probably fix it up. It might work out. I guess I can find you a cot."

"Thanks, I'll go check it out."

Grabbing his duffel bag and briefcase, Mike trudged up the dusty hill. He found the abandoned hut balanced precariously on ammo boxes. The shack featured a missing front door and large rips in the screen windows. Groaning, the weary traveler realized he had found his new home.

Buddy's observation had proven correct. Mike could view the ocean from the top of the sandy hill. He hoped his new home wouldn't end up as a VC target. The distraught man surveyed his surroundings before moving his duffel bag into the decrepit dwelling. The floor buckled and creaked under his weight. He gingerly settled down on an upturned wooden box. Burying his face in his hands, he considered his predicament. After traveling halfway around the world, his journey had ended at an old hut on top of a dirty hill in the middle of a war zone. The infantry lieutenant had no idea what other surprises waited. A sense of dread gripped his chest as he considered his prospects for the future.

The wind whipped sand across the top of the dusty hill. The boards in the old shack groaned with each new gust. Hardy left his perch on the ammo box to wander outside. His eyes watered in response to an instant invasion of grit. Blinking several times, he tried to clear his vision with a handkerchief. Through the haze, he noticed someone walking up the hill toward him. The newcomer stood about medium height, with a droopy mustache covering his upper lip, and dark aviator glasses obscuring his eyes. The man moved with a sense of purpose. When he came into close range, Mike could see lieutenant insignia on his collar.

"Hi, I'm Wiley Parks," the lieutenant called out. "Johnson told me we'd inherited an infantry officer. We don't get very many of you types around here, so I thought I'd come up and take a look for myself. Damn, if you don't look almost human!"

Smiling, Wiley offered Hardy his hand. Almost six inches shorter than Mike, Wiley projected none of the resentment expressed by the company commander.

"Mike Hardy. Thanks for the welcome, but the CO doesn't think I'm human. He hates grunts."

"Don't let Adams bother you. He'll come around,"

Wiley said. "I heard that he used to be in the infantry, but they threw him out. Now he's pissed off at the world because he didn't earn a Combat Infantry Badge. Don't take it personally."

"Not me. I need occasional rejection to keep me humble."

"Nice place you've got here," Wiley said. "We were thinking about blowing up this dump for practice, but now you can call it home."

"Is this the best you've got?" Hardy asked.

"We weren't expecting any more company, and our hooch only holds four. I think we have some extra cots on hand and screen for the windows. First thing we need to do is reinforce the foundation or you'll roll down the hill. Let's get some cement blocks. I'll give you a hand."

They worked for nearly two hours lugging the heavy blocks up the hill. Mike used a steel pole to lift each corner of the hooch while Wiley set the blocks in place. PFC Johnson arrived with a cot and mattress as they struggled with the foundation. After watching the two officers labor at the task, he hurried off without offering to help.

"There, that's a lot better," Wiley said. "You should feel pretty secure unless Charlie drops a rocket on your ass. By the way, you'd better fix up that old bunker over there. If we get attacked you'll need to jump in a good hole. I noticed some empty sandbags near the latrine. They smell like shit, but I guess they'll still hold sand."

Mike wanted to ask if the VC used the hill as a regular target, but he let it pass. "Thanks, you've been a great help." Mike shook his hand firmly.

"Hey, no problem," Wiley said. "I'm one of the few people around here who likes grunts. We truckers can be real snobs. Come on, let's go get a beer. We've earned it."

Hardy followed him to his hooch. Wiley made his way to a small cubicle, and offered Mike a seat on his bunk. The room had no chairs, only ammo boxes for furniture. The inhabitants kept their beer in a small refrigerator in the center of the room. Wiley hadn't exaggerated; no extra space remained for additional residents. He returned with a cold brew in each hand.

"Home sweet home," he said.

Mike quickly warmed to Wiley. Anxious to learn more about his new unit, he took several swigs of the cold beer. The beer provided temporary relief from the aches and tensions of the day.

"Adams and I live here with two other guys—Al Miller and Joe Tice. Al and Joe are both out on the road," Wiley explained. He went on to tell Mike about convoy duty and the unit mission.

"We have mostly truck drivers and maintenance types in the company, with a few cooks and administrative types thrown in. Convoys go out every day with one of us in charge, and we party every night at the club. That's about it—good duty and hardly anybody gets killed—on purpose."

Taking a long gulp of his beer, Mike encouraged Wiley to explain the getting killed part.

"It's no big deal. The VC take pot shots at us every once in a while. Most of our casualties are from accidents or drugs. Dumb shits fall off the trucks or overdose on *horse, smak, heroin,* or whatever they call the crap. GIs think heroin isn't addictive if they snort it, but it's 90% pure over here. They get hooked real easy, and then they're fucked. There's a rumor running around that the VC supply the shit to keep us spaced out. We had a guy get so high last week that he drove his truck into a rice paddy. He started screaming when we tried to pull him out. He thought we were trying to cut off his head. He's still locked up in a padded room. Take my advice and stick to beer or grass. Anything else will fry your brain."

They finished their beers and walked outside.

"Take some time to get settled," Wiley advised. "The old man won't put you on the road for a while. It took a month before he trusted me to go out alone. I'll come get you after chow, and we'll go to the club. They've got a floorshow tonight instead of a movie. We never miss live shows around here. Congratulations, you're about to be introduced to Chu Lai nightlife. See you later." Waving, he took off down the hill.

Hardy spent the better part of the afternoon settling into his new home. After finding a broom, he moved most of the dirt outside. He set up the bunk and unrolled his sleeping bag on the mattress. Additional chores included fixing loose boards, arranging empty boxes into furniture, and unpacking his duffel bag. Finding nothing else to improve his surroundings, he decided to delay any further upgrades.

Lieutenant Al Miller dropped by as Mike finished his work. Unlike Wiley, Al Miller had a large, bearish appearance. A thick layer of dirt covered his uniform, and he carried his M-16 by the handle. At first glance, he looked fearsome until he cracked a crooked smile.

"You must be Hardy. I'm Al Miller, the meanest road horse in gook land. How ya doing, Grunt?" Grabbing Mike's hand in his rough paw, he shook it vigorously.

"Word's out all over camp that we got us a grunt on board. Somebody sure did you wrong by sending you to the ol' 73d," he drawled.

"Yeah, it's nice to meet you, too." Mike rubbed his hand trying to bring back the circulation.

"Looks like you're all settled," Al observed. "We only provide the best quarters for our guests. Man, I'm parched. This gook dust dries me up faster than piss on hot asphalt. Let's go get a beer."

Mike followed him to the hooch. Reaching for a towel, Al threw the M-16 on his bunk.

"Have a seat, Hardy. I'll be right back."

Leaving his guest perched on an ammo box, Al left to wash off several layers of grime. Mike spent the time checking out the symbols of Al's existence. Photos on the wall showed Al with his arms around a pretty woman—his wife? Other photos portrayed him drinking beer with friends, holding up a string of fish, and sitting on the hood of a classic Ford Mustang. Mike smiled at these images of a regular guy enjoying his life.

Mike continued his visual search of the area. His eyes fell on a sign that read, 'Old truckers never die; they just run out of gas!!' He chuckled at the cartoon of a fat old trucker bent over to expel a fart. Now, he had a good idea about Al's sense of humor. The burly man had a penchant for slapstick.

"Hot damn, that feels better!" Al returned dressed in olive green underwear and carrying two beers in his hairy mitts. "Here, catch!"

He threw one of the cans at Hardy from across the room. Mike jumped from the ammo box to keep it from hitting the floor. Falling to his knees, the beer landed safely in his grasp.

"Nice catch," Al said. "We'll need you on our football team."

Puncturing his beer can, Al tossed the opener to Mike. The guy must have flunked Basic Etiquette 101. Snagging the opener with his free hand, Mike held the can at arm's length while he penetrated the top. Foam spewed out the hole in a volcanic blast. He tried to catch the spray in his mouth, but most of it ended up on his face. Finishing off his can of suds in three gulps, Al threw the empty at a trash box. Missing the box, the can clattered to the floor. Shrugging, Al reached for a Hawaiian print shirt.

"You heard about the floor show tonight?" he asked. "We always go early to get a table up front. Sometimes, the girls go topless and sit on our laps. I love it when they stick one of those things in my ear. Are you goin' to join us?"

"Sure," Mike replied. "Wiley said he was going to introduce me to Chu Lai night life."

"That Wiley is a pisser! Wait 'til you see him in action. Nice quiet boy with glasses—right? After a few beers, he'll be on his knees trying to sniff the girls in the crotch."

Lieutenant Joe Tice walked in as Al described Wiley's enjoyment of carnal pursuits. Joe sported a plump physique covered with dust from the road. He seemed out-of-place dressed in jungle fatigues with a forty-five-caliber pistol on his hip. To Hardy, he looked like a chef or an undertaker. The draft board probably overlooked his portly condition in order to meet some obscure monthly quota. A college education must have guaranteed his elevation to officer status. Joe didn't register surprise to see Mike drinking beer with Al. The word of Hardy's arrival must have spread throughout the unit, or he had grown accustomed to Al bringing home stray animals.

"Hey Joe, we got us a real killer assigned to the unit," Al announced. "Meet 2nd Lieutenant Mike Hardy, US Infantry."

"Hi," said Joe. "Why did they send you here?" He offered Mike a dirty, pudgy hand.

"Everyone asks me that. The army felt you guys needed some help to win the war."

Al threw his wet towel at Mike. "Shit, what war? I came here for the floor shows and the beer. Hurry up and get ready, Joe. Tonight, we're all going to get lucky. I'll even bet this cherry grunt gets to score. Move your ass!"

Laughing, Joe turned to Hardy. "You'll wish they'd sent you to the bush after hanging out with this bunch. I used to be tall and skinny. Look at me now." Sticking out his gut, he patted his paunch.

Al turned to Mike. "Do you have any party clothes?"

"Sure, but nothing like your flower shirt."

Al shoved Mike toward the door. "Move out, GI! Wiley will be here any second with the jeep. He doesn't like to wait for anyone."

Rushing outside, Mike walked quickly to his shabby quarters. He felt thrilled about spending the evening with his new associates. Hoping to fit in, he already sensed a degree of acceptance in their company. Things had started to look up. He could only see one hurdle left—Capt. Philip Adams. The captain had the potential of turning into a major nemesis. Hardy hated the thought of enduring more of Adams' wrath. Unless the company commander changed his opinion of infantry officers, Mike would end up spending a year in purgatory.

Setting aside his fears, he dug into his duffel bag for a pair of jeans and a pullover shirt. It felt good to shed his army garb. The last time he'd dressed like this, Clara had been with him in San Francisco. He splashed on some after-shave and pulled on his sneakers. Now, he felt ready for his first foray to the club. Tomorrow, he'd face the harsh reality of Capt. Adams.

What are you going to do now, lieutenant?

Mike would decide later.

One month in Chu Lai. Hardy had still not managed to work his way into the good graces of Capt. Adams. Adams wouldn't release him to command a convoy alone, but he had permitted him to accompany Wiley and Al on their trips. Joe Tice always made the run alone to Quang Ngai to pick up ice. Mike never received an invitation to go with him.

Christmas day, 1970, dawned with a brilliant sun rising above the horizon. Except for scattered sprigs of tinsel and occasional ornaments, the truck compound displayed few signs of the holiday. For many of the men, acknowledging Christmas would acknowledge loneliness and separation from families. So most of the GIs ignored the holiday. One local GI suggested that Santa Claus would have to bring presents to Vietnam with a machine gun on his sled. Another comedian suggested that Santa could best help the war effort by dumping reindeer shit on Hanoi.

The truck company had no time to celebrate Christmas. Convoys still made their regular runs to supply combat troops in the field. Mike, on the other hand, had earned a day off from the duty. He had just completed four straight days on the road. Two days earlier, Wiley had attempted to convince Capt. Adams that Hardy had exhibited the leadership skills necessary to command a convoy. In reply, Adams mumbled something about putting the grunt in command of the latrines. Mike wondered what it would take to break through the animosity. He felt frustrated by Adams' constant displeasure.

Hardy spent the morning in his bunk reading the last paperback novel in his possession. Skipping breakfast, he opened a box of C-rations for a can of pears and fruitcake. Unable to enjoy the luxury of having a refrigerator like his friends next door, he drank a can of warm soda from a stash under the bed. Warm beer and soda would continue until he acquired a compact Japanese model.

It occurred to him that the Japanese had mastered the art of reaping huge profits from the Vietnam War without spilling a drop of blood. Since World War II, they had learned to gain economic strength without direct involvement in the hostility. In every city, merchants sold Honda motorbikes, Toyota trucks, Panasonic stereo systems, Sony televisions, Seiko wristwatches, electric fans and refrigerators, *Made in Japan.* Japan held the Vietnamese—on both sides of the DMZ—hostage because of their hunger for electronic goods. In Mike's view, Japan would emerge as the only true winner in the Vietnam conflict. Ironically, the United States would gain nothing to profit from this war.

Mike hardly noticed the hooch maid when she entered to clean. He had obtained her services from Wiley. Already employed to clean the officer's hooch next door, she needed the extra income. For twenty bucks a month he could claim her services, too. After sweeping and mopping the floor, she made his bed, did the laundry, and polished his boots. The woman accomplished all this without any communication from him. He knew her only as 'Mama San.' She looked not old or young. Her appearance seemed average—not attractive or ugly. Hardy guessed her age somewhere in the late twenties. For the most part, Mama-San looked unremarkable. This woman, like so many others, just worked hard to survive the war.

Hardy glanced up several times from his novel to watch her work. At one point, she sat down on the floor to polish his boots. Every time she bent forward, he caught glimpses of her bare breasts beneath the loose pajama top. It occurred to him that her large breasts needed some restraint. Trying to focus on the words in his book, he kept returning to the view of her exposed flesh. Noticing a stirring in his lower regions, he wondered why he reacted so strongly to this rather plain-looking woman. She must have felt his eyes upon her, because she returned his stare without emotion. They had never shared any real eye contact until this moment. Neither of them said anything, so after a few seconds she returned to her task. Although he felt some guilt about his voyeurism, he made no effort to stop staring at her breasts. She, on the other hand, did nothing to restrict his view.

Mike waited for her to leave before rising from his bunk. The experience left him unsettled. He wondered if she had sent him a message. Upon further reflection, he dismissed the thought as foolish fantasy.

Moving to his desk, he decided to write a holiday letter to his parents. After several starts and stops, he reviewed the final product. The three pages seemed to convey the right tone. Devoid of any war news, he focused on his friendships, social activities, and admiration of the Vietnamese. He hated deception, but the truth might cause unnecessary concern. Americans had already received a full-dose of the 'truth' by watching the nightly news. His parents needed reassurance that he wasn't part of the *real* war. After stuffing the letter in an envelope, he carried it down the hill to the orderly room.

Mike found PFC Johnson hard at work opening cardboard boxes. Relieved not to see Capt. Adams in sight, he threw his letter in the mailbox. "Hey Johnson, what's up?"

The company clerk pointed to a pile of unopened boxes. "The Red Cross just dropped these off. They want us to have stuff for Christmas."

Mike ripped into a box filled with paperback books. "Wow, I can use some new books. I just finished my last novel."

Digging into the treasure chest, he pulled out two books at random: a modern romance and a directory of North American birds. Disgusted, he continued his search until discovering a spy novel and several mysteries. At last, he'd found good reading material.

"Hey, look at this!" Johnson yelled.

The company clerk had opened several boxes filled with red cloth bags. The bags contained toiletries, candy, writing materials, and Christmas cards. An elementary school child had signed each card. Some cards contained messages with requests for letters from soldiers in Vietnam. They counted out enough bags for everyone in the company.

"This is great, Johnson!" Hardy said. "We can use these to promote Christmas spirit. You and I are going to play Santa Claus."

"What do you mean?" Johnson asked.

"Almost everyone is out on the road or working in the garage. You and I are going to put one of these on every bunk. We'll also leave the books here for the taking. Christmas just got a little better. Let's go!"

"Got better for who?" Johnson complained. He hated the thought of doing anything outside the confines of his orderly room. Reluctantly, he followed Hardy on this mission of goodwill.

Spending over an hour making the deliveries, they finished just before evening chow. The convoys should return at any moment, and the maintenance crews had just wrapped up work for the day. Each man had his own plans for celebrating the holiday. Most plans included booze, drugs, and sex. Hardy had not heard of anyone planning to attend candlelight services at the chapel. The only damper on the festivities: a security warning of possible VC rocket attacks. The enemy loved to disrupt GI morale during the holidays.

Hardy dug out his best party clothes while waiting for his friends to return. Wiley trudged up the hill first. He looked tired from long hours on the road, but his spirits lifted once he saw Mike.

"Hey Grunt, you sure look pretty. Come here and give me a kiss." He made loud smacking sounds with his mouth.

"You're sick," Hardy said. "You've been spending too much time sniffing diesel fumes. Get your ass in gear, and let's hit the club. Al and Joe will be here any minute. Last one in the jeep buys the first round."

"Damn, it sure doesn't feel like Christmas. I hope Santa brings me something soft and warm to sleep with. I need company to get me through tonight," Wiley said.

"I'm sure he will," Hardy grinned. "You'll find a teddy bear on your pillow in the morning."

Wiley laughed. "Hey, that's no problem! As long as it's made of real fur, we'll get by."

Joe and Al turned up a few minutes later. As always, Al needed no encouragement to engage in wild celebration.

"Merry Christmas, shit head!" he called out. "Start the jeep. I'll be ready as soon as I wash my hog."

"You'd better sterilize it so your wife won't know where it's been," Hardy shot back.

"That'll never happen. It's always standing tall ready for inspection. Man, I really need a beer. Give me five minutes, and I'll be ready to tear into anything!" Al rushed off.

Al talked like an active participant in the sexual Olympics. Demonstrating an overt appreciation for the opposite sex, he mauled bar girls like a bear in heat. However, Mike never heard anything about the big man crossing the line into adultery. Deep down, Al fulfilled his commitment as a faithful husband. Hardy admired this resolve but, at the same time, enjoyed watching the burly man play out his fantasies in public.

Joe Tice shared little in common with Al. Even though he, like Al, wore a wedding ring, Joe never displayed any enthusiasm for debauchery. As a man with deep roots in the country, he outwardly pined for the girl he left behind. His wife, Wendy, married him right after high school. As far as anyone knew, she had served as his only sexual partner. Inwardly, Joe might consider expanding his sexual horizons, but any breach in fidelity would take place in deep secret. Even if he worked up his courage for the big event, once it happened ... BANG, guilt would consume him. Joe would drive himself crazy over the struggle of whether or not to confess his sins. Hardy couldn't decide if Joe would succumb to the allure of sex, or deny the temptation to avoid the guilt that would follow. It could go either way. What a bundle of contradictions, but that was Joe Tice.

They hit the club in full force before the evening rush. The club staff had finished hanging decorations. Little colored lights twinkled around the stage. A Filipino band unloaded instruments for the floor show. Two attractive women with the group assisted with the effort. Mike relished the prospect of watching them dance before him on stage. He tried to imagine them naked. He tried to imagine them naked with him in bed. He tried to imagine a night of unbridled passion in the arms of these island beauties. Totally distracted by the fantasy, he spilled his drink on the bar girl, Mary.

"Hey, you drunk already?" she snapped.

"I'm sorry, Mary," Hardy said. He handed over a five-dollar bill as a peace offering.

She tucked it away with professional ease. "No sweat, GI. Next time you spill on other girls, okay?"

"Hey Mary," yelled Al. "Make him lick it off until you're all clean. If he won't do it, I will!"

"You no lick me!" she bristled. Flipping her hair over her shoulder, she pranced off like a haughty debutante.

"Hot damn, that girl really loves me," Al swooned.

"Poor boy," Wiley patted him on the back. "He can't tell the difference between love and rejection. No wonder he stays horny."

They continued their banter for over an hour. Having secured a front row table, they drank in profusion until the start of the floor show. Three male performers opened the show in fluorescent green jumpsuits. The leader announced the band's name: *Body Heat* from Manila. They began with a pitiful version of *I Can't Get No*

Satisfaction by the Rolling Stones. The only redeeming moment came at the end of the song when the dancing girls appeared on stage. Dressed in the same jumpsuits as their male counterparts, they bounced and wiggled to the delight of the audience. The only difference in costumes— the women left the tops of their suits unzipped to their navels. Swooning in ecstasy, Al required physical restraint to keep from jumping on stage. His friends released him after he promised to control his compulsive behavior.

The show lasted for two hours during which the female performers exposed various parts of their bodies. At one point, Wiley screamed he could see nipples peaking through sheer bikini tops. Moaning loudly, Al begged both girls to sit on his lap. They both backed off to avoid his groping hands. The dancers probably realized that placing themselves in Al's grasp would have dire consequences. The performers looked relieved when the show drew to a close. Once the room began to spin, Hardy barely noticed their discomfort. The hours of drink and boisterous conduct had taken a toll on his sense of balance.

The band closed with the universal standard, *We've Got to Get Out Of This Place* by the Animals. Since GIs in Vietnam had adopted the ballad as their theme song, everyone knew the words by heart. Singing loudly, the audience pounded their fists on the table in time to the beat. When the number ended, the band appeared grateful to have escaped intact. They rushed off the stage shouting, "Merry Christmas!"

"Merry Christmas—shit," Hardy groaned. Having lost the spirit of the season, he observed the others in the room through a drunken haze. They, too, seemed to have lost the enthusiasm after the music stopped.

The party managed to regain life after taped music replaced the band. Mike found himself dancing with a pretty nurse—at least she looked pretty, considering his muddled state of mind. Wiley later informed him that she looked like a reject from the K-9 Corps. At this moment, she filled the need for female companionship as he held her in his arms. His loneliness had intensified in direct relation to an excessive intake of alcohol. Although intoxication had dulled his senses, he made a determined effort to stamp out holiday depression.

Sirens! The noise in the room screeched to a halt. Explosions! One of the women screamed.

"Incoming!" someone yelled. Mike froze, trying to comprehend what had just happened.

"Get down, Grunt!" Al yelled. He shoved Hardy toward the floor.

Mike vaguely remembered banging his head on a table during the descent. He experienced no pain as he moved in slow motion. When he attempted to focus his eyes the futile effort made it much easier to let them close. Surrendering to the impulse, he drifted away. As the noise and confusion faded, he sensed a general feeling of peace. In the distance, someone sang Christmas carols as snowflakes melted on his face. He had returned home to

New England for Christmas. The war in Vietnam had slipped thousands of miles away.

CHAPTER 8
Bloody Christmas

Al shook Hardy urgently. "Hey Grunt, are you okay?"

Mike tried to ignore the intrusion into his hallucinations, but Al continued the pressure.

"Come on, Grunt, we've got to get out of here. God Damn, he's bleeding! Look at his head. What a mess! Joe, bring me some ice."

Ripping up a tablecloth, Al filled it with the ice before applying it to Hardy's head. Returning to reality, Mike realized that a mammoth headache had replaced his peaceful delirium. When the fog lifted, he felt a sense of disappointment at landing back in Chu Lai.

"What happened?" Hardy gasped.

"Rockets," Wiley replied. "You fell and hit your head. Come on, we've got to get out of here."

Dragging him out of the club, they plopped him into the rear seat of the jeep. Suffering from pain and intoxication, he groaned with each jolt. His head throbbed while his stomach struggled to control the rising nausea. Once the jeep roared to life, gasoline fumes added to his stomach distress. He longed to release the pressure and turbulence by heaving his guts.

The sound of screaming sirens and sudden flashes of light assaulted Hardy's senses. Muted explosions filtered through the ringing in his ears. He'd never experienced greater misery.

Mike had no idea who drove the jeep, but a maniac had taken total control of his life. The racing vehicle moved at breakneck speed almost flying off the road. Losing control of his body movements, he prepared himself to embrace death. On further reflection, he prayed the perilous ride would end at his hooch. The final outcome of the ordeal could end in a toss-up.

When the jeep skidded to an abrupt halt, he lurched forward.

"Jesus Christ!" yelled Al. "Look at that!"

Hardy pulled himself from behind the front seat to see what had caused the unscheduled stop. He heard the screams of men suffering great agony. Opening his eyes with painful effort, he attempted to focus on the scene before him. Responding to fires caused by the VC rocket attack, a fire truck had driven off the pavement and jack-knifed against a utility pole. The collision had bent the truck frame, and flung firemen in all directions.

Hardy choked down another surge of nausea as he stumbled out of the jeep. He attempted to concentrate on the task ahead. Someone needed to take action to save lives; he wanted to help. Where to begin? Men rushed by him shouting orders, but no one seemed competent to handle the crisis. A dentist looked like the only medical official at the scene. Hardy recalled that his name was Doc Bowen. He remembered seeing the dentist drinking at the club earlier. Totally out of his depth, Doc could only scream, "Keep them breathing!"

Mike wobbled over to a Vietnamese fireman making gurgling sounds on the ground. With eyes opened wide in fright, blood pumped out of the victim's throat. The eyes begged for someone to save his life. Slowly spinning in space, Mike considered his options.

All right, Lieutenant, here's the situation. You have a man bleeding to death at your feet, and you are highly intoxicated. You must take immediate action or he's going to die. You must do something—NOW! What are you going to do, lieutenant?

"I don't know!" Hardy screamed aloud, pounding his fists against his head. This only increased the pain and confusion. Finally, with great hesitation, he knelt down to cover the gaping wound with an unsteady hand. Blood gushed through his fingers. He held his hand over the ruptured artery until the blood flow slowed to a trickle. The jerking body stopped moving; the pleading eyes froze in an eternal stare. The struggle ended with Mike doing little to help win the battle. He removed his hand in horror. Regarding the sticky warm blood running down his arm, he collapsed in despair.

"I didn't know what to do," Hardy sobbed. "What the fuck was I supposed to do?"

The fireman's eyes revealed nothing. They didn't convey gratitude or contempt. Had he done enough, or should he have gone for help? Who could have done better? Someone! Anyone! The silent fireman offered no response. The dead are content to let the living wallow in doubt and self-pity.

Hardy crawled a few yards away from the body before attempting to pull himself to his feet. His wobbling knees refused to cooperate causing him to fall twice before regaining his footing. The effort of these exertions put too much strain on his unsteady stomach. He ended up puking all over the fire truck. Still sobbing, he wiped his mouth with a bloody hand before realizing what he had done. He ended-up spitting out the remains of his vomit and the dead man's blood. At that moment, Mike's misery felt absolute.

"Keep them breathing! Keep them breathing!" Doc Bowen still tried to control the chaos.

Hardy knew the dentist longed for the security of his pristine office with its sterilized instruments. No one died in a dental chair. The only challenge came when he didn't monitor the flow of laughing gas. However, as a medical professional, the dentist felt compelled to handle this emergency. Doc did his best to put up a brave front, but he looked ready to panic.

"Hey, over here, there's one under the truck!"

Pulling himself together, Mike moved toward the voice calling for help. He found Al kneeling on the far side of the vehicle, reaching in desperation under the chassis as if looking for a lost object. Wiley and several other rescuers soon joined them.

"Is he alive?" Wiley shouted.

"Yeah," Al grunted with great exertion. "He's not too bad, but his legs are stuck. I can't move him. Quick, go to the other side and see what's holding him down."

Al continued to grunt and breathe heavily as he fought for leverage. He looked determined to save this life.

Wiley returned after a few minutes to give Al the report. "His right leg is caught under the drive shaft. It looks real bad."

Standing up, Al banged his fist against the side of the truck. "We can't move this piece of shit! He's trapped until we can figure something out!"

"Maybe, we can dig him out," a voice suggested from the rear.

"Fuck no," Al replied. "There's no room to move under there."

"Al," Wiley interjected. "We need the heavy wrecker to lift this thing. It won't have to lift it much to do the job."

"Right, call the company and get that thing here fast," Al said.

Wiley ran off to make the call on the radio.

"Who's left? Who else needs help?" Al shouted.

"I've got one over here," Doc Bowen replied. "C'mon, we've got to keep him breathing!"

Sirens wailed in the distance. Several more vehicles arrived on the scene to assess the damage. Hardy expected to hear more explosions from enemy rockets, but none came. The VC must have felt satisfied with the havoc they'd already created.

Hardy wanted to do something constructive, but he lacked the ability to handle the simplest task. He descended into a state of abject uselessness. Sobbing out of frustration, he wandered away from the scene. His path had no direction or purpose. Hoping to escape his torment, he tripped over a large piece of debris landing spread-eagle on the ground. Unable to move, he heard men shouting and the roaring sounds of engines—more yelling and then...nothing. His mind had slipped back to the security of his floating world. A deep sense of peace filled the blackness.

Tap, Tap, Tap. Hardy's head exploded with sharp jabs of pain. *Tap, Tap, Tap.* Sounds coming from nearby jolted him into consciousness. Opening his eyes, he jammed them shut in defense against the sunlight—sunlight? Where was he? He peered through the tiniest slits possible in his eyelids. Somehow, he had ended up in his bed. He heard muted footsteps.

"Oh, God," he groaned, and touched his head.

A bandage had replaced the torn tablecloth, and a cool washcloth covered his face. Someone started removing his clothes. Mike had no energy or desire to protest. Lifting the washcloth from his eyes, he saw Mama San undoing his buttons. Still smelling of vomit, he fought back the urge to retch. He muttered a hoarse, "Thank you." Somehow, she removed everything without creating additional discomfort. The awareness of his naked body caused him no concern. He'd sunk too low to worry about modesty.

Without saying a word, she returned with a bucket of hot water and some towels. Aware of his pain, she dipped one of the towels in the water, added soap, and began to bathe his soiled body parts. Not wanting to rush the process, she moved with caution. He allowed her to manipulate his limbs without protest. Lifting each arm, she washed both of his armpits. After raising and opening his legs, she reached for his pelvic area. Leaving nothing undone, she finished by washing his feet and toes. The healing process had begun.

Hardy dozed off several times during the long cleansing process. He attempted to pull the events of the past evening back into focus, but nothing remained except disjointed images. Aware what had happened, he couldn't return himself to the scene of the accident. During the mass confusion, he'd felt more like an observer than an active participant. Having done nothing substantial to help save those dying men, he suffered from a sense of ineptitude.

Waking several hours later, he found himself alone in the hooch. Touching his throbbing head, he found the bulky bandage still in place. The dizziness and nausea had subsided, but the headache still raged on. After reaching for his watch, he was surprised to see the dial read 2 p.m. He'd managed to miss most of the day after Christmas.

His throat felt sore and parched. Struggling out of bed, he perched himself on unsteady feet. Responding to a wave of vertigo, he swayed while attempting to gain his balance. He limped across the room in search of warm soda. Grabbing a cola from the cardboard case, he popped the top with a can opener. Foam exploded from the puncture drenching his hand, but he didn't care. Gulping down the warm liquid with relish, he reached for another. Mid-way through his second can, Al charged into the room.

"Hey, you're still alive. How ya feeling, Grunt?"

"I'm okay, except the hooch keeps moving."

"Man, did you get shit-faced last night!" Al slapped him on the back sending shock waves of pain to his brain.

Wincing, Hardy hobbled back to his bunk. "Yeah, and all the time I thought it was some other guy."

"It was you all right," Al said. "You need stitches in your head. I was too fucked up last night to take you to the hospital. We just bandaged you up and dropped you in the bunk. It's a helluva cut, but you'll be okay. You might even get a purple heart for it. I'll write you up for wounds sustained during an enemy rocket attack. No one needs to know you got drunk and fell on a table."

"Thanks, Mom will be proud," Hardy said. "By the way, what happened to the guys on the fire truck?"

"Well, you remember that anyway. I thought you'd want to talk about those dancing girls last night. I swear one of them kept looking at my crotch. She had a good eye for quality."

"Al, tell me about the accident," Mike insisted.

"There were six of them. Three dead, one critical, and

the other two will make it. I got the guy out from under the truck, but he might lose the leg. It was a bad scene—lots of blood. You were covered with it when we brought you back. I'm surprised that you remember anything."

"I remember it like a bad dream. I didn't do much to help."

"Don't worry about it. There were lots of other guys around. We saved the ones we could, and the rest would've died anyway. C'mon, I'll take you to the doc for stitches. I don't want your brain to fall out of the crack in your head." Pulling Hardy off the bed, he guided him to his jeep.

Al drove with great care on the way to the hospital. Aware of Mike's pain, he avoided bumps and sudden stops. Mike accepted Al's reasoning about the accident. No one could have done more to save lives. Understanding this, he still felt consumed by lingering uncertainty. He hated remembering his sense of helplessness and lack of self-control. A man had died in his grasp. Drunk or sober, nothing could change that reality. In the future, he'd analyze the event over and over trying to determine what else he could have done. Memories fade over the years, but guilt keeps the picture vivid. Hardy needed to come to terms with his conscience or face the burden of eternal doubt.

CHAPTER 9

Staging Area

"Hey Lieutenant, when's the rain gonna stop?"

Sergeant Willard Bates greeted Lieutenant Hardy as he sloshed toward the mess hall. The young NCO smiled and waved—he was a red-faced, beefy kid with a cheerful disposition. Bates seemed to thrive on adversity and performed at his best commanding *Bloody Mama*, a five-ton armored truck.

"I don't know, Bates," Hardy said. "Maybe, we should build us an ark and float back to the world."

"Ha, ha, you're right Lieutenant," Bates said. "I'd do anything to get us out of this shit!" Pleased with the suggestion, he would have gladly helped out with the project.

Mike loved convoy duty. Two weeks earlier, with Al's urging, Capt. Adams had cleared the infantry officer for command. Enjoying his new responsibilities, Mike benefited from the camaraderie and new discoveries. Through an unspoken agreement, the young lieutenant had accepted Sgt. Bates as his mentor. Now, he hung onto Bates' every word. Sharing a mutual respect, the difference in rank never interfered with their relationship. As a new convoy commander, Hardy learned to accept wisdom from a variety of sources. Sgt. Bates had his rough edges, but

Bates had a talent for dealing with challenges and adversity.

The mess hall was little more than a renovated shack built out of lumber and corrugated steel. Some lucky bastard back in the States had won an exclusive contract for corrugated steel—another example of capitalism at its best. The usual early morning din greeted them as they entered. Smoke from frying eggs and cigarettes saturated the atmosphere in the cramped space. After grabbing aluminum trays, they shuffled toward the serving line.

"You really enjoy this greasy slop, don't you Bates?" Hardy said.

"Sure do, Lieutenant." The young trucker patted his paunch. "I gotta keep up my strength to command *Bloody Mama*."

Hardy watched with amusement as Bates piled his tray with eggs, bacon, grits, pancakes, biscuits, toast, syrup, milk, coffee, juice and several bananas. They never experienced any shortages of food in the rear. Mike decided to settle for a meal of biscuits, bananas and coffee. Traditionally, officers ate apart from enlisted men, but no one bothered to follow this convention. Also, in keeping with the policy of relaxed discipline, most GIs neglected to salute their superiors in Vietnam. Everyone knew that enemy snipers could train their sights on the juicy target receiving the salute. Wisely, most army officers chose to ignore any displays of respect.

They found two empty places with some effort. The

table was sticky with syrup and sugar left by previous occupants. Most diners ignored the condition of the tables, but Hardy always carried extra napkins to improve his surroundings. Bates dropped his tray in the midst of old goo before chomping away at the trough. He fed his body machinery with the same dedication that he cared for *Bloody Mama*. Mike joined him after completing a little housekeeping.

Bates worked on a mouthful of eggs. "Where are we goin' today?"

"Duc Pho, I guess," Hardy said. "We should get MP clearance without much problem."

Duc Pho served as one of their usual destinations. As a major military combat base 120 miles due south of Chu Lai, it needed regular supplies of food, fuel and ammunition. The army base had weathered a series of attacks in years past, but enemy activity had slackened of late. The trip had become, more or less, routine. The truck convoy made the run on an average of five days a week.

Bates attacked his pile of pancakes. "Are you ridin' with us today?"

"Yeah, but it sure gets wet in the back of your truck. You've got no roof on *Mama*." Although large panels of one-inch thick iron surrounded the rear of the truck, nothing provided overhead cover for the crew manning the guns.

"Hell, Lieutenant, we like the fresh air. Besides, how can ya pass up the great company?" He pointed this out while licking fingers covered with syrup. "We'll find a way to keep ya dry."

Usually Hardy could choose to ride in any one of three positions in the convoy. The military police jeep always drove in front as the point vehicle. Convoy security required the commander to station a gun truck in the middle of the convoy and one at the rear. Gun trucks had 5 foot high armor plates attached around the truck bed, with M-60 and 50-caliber machine guns installed on rotating firing platforms. The convoy also had available an amphibious armored vehicle called a 'Duck' for additional protection. It carried a 20 mm cannon for use against fortified targets. Each one of these vehicles carried a radio transmitter so Hardy could control the convoy from a variety of positions. Lately, he'd been riding with Bates and his crew in the rear. Security procedures required him to change his command post on occasion, but he enjoyed Bates' company so he spent most of the trips on *Bloody Mama*.

"I'm glad you're goin' with us today, Lieutenant. I got a great deal for ya," Bates said.

"Oh God," Hardy groaned. "What's it this time?" He had been subjected to Bates' deals before.

Sgt. Bates leaned forward. "We got us a mini-gun," he whispered.

"What?" Hardy reacted with surprise. The mini-gun was the most advanced rapid-fire system in the army's arsenal. Hundreds of rounds could be fired in seconds.

Most mini-guns were mounted on aircraft to provide overhead firepower. Hardy had never heard of a mini-gun on a truck. "Where'd you get it?"

"Aw c'mon, Lieutenant, you know—Rodriguez. He traded some stuff for it." Bates grinned with satisfaction.

Staff Sergeant George Rodriguez served as the unit supply sergeant. He had a reputation for pulling off some of the most daring deals in Vietnam.

"What are you going to do with it?" Hardy inquired.

Bates beamed with anticipation. "We're goin' to put that little ol' gun on *Bloody Mama*."

"I've never heard of a mini-gun on the back of a truck. Are you sure you can do it?" Hardy asked.

"Shit, Lieutenant. No sweat, I've got all the gear. We'll do it tonight."

Hardy believed him. He believed the crazy bastard. Bates could do it and he'd give *Bloody Mama* a new credibility. He could almost imagine the faces on the Vietnamese as they drove through their villages. He almost choked on the thought.

"Damn you, Bates, you'll put both our asses in a sling!"

"Nah, I wouldn't do that," he replied. "You just tell the captain that it'll increase convoy security."

Mike relented with a smile. "Go ahead. It'll be worth the heat. Just don't tell anyone else where you got it."

"Not me. I keep my sources private."

Lt. Hardy greatly admired Bates' dedication to *Bloody Mama*. She filled a need that others found through sex and drugs. He ministered to her requirements with evangelical fervor. Nothing was too good for *Bloody Mama*. Hardy knew that Bates borrowed the name from the movie starring Shelley Winters. He vaguely remembered old Shelley chewing on a cigar as she fired her machine gun at the feds.

Bates applied a simple philosophy to his gun truck: "If you're real nice to her, she can be like your mama, but don't piss her off!"

The two men finished breakfast and deposited the remnants of their meal in an open garbage can.

The torrent continued outside the mess hall. They found *Bloody Mama* waiting to take them to the staging area. Sgt. Bates' crew had already begun to check the engine and the guns. He had them well-trained and they required no special encouragement to do their jobs. Each member of the crew had to love and care for *Mama,* or he'd face the wrath of Sgt. Willard Bates.

Bates' crew consisted of Private First Class Wayne Boss *(Basher)* from Independence, Missouri and Specialist Fourth Class Anthony Menetti (*Hit Man*) from Newark, New Jersey. PFC Boss and SP/4 Menetti received their nicknames from Sgt. Bates for singular acts of folly. *Basher* earned his name for having the audacity to put a dent in one of *Mama's* fenders. *Hit Man* won the distinction of being a crack shot after accidentally wounding a water buffalo while clearing his guns. Both men suffered at the hands of Bates because of this negligence. However, their dedication to *Bloody Mama* was clearly evident.

"Another day, same shit, right Lieutenant.?" yelled *Basher.*

"Where're we going, Duc Pho again?" *Hit Man* asked.

"Yeah, I guess so. I'll let you know as soon as I check for clearance," Hardy replied.

Hardy watched Bates work with his crew on the back of the gun truck and he felt cheered by their good-natured exchanges. Enjoying these early morning preparations, the men always appeared eager to get back on the road.

Bloody Mama was an impressive sight. What had once been an ordinary five-ton truck had evolved into a black war machine with one inch armor plating, two machine guns, and a red logo that screamed *Bloody Mama*. Hardy had often seen Vietnamese civilians stare in awe as she passed by.

The rain had almost stopped by the time they reached the staging area. Lt. Hardy jumped down, lit a cigarette, and walked away from *Mama.* He watched the blue smoke hang suspended in the damp air. Turning his Zippo cigarette lighter over, he read the inscription on the back. 'Fighting for peace is like screwing for virginity.' The other side read, 'Chu Lai, 1970.' He wanted to believe he'd arrived in Vietnam to fight for peace, but United States involvement seemed too contrived—too political. The current Vietnamese regime appeared so entrenched in corruption that little hope remained for creation of a democratic government. Vietnam presented a facade for the world to see. Behind the display of flags and rhetoric existed a political system in rapid decline. He could see it on the streets and in the eyes of the people. Meanwhile, the farmer tended to his rice paddy with no thoughts of political dogma.

Putting aside these disturbing images, Hardy concentrated on, 'Screwing for Virginity.' Something about this country, this climate, this war, filled him with sexual electricity. Sex and drugs were readily available everywhere, and he wanted to share in the bounty. He also attributed this 'electricity' to a general condition of horniness. After two months in country, he had yet to experience a real sexual encounter. Things had to get better!

Sloshing through puddles, he walked past trucks loaded with supplies, ammunition, and fuel. Drivers lounged in their cabs smoking cigarettes and listening to a variety of popular music. The loudest noise came from one of the fuel tanker trucks driven by Thomas Jackson, aka. 'Tex.' Tex, a young black man, contradicted all preconceived notions about black soldiers. Hailing from El Paso, Texas, he looked like a true cowboy with a six-gun and a cowboy hat. His favorite actor was John Wayne and his favorite music—real country. Hardy found him belting out a Johnny Cash standard.

> *I hear the train a comin'*
> *It's comin' round the bend...*

"Howdy, Lieutenant, come on in out of the rain."

"No thanks, Tex," Hardy replied. "You ready to go?"

"I reckon. Johnny and me are always ready for the highway," he said. "We love travelin' down that long road."

"Well saddle up, cowboy. We're ready to head off to the roundup," Hardy said.

"Ya-hoo, I love this place," howled Tex. "Just another day in paradise; see ya pardner."

Although a genuine character, Tex was one of the few soldiers able to project a tranquil state of mind without drugs. His only vice, beside loud country music, was warm beer out of a can. Mike admired Tex for his ability to maintain a sense of balance amid the chaos.

Hardy paused to visit with the crew of the other gun truck, *No Slack*. Sgt. Barry Hayes commanded the three-man crew without any of the fervor of Sgt. Bates. Hayes' men appeared more urban in character. They only focused on getting the job done and getting out of Vietnam. Each journey registered one more tick-mark off the clock—one step closer to home.

"Sixty-two and a wake up!" yelled out PFC Roger Blake. "I'm so short I have to reach up to tie my fuckin' boots."

Having reached the last two months of his tour of duty, Blake wanted the world to know his time in Nam was almost up. Always carrying a *short-timers'* stick, he added a notch as each day passed. No one dared touch his stick and it never left his sight. Every GI harbored some type of superstition in order to leave the country alive. Fellow soldiers respected these rituals without ever challenging a superstition—whatever works!

Hardy entered the dispatch hut after leaving *No Slack*. Master Sergeant Bubba Baldwin from Georgia served as the dispatch NCO. He had the responsibility for sending truck convoys off to their daily destinations. Bubba looked like the prototype of a transportation sergeant. He smoked cigars, drank whiskey, and nursed a forty-four inch waistline.

"Duc Pho, Lieutenant, ya'll should have clearance in about thirty minutes," drawled Bubba.

"Why the delay?" Hardy asked.

"Not sure," Bubba said. "I heard a rumor that *Charlie* was fuckin' with the road last night. The MPs are doin' a sweep of the area before we let you boys pull out." Flicking a cigar ash on his desk, he ignored the debris left on the paperwork. "Relax, Lieutenant. Take a break. Maybe the rain'll stop so you can work on your suntan."

"Yeah right, thanks, sergeant. Give me a yell when we're clear."

"Sure will. I don't like to keep you boys from havin' your fun."

"Thanks. I really love this place." Hardy left the comfort of the dispatch hut for the rain and mud.

Several of the transport trucks had already begun warming their engines. The smell of diesel hung heavy in the air. The new drivers always seemed eager to test the power of their engines. They acted like fighter pilots ready to plunge their aircraft into the heat of battle. Unlike the rookies, the veterans preferred to leave their machines in the hangar until the last possible moment.

Pausing by the main gate, Hardy watched a long line of Vietnamese waiting for clearance to enter the compound. They worked as laborers, hooch maids, bar girls and, on occasion, a VC infiltrator would slip in looking for juicy targets. The enemy always lived in their midst. Officially, whores never entered the compound to ply their trades, but after dark they ran loose in the barracks. In addition, a large number of hooch maids did double-duty during daylight hours to satisfy the physical needs of their employers.

The Vietnamese quietly accepted the indignity of body searches by the MPs in order to work in the compound. Some toiled for regular wages, while others looked for better ways to turn a profit. The black market thrived with any product in demand outside the gates serving as a prime target. The items of choice: cigarettes, booze, candy, and electrical appliances. Soldiers would trade these items for *grass* and *smak* (heroin). Vietnamese entrepreneurs could slip packages of drugs through the security fence at a number of unguarded locations without fear of detection. Over ninety-percent pure, most of the heroin was deadly to the uninitiated. Since GIs in Vietnam never experienced a shortage of anything illegal, a great number of them served their entire tour of duty in a drug induced stupor.

Two weeks earlier, an old woman had run past the MP station into an 'Off Limits' area. Two MPs yelled, "Stop" before dropping her with a volley from their M–16s. After searching her for weapons, they dragged the bullet-riddled corpse outside the gate for relatives to claim the body. Most of the Vietnamese accepted the incident with stoicism. Some of them considered it an inconsequential event, while others labeled the act as suicidal.

Lt. Hardy tried to shrug it off, too, but it still gnawed at his guts. Why did it have to happen? Could the old woman have been trying to make a statement? Maybe she just got tired of living in a country surrounded by armed foreigners —just another death, another mystery, in a land of mysteries.

He turned from the gate and headed back to *Bloody Mama*. Tired, cold and wet, he needed the good cheer of Sgt. Bates to lift his spirits. They would talk, laugh, and wait. The convoy stood poised to face the elements and, just possibly, the enemy.

Bubba's voice boomed over the radio: "Convoy cleared for departure."

"Let's move out," Hardy ordered the lead MP jeep.

Forty diesel engines roared to life at once. The rain had stopped, but the cold still chilled his bones. Sgt. Bates brought his crew to life by ordering the gunners to their assigned positions. Hardy stood by the radio wearing his communication helmet.

Each vehicle moved to its designated location in the convoy. Strategists had devised these position assignments for maximum security. Ammunition trucks never took up locations next to tanker trucks carrying fuel. If the convoy ever came under attack, the army hoped to prevent total disaster. The primary load consisted of ammo, fuel, various supplies and food. Refrigerated trucks called 'reefers' transported all cold food goods. Flatbed trailers carried most of the ammunition, dry goods and general supplies.

Slowly the convoy took shape as each truck fell into line. After the main gate opened, the MP jeep turned south onto the highway. *Bloody Mama* occupied a stationary position by the main gate as Hardy watched each truck pass. *No Slack* took up a spot in the middle of the convoy. Tex drove up in his tanker truck. Waving, he bounced to his music as he passed through the gate. *Bloody Mama* fell in at the rear.

The MP jeep had the responsibility for maintaining a legal speed limit of 50 miles per hour on the highway and 20 miles per hour through all villages. However, it didn't take long for the convoy to start rolling along at 60 on the open road. Traffic rules never applied much outside the compound. The landscape blurred as the truck speed increased. Outside the gates of Chu Lai the terrain looked flat to the east, but large sand dunes stood next to the highway up ahead. *Basher* tested his 50-caliber by firing short bursts into the dunes as they drove by. Peering to the west, Hardy could see hills and mountains. The VC had control of those hills, and they took advantage of the elevation by launching rocket attacks on Chu Lai at night. The rockets lacked accuracy, but the enemy still tried to hit prime targets. Fuel and ammo dumps were always the targets of choice.

The military police had designated checkpoints every two miles along the road to Duc Pho. Bridges, churches, schools and other significant landscape features made up each checkpoint. Every time the convoy passed one of these numbered positions, Hardy had to call in the location. If he didn't make the call within ten minutes, the command post would try to contact him. If they failed to make contact with the convoy, the command post would send out a search helicopter. The sand dunes served as checkpoint one.

"Charlie Papa One Sierra and rolling," Hardy announced over the radio.

"Roger," came the reply. The code words meant they had reached checkpoint one and were still moving south.

As usual, the convoy passed few vehicles on the highway; not many Vietnamese owned automobiles. They drove past a villager on foot carrying two baskets over his shoulders on a pole. Farmers bent over as they worked in their rice fields. Young boys rode water buffaloes. An old Mama San relieved herself at the edge of a rice paddy; human feces served as fertilizer. The landscape kept passing in a blur.

"Charlie Papa Two Sierra and rolling."

The truck convoy crossed a small bridge. Army engineers had rebuilt the bridge several times following VC attacks. Mike always held his breath at this location, expecting a command-detonated charge to blow them away. Foolish, he thought. They'd probably try to explode a tanker for more dramatic results. So far, *Bloody Mama* had led a charmed life.

The remains of an old Catholic church came into view on the left. The VC had shelled the stately structure to near oblivion. This church existed as a holdover from the days of French occupation. Hardy could never figure out if the VC had taken out their revenge on the religion or the French—probably both. The communists championed a simple philosophy: "Build a new society on the ruins of the old."

A school greeted them on the right. The wall surrounding the schoolyard featured pockmarks from bullet holes, but education for the young continued inside. A group of children occupied themselves with something in the yard. Using long sticks, they poked at an object in the bushes. Horrified, Mike watched as one child lifted up a three-foot snake on his stick. Having the distinct impression that all snakes in Vietnam were poisonous, he couldn't believe these kids had the audacity to flirt with death.

"Charlie Papa Five Sierra and rolling."

Sgt. Bates had not seen the incident with the snake. He remained busy with pencil and paper. When Hardy told him what the kids had done, he only shrugged. Bates had served too long in Vietnam to express any shock at such episodes.

"What are you working on?" Hardy asked.

"Look at this," Bates said. He had drawn a diagram of the new mini-gun on a platform at the center of *Bloody Mama.* "God, this is great! We can put the mother right here on a rotating mount and cover a 360 degree area. No one will touch us. We'll move the 50 caliber and the M-60 to the front and back corners. We'll be the best armed gun truck in the whole fuckin' world!"

"Great work, Bates," Hardy said. "I feel safer already."

Bates quickly returned to his sketching.

"Charlie Papa Six Sierra and rolling."

The convoy approached the first small village. The

trucks slowed to avoid rice drying in the road. The Vietnamese had little use for the asphalt highway except for drying rice. They neatly arranged the grain in rectangular patterns on both sides of the road. The drivers had to weave with caution through this obstacle course. Mama Sans squatted beside the rice always ready to jump up screaming if the trucks drove too close to their treasure.

The same smells always emanated from the village. The odors consisted of a mixture of smoke, drying fish, frying food, and human excrement. Because sanitation standards didn't exist, disease exacted a heavy toll. The surviving villagers lived to grow rice and avoid the war. Politics held little meaning for them. In spite of this political indifference, some propaganda whiz had painted South Vietnamese flags on many of their homes. Local residents displayed no interest in who ruled the country. They lived off the land.

Two Republic of Viet Nam soldiers (RVNs) walked down the road holding hands—a strange, but common sight to American GIs. In Vietnam, men exhibited no shame about open displays of affection in public. Mike had often seen men walking with their arms around each other. He had learned to accept the practice as a custom of the country.

On the other end of the spectrum, Mike had observed local men pitted against each other in brutal acts of violence. On this trip, while driving through the small city of Quang Ngai, he watched in horror as two RVNs tried to kill each other with their fists. Onlookers viewed the scene with detached interest. The stakes changed after one of the soldiers pulled a knife to stab his opponent. Mike never saw the outcome. American soldiers had received strict orders not to interfere with the civilians in any way. The convoy rolled on.

"Charlie Papa Nine Sierra and rolling."

The convoy passed more ruins and craters left by explosions. Bombs, artillery shells, mortars, or some other form of destruction had created the damage. Never repairing much of anything, the Vietnamese seemed content to work around the imperfections in the landscape.

The trucks slowed as the convoy entered another small village, once again dodging drying rice.

Small boys ran up to the trucks yelling, "GI numbah one. You souvenir me candy," or, "You give me cigarettes."

The mood changed after GIs brushed them off with "Dee, Dee" (Go away).

"You numbah ten, GI!" They followed this insult with obscene gestures. But the persistent hoodlums always came back for another try.

"Charlie Papa Twelve Sierra and rolling."

When the sun broke through the clouds, Hardy took off his flak jacket for relief from the heat. The damn things couldn't stop a high-powered round anyway. The same thing held true with the steel helmet. The army issued both items to give soldiers a false sense of security. He wished he had brought along his Boston Red Sox baseball cap.

The VC would never shoot a Red Sox fan.

They came upon a small group of RVNs gathered around two dead VC. The RVNs had carried the bodies out of the jungle like dead deer, with hands and feet lashed to poles. Devoid of any dignity, the corpses had started to bloat and decompose in the dirt. When the RVNs waved, the GIs returned their greeting with a half-hearted thumbs-up sign.

"Charlie Papa Fifteen Sierra and rolling."

Several miles later, they drove up to another dead VC by the roadside. This body, too, had bloated with flies swarming around the open wounds. Four boys poked the corpse with sticks. The act reminded Hardy of the kids in the schoolyard with the snake. If possible, these boys would have picked up the dead VC, like the snake, and thrown it around, too.

"Charlie Papa Eighteen Sierra and rolling."

Nothing else of interest came into sight during the remainder of the trip. At the outskirts of Duc Pho, Sgt. Bates argued with *Basher* about who would man the mini-gun. In the end, Bates decreed he would handle the duty until he found someone responsible to take his place. *Basher* protested, but he knew all along that Bates would claim the prize.

The gates of Duc Pho opened with the approach of the trucks. The convoy had arrived without incident. Once inside the compound, the trucks dispersed to their assigned unloading points. The whole process would take three hours before the trucks could return to Chu Lai. The sun had reached a halfway point in the sky overhead.

CHAPTER 11
Duc Pho

The army had fortified the town of Duc Pho to protect the highway and to re-supply troops fighting the VC in the surrounding hills. It also served as a point from which to launch long-range assaults against the enemy. Army infantry units had responsibility for protecting the base.

Sgt. Bates ordered his driver to stop *Bloody Mama* in front of the snack bar. Jumping to the ground, Hardy stretched his aching muscles after a tortuous ride on the five-ton truck. His body would continue to feel the vibrations for at least another twenty minutes.

The snack bar didn't have much to offer. With no embellishments or decorations, it provided a few tables and chairs for customers. One pinball machine existed as the only entertainment. The only items on the menu were cold soda, candy and snacks. These objects were displayed behind the counter guarded by Suzy, an attractive Vietnamese girl.

Hit Man entered the snack bar first. "Hey Suzy, how's your love life?"

Suzy glared at him in disgust. The truckers always made great sport of making her blush. *Hit Man* had launched the opening volley.

"No tell you," Suzy snapped.

"Aw c'mon, you can tell us." *Basher* had joined the game.

Everyone knew Suzy had a GI boyfriend, but she never revealed his identity. Truck crews took on the challenge to uncover the sneaky culprit.

"Suzy, what's that on your neck? Is it a bruise? Oh no, it's a hickey! Come here guys. Suzy's got a hickey," *Hit Man* teased.

"Ah-h-h!" Screaming, the distraught girl hid behind the counter.

"Come on Suzy, let me see your love bite. Is it a big one?" *Basher* asked.

"Oh-hhhh," Suzy moaned. Her embarrassment escalated.

Hit Man continued his persecution of the young girl. "You got any more of those, Suzy? Did he kiss you all over? C'mon show us, we won't tell,"

The young woman groaned from behind the counter.

"All right, you two knock it off," Sgt. Bates said. "I want a Coke,"

"We're sorry, Suzy," *Basher* said. "Come on, get up. Sarge wants a Coke,"

Suzy had no intention of facing her attackers. She remained crouched on the floor behind the bar.

"She won't get up, Sarge. I said I was sorry. I just wanted to see her hickey," *Basher* said with an evil smirk.

"Oh-hhhhh!" Another groan came from behind the counter. She remained frozen in place.

"I tried. She won't move, Sarge. I'll get you a Coke." Stepping over Suzy, *Basher* moved to the cooler. "All right, what'll the rest of you have? I'm your new bartender."

"That's enough, *Basher,*" Hardy said. "Bring some drinks over here and we'll play spades."

They always played cards during these breaks. On some occasions, Sgt. Hayes and his crew joined the action. Today, Hayes and his gang had found other diversions.

"They musta gone to the *Steam and Cream,*" said *Hit Man.*

Even as a small compound, Duc Pho offered one of the best bathhouses in the area. The girls, all handpicked, had undergone extensive training to provide a variety of pleasures. Service went way beyond a standard massage.

"I'll deal," volunteered Bates. He shuffled the cards and dealt out the entire deck.

"Hey Suzy, come on out. We won't bother you any more," said *Hit Man.*

"You go away. I hate you!" screamed Suzy. She refused to move.

"Leave her alone, shithead," said Bates. "She'll be pissed off for a month."

They left her alone to endure her misery. Turning their attention to the cards, the gun truck crew played for almost an hour. Suzy never reappeared during the entire time. With two hours left to kill, the card game had lost its fascination.

Stretching, Hardy pulled himself out of his chair. "I think I'll go see what Sergeant Hayes is up to," he said.

"Right, Lieutenant," said *Basher.* "After you find him, make sure you get all your joints greased, too."

"Try number 14," said *Hit Man.* "She'll blow your socks off."

Not bothering to respond, Hardy just waved as he walked out the door.

The steam bath was just a short walk from the snack bar. An old lady sat at the front desk to collect the 10-dollar entry fee. Mike didn't ask for number 14. Wanting to indulge in a new experience, he opted for room number 8, instead. Having visited the steam bath on numerous occasions, he had rarely drawn the same girl twice. He liked surprises.

The girl in number 8 rose from her stool the moment he walked into the room. He had never seen her before. Like many of the others, this one was attractive but unlike most Vietnamese women she had no trouble meeting his gaze. He liked that.

"You take clothes off," she said. Turning her back, the young woman moved to prepare the steam cabinet.

This bathhouse featured individual steam cabinets in each room. The box-like structures opened in front. Once inside, the customer sat on a stool, the doors closed, and only his head emerged from the top. Hardy liked that, too. Most of the other operations offered large group booths. He appreciated the intimacy of this setting. Removing his uniform, he hung it up on the rack.

"What's your name?" Mike asked.

"Leah." She guided him into the cabinet.

Once inside, she latched the doors and wrapped a towel around his neck. It took only seconds for the steam to begin its work.

"Okay, if I sing for you?" Leah asked.

"Sure," he said. No Vietnamese girl had ever sung to him.

Sitting on her stool, she began to sing softly in Vietnamese. The song had no meaning for him. However, it sounded like one of the sweetest things he'd ever heard. He waited until she had finished.

"What does it mean?" he asked.

"Old song," she said. "About boy and girl fall in love. Boy goes to war and dies. She left alone."

"It's not a very cheerful song. Don't you know any happy ones?"

"No. You ready come out now?"

"Yes."

After assisting him out of the cabinet, she rubbed him down with a towel. Next stop the shower—no stall, just a floor drain in the middle of the room. She held a hose with a shower attachment above his head. Mike squatted on the floor as she covered him with warm spray. Next, she soaped him down without missing any critical areas. He shivered when she washed his genitals. After a thorough soaping, she rinsed and toweled him dry.

"Now, you ready for massage?" she asked.

Taking hold of his hand, she guided him to the table. After stretching out on the table, she covered his midsection with a towel. Mike didn't know if she covered his groin for her benefit or his. The massage bordered on exquisite. Once she had warmed oil in her hands, she kneaded all his muscles. For a finale, she removed her sandals and walked on his back. Her small toes dug into his flesh as she moved—a magical experience. Climbing down, she whispered in his ear.

"You want me do this?" She rubbed her fingers gently inside his thigh.

"Oh yes," he said.

"Ten dollah," she quoted without emotion.

"Get my wallet, please."

Moving to the clothes rack, she returned with his wallet. Mike dug out ten dollars to pay for the service. After placing the money in her purse, she returned to the table. Without hesitation, she unbuttoned her blouse to reveal small pointed breasts.

"You touch me here, okay?"

He needed no other encouragement. Caressing her softly, he teased her nipples. Humming, she began to fondle him underneath the towel. As the pace accelerated, his breathing increased. As he neared climax, she leaned over to press her breasts against his chest. Her warm breath caressed his ear. Gasping, Mike melted onto the table. Savoring the sensation, it took several minutes for him to catch his breath.

"Was good?" She cleaned up the damage with a wet cloth.

"Great," he said.

"Come back see me. I be good for you again," she promised.

Sliding off the table, Mike dressed quickly. She helped by tying his boots. They shared no more touching or affection. With business completed, the time had come to leave. After he thanked her, she smiled and offered him a little wave. Next time, he would ask for number 8.

Feeling light-headed, he left the steam bath. He consulted his watch—almost an hour left before departure. He decided to visit Richard Chang. Richard was an infantry lieutenant of Chinese descent from California. Mike had met him a month earlier in Chu Lai soon after the new lieutenant arrived in country. Both men had attended OCS at Ft. Benning. Stranded, Richard needed transportation to his new assignment in Duc Pho. Recalling his own experience in Da Nang, Mike offered to give him a lift on the convoy.

Departing the next day, they rode together on *Bloody Mama*. Richard had a thousand questions and Mike did his best to give him answers. After all, he was a seasoned veteran of three months.

"How did you get assigned to a truck company?" Richard asked.

"I have no idea. Just unlucky, I guess."

"I should be so unlucky," Richard said.

The new lieutenant realized his destiny lay ahead in the jungle, where both men knew he had little chance for survival. Mike observed the all-too-familiar look of resignation in his demeanor. He'd seen the same expression on the faces of soldiers at Ft. Polk. He hoped that, somehow, Richard would overcome the overwhelming odds.

After arriving at Duc Pho, Mike deposited his passenger at his new battalion headquarters. Stalling the departure, Richard made him promise to visit on a regular basis.

"You're the only friend I have over here." Waving goodbye, Richard picked up his gear before walking off toward his infantry assignment.

This time, Mike found Richard in the barracks packing a rucksack.

"Hi, Mike, you found me. Great!"

"How's it going? Are you getting ready to go out?"

"Yeah, I've got to hit the chopper pad in ten minutes—just a short excursion into the hills. We need to clean out some rocket sites." He buckled up his pack.

"You look great," Mike lied. "The outdoor life must agree with you."

"Bullshit, I look like crap! I haven't had any sleep in two days. Something always comes up. We're short-handed at the moment. Walk with me to the chopper pad." Grabbing his gear and his M-16, he headed for the door.

"Sure," Mike followed him outside.

Other soldiers moved in the same direction. Mike felt conspicuous walking among these grunt warriors. Several of them stared at him, but no one said a word. A helicopter landed in a whirl of dust as they arrived at the pad. It unloaded two wounded GIs. One casualty had lost half his face and the other had lost a foot. Grimacing at the sight, Mike glanced at Richard. His friend displayed no emotion. This wasn't a good omen before a mission. Turning to him, Richard handed over an envelope.

"Hold this for me, Mike. Don't mail it unless you have to. You've been a good friend."

"Bullshit! Nothing's going to happen to you. You're going to make it. I'll be back next week."

"Right, just keep the letter. Thanks for everything." Leaving Mike standing alone in a swirling cloud of dust, Richard climbed aboard one of the waiting helicopters.

Hardy wanted to say so much more, but there'd be time —later. He'd come back for another visit next week. He shoved Richard's letter in his pocket.

Shit.

The convoy stood waiting by the gate when he returned. Hardy jumped aboard *Bloody Mama* ignoring wisecracks from Bate's crew. They expected him to share details of his visit to bathhouse.

Sensing his melancholy, Bates asked, "Are you okay, Lieutenant?"

"Yeah, move 'em out Sarge. Let's go home."

Mike heard helicopter engines fade in the distance. Leaving Duc Pho behind, the convoy headed north to Chu Lai.

Mike tried to shake off his feelings of remorse following the departure of Richard Chang.

I should be going with him, he thought. *Like Richard, I should lead a platoon of GIs into the hills to chase the VC. I should have the responsibility of leaving letters behind for loved ones. I should join Richard in preparing for death.*

As the convoy rolled toward Chu Lai, Hardy caught Sgt. Bates looking at him with genuine concern. He wondered why Bates cared so much about his state of mind. He tried to remember back to their first meeting. When had Bates first decided to adopt him? It must have happened the moment he expressed his admiration of *Bloody Mama*. At that point, Bates accepted him as an honorary member of the team. Now, they shared a mutual bond of friendship.

The return to Chu Lai always proved more eventful than the morning run to Duc Pho. Drivers pushed empty trucks hard on the trip back home. They punched the speed of the convoy well beyond the limits of safety. Acutely aware of this fact, pedestrians and cyclists took extra pains to stay out of the way. Careless Vietnamese had to dive into ditches in fear for their lives. The convoy ruled the road and most civilians accepted this intrusion as just another inconvenience of the war.

During this return trip, one of the flatbeds blew a tire.

Sgt. Hayes called Hardy on the radio from *No Slack*. "Mama, this is Baby Bear, over."

"This is Mama, go ahead, over."

"We got us a flat top with a broken wing. Please advise…over."

Considering his options, Hardy decided against stopping the entire convoy. Trucks parked on the roadside made juicy targets for the enemy.

"Baby Bear this is Mama. Take over my position in the rear, and I'll stay with the cripple. Do you read me, over?"

"Roger that. Baby Bear out," Sgt. Hayes replied.

They drove on until they came upon *No Slack* and the disabled flat bed. After *Bloody Mama* screeched to a halt behind the truck, Hayes took over the rear position in the convoy. Bates sent *Hit Man* and *Basher* to help the driver change his tire. Since VC snipers lurked everywhere, the crew could waste little time halted on the road. Bates and Hardy remained in back on the machine guns. Surveying the countryside, they relaxed after realizing the level terrain offered nowhere for a sniper to hide. Unless a VC popped out of the ground, they shouldn't have a problem. It had turned into a beautiful, clear day. Hardy decided to enjoy the temporary delay in their journey.

Hopping down from the gun truck, he checked the progress of the tire change. It would take twenty or thirty minutes to complete the job. Walking around to the front of the flatbed, he noticed a group of children heading toward them. Children always seemed to gather when trucks stopped on the road. He yelled up to Bates to throw down several oranges. Hardy had one of the oranges peeled by the time the children arrived. After breaking it into sections, he passed one piece to each child. Smiling, they thanked him for the fruit. He enjoyed watching the juice run down their chins. One little girl laughed as she tried to capture each drop before it hit the ground.

Busy with the children and a second orange, Hardy didn't notice an old Papa San standing at the rear of the group. The Papa San stood quietly with his eyes focused on the ground. The old man didn't speak or beg for attention. He waited in stoic silence for an acknowledgment or a rebuke.

When he finished peeling the second orange, Mike passed out all the pieces to the children, except one. Handing this section to Papa San, he waited for a reaction. The old man raised his head, looked Hardy in the eye, and gratefully accepted the gift. Observing a great dignity in him, Mike felt satisfied with the momentary contact.

Hardy picked up a third orange and before breaking the skin he passed it to Papa San—in a gesture of good faith. Accepting the prize, the old man regarded all the children who surrounded him. Slowly peeling the fruit, he broke it into sections before handing the pieces to his young audience. The last piece he offered to Hardy, but Mike insisted that he keep it. The old man smiled in gratitude once more. Hardy felt cheered by the warmth of the moment.

Sgt. Bates yelled down from the back of *Bloody Mama*. "Hey Lieutenant, I've got some extra ammo up here you can pass out. I bet they'd love to chew on that, too!"

"Save it, Bates. We might have to use it on the bad guys." Hardy climbed back up to join him.

With the tire change completed, the trucks made ready for departure. Waving to Papa San and the children, Mike left them in the distance surrounded by orange peels.

The flatbed raced down the highway at breakneck speed. The driver seemed determined to make up the time lost by the delay. *Bloody Mama* pushed hard to keep pace with him. The reckless driver blew his horn as he approached each village to give the inhabitants advance notice of his arrival. Hardy hoped the villagers had enough sense to get out of the way. He would have slowed the flatbed if possible, but he didn't have communication with any of the convoy trucks. As soon as the convoy returned to Chu Lai, he made himself a promise to kick the driver's ass.

Bates muttered and yelled during the entire pursuit. "Crazy bastard, I should shoot out his fuckin' tires; that'd slow him down. Son of a bitch must be high on smak."

Hardy yelled over the roar of the truck. "Do you know him?"

"Yeah, he hangs out with the dope heads. He used to be

a good kid, until he got fucked up. His name is Ames, PFC Robert Ames." Bates continued his condemnation of Ames and all dope heads.

Hardy wondered how a good kid could sink so low. After they returned to Chu Lai, he'd either settle for kicking the driver's ass or trying to bring the young man back among the living. Without some sort of rehabilit-ation, he wouldn't allow this dope head to drive in the convoy again. He already had too many drivers on the verge of self-destruction.

Thirty minutes later, the flatbed screamed to a halt outside of Quang Ngai. Ames almost collided with the main body of the convoy which had stopped on the road. *No Slack*, in the rear position, narrowly missed total destruction. Hardy saw Sgt. Hayes jump down from the gun truck screaming in frustration at Ames. He banged on the flatbed doors with his fists. Ames refused to budge from the truck cab.

Hardy rushed to the scene. "Why are you stopped?" He yelled at Hayes.

"Crazy fucker almost wiped us out!" shouted Hayes. He continued to bash on the truck door.

"Why are you stopped?" Hardy repeated louder.

"Aw shit, we hit a gook. MPs are up front trying to smooth things out. It's a bad scene. Gooks are blocking the road and won't let us leave."

"Cool off and quit hitting the truck. I'll deal with him later. Stay here until I get back."

Leaving Hayes behind still fuming, Hardy jogged to the front of the convoy. He arrived to find mass confusion. A young Vietnamese boy lay in a pool of blood in front of a tanker—quite dead. His mother kneeled by his side screaming.

One of the MPs tried to placate the boy's relatives and friends. "Things will be all right. Army will pay you *boo-coo* piasters. Trucks must go to Chu Lai…very sorry. Army will pay. Shit, I give up! Does anybody around here speak Vietnamese?"

Meanwhile, a dozen irate villagers had formed a blockade in front of the convoy by placing logs, bicycles, scrap metal, and themselves in the road. The convoy seemed stuck in the midst of a major incident. Hardy had no idea how to untangle the mess.

"Thank God you're here," yelled the frazzled MP.

Oh no, don't salute—too late.

He snapped Hardy a smart regulation salute. MPs always picked the worst times to display military courtesy. The salute targeted Hardy as a marked man. The Vietnamese crowd turned on him as a new object of their wrath. He had to endure poking, screaming, and shoving. At that point, he realized nothing more could save the situation. They had to get away.

Hardy grabbed the MP by the shoulders. "Call headquarters and advise them of our problem. Tell them we're leaving the scene before someone gets hurt—do not, I repeat, *do not* request assistance! I don't want them to send in the Marines. We can get out of this. Report back here to me after you've made the call. Do you understand?"

Nodding quickly, the MP made a hasty retreat to his radio.

Meanwhile, Hardy did his best to imitate a high-level diplomat. This proved something of a challenge because he'd never considered diplomacy as one of his strong suits. However, he made an earnest attempt to appear strong and sympathetic. The crowd refused to accept appeasement. The MP returned after what seemed a lengthy absence.

Hardy had reached the limit of his endurance. "Did you make the call?"

"Yes," he nodded vigorously.

"Do they understand our situation?"

"Yes, sir, they're standing by."

"Good. Now you stay here and wait for me to get back."

The MPs eyes opened wide in fright.

"Don't worry, I'll be right back." Hardy raced to the MP jeep to call *Bloody Mama.*

"Bates, this is Mama." He'd forgotten Bates' call sign. "Do you read me, over?"

"Roger, Mama. What's up?"

"Listen, we've got a big mess up here. In exactly five minutes, I want you to make a lot of noise—fire all the machine guns, yell, rev up the engine—whatever it takes.

Tell Hayes to do the same thing. Only do not, I repeat, *do not* shoot anyone. We need to get out of here alive. Do you read me, over?"

"Roger, we'll be ready."

Now, for the hard part: Hardy returned to the MP to give him new orders.

"Get into your jeep and drive it back into the convoy. We're getting out of here. I need a five-ton at the point. Go fast!"

The MP moved his jeep out of the way. Running to the flatbed in front, Hardy jumped into the cab on the passenger side. Meanwhile, the Vietnamese had started throwing stones at the trucks. Hardy didn't know the driver's name, but recognized him as a new kid in the unit. The driver looked scared.

Hardy tried to appear calm. "What's your name?"

"Sawyer, sir," he replied.

"You scared, Sawyer?"

"Yeah, a little," he said.

"Me, too, but it's going to be okay. When I give you the word, I want you to move forward slowly and do not stop. Blow your horn, rev up your engine, but do not stop. Do you understand?"

"Yeah, but there's gooks all in the road."

A rock slammed into the windshield cracking the glass.

"They'll move, Sawyer. Do what I say. Wait until I give the word, okay?"

"Okay, sir."

More rocks and sticks slammed against the truck. Hardy prayed they wouldn't break the windows. He also hoped that none of the villagers had guns. No one in the convoy wanted a firefight with the natives. Nervous tension raced up his spine as he waited for Bates' diversion. His saliva turned into paste. He didn't have long to wait. One minute later all hell broke out in the rear. The deafening noise caught the Vietnamese by surprise. Sgt. Bates had outdone himself. Ear splitting machine gun fire and horrific explosions shattered the silence. Most of the villagers scattered. Mama San dragged her dead son off the road. The human blockade began to disperse, except for a few stubborn souls who remained in position.

"Okay Sawyer, it's time to go. Move out, but slowly," Hardy said.

He hoped all the other trucks would follow their lead. Sawyer drove directly at the blockade pounding on his horn. The Vietnamese held on until the last possible moment before jumping out of the way. Moving forward, the flatbed pushed a path through the debris. Driving free of the blockade, Hardy looked behind to see the rest of the convoy following. The Vietnamese continued to throw rocks as each truck left the city. One mile past the scene, Hardy directed Sawyer to pull over so he could evaluate the situation. After walking back to the MP jeep, he called Sgt. Bates on the radio.

"Bates, this is Mama, over."

"Go ahead Mama."

"Is everyone clear?" he asked.

"Roger that, Mama! We're all out slicker than duck shit, over."

"Good. Keep your position in the rear. Send *No Slack* back to the middle. I'll wait for you here. Do you copy?"

"Roger, we're coming to get you."

After telling Sawyer that he'd done a good job, Hardy sent the MP jeep back on point. He waited for *Bloody Mama* as the rest of the convoy drove by. The drivers smiled and waved as they passed him on the road. They all seemed grateful to have escaped without sustaining serious damage. Mike realized that he'd just passed a leadership test, and felt deeply satisfied with the results.

Bates and his crew celebrated all the way back to Chu Lai. They felt thrilled that their little diversion had worked. *Basher* took credit for throwing the hand grenades. Bates grumbled that the diversion would have worked better if they had use of the mini-gun. The men discussed ways to improve their performance next time.

"There'd better not be a next time," Hardy said. "By the way, who was driving the tanker that hit the Vietnamese boy?"

"It was Spec/4 Bobby Waters," Bates said. "One of the drivers told us about it during the hold-up. Waters took it real hard. He tried to apologize to the boy's mama, but she kicked him. The MPs made him get back in his truck."

Waters, a black soldier from Detroit, had risen in stature as one of the best drivers in the unit. Al considered him steady and dependable. The young GI never used drugs or got himself into trouble. Hardy wished he had more drivers like him. Excelling as a basketball player, Waters loved to talk about professional teams in the NBA. Mike hoped he wouldn't grieve too much over the death of the Vietnamese boy.

Everyone in the convoy welcomed the return to Chu Lai. Once inside the gates, the compound closed like a safety net around them. The trucks headed for the motor pool to park for the night. After extending his thanks for a job well done, Hardy bade farewell to Sgt. Bates and his crew. Heading straight for Bobby Waters' tanker, he found the driver slumped over the steering wheel. Stepping up on the running board, Mike touched Bobby's shoulder.

"Waters, are you okay?" he asked.

"I never saw him," the young man replied. "We was going too fast, but I coulda stopped. I never saw him. I'm so sorry. I killed him."

"Waters, it wasn't your fault. It could have happened to anyone. We have to dodge kids all the time. You can't blame yourself."

"I keep seeing his face and all the blood. I did it to him," he sobbed.

Hardy grabbed his arm. "You've got to let it go. You're a good guy with a good heart. There was nothing you could do. It was just bad luck. Are you going to be all right?"

"Yeah, I'm okay," he said.

"Good. Go get some rest." Hardy left him alone with his misery.

Walking toward the orderly room, he thought about the need to write reports explaining the incident to Capt. Adams. Adams would probably criticize the way he'd dealt with the crisis. Hardy didn't care. Numbness had settled in behind his eyes, and a dull ache throbbed in his temples. The shock of the day had taken a toll on his body. Sleep would take care of most of it, but the rest would require healing over time.

Valentine's Day dawned bright, hot, and steamy. Every day in Vietnam either dawned bright and hot, or wet and hot. Humidity thrived in South East Asia, increasing the discomfort in those unaccustomed to the tropics.

Hardy didn't believe anyone could grow accustomed to this climate. Even the Vietnamese seemed to suffer during the hottest part of the day. They confined their labors to early morning and late afternoon. The rest of the day they remained indoors, or slept in the shade.

Most GIs didn't have the common sense of their native hosts. When the sun reached its highest peak, they hit the beach, played basketball, or worked under a hot truck. Beach sand burned their unprotected feet. The sizzling South China Sea offered no relief to swimmers. Asphalt on basketball courts melted, clinging stubbornly to sneakers. Medics had to regularly treat mechanics for heat exhaustion. So it went. Americans are always slow to adapt to a new environment. They systematically cling to their schedules and recreational activities, no matter what the conditions.

Tex Jackson existed as an exception to this rule. Enjoying his creature comforts, the young man from Texas always made it a point to never overexert himself. Between runs with the convoy, he sought refuge in his hooch with cold beer and hot country music. After several beers, he'd sing duets with Waylon Jennings or Johnny Cash.

He once explained to Hardy why he avoided the common pursuits of his peers.: "Hell no, I don't go to the beach, Lieutenant. Don't let nobody tell you that black folks can't get sunburned. We do, and I ain't gonna play in the sand. I love to relax in the shade drinkin' Budweiser lemonade."

Texas was well-known for extremes that included blistering temperatures and stifling humidity.

Tex also had strong opinions about drugs and whores. "I'm from the country. Mama raised us real strict. She taught us to work hard and stay away from sin. There's a whole lot of sin around here, Lieutenant. Some of these boys are in deep over their heads. Drugs will fry their brains and cheap sex will rot their peckers off. I'm goin' home to ride the range. I don't ever want to end up planted in Boot Hill for bein' stupid. I'm goin' out with a clear head and my guns ablazin', Ya-HOO!"

Mike considered Tex a piece of work. After ten months in Vietnam, this soldier had paid his dues. He deserved to make it home to his beloved Texas. Tex's mama should have felt proud of her son.

Stretching out on his bunk, Hardy relished the thought of enjoying the day off. Recent enemy activity had cancelled the regular run to Duc Pho. If necessary, the army could airlift supplies to troops in the field. The MPs had responsibility for clearing the roads before the convoys could go back to work. Mike thought about Richard Chang and the other grunts risking their lives to protect troops in the rear. Those soldiers deserved a lion's share of recognition as the true heroes in this conflict.

Mama San entered the hooch as he swung out of bed. Their relationship had changed since Christmas. They still spoke little, but Hardy treated her with new respect. Sensing his gratitude, she seemed to take pleasure in doing extra tasks for him. She started to clean off his desk, organize the clothes in his closet, add extra polish to his boots, and air out his bedding. He suspected that she took on these added duties to linger in his company, but Mama San offered no explanation. At times, they acted like novices at a high school dance. But, in spite of this awkwardness, they had formed a new bond. Mike gave her presents of C-rations and candy to take home. He knew she had a small son, but she never mentioned anything about a husband.

Vietnamese husbands rarely came up as a topic of discussion. Most women working in the compound had one—somewhere. The majority of their men fought with the South Vietnamese Army. Some husbands had migrated to the other side, so this restricted family contact to nocturnal visits. A number of others had returned home to nurse wounds or endure permanent disabilities. Many never returned, leaving their women behind as widows. The population of widows kept growing in Vietnam.

Family units grew tighter as a result of the war. Everyone had to contribute. Fathers and uncles toiled in the fields, or worked for the military as laborers. Mothers and aunts cooked and maintained the home. Young mothers left babies with the older women to work as hooch maids or bar girls. They distributed all the money earned for food and essentials. In Vietnam, the extended family had become the norm.

Bates entered after Mama San had finished making Hardy's bed. He seemed pleased to have the day off. After all, a day off from the road gave him the opportunity to do extra maintenance on *Bloody Mama*.

"Mornin', Lieutenant, let's hit the chow hall before we miss breakfast. They close down in twenty minutes."

"Okay, Bates, I'll help save you from starvation."

"It ain't me I'm worried about. You young lieutenants need to keep up your strength to lead us dumb sergeants."

"Give me a break," Hardy said. "You sergeants are the ones that keep the army running."

"You're right. I can't argue with that," Bates chuckled. "Just remember you're the one who said it, not me. Let's go."

They trudged down the hill to the chow hall. Hardy experienced some surprise that Bates had invited him for breakfast on their day off. They always shared breakfast on duty days, but never on days of rest. It occurred to him that a specific reason had prompted this invitation. Bates had something on his mind and Hardy was expected to play a part in any plot he might hatch. It always took Bates a while to drop his bombshells. He seemed to do his best scheming over meals.

Due to the cancellation of the trip, the chow hall served more diners than usual. Most of the drivers had slept late, rushing to eat breakfast at the last minute. Bates and Hardy found a spot next to the crew of *No Slack* and dug in.

"Happy Valentine's Day, Lieutenant," Hayes said. "Did you send your girl candy and flowers?"

Hardy thought for a while before responding. He realized he'd probably face a lonely day. "No, I really don't have a girl in the States. There was a girl in San Francisco, but I probably won't see her again. There are lots of girls back home, but no one special."

"Man, what a bummer," replied Hayes. "You really need a honey back home to keep your heart going. My girl swears she'll be faithful to me forever, even when she's out pounding some other guy. At least, I still have her heart, right?"

"Right," said PFC Blake. "I bet she'll get Valentine cards from half the swinging dicks over here."

Hayes glared at him. "You asshole, you've got no romance in your heart. It's not the girl, it's the memory of the girl that's important. All women are pure as snow in our dreams, and they save themselves just for us. That's the fantasy that keeps us going."

"Speak for yourself," Blake said. "If my girl even thinks about doing it with someone else—she's dead!"

The interchange continued like this for another ten minutes. The concept of love versus carnal lust always provoked heated discussion. Hardy kept his distance from the battleground, not wanting to reveal his lack of experience in these areas. It always seemed more prudent to stay out of the fray whenever he trod through unfamiliar territory. He allowed the debate to rage on without any interference.

Hardy supposed his sexual encounters matched or surpassed some of those at the table. He had no way of knowing. Everyone lies when it comes to revealing sexual conquests. The truth is either downplayed or exaggerated depending on the circumstances, or who's doing the telling. Hardy tended to lean more toward protecting the identity and dignity of his female partners—few as they might have been.

He'd known girls in college— even convinced himself that he'd fallen in love on several occasions. Mike and his female partners had gone through the motions by saying the right words, but each encounter ended as experimentation—not a lasting relationship. He'd experienced sex— rushed and awkward, but each event lacked real passion and commitment. Consequently, he left for Vietnam without leaving his heart behind. Now, he only had memories of San Francisco and a girl named Clara.

The breakfast banter came to a close as men emptied their trays of food. Some of them made hasty plans to visit steam baths or whores. No one ever mentioned drug use in the chow hall, but several truckers intended to snort smak or smoke marijuana as part of their activities. Too many GIs believed that snorting smak helped them avoid addiction. Most of them learned the deadly truth too late. Staggering numbers of clean-cut American boys turned into addicts during the war in Vietnam. Some of them never reached manhood.

Hayes and his crew picked up their trays, leaving Hardy and Bates to finish their meal. The chow hall doors closed, but no one bothered to rush them out. They finished their coffee at a leisurely pace.

"What are your plans today, Lieutenant?" Bates asked.

"Oh, I don't know. I thought I'd take a ride up to Hanoi to convince the North Vietnamese to surrender."

"Great idea," Bates said. "I'll drive you up in *Bloody Mama* and clear the roads. C'mon, what are you doing today?"

"I'm afraid to answer," Hardy said. "I have a bad feeling you've already made plans for us."

"You sure are sharp today, Lieutenant." Bates leaned forward. "We're goin' to have a Valentine's Day cook-out."

"Fantastic. What's on the menu?"

Bates looked sheepish. "Well, we had a little accident."

"Here it comes," Hardy groaned.

"Yesterday, we were loading up one of the reefers with cases of frozen steaks and lobster tails when that dumb *Basher* dropped some of the boxes. It was a terrible tragedy."

Hardy suppressed a grin. "I bet it was."

"It was. There was a lot of damage, and *Basher* felt real bad. That poor boy is always havin' accidents. I never should have trusted him with such an important job. There's no way I could send damaged goods to the generals. We salvaged what we could. We'll just have to make it up to them later."

Hardy shook his head. "So, when do we eat?"

"1400 hours on the hill, next to your hooch. Rodriguez found charcoal and a grill. We bought ten cases of beer. Sergeant Hayes invited a bunch of bar girls and a few nurses might even show up. We've got enough food for 50 people. I guess you can invite some of your officer pals. Only one thing—don't tell anyone about the accident, okay?"

"Bates, your 'accidents' are going to land us both in the slammer," Hardy said.

"Nah, I'm too careful. I'd never let anything happen to you, Lieutenant."

"Right, that makes me feel a whole lot better."

"C'mon, let's go. We've got work to do."

Bates grabbed the ruins of his breakfast, dropped off his tray, and headed out the door. Hardy followed after him.

Everyone declared the party a great success. None of the guests had the audacity, or the bad manners, to ask where the host had procured the food. No one ever questioned good fortune in Vietnam. Even Capt. Adams made an appearance without asking questions. After devouring his plate of steak and lobster, he disappeared without comment.

Al, Wiley, and Joe arrived to enjoy the exotic fare. Al took photos of the party-goers, threatening to make copies of anyone caught in revelry. None of the nurses dared to make the scene. The threat of being surrounded by 50 horny GIs raised the risk level too high. Several bar girls did join the fun. Lulu, one of the bar girls, bounced from lap to lap. She delighted in wiggling her tight little bottom against the panting victims until they turned rock hard. At that point, she jumped away with the admonition, "No, no, you bad boy!" This game went on for some time, until she reached Al.

A smiling Al said, "Lulu, do you know anything about the tradition of Valentine's Day?"

Lulu had no idea, but she suspected the worse. She'd had dealings with Al in the past.

"Valentine's Day is a day of love, and all women have to give themselves to men. I want you, Lulu!"

Grabbing her like a sack of flour, he flung the struggling woman over his shoulder. She screamed and kicked to no avail. Al carried her flailing body into Hardy's hooch. The crowd listened to her pleas for help for about five minutes. Many of the GIs cheered and yelled, "Go Al!"

Finally, she broke free from his clutches. In complete disarray, she carried her tattered blouse while attempting to readjust her brassiere. Fumbling to regain her composure, she yelled at Al before making her escape. "You numbah 10, I hate you!"

Al sprang from the doorway and shot back at her. "Lulu, how can you say that? This is Valentine's Day; come back to me!"

Sticking out her chin, Lulu strode off with as much dignity as she could muster. Mike never heard of her playing her lap games again.

The party lasted until the crowd had consumed all the beer and food. Hardy remained behind to help Bates and his crew clean up.

"Great party, Sergeant," Hardy said. "All of us needed to blow off a little steam."

"I knew that," Bates replied. "Everything just kinda fell into place."

"*Fell* is right! Just make sure *Basher* doesn't have any more accidents. Otherwise, we'll have a bunch of pissed off generals on our backs."

"I've tried to train the boy," Bates said. "I'll make sure it doesn't happen again, unless..."

"Unless nothing—I might be forced to make you a corporal."

"Right, Lieutenant. I'll be real careful."

Entering his hooch, Hardy cleaned up the destruction left by Al and Lulu. All in all, the day had turned out well. The VC had made it possible for the men to enjoy a little diversion. Tomorrow the roads would re-open, and the convoys could go back to work.

Joe Tice was the king of Quang Ngai. Somehow, he'd obtained a lock on the daily trip to the city. His little convoy consisted of two refrigerated reefers and one gun truck. Since the run was only half the distance to Duc Pho, Joe usually returned home right after lunch. They made the trip to Quang Ngai for the sole purpose of filling both reefers with blocks of ice from the local icehouse. The owner of the operation was a slick little Vietnamese named Mr. Van.

Joe refused to share the duty with any of the other three officers. Strangely enough, Capt. Adams supported this arrangement by doing nothing to upset the status quo. Adams preferred a peripheral role as commander. He didn't get involved as long as everything worked and the unit maintained balance. Hardy had upset Adams' sense of balance upon his arrival, but they had settled into an uneasy relationship. Adams kept his distance and let him do his job. Mike became a regular on the Duc Pho run, but Joe Tice owned Quang Ngai. Adams seemed satisfied.

Hardy questioned Al and Wiley about the mysteries of Quang Ngai. They both had made the run for Joe on the rare occasions when he needed a substitute. Al had made the trip for a whole week while Joe was on R and R with his wife in Hawaii. After returning from Hawaii, Joe grabbed the reins to reclaim his prize. According to Al, Joe seemed so relieved to be back in Chu Lai that he spoke little about the five-day reunion with his wife. The mystery deepened.

Al and Wiley exchanged theories about Joe's attraction to Quang Ngai.

"I bet he's got a little gook pussy down there," Al said.

Wiley figured the 'milk run' gave him more time to screw off. Joe enjoyed a lazy existence by doing little more than absolutely necessary. Appearing to crave time alone, he kept his distance from the enlisted men. Joe hated anything to do with leadership. He only wore his rank as protection from the masses. Joe revealed occasional displays of humor, but he still remained an enigma. Hardy made it his mission to solve the mystery of Quang Ngai.

Because Sgt. Hayes made regular ice runs with Joe, Hardy decided to start with him.

"Shit man, Quang Ngai's a piece of cake—in and out, no sweat. We grab the ice and run."

"What goes on there?" Hardy asked.

"Not much. The gooks load the trucks with ice and we hang out until they're done."

"Where do you hang out? Do they have a place like Suzy's?"

"No way, Mr. Van has an office or something like a reception room with couches, a stereo system and the works. Joe hangs out there, but they bring us gook food and Cokes—free."

"Does Lieutenant Tice stay in the reception room?"

"Sure, most of the time. He and Van take off sometimes, but he usually hangs out inside. Why all the questions?"

"I'm just curious about Quang Ngai," Hardy replied without conviction. "I'd like to make the run myself."

"No way," said Hayes. "Screamin' Joe would never let you onto his turf."

"Why don't Sergeant Bates and *Bloody Mama* ever go as escorts?" Hardy asked.

"Joe doesn't like Bates. I'm not sure why. Maybe he's afraid Bates would crowd him too much."

"Bates would never get in the way. He's a solid guy."

"Yeah, sure, but I'm more of a free spirit. Maybe, Joe likes that."

Hardy decided not to question the man further. Having learned as much as possible, any additional questions would only make Hayes more suspicious.

Hardy chose Al as his next target. Al confirmed everything Sgt. Hayes had said about Mr. Van and the waiting room.

"Man, they treated us like kings—hot food and cold sodas. They even had cold beer, cigarettes, and Hershey Bars. The guy must have a solid lock on the black market."

"Or, he must really like American GIs," Mike said.

"Hell, I don't know. The guy was real smooth, but you could tell he was in charge. He never asked for anything. He just wanted to be friends, or so he said. I had the feeling, I could ask for a '68 Corvette, and he could deliver —for a price. I'll bet that beneath the silky charm is a real dangerous character."

"I wonder why he didn't try to hook you into his operation?"

"I don't know? Maybe, he was afraid I'd squash his nuts. Maybe it was my honest face."

"He probably didn't have enough time to get to know you like we do," Hardy said.

"Quang Ngai's good duty. Joe's got it soft and doesn't want to give it up. That's all there is to it. Don't get bent out of shape."

Hardy realized Al had probably drawn the right conclusion. He was making too much of it. Everything in Vietnam presented at least two faces. The people, the politics and the country exhibited multiple personalities. Truth eluded discovery and it was easy to get caught up in the undercurrent of confusion. Mike decided he needed to keep his balance amidst the chaos. He'd try to adopt the oriental philosophy of eternal patience.

Hardy contented himself with regular duty to Duc Pho. By now, having entered his fourth month in Vietnam, he earned the privilege of adopting the swagger common to most veterans. After learning most of the basic survival techniques, he could start hazing the 'cherries.' His jungle fatigues had faded after hours of exposure to the sun and multiple washings. Thirty percent of his tour stood behind him. Joe Tice had reached the ninety-eight percent mark. Joe would leave Chu Lai for home in two weeks.

Much discussion followed about who would assume the throne of Quang Ngai. Joe seemed reluctant to pass the scepter to anyone. Hardy guessed Joe had the closest ties to Wiley. Since Al had made him feel like a chump too often, the big man had little chance of competing for the job. Adams, however, made one of his rare leadership decisions. He decreed Quang Ngai duty would rotate among the three remaining officers. Rotation would continue until one of them left, or they were blessed with a new officer replacement.

"They'll probably just send me another God damned grunt," Adams muttered.

It appeared obvious that Hardy had still not made Adams' list of favorite people. In retrospect, Mike felt certain that the company commander held no one in close regard. He stretched his memory to name more than 2 or 3 of Adam's most trusted confidants. Determined never to enter Adams' circle of influence, Mike opted to avoid the man whenever possible.

Joe took on the responsibility of training his three replacements within the space of a week. Hardy made his first journey to Quang Ngai two days later. Joe appeared solemn during most of the trip with little to offer in the way of advice. They drove by the same familiar checkpoints

Hardy passed every day on his way to Duc Pho. Joe called them in with little enthusiasm. Hardy pressed him for conversation.

"You must be excited about going home next week?"

"Yeah, I guess so," Joe replied.

"Your wife will be glad to have you back," Hardy said.

"Sure, she writes to me every day."

"What's the first thing you're going to do when you get back to the States?"

"Hell, I don't know, Hardy. Kiss the dog and pat my wife. I'll send you a telegram," he snapped.

At this point Mike lost his cool. "Damn it, Joe. What's wrong with you? You should be excited about leaving this hellhole. You're going home alive!"

Joe didn't react immediately. He appeared to consider his response for several minutes. Finally, he replied in a measured tone. "You don't know anything about me, do you? None of us knows anything about each other over here. We talk, we tell lies, but no one really tells the truth. It's easier to play games and hide what's inside. You want the truth, Hardy? I don't want to go home. I want to stay here a while longer."

Joe's candor unsettled Hardy. "You're kidding. This place will kill you if you stay here long enough!"

"I've never felt so alive in my life," Joe replied. "I never had a real life, 'til I got over here. I grew up in a small town and married my high school sweetheart. This is the real world. Over here, people struggle to exist and just stay alive. You can feel the energy, the electricity. I was dead before I got here. This has been the greatest adventure of my life."

"This is no game, Joe. You can get killed and lose the life you're enjoying so much."

"You don't get it. The danger is the best part. I enjoy simple things I never enjoyed before—the smell of coffee, the taste of beer, and riding in the open air. Even diesel fumes and waking up at 5 a.m. are easier to deal with. I'm going to miss it a lot. It's depressing to know I'll never feel this way again."

Hardy had no more answers. He studied the church ruins and rice fields as they drove by. Nothing looked different. Everything was in place. Nothing had changed, except him. Although disturbed by Joe's confession, he knew what he had meant. Like Joe, he felt the same thrill of the road. He wondered why it surprised him to hear someone else admit it. Mike had received more information from Joe Tice than he ever expected.

The rest of the trip proved uneventful. Turning down a small street in Quang Ngai, they stopped in front of the icehouse.

Mr. Van appeared smiling with his arms open. "Welcome, American friends. You bring new officer to meet me Lieutenant Joe. Come inside we eat."

The reception room looked just like Sgt. Hayes had described it. Low couches and teak coffee tables decorated the room. Incense burned in the corner and Vietnamese artwork adorned the walls. This room had been designed to impress visitors. Although the clock read only 10 a.m., Van insisted on feeding them lunch. A middle-aged woman appeared carrying cans of ice-cold cola, followed by a young Vietnamese girl carrying trays heaped with steaming food. Platters of french fries, steamed vegetables, fried meat and bowls of rice and soup filled the table. One of the platters contained chunks of fried meat with tiny ribs. Visions of various local rodents appeared in Hardy's mind. He ended up nibbling on the french fries and eating a little rice.

"You not hungry?" Van asked.

"No, but the food looks great," Hardy said. "I'm still pretty full from breakfast."

It occurred to him later, he'd probably shouted his response at Mr. Van. Americans always seem to address foreigners as if they're hard of hearing. Somehow, the speaker feels that shouting helps the listener better comprehend the English language. In reality, the reverse is probably true and the victim is forced to endure the insult.

Following the meal, Hardy walked outside to the street. A group of children approached and stood around him smiling. As usual, he carried hard candy in his pocket for these occasions. The children gleefully accepted the goodies. One little boy reached up to hand him a notebook. Inside the book, he found English lessons along with attempts by the boy to capture the letters of the alphabet. Having formed several words like *cat, dog* and *boy*, the boy seemed proud of his efforts. Some Vietnamese kids worked hard to identify with the Americans stationed in their country. Others harbored the futile hope of leaving Vietnam for a new life in America. Most of them just wanted to take advantage of the GIs for as long as possible. Mike couldn't blame them for wanting a better life. Patting the little boy on the head, he gave him a 'thumbs up' sign. The boy smiled and beamed with pride.

Two hours later, the reefers made ready to leave after loading up with ice. Van offered dramatic gestures of parting. Waving until the last truck passed out of sight, it looked like he was saying goodbye to his best friends in the world. Mike found it difficult to accept Van's sincere admiration for Americans. Something ominous had permeated the atmosphere—like an ax waiting to fall. However, the man gave no hint of his ulterior motives. Hardy knew that he and Mr. Van would meet again.

Joe wasn't willing to share any insights about Mr. Van's behavior during the ride home. His only response: "Mr. Van's okay. He's always treated me well."

After that, Mike tried to encourage Joe to share his road duty experiences. Applying an unassuming approach, he asked Joe's advice about running convoys. The morose man brushed off Hardy's overtures by refusing any form of conversation. Joe had already said he didn't want to go home. And, Mike concluded, he resented leaving others behind to fill his shoes. With nothing else say, they returned to Chu Lai in silence.

Unable to solve the mystery of Quang Ngai on his first excursion into the city, Hardy's instincts warned him to avoid Van's operation. He hoped to keep his distance from the icehouse gang.

Joe Tice was another matter. Mike had tried to develop a friendship with him during the past few months, but Joe dealt with people on his own terms. Except for the momentary outburst on the road to Quang Ngai, Joe never revealed anything more about himself. He would always remain an enigma, but Mike Hardy would never forget Joe Tice.

CHAPTER 15
Farewell Joe

Hardy often thought about the old saying: "War brings out the worst in men." While recognizing great truth in the adage, he recalled witnessing numerous acts of senseless violence during his first four months in Vietnam. Soldiers thrust into war shared something in common with the James Bond character—a license to kill. The army expected this license to carry maturity, sensitivity, and common sense as prerequisites. Unfortunately, GIs who lacked these essentials took great pleasure in inflicting pain on the helpless—often without fear of recrimination. The army never exerted much effort to screen recruits for this character flaw. They gave them guns and trained them to kill without hesitation. Some men excelled in the business by destroying the enemy with great relish. The army was pleased. Those soldiers not assigned to combat units had to find other targets of opportunity.

Mike and Joe ended their one and only run to Quang Ngai on a sour note. Joe remained bitter after his earlier outburst and appeared agitated during the return trip. Hardy gave him as much space as possible on the gun truck. However, once they passed through the gates of Chu Lai, Mike made the mistake of trying to make amends.

"Joe, I'm sorry. I should have kept my mouth shut back there. I didn't mean to push so hard."

Joe stared ahead trying to ignore his presence.

Determined to press his apology, Mike continued. "Joe, I'm sorry. You pissed me off with all that talk about not wanting to go home."

Joe turned on the attack. "Fuck you! You think you've got all the answers don't you, Hardy? Do me a favor. I've got one week left—just keep out of my way."

That was Mike's last attempt at trying to make peace with Joe Tice.

Returning to the company area, they found the compound in turmoil. Hardy heard yelling and shots fired close by. Trying to make sense of the situation, Mike assumed the company had come under attack by the enemy.

PFC Johnson approached them running from the orderly room.

Jumping down from the truck, Hardy confronted the breathless man. "What's going on?"

"We're shooting all the dogs. The old man heard a rumor about rabies in the area. He told us to kill all the dogs in the company."

Without waiting for a response, Johnson rushed off.

Dumbfounded, Hardy observed the chaos. Many of the truckers kept pets and fed them scraps from the mess hall. The animals provided companionship during off-duty hours. Mike always enjoyed watching the dogs line up to wait for their masters to return home. Since the animals were a prized possession, he couldn't believe Adams had ordered the slaughter. GIs returning from convoy duty would react with fury at finding their beloved canines exterminated on a sudden whim of the commander.

Hardy didn't have a dog, but Al kept a little brown mutt in his hooch. All the residents took turns with his care and feeding. As the only pet on Sand Hill, he clearly belonged to Al. Pretending the mutt had little value, Al made a point of calling him *Turd.* "He looks like a turd and ain't worth a shit."

In spite of this inglorious name, anyone could see a deep attachment between dog and master. At this moment, Al was away from the compound on road duty. Without a moment of hesitation, Mike made up his mind to protect the beast. The big man would be crushed if anything happened to his little mutt. Mike rushed toward Al's hooch on the errand of mercy.

Halfway up the hill, he ran into Capt. Adams. Agitated, Adams waved his arms like a crippled buzzard. "Give me your .45," he ordered.

Instinctively, Hardy's hand went down to the holster holding his pistol, "What for?"

"Don't give me any shit, asshole!" Adams shouted. "I'm going to shoot some dogs. Give it to me!"

Standing face to face with a crisis, Mike realized this confrontation called for a leadership decision. Staring at Adams, he understood his entire career depended on obeying the man. Refusing a direct order could land him in the middle of a court martial. Knees shaking, he tightened his grip on the pistol. After a moment of hesitation he replied, "I can't give it to you. I'm signed for it."

Eyes bulging, Adam's face turned beet red. "Give me that weapon right now, or I'm going to kick your sorry ass down the hill!"

Hardy prepared himself for the attack. "No sir, I'm sorry I can't do that."

The next few seconds flew by in a supersonic blur. Grabbing at Mike's uniform, Adams started pulling at the pistol. Hardy resisted the temptation to hit the pock-marked face. Any assault on the company commander would only make the situation worse. During the struggle, Mike exerted more strength than his furious opponent. Over-matched, Adams released his grip when the younger man forced him to his knees. The defeated man scrambled to his feet while giving his subordinate one last shove.

"You're in deep trouble, shithead!" he screeched. "I'm going to bring you up on charges. You're confined to quarters until I decide what to do with you. Get out of my sight!"

"Yes, sir," Hardy replied.

Preparing to leave, he turned around to face Adams. "I'm going to my hooch, but I'm taking Al's dog with me. If anything happens to the dog, you'll have to answer to Al."

"Fuck you!" Adams shot back. "Keep talking and

you'll get yourself in more trouble." Glaring at Hardy one last time, he stumbled toward the compound.

Racing to the top of the hill, Mike found Turd hiding under Al's hooch. It took some coaxing, but the little mutt eventually left his sanctuary. Lifting the dog off the ground, he cradled him in his arms. Safely inside his hooch, Mike locked the door behind him. Hardy realized that his entire career stood in jeopardy. With reckless abandon, he'd made up his mind to protect the little dog. Having defied Capt. Adams, he had no other option but to wait for whatever punishment would follow.

Shots rang out in the compound for the remainder of the afternoon. Hardy cringed every time he heard the muted explosions. Each shot raised the possibility of more lives being lost in the slaughter. Mike held onto his .45 while Turd shivered in his lap. Having no idea what else to expect, he visualized Adams returning at any moment with an armed escort. No one came. After a while the shooting stopped; the massacre had ended. Hardy wondered if Al's dog remained as the sole survivor of the carnage.

Al returned several hours later yelling for his mutt.

Hardy stuck his head out the door. "He's in here with me, Al. He's okay."

Al rushed into the hooch. "God damn, they're all dead. The place has gone crazy. Thank God, you're safe, Turd. Come here boy!"

Jumping up into his arms, the little dog started licking

his face. The joyful reunion justified all the trouble Hardy had endured.

"Thanks, Grunt," Al said wiht gratitude. I really appreciate you taking care of him. Tell me what happened."

Hardy related all the details of the experience. He gave him a complete account of his confrontation with Adams.

"That son of a bitch, I'll crush his balls with a hammer. Don't worry Grunt. I'll take care of Adams. He pissed off a lot of people today. I appreciate you sticking your neck out for my dog. Adams won't touch you, I promise."

"Thanks. I keep waiting for the MPs to show up and take me off to jail."

Al laughed for the first time since his arrival. "Don't you worry about a thing. Adams is a weasel. I can handle him. You did me a big favor, and I won't forget it. Adams will be lucky to survive the week without someone blowing him away. Are you okay?"

"Yeah, sure."

Hardy felt secure for the first time that afternoon. Shaking his hand, Al thanked him again before carrying his dog back to his hooch.

Mike spent a sleepless night in his bunk. Hoping to escape serious retribution from Adams, the magnitude of his defiance remained with him. He couldn't remember committing a more serious offense in his life. In spite of his lofty motives, he'd refused to follow a direct order. During wars in the past, soldiers faced firing squads for committing the same offense. The thought of standing in front of a dozen loaded rifles didn't make for peaceful slumber. He tossed and turned at regular intervals.

Hardy awoke at dawn not sure of his status. Although scheduled for the Duc Pho run, he didn't dare leave his hooch. Having no choice, he waited for the final verdict.

Al showed up an hour later with breakfast on a tray. "Good morning, Grunt. You did call for room service, right?"

"Thanks. What's going on?"

"All hell's breaking loose. Lieutenant Colonel Hollins, the battalion commander, has been behind closed doors with Adams for over an hour. Someone threw a tear gas grenade under Adams' office last night. I bet he's really pissing in his pants. He's lucky it wasn't a real one. They'd better get him out of here fast, or he's a dead man."

"Jesus," Hardy gasped. "What am I supposed to do?"

"Sit tight for now, Wiley and Joe will cover for you. Hollins told me to stick around. I'll let you know when something develops. Eat your breakfast before it gets cold." He slapped Hardy on the back. "Don't worry, you'll be okay. Remember, I promised, right?"

"Thanks, I'll be here if you need me," Mike said.

"Clean this place up. It looks like shit. It looks almost as disgusting as my dump." Squeezing his arm, Al left him with cold eggs and bacon.

Due to his confinement, Hardy had missed dinner the night before. Feeling faint from the effects of hunger, he dug in.

Mama San walked in as he cleared the remnants off his tray. He wondered how much she had heard about the previous day's events. She started cleaning without saying a word. Mike tried to stay out of her way, but he felt restless in his cage. He paced the floor hoping Al would return with news of his pardon. The minutes dragged on with no sounds except for those made by Mama San sweeping. In a daze, he sat on the edge of the bed to watch her work.

Approaching him at one point, she gestured her need to sweep under the bed. Moving out of the way, he watched as she bent over to perform the task. The motion of her body had an intoxicating effect on him. Without thinking, he put his hand on her waist. She didn't resist the contact. She acknowledged the touch by putting her hand over his. The broom slid slowly to the floor. Looking at him with curiosity, she didn't resist when he pulled her closer.

Hardy made a half-hearted attempt to listen to the inner voice warning him to stop touching her, but his pent-up sexual frustration took control of his actions. Nerves raw, a pulse throbbed in his temples. Moving his hand under her pajama top, he reached for one of her heavy breasts. Massaging the silky flesh, her nipple responded immediately to his touch. She moaned when he slipped his other hand between her legs. After guiding her down on the bed, he removed the pajama top. Taut nipples stood fully erect.

Content to let him control their lovemaking, she

watched his hands slide to the elastic of her pajama bottoms. As he pulled the bottoms down, she lifted her hips to ease the task. His hands traveled up and down her body. Her flesh felt soft and warm to his touch. His mouth moved to her nipples. Her skin tasted like an exotic musk. When his fingers touched her sparse pubic hair, she opened her legs. The wetness seemed to reach out to him. Without hesitation, he responded to the invitation. Each caress felt like a soothing balm. Each thrust released more of his repressed tension. Each moan sounded like a symphony of contentment. He had found temporary refuge in the arms of this Vietnamese woman. The world outside seemed far away.

The end came too quickly, but the final seconds pulsed with exquisite pleasure. Mike had never experienced a more powerful release. He held her until the waves of passion had subsided. After regaining control of his breathing, he rolled over on his back to indulge in the lingering sensations. Mama San's face still glowed from the intensity of their union.

Leaving him lying on the bed, she walked naked to the washbasin. After she returned with soap and a wet washcloth, the two lovers took turns washing off the remains of their encounter. Hardy recalled another occasion when she had given him a thorough washing. At that time, she'd shown him great kindness. Moved by the memory, Mike searched for a sign that mutual need, not charity, had prompted her participation in their lovemaking.

He was unable to read her thoughts. Mama San remained inscrutable.

Not wanting to cheapen the experience, he resisted the urge to give her money. In the end, he gave her some candy bars for her son. She thanked him and left. Mike watched with sadness as she walked down the hill, but he would have more opportunities to explore the relationship.

Several hours later, Al arrived with the news that Capt. Adams had received orders for immediate transfer to another unit. Al also announced that Mike had dodged major punishment for his breach in discipline. However, as an alternative to a court martial, he would have to undergo a verbal reprimand from LtCol. Hollins.

"It's no sweat," Al assured him. "Nothing goes on your record and the case is closed. You can go back to work tomorrow."

"Thanks, Al. By the way, who's going to replace Adams?"

"You won't believe this shit—me. Hollins said I was the ranking man since no captains were available. I guess you're stuck with me, until I get blown away or fired."

"Hey, that's great. I might really get to like this place, after all."

"You might, but if you ever disobey a direct order from me you'll be wearing your ass around your shoulders."

Punching him lightly in the stomach, Al turned to leave. "Oh, now that I'm in charge of this dump you're officially off confinement. Let's go to the club to celebrate."

Hardy pulled on a clean shirt before joining him outside.

Three days later, the Sand Hill gang held a farewell party for Joe. Joe had asked his fellow officers to keep it low-key. No naked girls jumping out of cakes, no drunken orgies, and no expensive gifts. Mike had paid a Korean craftsman to make a brass engraving of a gun truck with the words, *QUANG NGAI, 1971.* Joe accepted the plaque with his thanks. A few other officers joined the party to wish him well. No one made speeches, shed any tears, or expressed regrets. Joe merely said, "Thank you" and wished everyone well.

Another tour of duty had ended. Unable to resolve their personal conflict, Mike and Joe parted less than friends. Maybe Joe would find some inner contentment after leaving Vietnam. Mike knew he'd carry the memory of Joe Tice with him whenever he made the Quang Ngai run in the future. The legacy of the King of Quang Ngai would continue for a while longer, but Mike Hardy had no intention of assuming the crown.

It didn't take long for life in the truck company to return to normal. Convoys still left to make their daily runs. Al moved into Adams' old office to assume his new duties. Everyone seemed pleased with the appointment. The transition process proceeded smoothly, even though Adams didn't stick around to pass on the reins of command. He departed without notice or ceremony.

As the new company commander, one of Al's first acts was to request two more officers for convoy duty. Adams never went out with the trucks, but Al remained in the rotation continuing to take his turn. He pledged to share the responsibility until more help arrived.

Two days after the dog massacre, Hardy reported to LtCol. Hollins' office. After offering the colonel a crisp salute, Hollins gestured for him to sit down. The battalion commander seemed friendly enough. He asked for an explanation of what happened.

Hardy offered his version of the confrontation with Adams. He explained why he had refused to relinquish the pistol. "I was confused and afraid to give up my weapon. Captain Adams acted totally out of control. Looking back, I probably made the wrong decision, but at the time it just didn't seem right to give it to him."

"Well, that's all behind us now." Hollins drawled in a thick North Carolina accent. "Lieutenant Miller tells me you're a good officer. Sometimes good officers make mistakes. Let's just say you made a mistake, and it won't happen again. Am I right?"

"Yes, sir," Hardy jumped to his feet. "I want to stay in the company. I'll do a good job."

"I know you will, son." Moving from behind his desk, Hollins placed a big hand on Hardy's shoulder. "Sometimes, we think we're so right that we don't leave room for any other point of view. Once you get a little more experience under your belt, things won't always look so black or white to you. Good officers weigh all the evidence before they take a stand. I think you'll do all right." He shook Mike's hand.

The young lieutenant saluted and left his office.

Hardy's heart pounded like a kettledrum as he surged out of the building. Having avoided serious punishment, he felt rejuvenated. Even though he'd received a subtle rebuke, the battalion commander's encouragement had left him feeling buoyant. Hollins had made a point not to shatter his ego; he had allowed the lieutenant to walk away with dignity. Sometime later, it occurred to Mike that the two greatest contributions we can bestow on others are the gifts of respect and dignity. He made himself a promise to always remember that lesson during his future dealings with others.

Mike found Sgt. Bates yelling at *Hit Man* as he walked

past *Bloody Mama.* "You stupid asshole, you left the machine gun uncovered last night and now it's full of rust! You ain't worth a shit!"

Hardy made a note to himself to have a talk with Sgt. Bates about human dignity as soon as possible.

In addition to their regular duties, company officers also had responsibility for night security detail. Each lieutenant in the unit took his turn at the job twice a week. Surrounded by barbed wire and sandbags, the 73d Transportation Company had orders to guard an assigned sector every night. Required to post two guards in each bunker, the duty officer had make sure they stayed alert at all times. Intelligence officers had issued warnings that enemy sappers could slip through the barbed wire in the darkness, cut the throats of sleeping guards, and set off explosive charges. These sappers, or specialists trained in breaching enemy defenses, could crawl in on the land, or swim in from the sea to reach their targets. If left unprotected, nothing of strategic importance could escape the reach of the enemy. Truckers by day turned into warriors at night for guard duty. Most of them were uncomfortable in the role.

This particular night, Lt. Hardy had Sgt. Bates assigned as his duty NCO. Their first responsibility was to inspect the troops before sending them to the bunkers. Following the inspection, the two men had to make sure the guards had weapons and enough ammunition for the job. In addition, Lt. Hardy had to quiz his guards on their duties, and pass on any orders of the day. Recent reports advised that enemy activity had increased in the area. Hardy's instructions included an upgraded alert status for Chu Lai. After observing the sorry state of his troops, Mike shook his head in dismay. He had little confidence that they could live up to the challenge.

The company had the job of manning six bunkers on the beach. The plan called for two men assigned to each bunker. Each watch lasted two hours. One man always remained awake while the other slept. Unfortunately, that plan didn't hold water. In reality, both men slept all night after snorting smak or smoking joints. During an earlier night duty assignment, Hardy had informed Bates that he wanted to inspect the bunkers.

Bates recoiled in horror. "Are you crazy? If you go down there and wake them up, they'll think you're a gook and blow you away. Stay away from those dope heads, and you'll live a lot longer."

Hardy took his advice. After that, the VC had an open path into the bowels of Chu Lai, courtesy of the 73d Transportation Company.

This night, Hardy expressed his outrage at the sorry state of the GIs on duty. Several of them appeared stoned and incoherent. When he looked into the eyes of PFC Ames, the man returned his gaze with a blank, glassy stare. Unable to focus, Ames had no idea who he was or why he stood in formation.

Hardy pulled Sgt. Bates aside. "I can't send him to the

bunker. That's the same junkie who almost caused the wreck in Quang Ngai."

"You've got to, Lieutenant," Bates said. "He's too fucked up to drive tomorrow, and we can't replace him with one of the good men. We need drivers."

"The rest of these guys aren't much better off," Hardy said. "I won't be able to get any sleep tonight with them on watch. Charlie could slip in and blow us all away."

Bates offered a sympathetic shrug.

Unable to do anything more to solve the problem, Hardy resigned himself to accept the situation. He couldn't believe how much military discipline had eroded during the course of the war in Vietnam. Although he had no intention of signing on as a career soldier, he still felt obligated to do his duty. Political maneuvering and the anti-war demonstrations back home had changed everything. Some GIs used these events as excuses to lead wasted lives. Although he felt some sympathy for their predicament, he refused to join their ranks.

With reluctance, Hardy took Sgt. Bates' advice by sending all the guards to their posts. On the way back to the orderly room, they passed the nightly *meat wagon*. A small group of ragged whores jumped from the back of an army truck. Sgt. Rodriguez controlled the operation, but he wasn't in sight. Normally, duty officers ignored this nightly ritual because they considered it harmless recreation for the troops. In spite of medical briefings about the benefits of wearing condoms, unprotected sexual activity continued unabated. Those soldiers throwing caution to the wind paid the price by contracting several different, virulent strains of venereal disease. Usually, the unpleasant experience convinced the participant to refrain from further unprotected sex. One popular rumor circulated that an incurable form of VD, found only in Southeast Asia, could result in genital amputation. In spite of the risks, the games continued.

Bates and Hardy watched the girls as they giggled their way toward the barracks. Shocked, Hardy observed that the last girl in line looked about six months pregnant. He couldn't understand why she continued to ply her trade in her present condition. When he called out to her, she ran up to him smiling.

"Hey, GI. You want numbah one boom-boom—five dollah?"

What a night! Hardy thought. *Dope heads asleep in the bunkers and pregnant whores in the barracks.* But as he pointed to her belly, what he said, was, "No boom-boom. You have baby san."

Smiling, she patted her extended abdomen. "No boom-boom, okay." Still giggling, she ran off to join the others.

Hardy snarled at Sgt. Bates. "This place really sucks!"

"Well, look on the bright side. At least you ain't the daddy." Bates gave him a devilish smirk. "You're not the daddy, are you, Lieutenant?"

"Fuck off, Bates! You know better than that. I don't chase whores."

"That's too bad. You could use a little nookie to lift your spirits."

"My spirits are fine. This damn army needs the help, not me. We're dragging ourselves through a sewer."

"Don't worry, we'll clean up the sewer—you, me, and *Bloody Mama*. We'll get rid of all this shit in no time." So it went.

After entering the orderly room, Hardy and Bates continued their discussion about corruption in Vietnam. Bates had risen above the illegal pursuits of his peers by dedicating himself to a useful purpose. He lived to command *Bloody Mama* and protect the convoys. This commitment gave meaning to his existence, along with a reason to get out of bed each morning.

"Most of these boys are homesick and scared. They feel like they've got no reason to be here. Drugs either help them kill the time, or they end-up killing the smak-head. Every one of them has to pay the price. You can't do anything to change that, Lieutenant."

Not able to accept this advice, Hardy felt the need to confront the problem. He considered taking on Private Ames as his special project. Sensing Ames was a decent kid at heart, he hoped to bring him back to life with some encouragement. He just needed to find the right key.

Just before midnight, four MPs entered the orderly room. They advised Lt. Hardy that they intended to make a "health and welfare" inspection of the barracks. An obvious ruse, the inspection gave them an excuse to confiscate drugs and arrest whores. Hardy and Bates had no choice but to go with them.

Mike heard loud music and smelled marijuana as they approached the barracks. Since the residents held parties every night, the MPs had no trouble collecting evidence. The military cops could choose their targets at will. Fortunately, they rarely conducted these raids, preferring to leave law enforcement in the hands of the unit commander. Unfortunately, they chose tonight as an exception to that policy.

Although he never entered the barracks after dark, Hardy expected the worse. Already aware that whores worked inside, he could only guess what else waited for them. He hoped the MPs had enough common sense not to barge into the rooms. Once they started banging on doors, any number of dangers waited on the other side. A crazy, hopped-up GI, fearing an attack by the enemy, could start firing his M-16 at the intruders. Aware of this danger, Hardy noticed that the MPs knocked gently, and stood aside before entering each room.

They found three truck drivers in the first room smoking grass. The occupants didn't hear the intruders because of their loud music. Once alerted that the Gestapo had arrived, they hastily deposited their joints in butt cans.

"What are you boys doin' in here?" asked the head MP. "Smells like ya'll are burnin' incense. Is that right?"

They all stammered at once. "Right, right, right."

"I thought so. You boys got any hard stuff in here? Let's open those wall lockers."

Each one the men fumbled for keys before opening their lockers. The MPs sifted through all their belongings. They found porno magazines, switchblade knives, a small bag of grass, and a pair of handcuffs.

"Damn, these are better than mine," said one of the MPs. "What are you doing with handcuffs?"

One of the drivers blurted out in desperation, "We're goin' to use them on enemy prisoners."

"Shee—it, you truck boys don't never see Charlie, unless he decides to shoot at your ass. What's in this little ol' plastic bag—some of that incense?"

"Right," the truckers agreed in unison.

"Well, we'll take it with us. We don't want you boys to burn down the building. Whew, you need to open a window to let in some air. The incense smell is strong in here."

One of the residents rushed to the window, while the other two fanned wildly at the clouds of blue smoke.

"You boys be careful and don't play with matches. Be good now."

They exited the room leaving the GIs madly clearing out the smoke. The MPs were after bigger game.

They found one of the girls in the next room. Having just completed her community service, she was in the process of getting dressed. Startled, the terrified prostitute attempted to cover the exposed parts of her body. Her unlucky customer didn't know how to react, so he covered his head with a pillow.

The senior MP walked over to pull the pillow away from his hapless victim. "Hello, you're not tryin' to hide from me, are you boy?"

Sitting up quickly, the GI covered himself with the sheet. "No—No, I was just..."

"I know, I know," The MP replied in a soothing tone. "You were just getting ready to say goodbye to your sister. This is your sister, isn't it?"

Appearing totally confused, the young man could only blink in response.

"That's all right. We'll take her with us when we leave. We'll make sure she catches her plane back home. You know it's funny that I don't see any family resemblance. She almost looks like a local girl. Well, we'll sort things out. By the way, let's have a look in your locker."

They conducted a thorough search without finding any drugs, but uncovered a live hand grenade.

"Damn, son—you're not supposed to have this in your room. You could blow yourself up. We'll take it along with us. You behave yourself. Next time, keep your sister out of the barracks."

The GI nodded in agreement. The MPs went after more prey.

The raiders found the next room empty because the occupants were on guard duty. One of the wall lockers stood open with the name AMES above the door. Pawing through the contents, the MPs found several small, plastic containers, each about the size of a thimble. The containers looked empty, but traces of white powder residue remained.

"Bingo," said one of the searchers. They found several other containers hidden in the room.

"Lieutenant, since we found evidence of drugs we're going to break all the locks."

Hardy didn't appreciate this invasion, but nodded his consent. The MPs quickly snapped all the locks before discovering more containers. They placed all the drug evidence in marked plastic bags, made notes on the men involved, and moved on.

Finding the door of next room ajar, the raiders entered without knocking. Hardy reacted with shock at the scene before him. One of the beefy mechanics was fully engaged in sex with one of the whores. Startled by the intruders, the woman screamed. The stunned mechanic quickly withdrew himself from his agitated partner. Disengaged, he sat up, fully erect, with his massive belly heaving. The poor girl made no move to conceal her body, staring at the search party like a cornered feline. Her legs remained wide open from the effort of accommodating her bulky customer. Hardy hoped she'd move quickly to cover herself, but she didn't. One of the MPs had to throw her a blanket.

"Well, what do we have here?" asked the senior MP. He appeared unfazed by the scene before him.

"Oh, shit." Groaning, the mechanic dropped his head into his hands.

"It looks to me like you're interrogating a VC prisoner. Is that some kind of secret technique? We should try it ourselves. You got any drugs or contraband in here?"

The portly GI shook his head and the subsequent search revealed nothing. The MPs ordered the girl to get dressed before escorting her out of the building. They left the mechanic behind, red-faced, and dazed.

The search continued for another hour until all the girls were apprehended and taken outside. They discovered more truckers smoking grass, but released them without filing any charges. The searchers found more plastic containers and marked them as evidence. The inspection had proven productive. Before leaving, the MPs filled out the paperwork in the orderly room. They promised to send copies of their report to Al.

Except for a burst of M-16 fire at 3 a.m. nothing else interrupted the night. One nervous GI called from the bunkers to report movement in the wire. The caller thought he'd seen something when he woke up to take a leak.

"Do you see anything now?" Hardy asked.

"Nah, I must've scared him off."

"Okay, let me know if you see anything else."

The rest of the night passed without incident.

At dawn, the guards stumbled up from their bunkers to eat breakfast at the mess hall. Hardy logged in the events from the previous night for Al to read. The company had escaped infiltration by the enemy, but the unit had endured an assault by the MPs. At some point, an obscure authority figure in the legal office would file charges. Disciplinary action would follow, but nothing would change. Drug use would continue and the whores would return tomorrow. Mike climbed up the hill to his hooch, collapsed on his bunk, and fell into a deep sleep.

Al exploded when he read the MP reports on the barracks raid. "Those bastards had no business tearing into our company. Every unit has drug problems. They wrote us up for prostitutes in the barracks, numerous cases of marijuana use, and cited six individuals for possession of heroin. Lieutenant Colonel Hollins told me to clean things up so he doesn't have to get involved."

"What are you going to do?" Hardy asked.

"Shit! I'll have to give Article 15 discipline to the smak heads. After that, we'll try to clean them up. I want you to talk to Rodriguez about controlling his whores. The whole barracks is on notice to straighten up, or I'll knock some goddamn heads together."

Life in the barracks had already started to change. Immediately following the great raid, stronger security measures went into effect. Residents took extra pains to keep their drugs out of sight. Security guards always stood in place to watch for MPs. Trucks stopped unloading prostitutes in the middle of the compound. Their handlers slipped them in after dark through a side door in the barracks. Vice continued, but in a more controlled environment. In spite of all these changes, Hardy still needed to talk to Sgt. Rodriguez.

Mike had first met Sgt. Rodriguez after he and Wiley finished repairing the Sand Hill hooch. At that point, Wiley encouraged him to visit the supply room for bedding and cleaning materials. Everyone knew Rodriguez maintained the best-stocked supply room in Vietnam. Hardy would soon discover the full scope of the operation.

Staff Sergeant George Rodriguez hailed from Phoenix, Arizona with eight years of army experience. He had twinkling brown eyes, a car salesman's smile, and a politician's handshake. Supply was his life and he knew how to play the system like a concert violinist. At some point, during two tours of duty in Vietnam, Sgt. Rodriguez had perfected the art of wheeling and dealing.

"Welcome to the company, Lieutenant. I heard we had a new officer. What can I do for you?"

"I need a broom, mop, bucket, cleaning supplies, blankets, sheets, a pillow and some other stuff. Do you have them?"

Rodriguez laughed. "Sure, that's easy. I've got anything you need. Let me explain something to you." He held up a thick notebook. "I tell this to all the new officers. This book contains everything we're supposed to have in the company supply room. We've got it all. I also keep a back-up warehouse with extra supplies of everything we're authorized to have and some things we're not. None of the extra stuff is in our books. You never know when we'll need the extras. I also handle special orders. You need something hard to get, and I'll get it. We can always work out some arrangement. My only rule is—no drugs. GIs will never get drugs from me. I don't mind handling some of life's other pleasures, but no drugs. We've got a good thing going here, Lieutenant. I'm always ready for inspection, and I always pass with flying colors. I tell you this in good faith. I can always use more partners, but if you're not interested, don't get in the way of my operation."

Hardy bristled at the veiled threat.

Rodriguez gave him a knowing smile and continued. "You need me Lieutenant—maybe not now, but you will some day. I always take care of my people in the company first—that's a promise. Now, tell me what you need and I'll have it delivered."

Experiencing conflicting sensations of discomfort and awe, Hardy felt some discomfort at Rodriguez's unabashed candor and the massive scope of the supply operation. Having placed all his cards on the table, the supply sergeant waited for the new lieutenant to play his hand. Mike had no intention of delving into the workings of the man's inner sanctum. But in spite of everything, he appreciated Rodriguez's ingenuity and admired his spirit.

Hardy offered Rodriguez his hand. "Thanks for the briefing, Sergeant. It's a pleasure to meet you."

Rodriguez grabbed a notepad. "Okay, now give me that list of all the stuff you need."

Two hours later, a truck parked in front of Hardy's new residence. Rodriguez supervised as an assistant unloaded the supplies. In addition to the items Hardy had requested, the delivery included 10 cartons of cigarettes, a canned fruitcake, 5 cases of beer, an M-16 rifle, and an M-2 carbine with extra magazines. Mike already owned an M-16, but Rodriguez advised him to keep an extra in case he needed it. The M-2 carbine had done duty as a combat staple during World War II. With the advent of the war in Vietnam it had found new popularity. Simply by owning one, carbine owners attained special status. The rugged weapon was lightweight, accurate, and dependable. Meanwhile, jungle troops complained about the M-16 jamming during the heat of battle. The supply sergeant claimed he had found it just lying around.

When Hardy thanked him for the extras, Rodriguez made light of the gesture.

"They're just a few little *Welcome Wagon* gifts, Lieutenant. I look forward to working with you."

He drove off leaving Hardy surrounded by the bounty. That ended the first encounter with Staff Sergeant Rodriguez.

Mike made it a point to maintain a cordial relationship with Sgt. Rodriguez during the months that followed. He rarely requested special favors, or interfered with supply room business. Rodriguez seemed content with the arrangement, but today was a different matter. Hardy needed the supply sergeant's help to keep Al out of trouble. He entered the supply room. "Sergeant Rodriguez, we need to do something about the whores in the barracks."

"I know," he replied. "Things got out of hand. I should have seen it coming. Next time, I will."

"How are you going to stop the MPs?"

"I'm not, but now I've got a friend who'll warn me when they're coming. I should have had someone inside before, but I didn't think it was necessary. Don't worry, it won't happen again. We're taking precautions, but I'll keep a sharp watch out anyway. Tell Lieutenant Miller there won't be any more trouble from the MPs."

"Thanks, Sergeant Rodriguez. Al's a great guy and he doesn't need the heat."

"Don't worry, everything's under control," the supply sergeant said. As far as Hardy knew, Rodriguez always kept his promises.

Al took care of the necessary discipline. He called in all the GIs charged with heroin possession to offer them a choice. If they wanted to plead guilty, he could give them Article 15 punishment to close the matter. If they pleaded innocent, he would arrange for a Summary Court Martial. Punishment from a court martial could have severe consequences. Fortunately, all the accused men pleaded guilty so Al reduced them one grade in rank. PFC Ames would now be Pvt. Ames. In addition, Al offered each soldier the opportunity for rehabilitation. They could go to a hospital for treatment with no penalty attached. None of the men took the option, declaring they could handle things themselves. These GIs, like many of their comrades, still held onto the fantasy they could quit their drug habits at will.

The army knew it had a serious drug problem in Vietnam. To counteract the growing trend, they offered medical intervention to addicted GIs, but few took advantage of the program. Drug screening and discipline served as the last line of defense. Every soldier leaving Vietnam had to take a urine test. Those detected with drug traces in their urine, were detained until they dried out. Unable to stem the growing tide of addicts, the army focused on a public relations campaign to deal with the dilemma. A flood of pamphlets arrived warning about the physical dangers of drugs, along with unveiled threats to prosecute the violators. Like most other army propaganda, the majority of GIs ignored the warning.

Hardy went after Pvt. Ames. Pulling him aside one afternoon, he gave him some options.

"Ames, I'm going to help you. Do you want help?"

"What for?" he mumbled.

"You're a smak-head. You're hooked. If you don't turn things around, you're dead meat."

He stared at Hardy without emotion. "I can handle it."

At least he didn't deny having a habit. "You can't. You know you can't. Why don't you tell me about your family?"

Ames looked skeptical, "What for?"

"You're going home some day. The war will be over for you. Look at yourself. Is this the way you want them to see you?"

He backed away from Hardy. "I can stop. I'll stop before I leave."

Mike grabbed his arm. "You can't wait. You've got to start now. Where's your home?" Hardy waited for a response.

"Dayton, Ohio," he replied.

Hardy felt they were beginning to make progress. "What does your father do?"

Ames dropped his head refusing to look at the lieutenant. "He's a school teacher."

Hardy pressed on. "What does your mother do?"

"She's a secretary," he said. The memory of his parents seemed to cause him great pain.

"Do you have any brothers and sisters?" Hardy asked.

"Yeah, I've got a little brother." He rubbed his eyes with both fists.

"Sounds like a real nice family." Mike waited for the impact to register. He switched topics. "Do you like baseball?"

Ames seemed more comfortable with this line of discussion. "Yeah, I like the Cleveland Indians."

"Did you ever go to the ball games?"

Ames reflected for a moment. "Dad took us sometimes." He stared past Hardy, as if trying to focus on the memory.

"Ames, it sounds like you've got a great life to go back to. A lot of guys over here don't have that. Did you ever use drugs in the States?"

He shook his head emphatically. "I smoked a few joints, but nothing else."

Mike knew he was telling the truth. "Okay Ames, here's the plan. Effective immediately, I'm pulling you off duty as a truck driver. I won't have you driving in the convoy while you're fucked-up. I'm assigning you to Sergeant Bates and *Bloody Mama*. You'll work the rear of the gun truck. I want you report for duty each morning with a clear head. If you don't, Sergeant Bates will bust your balls. If you get cleaned-up, I'll put you back on as a driver. If you stay clean, you can go home with your head held high. That's it. If you don't agree, I'm done with you and the army can throw you into a padded room. What do you say?"

Silence formed like an invisible wall between them. Hardy looked for a reaction, but Ames kept his face down.

After a moment of reflection, he raised his head. "Okay, I'll do it."

"Do you mean it, Ames? Do you really mean it?"

Ames wrapped his arms around his chest. He tried to form words into a sentence, but they emerged with difficulty. "Yeah, I want to stop. I've tried before. I can do it—this time."

Hardy searched his face for some sign of commitment, but he only observed desperation. "Good. Make sure you report to *Bloody Mama* first thing in the morning. Remember, I want you straight."

"Okay and Lieutenant—thanks."

Hardy's spirits soared after Ames departed. Maybe there was hope. On the other hand, maybe the addiction held too firm a grip on the young man. Mike wanted to believe otherwise. Only one major obstacle stood in the way of the plan. Sgt. Bates had no idea about his role in Ames' recovery. Hardy had improvised that part of the strategy on the spur of the moment. He found Sgt. Bates tinkering with his mini-gun and gave him the news.

"You what?" Bates shouted. "I'm not goin' to have a dope head on *Bloody Mama*. I've got enough trouble with the two dickheads I already got. At least, they don't use drugs."

"Sergeant Bates, I'm asking you to help me—to help Ames," Hardy replied. "I think there's hope for this kid. He needs a little discipline, and you can give it to him. If it doesn't work out, we'll throw him back. I'm asking you as a favor. Let's give him a chance."

Looking physically ill, Bates gulped several times before he attempted to reply. "Damn it, Lieutenant, I wish you wouldn't put it that way. I've got to think about what's good for *Bloody Mama*."

"I know I'm asking a lot, Bates. I just can't think of anyone else better to do the job."

"Shit, you know I'd do anything for you. This just doesn't seem right."

"I know it might not work. I need to give him a chance. Bust his ass if you have to, but make him feel part of the team—that's important. Will you do it?"

Bate's face flushed crimson. "I'll do it. I just don't like it. There's only one thing—I decide if it's not workin' out, okay?"

Hardy grabbed his hand. "It's a deal, but you need to give him a real chance to get his feet on the ground. It might take a while."

"He'll get his chance."

Turning away, Bates went back to work on the mini-gun. Hardy feared he had asked too much. He worried about the strain he'd placed on their friendship. Only time would tell.

True to his word, Pvt. Ames reported for duty on time the next morning. He looked a little ragged with bloodshot eyes, but he seemed in control. Hardy held his breath.

As promised, Sgt. Bates treated him well. He introduced him to *Hit Man* and *Basher*. Bates had one basic rule: Take care of *Bloody Mama* first, last, and always. After that, Bates told him to complete every job assigned, or he'd do it over until he got it right. Bates also stressed that Ames would have to pull his weight in order to earn a place on the team. Nodding agreement, the young man went straight to work.

Hardy let out a sigh of relief after clearing the first hurdle. Sgt. Bates shot stern glances at him several times during the introductions, but Bates seemed to warm-up after they left the staging area. This was just another trip to Duc Pho; it almost felt like old times.

They arrived at Duc Pho without incident. During the trip, Ames suffered the wrath of Sgt. Bates when he appeared to nod off on the machine gun. Otherwise, he had survived his initiation. When the crew stopped at Suzy's for a card game, they invited Ames to join them. He did. Suzy didn't display any marks of passion this time, so she escaped serious taunting from the crew. However, she couldn't avoid the usual teasing. This time, she handled all the jibes with ease. Hardy played cards for a while before leaving the group. As he departed, he took some flak about going to the *Steam and Cream*. Considering his options, he decided to forgo a trip to the bathhouse in order to visit Richard Chang.

More often than not, Richard was on patrol when Mike came to call. This time, he found the infantry lieutenant in the orderly room filling out paperwork. Richard looked better than he had during past visits.

"Hi, Mike, come on over and sit down. I'm almost finished."

"What are you doing?" Hardy asked.

"Patrol reports—I have to fill these things out after every trip to the bush. We got back yesterday, and they're due today."

"How did it go?"

"Not too bad. One of our guys took a hit, but he'll be okay."

"How are *you* doing?"

"I'm doing fine, Mike. Things are looking-up. I'm learning how to survive in the bush; each trip out gets a little easier. I slept great last night. Let me finish this stuff and we'll go to my hooch for a beer."

It took him ten minutes to complete the work before

they left for the hooch. The beer retrieved from Richard's small refrigerator tasted ice cold. After he returned to Chu Lai, Hardy made a silent promise to visit Sgt. Rodriguez to request one for his hooch.

"Seriously Mike, I'm doing great. There hasn't been much action lately, and I'm getting more time off. We've even got some replacements in to help handle the load. Eight more months, and I'm out of here."

"That's great. Listen, when you get a few days off, come see me. I'll show you the sights of Chu Lai. I'm offering you an open invitation to ride with the convoy at any time to escape from here."

"Thanks, I'll take you up on that. There's something else—I've found a girl."

"Great." Hardy knew Richard had a reason for his new upbeat attitude. "Who is she?"

"I haven't told anyone else. She only visits me at night. She's one of the bathhouse girls, but she's special. She sings to me in Vietnamese."

Gulping, Hardy recalled a *special* Vietnamese girl who had sung for him. He made a point of not asking her name.

"That's wonderful," Hardy replied. "You deserve someone special."

They talked for over an hour about plans for Richard's visit to Chu Lai. Hardy brought his friend up-to-date about convoy duty, along with his past problems with Capt. Adams. Richard displayed a talent for listening, but seemed unwilling to share much about his experiences in the bush. Mike had observed this reticence in other infantry GIs. Having received little eyewitness feedback from the front lines increased his curiosity about combat. It also deepened his sense of guilt about missing the action. Parting with a handshake, the two men vowed to spend more time together soon.

The return trip to Chu Lai ended without any difficulty. Ames still looked shaky on the job, but the new crew member responded quickly when Sgt. Bates barked an order. Halfway to Chu Lai, Ames asked about acquiring a nickname like *Hit Man* and *Basher.* Glaring at him, Bates announced that he'd have to earn one. All in all, the experiment had succeeded during the first run to Duc Pho. From now on, they would take it one day at a time.

First Lieutenant Mike Hardy

Mike liked the sound of it.

Effective 9 April 1971, you are promoted to the rank of First Lieutenant, US Army.

Now, he could ditch his gold bar, replacing it with the silver bar of a senior lieutenant. Standing one promotion away from captain, he felt older and more experienced. He spent the next thirty minutes with a black pen, coloring over the gold insignia on his jungle fatigues.

In order to celebrate the event, Mike invited his friends to the club. He bought the drinks while Wiley and Al improvised the entertainment. Since the club had no floor show scheduled, they held cockroach races, a beer drinking contest and entertained themselves with "Toss the Bargirl." The idea was to hurl a girl to her male partner over the longest distance. Al won that contest by tossing Mary, one of the more attractive bar girls, for a new club record. Of course, winning the game required a clean catch or the toss didn't count. Invariably, the girls ended up with an assortment of bumps and bruises. The women hated the game, but they played for the tips. The girl on the winning team received a cash bonus.

Al had adopted a more restrained attitude since his appointment as company commander. In spite of his new responsibilities, he still enjoyed having fun. Toning down his more overt acts of lechery and exerting remarkable self-control, he still continued to covertly squeeze his prey. Hardy caught him giving Mary quick feels before each toss. The irate girl kicked and fussed after every illicit pinch. Later, Al explained that this contact was an essential part of his throwing technique. It helped him pump-up before throwing Mary across the room. No one accepted this reasoning, but the explanation fit Al's quirky sense of humor.

Wiley had a special reason to celebrate. In two days, he was scheduled to leave for Bangkok on R and R. After passing the seven-month point in Vietnam, the army authorized him to take one week off for rest and relaxation. The young stud strained at the bit to engage in unrestrained carnal pursuits. Bangkok specialized in offering a bountiful array of beautiful women, of low moral character, for the lonely tourist. For $200 or less, a soldier could secure a companion, lover, and tour guide for an entire week. Or, Wiley could elect to sample a variety of Bangkok delights. Some girls sat in windows, like their counterparts in Amsterdam, while others engaged a referral service to schedule their assignations. Beautiful Thai girls flourished for the diversion of US servicemen. Wiley could hardly contain his anticipation.

Still short of officers in the company, Al and Mike agreed to rotate duty between Duc Pho and Quang Ngai during Wiley's absence. In the event of an unscheduled trip, a senior NCO could command the convoy. LtCol. Hollins still promised to obtain officer replacements for them as soon as possible. Hardy was scheduled for the Quang Ngai trip in the morning.

The young lieutenants celebrated like the *Three Musketeers*. Al, Wiley, and Mike left the club singing with their arms around each other. It had been a great night. Hardy had developed a strong liking for these two men and felt secure in their company. The three friends could carouse without restraint, or fear of rebuke from one another. Having been accepted by Al and Wiley, Mike couldn't ask for better companions. The men had been thrown together by chance, but they took advantage of the opportunity by developing a concrete bond of friendship.

Hardy left for Quang Ngai early the next morning. With no reports of enemy activity or bad weather on the horizon, the small convoy left on schedule. Mike rode with Sgt. Hayes on *No Slack*, followed by the two reefers. This was his first trip to Quang Ngai since the fateful journey with Joe Tice. Still having reservations about associating with the icehouse gang, he made an effort to mentally prepare himself for the task. He planned on loading the ice without delay in order to leave town without any entanglements. After returning to Chu Lai, he had an appointment with Sgt. Rodriguez.

Mr. Van greeted them at the doorway as they drove up. He welcomed Mike warmly.

"Loo-tent, welcome—my friend, Joe—go home, yes?"

"Yes, he went home last week."

"So sad—Joe very good friend—we be friends now—yes?"

"Sure," Hardy replied without conviction.

Van grabbed one of Mike's hands. "Tell me your name again, Loo-tent."

"Mike—Mike Hardy."

"Good. I call you Mike—okay? You call me Van."

"Sure—ah—Van."

"Good, now we eat—come."

Trays of food appeared magically as Hardy followed his host into the reception room. He had not seen Van signal for service. The offerings looked about the same as last time. Hardy sipped from a bowl of soup while nibbling on a few french fries. He also tasted some of the steamed vegetables. Van seemed to enjoy watching him eat. The ice plant owner made sure Mike had a cold soda in front of him at all times.

During the meal, Van spoke to him earnestly in broken English. "Quang Ngai once beautiful city. Not now, yes? VC come steal food and money. VC very bad; I hate VC!" Curling one of his hands into a fist, he shook it above his head. "VC kill Quang Ngai people, take women, kill children—very bad. Now, Quang Ngai people very afraid. American Army come—VC run away fast. Americans very good—give us food, help fix city. Quang Ngai people very happy now; I love Americans. We be friends, Mike?"

"Sure, Van," Hardy replied. "I hear that some VC are still operating in Quang Ngai."

Van jumped to his feet in anger. "No VC here! VC come to Quang Ngai—I kill them. I hate VC!"

Disguising his skepticism, Hardy observed his host with interest during this tirade against the Communist devils. Van seemed determined to convince his guest of his hatred for the Viet Cong, and his total loyalty to the American Army. Mike sensed that the man had designed this outburst to establish the groundwork for his personal agenda.

Immediately following Van's proclamations, Hardy heard a commotion in the street. The front door flew open, followed by a Vietnamese man stumbling into the room bloodied and bruised. Blood poured from deep cuts on his face. Reaching out to Van, he begged for help. It seemed obvious the two men knew each other. Van's face flushed crimson with anger as he yelled at the intruder to get out. Four RVN soldiers rushed in to pull the helpless victim back into the street. The battered man's pleading eyes searched for a sympathetic face. In desperation, Mike jumped to his feet.

Van grabbed his arm to prevent interference. "No Mike! Man very bad—maybe VC. Soldiers take him away. You stay here."

Van ordered one of his associates to hold Hardy under control. Mike watched as the soldiers pounded the victim with their rifles and boots. After the torture ended, the soldiers dragged the unconscious victim away. Hardy couldn't believe he had just seen the face of the enemy. Something else was going on—something beyond his understanding. Having been warned not to involve himself in Vietnamese affairs, he had not interfered with the violence. The bloody pulp in the street could not have been a VC, he reasoned. The enemy existed somewhere else—somewhere else nearby.

Van attempted to divert his attention away from the incident. He guided Hardy back to the lounge chair. A Vietnamese woman appeared with a bucket to mop up the blood on the tile floor. When everything returned to normal, Van recovered his smile. He did his best to help Hardy forget what had happened. In spite of these efforts, Mike knew he wouldn't forget the brutal beating.

Before leaving, Van handed him a present wrapped in colored paper tied with a ribbon. It weighed heavy in Mike's hands. "For my friend—in Vietnam, friends give presents."

Smiling, he patted Hardy's arm. Mike wanted to throw it back at him, but decided to avoid acting like an ugly American. The army had trained him to respect Vietnamese hospitality, and he didn't want to make a scene. He accepted the gift with feigned gratitude. Van looked pleased. With great relief, Mike left the icehouse and the city behind.

Sgt. Hayes pointed at the package. "You know what that present means, don't you?"

"No, what?"

"Van gave you a gift and now you have to give him something in return. It's a Vietnamese custom. Open it up and let's see what you got."

"Oh no," Hardy groaned.

An unknown force had shoved him onto a treadmill that kept going faster and faster. From his school days, he recalled a line from *Alice In Wonderland*, by Lewis Carroll: *And the Red Queen said to Alice, If you want to stay in one place around here, you must run as fast as you can. If you want to go somewhere else, you must run twice as fast.*

Hardy opened the package to find a Smith and Wesson .38 caliber revolver inside, complete with holster and ammunition. It didn't look new, but someone had maintained it in excellent condition. He now owned another gun. Everyone kept giving him guns. If this trend continued, he could open up his own firearms business.

"Wow, what a piece of work!" Sgt. Hayes exclaimed. "Man, you can dump that sorry ass .45 and strap on the .38. You'll be a real cowboy, Lieutenant."

"No thanks, I'll keep the .45," Hardy said. "I'll put this away until I figure out what to do."

"Don't forget," Sgt. Hayes said. "You've got to get Van a gift, or it'll be a major insult. I'm just covering your ass."

"Thanks. I sure would hate to insult Mr. Van." Considering his options, Hardy placed the revolver back in the box.

They arrived back in the company area at lunchtime. Skipping the mess hall, Hardy went straight to his hooch. Mama San had just finished her chores. He gave her a hug and a pat on the bottom. Preoccupied, he didn't want to indulge in any advanced physical activity.

Looking disappointed, she waved goodbye. More opportunities waited in the days ahead to enjoy her company. Securing the revolver in his locker, he left to find Sgt. Rodriguez. He found the supply sergeant going over some records.

"Hi Lieutenant, what's up?"

"I need a favor, Sergeant Rodriguez."

"Sure, anything you need. Like I told you before, all you have to do is ask."

"I need a small refrigerator. There haven't been any for sale in the PX for months. There's no telling when they'll get in another batch."

Rodriguez grinned. "Yeah, I heard they had a problem with the shipment. I think it got lost somewhere, but I can get you one—no problem."

"Thanks, I'd really appreciate it. It'll be great to have cold soda and beer. By the way, how much do I owe you?"

"Nothing, I told you we can always work something out." Rodriguez considered his response. "All I need is a small favor from you. PFC Sullivan works with me. You know him don't you?"

Hardy nodded.

"He's a good GI, and I'd like to give him some time

off. He's been working hard around here. I want him to get a twenty-four hour pass so he can go to Da Nang. You can authorize it. Can you help me out?"

Hardy felt skeptical, but the request sounded reasonable. "Sure, that should be no problem."

"Great, thanks. Oh, he'll need some transportation. Would it be okay if he checks out a small truck? He'll only need it overnight. That way he can make a pick-up for me on the way back. I'd really appreciate it."

Now, Mike understood the full scope of the request. Rodriguez had arranged for PFC Sullivan to run an errand and Hardy had signed on to support the caper. He felt the pull of manipulation, but this one small indiscretion seemed like a miniscule price to pay for cold beer. After some hesitation, he agreed.

"Great, Lieutenant. I told you we could help each other out. I'll have the refrigerator delivered today, and you'll be drinking cold beer tonight. If you ever need anything else, come see me. I like working with you."

They shook hands. Hardy left the supply room feeling some pangs of guilt. During the return to Sand Hill, Mike attempted to convince himself that the minor compromise wouldn't have lasting implications. He could avoid further involvement with Sgt. Rodriguez whenever he wanted. Deep in his heart, he knew there would be a next time— probably in the near future.

Before arriving at his hooch, Mike ran into a stranger. The confused man looked like a lost soul trying to find his bearings. The newcomer appeared caught in the dilemma of either climbing to the top of Sand Hill, or heading back to the company area.

Moving closer, Hardy noticed the 2d Lieutenant bars on his collar. He called out, "Can I help you?"

"Yes, thanks. I'm Lieutenant Harris—Lance Harris. I think I've been assigned to your company."

Lance looked ill at ease in his baggy jungle fatigue uniform. Obviously out of shape, the man's swollen face radiated fiery heat from the effort of dragging his paunchy body up the hill. Sweat dripped from his receding hairline onto a hairless upper lip. His darting eyes seemed unable to settle down in their sockets.

Hardy reached out and shook his hand. "Mike Hardy. You're not a grunt are you?"

Harris looked flustered for a moment, but regained his composure. "Oh, no—I'm AG. Most of my experience has been in military personnel."

AG stood for Adjutant General Corps. This guy was a desk jockey who dealt in military assignments and personnel matters. He'd probably never worked outside an office in his life. Hardy almost laughed out loud. If Adams hated grunts, he would have strangled this administrative puke. He almost wished Adams were here to greet the new arrival.

Mike regarded Lance thoughtfully. Why would any mother want to call her son Lance? Names like Lance, Rock, and Tab sounded unmanly. Lance didn't act gay.

Although he looked a little skittish, he seemed pretty straight. Hardy noticed he wore a wedding ring.

"Well, Lance, have you checked in yet?"

"Yes, I left my orders with that smart-ass clerk in the orderly room."

"Ah, yes, PFC Johnson. He's not much, but he's all ours. He hasn't been the same since his daddy went away. Captain Adams—but that's another story. Where's your gear?"

"I left it in the orderly room."

"Come on, I'll help you carry it to your new home."

They hauled the duffel bags up the hill. Once they arrived, Hardy dropped Lance's belongings on Joe Tice's old bunk. He hadn't consulted with Al, but this seemed like the right place for Lance. Wiley and Al had the large hooch all to themselves. Wiley had already left the company area to make travel arrangements to Bangkok.

"Welcome to your new home," Hardy said. "Are you sure you're supposed to be assigned here?"

"Yes," he replied. "I was working AG in Da Nang, but there were too many of us. Somebody screwed up by doubling our authorizations. We got word they needed officers in Chu Lai, so I volunteered."

Mike gave him one of Al's cold beers and laughed. "You do realize you were a lot safer in Da Nang. There's a war down here. Charlie shoots at our trucks by day and fires rockets at us at night. Are you married?"

"Yes," he beamed. "I have a beautiful wife in

Michigan, near East Lansing. She works for a restaurant chain. We're going into business together when I get back. Here's a picture of her."

By Mike's assessment, she looked like someone from a Rueben's painting—pink, plump, blonde, and buxom. He visualized an image of her nagging poor, timid Lance to take out the garbage.

"She's lovely." Hardy managed. "So, you're Lance from Lansing?"

"Yes, people always joke about that."

"Well, Lance, welcome to the 73d Transportation Company." Raising his beer can, Hardy took a long drink.

Mike couldn't wait to introduce Lance to Al. Living in different worlds, the two men shared nothing in common. If Lance could survive occasional humiliation, he'd probably do all right. Hardy wasn't sure how he'd fit in with the rest of the company, but they needed the new officer for convoy rotation. He left Lance alone to unpack.

Hardy's mind wandered back to the events of the day. Mr. Van and the beating in Quang Ngai still caused him to clench his teeth in disgust. The deal with Sgt. Rodriguez stuck like flypaper on his conscience. Having experienced another rite of passage, he felt uncertain about his next moves. In the space of a few hours, his whole concept of morality had blurred. At the moment, he had no idea how to adjust the focus.

True to his word, Sgt. Rodriguez delivered the refrigerator the same day. Hardy ripped open the new box with eager enthusiasm. After plugging his new appliance into the only outlet in the building, he immediately stocked it with beer and soda. Mike looked around the hooch with satisfaction. What had once been a run-down shack now provided him with many of the comforts of home. Surviving several thumb hits with a hammer, he had built bookcases, chairs, and a table out of spare wood and ammo boxes. Wall shelves displayed special photographs and memories of New England. Curtains, made out of the remnants of an old parachute, covered the windows. Although enough room remained for one more resident, he purposely filled the empty space with personal belongings to discourage additional tenants. Not ready to enter his hooch in *Better Homes and Gardens*, it still met his basic needs. The arrival of the new refrigerator filled the last remaining requirement for relative comfort.

When Al returned from Duc Pho, Hardy introduced him to Lance. Looking puzzled, Al managed to give the new officer a warm welcome. Unable to believe the truck company had inherited an AG officer, he asked Lance if he had any transportation experience. Lance listed some minimal training on trucks during ROTC. For some unknown reason, that experience provided enough justification for an assignment to the transportation company. Shaking his head in disbelief, Al asked Mike to show Lance the ropes.

Later, Al came to Hardy's hooch. When Mike offered him a cold beer, Al expressed his admiration for the new refrigerator. He asked where he had gotten it. With some discomfort, Mike confessed Sgt. Rodriguez had helped him out. Nodding with understanding, Al didn't inquire further about the acquisition. At that point, the conversation turned to Lance.

"I don't know about that guy, Grunt. He's not a real man—I mean—it's not that he's swish, but if he didn't have a wife, I'd swear he was—you know. I need leaders to run the convoys. I don't know if he can hack it. The drivers will tear him to pieces."

"He's different," Hardy agreed. "I'll train him hard to see if he can make tough decisions. Maybe, we can turn him into a transportation officer. We need the help. Hollins might not send us replacements for a long time."

"Do your best, but I think he's a lost cause. I'm not really sure if the boy pisses standing up."

After reaching for another beer, Al stretched out in one of Mike's homemade chairs. He put Lance out of his mind for the moment.

"Damn, I'll bet old Wiley is foaming at the mouth to

get to Bangkok. He should be there tomorrow. He's going to get so much pussy his dick will need R and R for a month after he gets back. I envy that boy."

"Maybe he'll bring back photos," Hardy said.

"Nah, I don't want pictures—I want the real thing. I want to smell it, touch it and taste it. If it ain't the real thing, I don't want nothing to do with it."

They carried on well past sunset. Mike always enjoyed Al's impromptu performances. He made sport out of encouraging the big man's outrageous sense of humor. Al loved an audience. It took little incentive for him to launch into his routines on cue. Time passed quickly as the two friends speculated about Wiley's sexual exploits in Bangkok.

Suddenly, the scream of sirens pierced the night.

Al jumped to his feet. "Shit—rockets! Go grab the cherry and get to the bunkers. I knew they'd hit us tonight." He took off out the door.

Rocket attacks commonly occurred in Chu Lai after dark. The military compound suffered these assaults several times a week. In most cases, the VC fired only one rocket at the compound at a time. On occasion, they arrived in groups of two or three. Woefully inaccurate, the missiles usually exploded without doing much damage. However, everyone in the targeted area maintained a healthy respect for the unpredictable flying objects.

Hardy ran to find Lance. He located him sitting wide-eyed on the floor of the hooch. "Come on, that siren means incoming rockets. Get your ass into the bunker."

Hearing an explosion in the distance, Lance jumped to his feet. Looking visibly shaken, but followed Hardy to the bunker.

"Don't worry," Mike said. "The first time is the worst. You'll get used to it. Besides, I think the rocket has already hit. We heard the explosion."

"Will there be any more rockets?" he stammered.

"Usually, Charlie only shoots one at a time. He just wants to keep us on our toes. Sometimes we get more, but—"

BOOM!

The explosion shattered the silence. The rocket landed so close, dirt flew into the bunker. Hardy fell to the ground landing on top of Lance. The newcomer shivered and moaned beneath him.

"Are you okay?" Hardy asked. "That was close."

"Yeah, I'm all right," he replied.

'I never had one hit that close before. It scared the shit out of me!" Hardy lifted himself off the ground, dusted himself off, and helped Lance to his feet.

"Jesus, you told me you had a war here," Lance coughed. "I guess I'll have to get used to it." Lance brushed himself off. "Shit, I think I just pissed in my pants."

After that, and much to Mike's surprise—Lance smiled. Hardy couldn't believe how quickly the newcomer had recovered. Mike still felt like a mass of raw nerves, but Lance stood tall with a self-conscious grin on his face. Maybe, the new guy would work out after all.

Hardy lurched out of the bunker to see where the rocket had landed. Peering down the hill, he focused his gaze toward the sea and the distant guard bunkers. Observing black clouds of smoke in that direction, he couldn't assess the damage from his vantage point. After directing Lance to stay put, he ran into the hooch for his M-16.

Returning to the bunker, he informed Lance, "I need to go down there to check the bunkers. I've got to make sure none of our guys are hurt. Are you okay?"

Nodding, Lance indicated for him to go ahead.

Hardy worked his way down the hill. Thick underbrush and broken glass impeded his progress. His flashlight beam struggled to cut through the dense smoke. The acrid residue from the explosion assaulted his nostrils. Clutching the M-16 tighter, he moved with caution toward the guard bunkers. He remembered Sgt. Bates' warning about approaching the guards at night. If they had survived the attack, the skittish guards could pose a threat to his safety. The combined effects of drugs and the rocket attack made them highly unpredictable. He forced himself to move on. Fortunately, the smoke provided good cover.

When he arrived within earshot of the first bunker, he flattened himself on the ground before calling out. "This is Lieutenant Hardy. Can you hear me?"

No one answered. After releasing a long breath of pent-up tension, he decided to crawl a little closer.

"This is Lieutenant Hardy. Is everyone okay?"

Hearing some muffled sobbing off to his right, he crawled off in that direction.

"Hold your fire! This is Lieutenant Hardy. Can I come in?"

The sobbing stopped for a moment. He heard a hoarse reply. "C'mon in—hurry!"

Jumping to his knees, Hardy scrambled into the bunker. His eyes took in the scene. "Are you guys okay?"

One of them sat on the ground, while the other stared intently toward the sea. His M-60 machine gun stood cocked and ready. Mike crawled over to the man on the ground. He recognized Spec/4 Sanchez.

Sanchez sobbed on the floor of the bunker. "I was asleep. Man, I thought I was dead. The noise—my ears hurt like hell. Oh shit, man!"

"Take it easy, Sanchez. It's all over. It was a rocket and you're not hurt. Come on breathe easy. You're okay."

Sanchez attempted to control his panic.

The other GI didn't turn around. "The fuckin' VC are still out there. I heard a noise in the wire."

Hardy attempted to diffuse their anxiety. "It was only a rocket. It's over. Keep an eye out, but it should be quiet now."

After a few minutes they both seemed to regain some self-control. Hardy patted each man of the shoulder before he crawled away.

Reaching the next bunker, he found the guards in about the same condition—they looked stunned and afraid. If drugs had dulled their senses before the explosion, fear now rendered the two men stone sober. Both seemed unhurt, so Hardy told them to take it easy as he crawled away. At that point, he decided to curtail his inspection. The other guard posts were located a distance away from the impact site. He didn't relish crawling up to any more bunkers in the dark. Satisfied, he returned to the relative safety of his hooch.

The next morning, Hardy and Al visited the impact area. They found a crater halfway between two of the bunkers about twenty feet wide and six feet deep. Pieces of the rocket remained visible at the center of the crater.

They left the fragments untouched. The explosive ordnance team would want to inspect the debris.

Al expressed his awe at the power of the device. "I had no idea those things could cover such a wide area. Look, the shrapnel fans out in all directions from the hole. Anyone within a hundred feet of the blast would end up mincemeat. Our guards lucked out."

Confirming the guards' good fortune, they picked out chunks of twisted metal from the sandbags around the bunkers. If the rocket had landed much closer, the occupants would have faced certain death.

When Hardy met Sgt. Bates for breakfast he filled him in on the rocket attack. Bates had heard the explosion, but didn't know it had landed close to the guard bunkers. Mike also gave him the details about Lance.

"It looks like he's going to be traveling with us. I think I'll break him in on *Bloody Mama*."

"Poor *Mama's* been forced to take on all the orphans lately," Bates complained.

"How's Ames doing?" Hardy asked.

"Not too bad. He seems pretty straight and wants to help out. I keep waiting for him to slip back into his old ways. The boy is still pretty shaky."

"Keep working with him, Bates. You're doing a great job and I appreciate it. I really want him to beat this thing."

Bates shoveled in a mouthful of eggs. Conversation trailed off for a while. Hardy knew something else worried the truck sergeant.

Three minutes later Bates broke the silence. "We got another problem. Bobby Waters came to see me. He says he's in love and wants to get married. He wants to talk to you and Lieutenant Miller about getting permission."

Hardy remembered Spec/4 Bobby Waters as the driver who had killed the Vietnamese boy in Quang Ngai. Although pleased the young driver had found someone to love, he didn't like his chances of marrying a local girl. The US Army tried to discourage such unions by intentionally lining the road to marital bliss with bureaucratic obstacles.

"I'm glad he found a girlfriend, but it'll be tough for him to marry her," Hardy said.

"You won't be very glad when you see her. She's an old Mama San. I bet she's almost fifty years old."

Hardy couldn't suppress his surprise. Bobby possessed

enough good looks and intelligence for any young woman to consider him a great prospect for marriage. And yet, he claimed to love someone old enough to be his mother. Something felt wrong. While his mind searched for answers, the image of the Mama San holding her dead son jolted his memory.

"That's it," Hardy said.

"What do you mean?" Bates asked.

"He wants to make up for killing that boy. He's found a lonely old woman. He thinks he can make her happy as her husband, or by taking the place of her lost son."

Sgt. Bates stopped eating. "God Damn, that's sick! I know Bobby's screwed-up, but he can't be that fucked-up."

"Don't you see—it fits. Why else would he want to marry someone that old?"

"I don't know, Lieutenant. Things have been getting real strange around here lately. I'm not sure of anything anymore."

"I know what you mean," Hardy replied. "Be patient and everything should return to normal soon—whatever normal is. I'll talk to him after we get back from Duc Pho."

Bates looked skeptical, but summoned up enough reserve strength to finish off his breakfast in short order.

The trip to Duc Pho ended without incident. Before leaving Duc Pho, Hardy intercepted Bobby to tell him they needed to talk after returning to Chu Lai. Flashing a big smile, Bobby said he could hardly wait. He promised to bring his 'girlfriend' to the meeting. The young man looked genuinely happy. Feeling perplexed, Mike felt uncertain about how he should handle the situation. If he attempted to discourage the marriage, Bobby could slip into deep depression. If he gave his blessing to the union, he'd act in total opposition to his judgment. No reasonable solution seemed possible. He hoped to find the answer before his meeting with the couple.

The return to Chu Lai seemed to take longer than usual. Hardy dreaded the possibility of having a confrontation with Bobby.

Sgt. Bates could offer little advice. "Sorry, Lieutenant, but I'm glad it's your problem and not mine."

Sgt. Willard Bates' sense of balance had already been threatened by having a junkie on *Bloody Mama,* and by knowing he had to train some new, unknown officer. The Bobby Waters' dilemma had infused within him more anxiety than he could handle.

Hardy met Bobby Waters and the Vietnamese woman in the orderly room. She looked as old as Bates had described her. Rolling his eyes, PFC Johnson stared at the unlikely couple. Hardy suggested that they meet in Al's empty office. The young man and his elderly partner followed behind holding hands. Once inside, Hardy closed the door and offered them the couch. Waters waited for the woman to settle in place before he sat beside her. They continued to hold hands. The sight of this handsome black man, holding the wrinkled hand of an old Vietnamese woman unsettled Mike. Pausing to compose himself, he looked for a way to open the discussion. During the momentary silence, Waters' and the woman's eyes remained fixed on each other.

Hardy coughed politely. "Sergeant Bates tells me you two want to get married. Is that true?"

"Yes, sir," Waters grinned. "We love each other and want to get married as soon as possible."

The woman stared straight ahead without any emotion.

Hardy searched for the right words. "This is...ah...very difficult thing you want to do, Waters. I'm sure you love her, but the army frowns on GIs marrying the Vietnamese."

"I know that, sir. I don't care what it takes. I want to marry her." He put his arm around the woman protectively.

"There's tons of paperwork, and you have to get approval from the army, as well as the Vietnamese Government. The embassy has to grant her a passport and a travel visa. It could take months."

"I don't care," Waters insisted. "We can do it."

"Are you sure, Waters? Why don't you think about it and enjoy each other's company while you're still here. After you get home, you might be able to return to Vietnam and bring her to the States."

"No way, Lieutenant! She's going home with me, or I'll get out of the army and stay here with her." There seemed little purpose in arguing with him.

Hardy hesitated before deciding to try another approach. "Do you go to church, Waters?"

He looked at Hardy with curiosity. "Sure, back home."

"Will you do me a favor? I want you to talk to one of the chaplains. They're experts in these matters, and I'm not. The chaplain can explain all the paperwork and procedures. You're a good man, Waters, and I want to do right by you. Will you see the chaplain?"

"Sure, I guess."

"I think that's the right thing to do. After you're done with the chaplain, we'll talk again, okay?"

"All right, I'll come back," he said.

Bobby Waters rose from the couch before walking out of the office, hand-in-hand, with the woman he wanted to marry.

Hardy sat frozen in place after their departure. Sgt. Bates had summed up the situation—things had gotten strange lately. Mike didn't feel confident that the meeting had accomplished very much. In spite of everything, he'd only transferred the problem to the chaplain. Ultimately, Waters would have to find his own solution. Men in love, or men who *think* they're in love, are not inclined to take advice. Hardy's only remaining options: wait for the unavoidable outcome and stand ready to pick up the pieces.

Al shook his head when Hardy told him about the Waters' problem. Al knew Bobby well, and held him in high regard. He hated to see one of his best drivers involved in personal turmoil.

"I knew the accident screwed him up, but this is too much. I should've sent him to a shrink long ago."

"None of us saw this coming, Al. Most guys with emotional scars heal over time. I guess Bobby couldn't shake off the guilt. Maybe, in a crazy way, he thinks he's doing some good."

Mike explained how he had handled the meeting. He included the referral to the chaplain.

"That was good, Grunt. I don't think the chaplain will help much, but it buys us some time. I'm sending him for mental screening as soon as possible. In the meantime, he pulls road duty every day. I'm going to work him so hard he won't have time to think about Mama San."

Waters didn't complain about the extra duty. He continued to do his job like a true professional. After visiting with the chaplain, Bobby left the session disheartened by the results. The chaplain had done his best to dissolve the relationship. He reminded Waters of his duty, and his responsibility to his family back home. In the end, the church, and the US Army, refused to bless the marriage. Speaking to him after the meeting, Hardy could see the young man still suffered fallout from the decision. In spite of an earnest attempt to boost Bobby's morale, Mike's words of encouragement had little effect on the distraught soldier. No amount of consolation could alter the situation. Dropping his head, Bobby walked away in defeat. Three days later, Bobby Waters disappeared. Al had no choice but to list him as AWOL, or absent without leave.

Al and Mike continued to rotate duty between Duc Pho and Quang Ngai during Wiley's absence. Required to complete his administrative in-processing, Lance couldn't help with road duty. Al gave him a few extra days to finish up before settling into the convoy schedule. At that point, he would start traveling with Mike on a regular basis.

Hardy agonized about his upcoming trip to Quang Ngai. Feeling compelled to take Van a gift in return for the revolver he turned to Sgt. Hayes for a suggestion. Hayes recommended a good bottle of scotch whiskey. It seemed that Mr. Van had expensive tastes in fine liquor. Finding a good bottle of scotch seemed like an impossible task. Anxious to put the obligation behind him, he went to see Sgt. Rodriguez.

Rodriguez greeted his visitor with a smile. "Hi, Lieutenant, how's the refrigerator?"

"Great, thanks, Sergeant Rodriguez. I wonder if you could help me out with a problem?"

"Sure, what do you need?"

"I need a bottle of scotch—fairly expensive."

"That's no problem. What's it for, a gift?"

Hardy described the situation with Mr. Van.

"Sure, I understand. Sergeant Hayes is right. We do business with these people and can't afford to offend them. You're doing the right thing. I just happen to have a bottle in back. I'll get it for you."

Returning with a bottle, Rodriguez placed it on the counter. Hardy recognized the scotch as old and expensive.

"This should do the trick." With a wink, he handed Mike some wrapping paper and a ribbon. "And, here's something to make it look pretty. You'll impress the hell out of Mr. Van."

"Thanks, I really appreciate this. How can I make it up to you?" Mike waited for the inevitable request.

"There is a way you can help me out. I do a little business with Mr. Van, from time to time. In fact, I've got a package here that needs to go to him. Believe me, it contains nothing illegal. If you make sure he gets it, we'll call things even."

With reluctance, Hardy resigned himself to deliver the package. "Sure, I'll make sure he gets it."

"Great. I'll be right back."

Returning from the back room, Rodriguez carried a package about the size of a shoebox wrapped in brown paper.

"This is it. I really appreciate it. Let me know how it goes, Lieutenant. If you need anything else come see me."

Hardy scooped up the bottle of scotch, tucked Van's package under his arm, and made himself a promise. After making this final delivery he'd retire from the gift exchange business for good.

When Mike arrived in Quang Ngai, Van showered him with thanks for the scotch and the package from Sgt. Rodriguez. The convoy lieutenant waited to see if Van intended to hug him, or kiss his hand. Treated as Van's special guest, Hardy felt the pressure of more obligations waiting to test his resolve. During the professions of gratitude, Van slipped the secret package to one of his assistants who spirited it out of the room.

"How is my good friend, Sergeant Rodriguez?" Van inquired.

The food arrived as Hardy settled onto the couch. Everything looked familiar except the soup had a different color, and several things on the tray looked like egg rolls. He picked carefully at the contents on his plate.

"He's fine. He asked me to give you his regards."

"Sergeant Rodriguez is very good man. I send him a little present. Will you take for me?"

Hardy groaned. When was this going to end? He hoped Van had no more presents for him. After a moment of hesitation, knowing he'd regret his decision, he replied, "Sure."

Calling to one of his assistants, Van spoke to him in rapid Vietnamese. The man hurried off on his task.

Van patted Mike on the arm. "Very good, you make me happy."

Hardy's thoughts turned to the victim he'd seen beaten in the street. "Last time I was here a man was beaten by the RVNs. Do you know what happened to him?"

Van's face clouded over, and the perpetual smile disappeared. "No," he replied with emphasis. "He bad man...VC...probably dead. No problem."

"Probably dead" meant, he *was* dead. Hardy had no doubt that Van knew the outcome of the incident, and had most likely played a role in the man's demise. Mike recalled a vivid image of those pleading eyes begging him for help. This was the second time that someone had begged him for rescue. Shifting uncomfortably in his seat, he experienced a sharp pang of guilt over his lack of response in both incidents.

Forcing a smile, Van attempted to recapture the light-hearted atmosphere. "Do you have girlfriend?"

"No, not in Vietnam," Hardy said.

"That's too bad. You young man, young man need woman to stay strong. You need a girlfriend."

"I'm all right." Hardy suspected what Van had in mind.

"Many pretty women in Quang Ngai. You are important man, American officer—great honor to make you happy. I bring pretty woman here to meet you, okay?"

"No—No thank you, Van. I have a beautiful woman in the States. She will be my wife," he lied.

Smiling widely, Van clasped his hands together. "Yes,

wife is very good. I want you to be happy. If you want Quang Ngai girlfriend, you tell me. I find you the very best," he promised.

"I'll let you know," Hardy said.

They spent the rest of the time discussing trivial matters.

After a lapse in conversation, Mike walked outside to find the children waiting for him in the street. He passed out all his candy. Before leaving, Van gave him a small gift for Sergeant Rodriguez. Hardy had the distinct feeling the package contained a large sum of money. Tucking it away, he left Mr. Van and the icehouse gang behind.

That night, Hardy departed for the club alone. Al had begged off due to a bad cold and Lance had stayed behind to write letters to his wife. Making it clear that he preferred solitude in the evenings, the newcomer had visited the club on only a few occasions since his arrival. Clearly suffering from homesickness, he used the isolation to maintain an emotional bond with his wife. Hardy had no doubt the woman possessed a devoted husband. Mike, on the other hand, needed the atmosphere of the club to shake off the events of the day.

Business appeared a little slow when he entered the club. The bar girls had no trouble meeting the needs of the few customers in the place. Hardy searched the room for a familiar face until he spotted Lt. Jefferson Swift sitting alone. Having socialized with the good-natured officer once before, he remembered enjoying his company.

Lt. Swift had responsibility for total control of the local property disposal yard. He called himself, 'The Chu Lai Junk Man.' Most scrap metal and debris from the war ended up in property disposal. The job entailed moving or selling the scrap at the convenience of the army. No one ever explained what happened to the funds once they reached the US Treasury. Jefferson didn't care who spent the money as long as Korean and Vietnamese business-men clamored to keep buying the stuff. He never had any trouble finding customers, or junk dealers anxious to gain his favor. As a successful entrepreneur, 'The Chu Lai Junk Man' enjoyed a controversial and lucrative lifestyle.

Lt. Jefferson Swift hailed from the great city of Austin, Texas. After attending Texas A&M, he obtained his army commission through the ROTC program. As a loyal 'Aggie,' he loved to talk about the football team, but had nothing positive to say about ROTC. The man from Texas harbored no love for the military lifestyle. He pushed the army's personal appearance regulations to the limit. Long, dark hair fell over his ears and a bushy mustache drooped to his chin. He looked like a holdover from an earlier time —possibly the Civil War. Smiling, he waved Mike over to his table.

"Hi, Jefferson, how's the junk business?"

Lt. Swift had made it clear during their first meeting that his first name was Jefferson. Hating nicknames, he felt obligated to honor his namesake Thomas Jefferson. In spite of a casual demeanor, he seemed imbued with a strong sense of southern tradition.

"It keeps piling up. How's the truck business?"

Hardy shared some of the details about the Quang Ngai trip, along with a few of his other, less controversial adventures. After that, extolling the attributes of oriental women, the two men speculated about Wiley's leave in Bangkok. Jefferson loved Asian women, confessing that he'd miss their company after returning to the States.

Mary, the bar girl, approached the table to take drink orders. The attractive woman leaned over to whisper something in Jefferson's ear. Her affection for him appeared obvious.

"No, no," he laughed. "Just bring us some more drinks."

With blatant familiarity he patted her round little bottom. She just smiled over her shoulder before skipping off on her errand. If anyone else had touched her like that, he'd end up wearing her serving tray as a new hat.

Mike leaned over to scold Jefferson. "You sly dog. Have you been taking unfair advantage of that poor, innocent girl?"

"A real gentleman never discusses affairs of the heart," Jefferson said. "Her virtue and reputation are safe with me."

"Right, just make sure I get invited to the wedding. I'm sure you'll need to make an honest woman out of her."

"Never! There are too many fields left to plow, too

many flowers yet to pluck, too many universes left to explore, too many—"

"All right, give me a break!" Hardy raised his arms in mock surrender. "Just throw a few crumbs in my direction, okay?"

Jefferson leaned forward. "My friend, I'm willing to help you discover the best women this country has to offer."

Grateful, Hardy thanked him for the generous gesture. The two men continued their lively chatter. Since the club had no floor show scheduled for the evening, they discussed the pros and cons of staying for the nightly movie. Before reaching a decision, a loud clattering noise and a POP on the roof interrupted their conversation.

"What the fuck?" Jefferson exclaimed.

Hardy knew immediately what had happened. "Quick, let's get the hell out of here—gas!"

Some of the enlisted troops had decided to have fun at the expense of the officers. Tear gas came in different forms—fired from a launcher, or thrown like a hand grenade. Once released, the tear gas exploded from a canister to disperse its' torment in all directions.

"C'mon, run!" Hardy yelled.

They'd almost reached the door when Hardy gulped in a lung-full of the stuff. A raging fire burst open in his chest. His throat started to spasm and tears streamed out of his eyes. Coughing uncontrollably, he scrambled for fresh air. Once outside, he fought for oxygen. Jefferson had also received a strong dose, so they hacked in unison. After several agonizing minutes, the pain and irritation subsided.

"Well, so much for the movie," Jefferson rasped. "Let's go to my place—it's safer."

Agreeing, Mike followed him away from the club.

Never having visited Jefferson's hooch, Hardy expressed amazement at the opulence of the quarters. Decorated with expensive teak and mahogany furniture, the hooch contained a state-of-the-art music system arranged on wall shelves. Two speakers, the size of Hardy's refrigerator, stood ready to pump out the amplified sound. In another corner of the room, a fully stocked wet bar waited to serve guests. A tasteful display of oriental sculpture glistened from several locations around the room. Rounding out the lush interior, silk drapes adorned the windows and plush oriental carpet covered the floor. The extravagant décor left Mike speechless.

"I don't bring many people in here—men anyway," Jefferson winked. "It's hard for me to explain all this."

"I can imagine it is." Hardy fought to suppress his burning curiosity about how Jefferson had accumulated the costly furnishings.

Jefferson anticipated his interest. "Before you ask, most of this came as gifts from friends, and I bought the rest. I love oriental art and furniture. My friends have been very helpful in assisting me choose the right items. I really need a beer; how about you?"

Hardy nodded agreement. Jefferson reached into his refrigerator behind the bar while Mike settled himself on a small couch.

"I felt I could trust you to keep my secret. That's why I brought you here. I like showing the place off, but the wrong people could mess this all up."

"Don't worry, your secret is safe with me." Mike arched his neck. "Nice dump you've got here."

Jefferson turned on his tape deck. Instantly, the music of George Harrison filled the room.

"I need something stronger than beer. How would you like to smoke a little weed?"

"Sure," Hardy replied. He hadn't smoked much pot since his arrival in Vietnam, but he and Wiley had shared a joint from time to time. Al never joined them. Al's drug of choice was cheap beer.

Jefferson returned with a plastic bag. "I get this stuff in sandbags. I've got more than I'll ever use. I'll give you some to take with you. It's a special batch. The Vietnamese sprinkle it with magic powder."

Jefferson hadn't exaggerated about the potency of the weed. After inhaling twice, Mike began to feel the effects of the drug. Finishing the first joint, he lost some muscle coordination and a large portion of his comprehension. Later, aware that he and Jefferson had laughed for hours, he couldn't recall—why. The next day, searching through the murkiness of his memory, he remembered leaving for his hooch only to collapse on his bunk in a total stupor.

Four days later, Wiley returned looking pale and exhausted. Out of sympathy, Mike agreed to let him rest before forcing him to share his R & R adventures.

Al wouldn't hear of it. "You tell me right now what happened you little skunk, or I'll use your balls for ping-pong practice."

Dropping his gear, Wiley sat heavily on his bunk.

Al handed him a cold beer. "Now talk!" he demanded.

Wiley took a long drink of the beer, wiped his mouth, and gave them both a tired smile. "Well, let me see, where should I begin?" He paused for effect.

"You'd better begin right now, or your family will collect death insurance," Al threatened.

"Okay, here goes…" Wiley broke into a long discourse on the exotic delights of Bangkok.

After he checked into a downtown Bangkok hotel, a man selling the services of tour guides approached him. Wiley followed the man to a nearby office. Upon entering the building, 20 beautiful women extended a greeting with seductive smiles. For 40 dollars a day, or 200 dollars a week, he could secure the services of one of these Thai beauties. He selected one of the most stunning ladies before returning to the hotel for his tour of passion in Bangkok. After shedding their clothes, the two of them bathed together. Later, the stunning woman gave him an exquisite massage. Following the massage, they engaged in a night of uninhibited sex. Wiley's companion committed herself to fulfilling all his desires. The next day, she satisfied her obligation as a tour guide by escorting him throughout the city. They parted with some reluctance, but Wiley had dedicated himself to purchasing a different partner during each day in the city.

All of the women, without exception, possessed exquisite oriental beauty along with a willingness to please. Wiley did his best to keep up a torrid pace, but he started to slow down by the end of the week. Exhausted, he began to sleep more and engage in sex less often.

"You what?" Al screamed. "You fizzled out? How can you say that? I thought you were a *real* man?"

Wiley defied anyone to survive a week of continuous sex in Bangkok. Al vowed he could do it.

Wiley held them in rapt attention for nearly an hour. Al let him off the hook after he agreed to provide more details about the adventure the next day. The exhausted traveler promised to cover every minute of the experience.

Returning to his hooch, Mike felt relieved to have Wiley back. Wiley's return completed their circle of friendship. Still worried about the problem of Lance and how he'd fit into the unit, Mike also thought about Bobby Waters' desperate attempt to find a new life. The young man remained in hiding out there—somewhere. With any luck, the authorities would return the poor guy to the safety of the compound. Otherwise, Bobby Waters would join the ranks of the other souls lost in the abyss of meaningless conflict.

Bobby Waters returned three weeks later—not willingly, but in handcuffs and under arrest. Now that the MPs had found their man, Bobby would pay for his indiscretion. The army maintained a low tolerance for those who wandered off without permission. This was war, and Bobby had committed a grievous act. Military justice had to decide whether to charge him as AWOL or for desertion. The latter carried a much stiffer penalty.

Bobby had not wandered far. Some RVNs had found him in a small village only twenty miles from Chu Lai. After ditching his uniform, he'd changed into black pajamas. He and his Mama San had set up housekeeping in a grass shack. A six-foot black man, living in a Vietnamese village, was bound to attract attention. It didn't take long for the RVNs to locate him and turn him over to the MPs. Bobby's experiment in native living had gone sour.

Al did all he could to assist in Bobby's defense. He made sure the distraught soldier received counseling from an army psychiatrist. In addition, he convinced the military judge to charge Bobby with Absent Without Leave. Al, also, provided strong testimony in his defense.

The psychiatrist confirmed that his patient suffered from different degrees of shock, trauma, and guilt as a result of the Quang Ngai accident. The doctor advised the court that Bobby would need additional therapy to recover from his difficulties.

The court panel considered all the arguments and, in the end, recommended leniency. The military judge agreed. He reduced Bobby to the lowest rank possible, ordered a bad conduct discharge, and sentenced him to six months of probation. As long as he continued to seek counseling for his mental distress, he wouldn't serve any jail time. Sitting in silence during the sentencing, Bobby nodded his agreement to the counseling stipulation. Bobby Waters, a good soldier, departed for home in disgrace. Hardy knew he would never hear from him again.

Both Al and Mike felt saddened by the outcome. They agreed it could have been worse, but Vietnam had ruined another good man—this time not by enemy fire or drugs. Regardless of the circumstances, the war had claimed another victim.

*****

Mama San sat on Hardy's bed waiting for him to return from the trial. When he entered the hooch, she stood up searching his face for a sign of welcome. Sensing her uneasiness, Mike opened his arms. Without hesitation, she closed the distance between them.

He held her face in his hands. "Did you miss me, Mama San?"

Pulling her tighter against his chest, she returned his embrace.

"Today was very bad. We lost a good GI. I wish I could have done more for him."

Hardy knew she didn't understand anything he said. He just needed to say the words out loud. She held onto him in silence.

"I really think you like me, Mama San. I hope I don't do anything to hurt you. My track record hasn't been very good lately."

Moving her away from him, he placed a hand on one of her breasts. Closing her eyes, Mama San tilted her head backwards. Mike did not consider her attractive. Her round face and wide nose distracted from an otherwise pleasing appearance. Oblivious to these imperfections, he felt stirred by her desire for him. At this moment, he thought of her as uniquely beautiful.

Removing her top, Hardy marveled as her chest heaved with each breath. He moved behind her to cup both breasts in his hands. She stood transfixed, willingly submitting to his manipulation. Dropping to his knees, he pulled her pajama bottoms down over her hips. Standing uncovered before him, she exhibited no shame or embarrassment.

When he rose to his feet, Mama San guided him toward the bed. Stopping beside his bunk, the naked woman removed each piece of his uniform, all the while caressing him with her fingers. His heartbeat quickened as she explored every part of his body. With no need to hurry, the two lovers prolonged the sensual contact. Finally, with nerve ends on fire, they joined their bodies in a frenzied union.

It took an eternity for Mike to resume normal breathing. Mama San had already recovered, but waited for him to recuperate before leaving his side. When he attempted to stir, the Vietnamese woman gestured for him not to move. Slipping away from the bed, she glided across the room. Fascinated, he watched each one of her graceful movements. Taking hold of the washbasin, Mama San filled it with clean water. As she reached for the soap, and one of her neatly folded towels, Mike expected her to wash him. Instead, she placed the basin in the middle of the floor. Displaying no hint of modesty, the lithe woman lowered herself over the washbasin. As she began to soap herself, Mike could not recall witnessing anything more intimate. This exceptional woman took pleasure in sharing a private moment with her lover. The intimacy of the act conveyed her intent to eliminate any secrets between them.

After drying herself, Mama San emptied the basin, refilled it with clean water, and returned to the bed. She washed Hardy from head to toe. Immediately after the cleansing process, she massaged his entire body. Mike surrendered himself to the hands kneading his flesh. He had never enjoyed a more stimulating experience. She worked down the entire length of his body until her fingers lingered inside his thighs. At that point, they made love for the second time that afternoon.

Hardy knew she couldn't stay any longer. All hooch maids were required to sign out of the compound before dark. Realizing the time, she pulled on her clothes. Before leaving, Mike gave her some candy for her son. She walked out the door after hugging him one more time. Mama San waved a mournful goodbye as she disappeared down the hill. Hardy took a deep breath before collapsing exhausted on his bunk.

Al and Wiley pounded on his door after dark. Mike had already missed supper. He would have gladly slept the rest of the night away.

Al had other plans for them. "C'mon, get up Grunt. We're going out."

Hardy tried to dodge the invitation, but Al refused to relent.

"I said, let's go. I have great plans for us tonight. Whew! What's that smell? Wiley, does it smell like someone had sex in here?"

"It sure does," Wiley grinned. "Come to think of it, I saw your dog walking a little funny tonight."

"What?" Al screamed.

Jumping on top of Mike, Al wrapped both hands around his neck, and bounced on his back. "You had relations with my dog? You sick pervert! I heard all grunts were queer, but for you to attack an innocent little dog—I hope your pecker gets rabies!"

"Get off me," Hardy choked. "I can't breathe."

"Good, maybe you'll learn your lesson. Are you awake yet? Okay, let's get going."

"Where are we going?" Mike asked.

Al wrapped a hairy arm around him. "I got a hot tip from Sgt. Rodriguez. The AMERICAL NCO Club is having a Filipino floor show tonight."

"So what? We see floor shows all the time."

"Not like this." Al poked him in the ribs. "These girls take off all their clothes and dance naked. Rodriguez swears it's the truth."

"We can't go to the NCO Club," Hardy said. "If they find out we're officers, they'll kick us out."

"How will they find out? They don't know us over there. We'll wear our party clothes and blend right in. Besides, with your baby face no one would ever guess you're an officer. Come on, let's go!"

Since Lance didn't have any interest in going with them, he agreed to serve as duty officer. As long as one officer remained in the compound, Al could enjoy his freedom to prowl. Unleashed, the three men escaped the compound to spend the night in animal pursuits.

The NCO Club was jammed by the time they arrived. Hardy hoped they would avoid running into any familiar faces. After they worked their way to the bar, Al ordered two beers for each of them. He wanted to delay a return trip for as long as possible. The crowd noise increased as the start of the floor show grew closer. The bar girls had given up trying to serve customers. Whenever they attempted to brave the masses, they faced severe mauling. One girl lost her panties in the performance of duty. That was enough. Now, all of them cowered behind the bar refusing to budge.

Mike and Wiley followed Al as he attempted to navigate his way closer to the stage. Bodies did not move willingly, but no one deliberately impeded their progress. Al had come to see naked dancing girls at close range; he wouldn't settle for balcony seats. They advanced within ten feet of the action before settling themselves onto the floor. Screaming GIs surrounded them clapping their hands with anticipation. The crowd had grown restless waiting for the arrival of the main event.

The stage looked ready, the band had moved into place, but the performers had not appeared. The club manager stood on stage engaged in a heated discussion with the manager of the group. No one could hear the conversation, but the club manager kept poking the Filipino in the chest with his finger. The little man cringed while gesturing helplessly at the crowd. Apparently, the Filipino had some reservations about bringing his girls into the midst of these savage beasts. No one could blame him, but a riot would erupt if he didn't comply. Without the immediate appearance of naked dancing girls things could get ugly.

The hand clapping turned into foot stomping making the din unbearable. The club manager begged for control while holding up his hands to plead for quiet. After the volume had decreased to a tolerable level, he addressed the raucous audience.

"Okay, settle down you guys. The girls will be out in a few minutes if you obey a few rules."

Loud whistles and catcalls followed.

"Okay, that's enough. The rules are simple—keep the noise down, stay off the stage, and no touching the girls. Does everyone understand?"

The audience replied in unison. "Sure!"

Followed by, "Bring on the girls!"

"Bring on the girls!!"

The club manager looked skeptical, but he signaled for the band to start playing.

The music quieted the mob as they waited for the dancers to appear. By the second warm-up number, the performers had still not made an entrance. The crowd began to show its displeasure by more foot stomping. After an eternity, four pretty Filipino girls stepped cautiously onto the stage. Dressed in skimpy bikinis, the frozen smiles on their faces looked more like grimaces. No one seemed to notice the girls' discomfort. Enthused, the audience cheered them on to new levels of accomplishment.

The dancers seemed to gain a little confidence after the first number. One of the girls bravely removed her bikini top, waving it in the air. The crowd cheered and begged for more. The other three dancers followed suit by removing their tops. The music continued as the girls danced topless for about ten minutes. The NCOs loved it, but the club had promised them *naked* dancing girls. Out of desperation, the crowd started throwing money on the stage. Bravely, the performers continued to dance as they dodged flying quarters.

Finally, the music stopped and a drum roll announced that the big moment had arrived. One by one, each girl removed her bikini bottom to stand fully exposed in front of the audience. Al grabbed his heart as he swooned in mock ecstasy. Everyone else applauded and whistled his appreciation. Two hundred sets of hungry eyes focused on every little movement.

The music resumed while the dancers moved seductively to the beat. Mike watched with interest as all the girls competed for attention. Each one attempted to outdo the others by performing erotic movements. The audience shouted for more. When one unfortunate dancer wandered too close to the edge of the stage, an onlooker grabbed her ankles. The assailant almost dragged her off the stage, but the naked performer escaped intact. The terrified girl retreated to a safe distance away from the clutches of the mob.

The show lasted another thirty minutes without further incident. At that point, the performers appeared ready to retreat. Blowing kisses of farewell, the girls headed for the wings while the crowd attempted to delay their departure with a shower of more quarters and rolled up bills. The aroused audience wanted to see one more dance. Shaking their heads in refusal, the dancers made the critical mistake of dropping to the floor to collect their bounty. The sight of four naked girls, crawling on the stage, was too much for one drunken GI. Charging forward, he grabbed one of the girls from behind. As he pawed at her body, the other dancers made a hasty retreat leaving their unfortunate colleague to deal with her tormentor.

The drunk's friends cheered as three more spectators decided to join in the fun. Now, all four GIs grabbed at the helpless dancer struggling on the floor.

Al erupted in fury. "Those assholes can't do that!"

Jumping to his feet, he pushed his way onto the stage. Mike and Wiley followed close behind. Not thinking it wise to attack four NCOs in front of two hundred of their friends, Mike still couldn't let Al face the threat alone. Members of the crowd stood in the way to prevent them from interfering. In spite of this obstacle, the two young officers fought their way to the stage. Al had already started to shove the attackers away from the Filipino girl. Looking over his shoulder, Hardy observed a dozen angry faces coming to the aid of their buddies.

Three minutes later the MPs arrived blowing their whistles. The shrill blast startled most of the combatants enough to force a retreat, but several others stayed behind to fight. Hardy absorbed a flurry of punches from flying fists. He fought back valiantly, but he and Wiley were outnumbered. One punch landed squarely in Mike's face causing him to crumple over in agony. The MPs saved them from total annihilation by beating off their assailants.

Looking up from the floor, Hardy watched Al gather up the naked dancing girl in his arms. Holding her tenderly, like a small child, he carried her off the stage. After leaving her in the protection of her friends, he dusted himself off. The Filipinos responded with profuse expressions of gratitude.

Unable to escape from the club, the MPs detained the three officers for questioning. Attempting to avoid expo-sure, the battered intruders gave the MPs false names and ranks. Al explained that the three of them had just arrived from Da Nang to visit friends. He attempted to convince the MPs of their efforts to protect the girl, and not harm her. Although skeptical, the MPs released the men to seek med-ical attention. Hardy sighed with relief as blood streamed from his nose. Once freed from the club, the injured officers drove back to Sand Hill nursing their wounds.

"Well Al, that was certainly exciting," Wiley said. "Next time you invite me to a party, I'll bring my brass knuckles."

Al laughed in spite of his pain. "You two are damned lucky I was there to protect you."

Groaning, Mike held a handkerchief up to his face. Al had performed a great act of gallantry. Although the big man loved playing the role of a philanderer, he would never tolerate seeing anyone abused. Hardy swelled with pride at having such a courageous friend.

The next morning, Mike awoke sporting a swollen nose and two blackened eyes. Desperate to crawl back into bed with an ice pack, he forced himself to prepare for a scheduled run to Duc Pho. After taking some aspirin, he put on his sunglasses to mask the damage. Remembering that Lance would accompany him today, he stopped by his hooch before heading to the mess hall. Wiley had already told Lance about the fight, so Mike didn't have to answer relentless questions about his injuries. Taking a long look at the battered face, Lance extended his sympathy without further comment.

Sgt. Bates met them at the mess hall for breakfast. Unprepared for the sight of Hardy's bruises, Bate's exclaimed, "Damn, Lieutenant, what happened to you?"

"Lay off, Bates. I fell out of bed."

"Sure you did. It looks like you tangled with an angry husband."

"Can it, Bates. Let me suffer in silence."

"Okay, but next time you get into trouble make sure I'm around to help get you out."

"Thanks, I had help." Mike touched his nose gingerly.

Hardy had to endure taunts throughout breakfast. Sgt. Hayes dared him to take off his sunglasses. Ignoring the challenge, Hardy continued eating without removing the eye protection. Rushing to finish breakfast, he made a premature exit from the mess hall. On the way out, he grabbed a *Stars and Stripes*.

The *Stars and Stripes* was published every week. Except for old newspapers from home, it served as the only written news the troops received. The paper billed itself as an *unofficial military publication*, but it carried mostly news about the war. The newspaper never mentioned anything about peace demonstrations back home, but it always published a weekly list of war casualties on the front page. Hardy tucked it under his arm to read later.

During the trip to Duc Pho, Mike attempted to instruct Lance on the duties of a convoy officer, but with little success. His head throbbed too much from the pain of his injuries. Fortunately, Sgt. Bates jumped to the rescue by taking over the training. Thanking him, Hardy retreated to a quiet corner at the rear of the truck. After easing himself into a sitting position, he pulled out the newspaper. The headlines announced news stories of little interest to him: *US airplanes still bombed Hanoi. The North Vietnamese had launched a new offensive.* His eyes fell to the bottom of the page where he started to read the names of seventy or eighty men killed in action during the previous week. Halfway down the list, he stopped in horror at finding a familiar name:

Lt. Richard O. Chang
C Company, 3rd Battalion
23d Infantry Division, AMERICAL

Oh no—not Richard! Richard couldn't be dead.

Hardy covered his face in disbelief. Why hadn't someone told him? How could it happen? Without the benefit of an explanation, he dropped his head to his knees.

Sgt. Bates observed his distress. "What's wrong, Lieutenant?"

Mike handed him the newspaper.

Bloody Mama vibrated and roared down the highway toward Duc Pho. Each bump in the road slammed a jolt of pain through Hardy's body. He almost welcomed the agony as atonement for his shame. Unable to fully understand this feeling, he knew it had something to do with his guilt over Richard's death. Richard had faced his fate bravely, while Mike struggled with day-to-day existence at a safe distance away from the fighting. As he mourned the loss of his friend, Hardy convinced himself that he could never emulate Richard's sense of duty.

Mike caught Sgt. Bates watching him at regular intervals. Bates seemed torn between lending his support or leaving him alone to grieve in silence. Hardy had never experienced the pain of losing a friend. And, at this moment, he found it difficult to accept the reality of Richard's death. He'd known other men killed in action, but they had been assigned to someone else. During this time of reflection, the need to safeguard his own mortality tugged at his conscience. For some unknown reason, the hand of fate, or God, had kept him out of combat. In reality, Mike knew that as a combat officer he would have done his duty until meeting the same end as Richard. Instead, someone, or something, had stacked the odds in his favor. Guilt evolved into a feeling of gratitude. With new awareness, he praised his good fortune at dwelling in the safety of *Bloody Mama's* womb. Now, surviving Vietnam took on more significance than ever.

Hardy pulled himself to his feet by holding onto the side of the gun truck's armor plating. As he watched the landscape rush by, he observed the familiar sights. Mama Sans still tended their rice on the roadside. Children played in the schoolyard. Papa Sans worked in the fields. South Vietnamese soldiers displayed dead VC on the side of the road. Nothing had changed—just another day on the road to Duc Pho.

He moved toward Lance and Sgt. Bates. Ames expressed his regret for Richard's death as Hardy passed by his machine gun position. Mike patted Ames on the shoulder, thanking him.

Bates extended his hand. "I'm sorry about Lieutenant Chang. He was a good man."

Bates had only met Richard once or twice, but he knew that the two had been friends.

"Thanks, Sergeant Bates. He *was* a good man. How's everything with the convoy? Any problems?"

"We're in good shape. We'll hit Duc Pho in about thirty minutes."

"Good. How are you doing, Lance?"

"I'm okay." The newcomer twitched with discomfort.

"Do they always put dead VC on the side of the road like that?"

"Yeah, all the time," Hardy replied. "They want us to see how much they're helping to win the war. Everytime they kill a few VC, we give them more guns and equipment. It's strictly supply and demand."

"God damn, Lieutenant, you've been over here too long. You're startin' to sound like the rest of us," Bates said.

"Seven more months, Bates; I still have a long way to go."

"No sweat. As long as you stay close to *Bloody Mama* you'll make it with no problem."

These words of assurance echoed Mike's earlier thoughts. Welcoming the security of the armor-plated gun truck, he returned to the task of training the new convoy officer. "Lance, I should warn you not to listen to this crazy sergeant, but he's managed to keep me out of trouble —so far. You could do worse."

"He's a real good teacher," Lance responded. "He'll deserve a medal if he can turn me into a trucker."

Bates shook his head in mock frustration. "Shit, no one told me I'd end-up training lieutenants. I thought officers were supposed to lead us."

"C'mon, Bates, you don't really believe that," Hardy said.

"You're right, Lieutenant. I guess I lost my head for a minute."

It felt good to laugh again. Life had started to return to normal.

Driving through the gates of Duc Pho, Hardy watched the trucks scatter to their assigned unloading points. He left Lance with Sgt. Bates at Suzy's while he headed to the clinic. After tolerating the heat and truck vibrations for the last several hours, he needed some painkillers and an ice pack for his face. The medic on duty expressed amusement at seeing an officer with two black eyes and a swollen nose. Suppressing a chuckle, he gave Hardy an icepack and codeine pills. The ice provided immediate relief to his face. The pills would take care of pain over the long-term.

Hardy thought about going to the steam bath, but he opted to visit Richard's unit instead. Anxious to know how Richard had died, he felt certain someone could give him the details. After arriving at Richard's hooch, he went inside. He found the bed stripped and Richard's belongings removed. Combat units had perfected the art of dealing with their dead. They dispatched bodies and personal effects out of sight with great efficiency. The infantry took pride in cutting their losses in short order to continue on with the mission.

After Hardy walked to the orderly room, a clerk directed him to Sgt. Fallon, who had served as Richard's platoon sergeant. Mike found the man in his hooch writing a letter. Shirtless, Fallon only wore a pair of cut-off shorts.

"Sergeant Fallon, I'm Lieutenant Hardy. I was a friend of Lieutenant Chang."

Looking up, he waved Hardy in. Fallon looked youthful with close-cropped blonde hair and steel blue eyes. His tanned body featured a number of scars and deep scratches from months in the bush. In spite of his youth, he had the look of a seasoned veteran.

"Have a seat. Do you want a beer?"

"Sure, thanks."

Sgt. Fallon rose from his chair to round up two cans of cold suds. When he returned, he stared at Hardy's face with unrestrained interest. "It looks like you tangled with a rough customer."

Adjusting the ice pack over one eye, Mike took a long drink of the frosty cold beer. "There were about six of them. I just happened to be in the wrong place, at the wrong time."

"God damn, I thought it was dangerous in the bush." Fallon popped open his beer with a can opener. "I guess you want to know what happened."

"Yeah, if you don't mind; I'd like to know how he died."

"No problem. I've got a copy of the report here. You can read it if you want, but it doesn't tell the whole story. We always clean up the details and keep it short. Once a guy gets blown away it really doesn't matter how it happened."

"I guess you're right. I'm just trying to close the book on a friend."

"I understand. Lieutenant Chang was a good man. I don't like officers very much—no offense, but Lieutenant Chang was one of the few good ones."

Smiling, Hardy replied that no offense was taken.

Sgt. Fallon continued with his story. "Lieutenant Chang knew how to deal with people and he wasn't all hung-up on rank. He listened and asked good questions. I really thought he was going to make it. He learned fast and had a good feel for the bush. I trusted him."

"What happened?" Mike asked quietly.

"It was crazy. There'd been no action for days. Charlie was nowhere to be found. It was a routine patrol, and our guys had started getting careless. In order to maintain discipline, Lieutenant Chang tried to tighten everyone up. He told me he had a bad feeling. During one of our rest stops, he chewed out some guys for 'smoking and joking.' On the way back to the front of the line, we heard a shot and he went down. A sniper got him in the neck and he was bleeding real bad. We tried to help him out, but there was too much damage. He died after a few minutes. I sent a patrol after the sniper and they shot him out of a tree. The asshole was still alive when they dragged him back to me. He was just a kid and looked like he was only twelve years old. There was a hole in his gut and he looked real scared. I could tell he was in pain, but I was real pissed off. I took out my knife and finished him off. We left his body tied to a tree, as a warning. I didn't put that part in the report. I just reported that Lieutenant Chang had been killed by sniper fire and we'd shot the sniper. The real story never leaves the bush. It's a dirty war out there and we do shitty things to survive. Lieutenant Chang knew that, but he was one of the good guys. He was just unlucky. That's what happened."

Hardy observed him during the entire monologue. Fallon had provided a matter-of-fact, clinical description of the episode. It seemed like he had disassociated himself from the event by taking on the role of spectator. Hardy didn't see a cold-blooded killer before him, just someone who had learned to cope with violence. Mike wondered how Fallon would readjust to civilian life. He thanked the combat NCO, shook his hand, and walked out into the hot sun.

Mike felt some relief after learning the details of Richard's death. Satisfied with knowing how Richard had died, he also felt gratified to hear about Fallon's respect for his friend as an officer. Richard's death still seemed like a senseless waste—just another death in this senseless conflict. As Hardy walked away from Richard's unit, he mentally closed the chapter on his grief. He would miss his friend, but nothing could change the outcome of the tragedy.

On the return trip to Chu Lai, Hardy turned over control of the convoy to Lance. Lance had proven himself a good student by calling in all the checkpoints with relative ease. The codeine and beer had taken effect on Hardy's brain, so he spent most of the trip in a drowsy stupor. In spite of this handicap, he managed to quiz the new lieutenant on some operational procedures. Sgt. Bates also seemed pleased with the new officer's progress. All in all, Lance seemed right at home on *Bloody Mama*. It looked like they had groomed a real AG combat trucker.

Visiting the club later that night, Mike found Jefferson in his usual spot. The lieutenant from Texas was engaged in deep conversation with Mary. She seemed annoyed by the unwelcome interruption, but smiled when she observed Hardy's bruised face.

"What happen to you, GI? You get fresh with bar girl?" She seemed to take delight at his appearance.

"No Mary, I got kicked by a water buffalo."

This sent her into sudden gales of laughter. "You bad boy—get fresh with water buffalo!"

Jefferson erupted into laughter. Even though they laughed at his expense, it felt good to spend time with happy people. The three of them enjoyed the merriment until Mary breezed away still chuckling. Mike watched her leave with great interest. Moving away with a professional sway in her hips, she knew how to display her assets.

Squirming in his chair, Mike said to Jefferson, "Whew, that girl is a little oriental tiger."

"She does have spirit. I wonder how her act would play in Texas?"

"You're not going to take her home with you?"

"No way; I'd just like to see her act in Texas. So, fess up. What happened to your face?"

Mike went through all the details of the NCO Club adventure by describing every painful moment. Jefferson expressed his admiration of Al's intervention. He liked the way they all had defended the dancer. Hardy also shared the details of Richard's death, without discussing the way

Sgt. Fallon had dealt with the sniper. He'd never reveal that part of the episode.

"You've had a rough time in the past twenty-four hours. You need a party. There's a bash at the hospital tonight. One of the staff just got promoted and they're giving some of the nurses a send-off. We're invited."

"I'm not invited."

"Sure you are. I have an open invitation to bring a friend any time. We'll stop at my place for a little smoke before we hit the party. What do you say?"

Hardy didn't feel in the mood to party, but he needed the company of cheerful people.

"Let's go."

After leaving the club, they drove to Jefferson's hooch. When they arrived at the luxurious quarters, Jefferson pulled out several joints. The lingering effects of the codeine along with a new infusion of marijuana began to take a toll. Mike slipped into a state of total relaxation. He experienced no pain, no stress, and no remorse. Hostile images turned into fuzzy blurs. The painful residue from his injuries slipped away until he felt only numbness. He could have remained in this condition indefinitely. Jefferson shattered the spell by insisting that they leave and go to the party.

They found the celebration in one of the hospital lounges. The room had filled with people and cigarette smoke by the time they arrived. Jefferson worked his way through the crowd. Periodically, he would stop to carry on a conversation with an acquaintance. Hardy tried to avoid any conversation. He didn't trust his tongue to perform as it should. In spite of his best efforts, he couldn't avoid a confrontation with a sympathetic young nurse.

"What happened to you?" she gasped.

Tired of explaining his facial condition to the curious, he mumbled something about a helicopter crash and an attack by the VC.

"You poor thing, you must be in terrible pain."

"No," he smiled crookedly. "I'm in no pain. I'm taking...ah...medication. I feel okay."

"That's good. Let me know if you need anything else. I hope you feel better. Bye."

He wondered what she'd look like without the loud buzz in his brain or the pressure behind his eyes.

As he wandered aimlessly through the crowd, he imagined the attention of the party-goers had focused on him. He couldn't decide if they stared at him because of the black eyes, or because he looked stoned—probably both. He felt a rush of dread that someone would discover his secret. Coming face-to-face with a colonel, he attempted to focus on the man's features. The colonel seemed to exist in another dimension. Mike's heart pounded rapidly.

"Are you all right, son?"

"Oh, yes sir. I had an accident, but I'm taking some strong medication for the pain."

"Well, you'd better get to bed before you fall down."

"Yes sir, I will." Hardy made a swift escape to the opposite side of the room.

The celebration continued well past midnight. Mike made some new friends, but couldn't remember their names. When he found Jefferson, he pleaded for escape from the probing eyes of the party-goers. They made their way to the jeep. Jefferson asked how he was doing.

"Man, I'm blasted!"

"See, I knew you needed a party."

After landing at his hooch, Hardy fell into his bunk. Time and place ceased to exist. He drifted off into nothingness.

Splashing water on his face the next morning, he checked his facial damage in the mirror. The swelling had subsided, but both eyes still sported yellow-tinged black bruises. Although his nose didn't seem broken, it felt tender and sore. Dressing for breakfast, he remembered an important errand to perform. Recovering Richard's letter to his family, he dropped it into the mailbox on the way to the mess hall.

Another month ticked by without incident. The war raged on, but it seemed far away. Chu Lai still suffered rocket attacks every night, but the rockets landed outside the company area. Numbed by the routine, the truckers started showing the effects of complacency. Danger still loomed on the highway, but the convoys charged on with reckless abandon. Every assignment brought them one day closer to going home. The drivers acted like they could speed the process by tearing-up the road.

Hardy made a futile attempt *not* to count the days remaining in his tour of duty. Remembering Hank the bartender's admonition about *short-timers,* he still couldn't avoid looking at the calendar. In spite of his best efforts, he felt drawn to the process as a route to deliverance. The army promised to send every GI home after one year of duty, providing they survived Southeast Asia. According to his most recent count, only six months remained before his scheduled departure. Even better, the army could grant him an early release to return to college in September. September was only four months away. At this point, surviving the challenges of campus life seemed like a much better option than risking further exposure to VC rockets. Mike waited with great anticipation for approval of his early release application.

Lance had made great progress as a convoy commander. Although he didn't fit the macho stereotype portrayed by actors in training films, he earned the respect of subordinates in his own unique way. By listening and making decisions based on the good advice of veterans, he gained acceptance and performed well beyond all expectations. After three weeks of training, Al released him for command.

Hardy still worried about Lance's brooding relationship with his wife. She seemed to control his behavior through the force of her letters. Refusing to discuss the true nature of their partnership, Lance always spoke of her in glowing terms. Greeting each letter from home with great antici-pation, he inevitably turned somber after digesting its contents. He acted like a character caught in the middle of a marriage skirmish with little chance of surviving intact. Hardy viewed the struggle as the unfolding saga of a bad television drama.

During the past month, Mike had made an earnest attempt to avoid excessive involvement with Sgt. Rodriguez. But, from time to time, he granted Rodriguez small favors. By restricting his indiscretions to approving twenty-four hour passes and vehicle dispatches, he still enjoyed the benefit of extra food, booze and cigarettes. Enjoying the bounty from the collaboration, he saw nothing wrong with his limited involvement in the operation.

Late one afternoon, Sgt. Rodriguez called him to the supply room. "Hey Lieutenant, how's it going?"

"Great, Sergeant Rodriguez. I really appreciated the case of beer and the vodka you sent over. I like to get a kick out of my orange juice."

"No problem, you've been a great help to me. That's why I asked you to come down here. I just came into possession of this brand new Seiko watch."

He presented Hardy with a gold, automatic self-winding watch still in the display box. "Really, it's no big deal. Someone just gave it to me. I could sell it or trade it, but I want you to have it. It's my way of saying *thank you* for helping me out when I needed it."

Mike was awestruck by the beauty of the thing. "Thanks, but I really can't accept this."

"Why not? It's just another little gift like the beer and cigarettes. It's important that I show you my appreciation. I'll be very disappointed if you turn me down. C'mon Lieutenant, take it. It'll look good on you."

Hardy felt caught in the midst of an ethical dilemma. Knowing it was wrong to accept the watch, he recognized the fact that he had accepted Rodriguez's gifts in the past. After all, he wouldn't be doing anything out of the ordinary. Besides, he couldn't afford to offend the supply sergeant; he might need his help sometime in the future.

"Thanks, I'll take it. You've always been fair with me, Sergeant Rodriguez." Hardy claimed his new prize.

"No sweat. I told you before that I always take care of

my people. This is business, and we can all share in the profits if we help each other."

Mike nodded his agreement but had trouble swallowing. He had expanded his involvement in the operation more than he ever imagined possible. "Thanks, I'll do what I can, but there are limits. I can help out in small ways. I just can't get too involved—if you know what I mean."

"Sure, sure, no problem, we'll just keep things as they are. If you do me a favor once in a while, I'll do the same for you."

"Okay, count me in. I'll need favors from time to time, too."

After they shook hands, Hardy walked out of the supply room with a new watch, and another package for Mr. Van. He was scheduled to leave for Quang Ngai in the morning.

The next day Mike awoke with the new watch on his wrist. It was the most expensive timepiece he had ever owned. He savored the luxury of it for several minutes, until his eyes fell on Mr. Van's package. Losing the momentary reverie, he plunged into regret. Everything had a price, but he hadn't expected to make the payments along with installments of a guilty conscience. Now that he'd entered the black market arena, all the escape routes appeared blocked. Grabbing the package in disgust, he left for the mess hall.

He found Sgt. Hayes and his crew eating breakfast when he entered. Hayes glanced quickly at the package giving him a knowing look. Hayes gestured for him to join the group for breakfast. Mike noticed a new guy sat at the table. Now that PFC Blake had departed for home, PFC Scott Calhoun had arrived from Los Angeles as his replacement. Calhoun looked like a displaced surfer, with beach-blonde hair and a peace symbol tied around his neck. On the surface, Mike considered him a good fit for the *No Slack* bunch.

After breakfast, Hayes shared his philosophy of survival for the benefit of the new crew member. "Charlie's out there everywhere. He watches us all the time. He's also enlisted people to spy on the inside. Any of the hooch maids or gooks working for us could be working for the VC."

"No way," Calhoun scoffed. "If he knows everything, he could take us out any time."

"That's right. You've got to stay alert. If you start every morning believing today is the day he hits us, you'll be ready. Charlie will see that, and he'll hold off until he sees you slacking off."

"Man, I'd go nuts stayin' on edge all the time. He'll hit us when he wants. Why get all uptight waitin' for it?"

"You'd better keep the edge if you want to live. Stay alert on the road and your chances are better if we get attacked. Kick back and relax only when you're home safe in your hooch. Am I right, Lieutenant?"

Having heard all this rhetoric before, Hardy had only half-listened to the conversation. His attention had drifted back to his discussion with Sgt. Rodriguez a day earlier.

"Yeah, that's right. We've been lucky so far, but we're due to get hit. The VC can't afford to let us drive up and down the highway every day without an attack, or they'll lose face. Their strategy is based on fear so they'll strike when we least expect it. Stay afraid and you'll live longer. C'mon, let's get out of here and hit the road."

The *No Slack* crew followed him out the door.

They made the trip to Quang Ngai in a steady downpour. Rain parkas offered some protection, but the rain always ended up saturating Hardy's neck area and legs. He observed Calhoun during the trip. The new guy seemed more concerned about staying dry than watching for the enemy. Sgt. Hayes would have to do more training.

Mr. Van waited for them in the doorway. He offered up a big towel when Hardy ran into the reception room. One of Van's assistants helped Mike out of his rain gear. Hardy rubbed his wet hair vigorously with the towel. A pretty girl brought him a pot of tea, pouring some of the hot liquid into a cup. Like other servers in the past, he expected her to return to the kitchen, but this girl remained seated beside him. He accepted the proffered cup of tea from her delicate hands. Viewing her with interest, he rubbed the feeling back into his upper body. As she stared demurely into her lap, Hardy shot Van a questioning look.

Van replied with his gold tooth sparkling in the light. "You need hot bath. This lady will take you in back. I have hot water ready. You go now, Mike."

Hardy wanted to argue with him, but the offer of a hot

bath sounded appealing. Handing Van the package from Rodriguez, he followed the Vietnamese girl toward the rear of the building. Van patted him on the back as he departed the reception room.

The tile tub was constructed below floor level. Soap and towels waited nearby on a rack. Hardy sat down on a stool to remove his boots. The girl knelt before him to loosen his wet laces. After pulling his boots off soggy feet, she continued to remove the rest of his clothing. He allowed her to complete the task without offering any resistance. When she had removed everything, she guided him into the tub. The water felt hot, but not too hot to tolerate. Slipping below the surface, only his head remained exposed. The warmth of the water had an immediate soothing effect on his chilled body.

After he had settled into the tub, an old woman arrived to remove his wet boots and uniform. The girl exited behind a screen in the far corner of the room. She appeared minutes later, dressed in a short silk robe. Hardy watched with interest as her lithe body moved to the edge of the tub. Standing above him, she slowly untied the belt of her robe. It fell lightly away from her. Her naked skin gleamed in the lamplight illuminating her mesmerizing beauty. With dance-like precision, she stepped into the tub and settled down beside him.

Obviously, Van had planned this encounter. He must have realized that Mike wouldn't just walk off with a pretty girl. He'd waited until the lieutenant had shown up wet and miserable. With the arrival of the rain, Van had allowed nature to take its course—it worked. It's almost impossible to ignore a beautiful, naked woman sitting beside you in a hot tub of water. Surrendering all his misgivings, Hardy gave into the moment.

Reaching for a bar of scented soap, the young woman washed his back with soft hands. He closed his eyes as she massaged the last traces of cold from his muscles. Her fingers touched and teased without restraint. With a long sigh, he submitted himself to the sensations of pleasure. When she increased the pace of her movements, Hardy had to gently restrain her hands. He wanted to prolong the experience for as long as possible.

When she finished with the soap, Mike took the bar in his hands to return the favor. He rubbed and caressed her golden flesh. Leaning against him, she offered herself without hesitation. Soaping her breasts, he teased her nipples until they stood fully erect. Massaging her firm belly, he allowed his fingers to slip between her legs. As he touched the intimate parts of her anatomy, she pushed tighter against him. She offered her steaming body as an open invitation for erotic discovery.

The water in the tub began to cool. At that point, the woman rose to her feet. Stepping out of the water, she offered Mike her hand. Joining her on the deck, she wrapped a towel around him. She arranged more towels on a soft mat before returning to his side. They took turns toweling each other. Warm and dry, she guided him to the mat. Stretching out, she opened her arms in invitation. Without hesitation, he entered her body with no feelings of regret.

The Vietnamese girl remained with him for a short while after their intimate encounter. Before leaving, she washed and dried him one more time. Bending over, she kissed him on the forehead before wrapping him in a dry towel. Smiling, he waved goodbye. Later, it occurred to him that she hadn't spoken a word during their time together.

The old woman returned with his uniform. It had been dried and pressed. The boots still felt damp, but she had dried the socks. After dressing, he found Van waiting for him in the reception room.

Grinning, Van put his arm around him. "You have good bath?"

Hardy wanted to pull away, but resisted the impulse. "Yes, thanks."

Van smiled a gold, toothy grin. "Very good. Same lady wait here for you next time."

"I'll let you know, okay?"

Looking disappointed, the man recovered quickly. "Okay, you let me know. You want different lady?"

"No, that's not it. I'll let you know when I need a lady."

"Okay. We still friends, Mike?"

"Yeah, sure, we're friends."

Shaking his hand warmly, Van gave him a package for Sgt. Rodriguez. Hardy stuffed it into his pocket before walking out into the rain.

On the trip back, the rain continued its assault. It didn't take long for Mike to start shivering from his rain-saturated clothing all over again. The Vietnamese farmers still toiled in their fields, oblivious to the elements. Mike attempted to block out his misery by recalling the events of the past two hours. Van had manipulated him into contact with the seductive lady, but the experience had given him great pleasure. He knew that he'd pay a steep price for more pleasures of that sort. In spite of an afternoon of passion, he felt reluctant to plunge any deeper into Van's debt.

After returning to the company area, Hardy headed straight to the supply room. Anxious to unload Van's package on Sgt. Rodriguez, he wanted to retreat to the warmth of his hooch. He found Rodriguez talking with his old friend, Sgt. Buddy Wallace. Buddy had provided Mike with his first ride to Chu Lai, along with an introduction to the black market. True to his promise, Buddy had returned to check up on him.

Hardy shook his hand. "Buddy, I didn't know you knew Sergeant. Rodriguez."

"Sure I do. George and I do business every once in a while. You've got a great supply sergeant here. He's done a lot to help me out. So how's life in the trucking business?"

"Great. We've got a good company and the work is steady. How are things with you?"

Mike had intended to pass Van's package to Sgt.

Rodriguez and make a hasty retreat, but he decided to wait for a more opportune moment. Unfortunately, Buddy looked like he was in no hurry to leave.

"I told you about my colonel. He still hates my guts, but wants more young pussy. I'm here to see if you guys can send me some."

Hardy held up his hands in protest. "That's not my department. The supply sergeant handles all special orders."

"We'll try to help him out, Lieutenant," Rodriguez chuckled. "Did you bring me anything from Quang Ngai?"

Digging into his pocket, Mike pulled out the package. "Mr. Van sends this to you with his compliments."

Although Hardy attempted to make light of the delivery, Buddy observed the exchange with great amusement.

"Well, it looks like you guys are working well together. I figured you'd fall into the business." He playfully poked Mike in the ribs.

Hardy reacted as if struck by a hot iron. "It's not business. Sergeant Rodriguez has done a lot to help me out, so I'm just returning the favor. Listen, I'm wet and cold. I've got to go to my hooch to dry off. It was good to see you again." He shook Buddy's hand.

"Sure," Buddy replied. "Let me know if you ever need anything."

"Don't worry, I'll let you know."

Finished with the good-byes, Mike left the supply room

behind. He could hear them laughing as he walked back into the downpour. Their cynical delight cut deeper than the driving rain. Thoroughly soaked and humiliated, he longed to escape his obligations to Sgt. Rodriguez. Unless he found a way to sever the alliance, he'd run the risk of losing his last shred of self-respect.

After arriving at his hooch, he replaced his wet uniform with clean jungle fatigues. The dry clothes cured the wetness and cold. He needed another cure. He needed to find a way to end the Quang Ngai connection.

CHAPTER 24
Bon Voyage

Al had a date to keep with Bangkok. He'd talked of nothing else since Wiley's return. At every opportunity, he harangued Wiley to repeat every detail of his Bangkok experience—over and over.

Unable to endure this relentless pressure, Wiley exploded."God damn it, Al! I told you that part a million times already. Give me a break!"

"Don't be so touchy, little man. I want to hear it again. Tell me how she got down on her hands and knees in front of you."

"Oh, shit. Okay, we were naked in the hotel room. She got down on her hands and knees. I got down behind her and we made love—that's it."

Jumping off his bed, Al flung his arms around Wiley's chest and squeezed. "No, no, you cheap little prick. Tell it the long way—step by step—like it really happened."

"All right, let me go you big ox!"

Al dumped his squirming victim on the floor with a warning. "You'd better not leave anything out."

Groaning, Wiley retold the entire episode with all the sordid details intact. So it went.

Al had not always intended to visit Bangkok. Initially, he expected to follow the Joe Tice plan by meeting his wife in Hawaii. After Wiley returned from R and R, Al transformed into a man possessed. He vowed to rearrange his itinerary to immerse himself in everything Bangkok had to offer. Whenever anyone mentioned the city, his eyes turned wild and unfocused. Everyone close to Al tried to avoid the topic completely. Ignoring this strategy, the burly man forced the issue at every opportunity. If he didn't make the pilgrimage soon, Mike and Wiley agreed to put him out of his misery.

Al's deliverance from Hawaii came at the hands of his mother-in-law. The elderly woman required some type of surgery. With deep regret, his wife wrote that she needed to remain at her mother's side during the lengthy recovery period. In response to his wife's letter, Al wished his mother-in-law a speedy return to health. Outwardly, he expressed his disappointment about the canceled plans. Inwardly, he could hardly contain his good fortune. The fates had intervened so Al could travel to Bangkok.

As the time of departure grew closer, Al's anticipation increased. With restless energy, he paced the floor of his office for long intervals. All too often, he'd give an order only to repeat it several times without thinking. Forgetting small details, he had difficulty maintaining his train of thought. Fortunately, Mike and Wiley could jog his memory often enough to save him from total embarrassment. They'd never seen anyone in such a state of distraction.

After what seemed like an eternity, the departure day grew close enough for Al to pack his bags. His flight to the carnal paradise would leave the next day. Rushing around like a wild man, Al threw his clothes haphazardly into a travel bag. At this rate, he'd win the award for the most wrinkled tourist in Bangkok. He had no intention of packing an iron; his focus far exceeded mere concerns about clothing. Although he treated his travel wardrobe like a major inconvenience, he constantly pestered Wiley for more suggestions on what to pack.

Wiley refused to buy into his friend's hysteria. "Cool it, Al. Take enough for a couple of days and buy the rest when you get there. Bangkok has great clothes for sale."

"Right, right," he mumbled. "What about money? How much money should I take?"

"Take enough," Wiley replied with a sneer.

Jumping to his feet, Al grabbed the smaller man by the throat. "Don't bullshit me, you worm! Tell me the truth, or I'll use your head for batting practice."

"Okay, let go!" Wiley choked. "Take four hundred dollars for a good time, or six hundred dollars for a great time."

Al considered this for a moment. "I'll take seven hundred and fifty."

Since this trip offered an once-in-a-lifetime experience, Al wouldn't risk scrimping on anything.

The Sand Hill Gang would never allow Al to depart without an appropriate send-off. The night before his flight, Mike and Wiley organized *Bon Voyage* party at the club. After inviting all of their friends to attend, they coerced the bar girls into wearing bikinis for the occasion.

The girls reluctantly agreed after each of them received a twenty-dollar incentive. Mary looked absolutely stunning. The bikini accentuated her full breasts and tight little behind. She moved like a gazelle. Jefferson beamed proudly every time she leaned over him. No one had any doubt about his right of ownership.

Al relished the atmosphere his friends had created for him. The bar girls took turns sitting in his lap, enduring his wandering hands with tight smiles. Relief flooded their faces whenever they escaped from his clutches. Having promised to conduct themselves as good sports, they accepted the onerous duty with relatively good humor.

At one point in the evening, Wiley arranged for one of the girls to place a wreath on Al's head while the others fed him grapes. Unfortunately, when the ladies didn't move their hands fast enough, Al attempted to bite their fingers. After her first nip from the chomping teeth, Mary threatened to go on strike if someone didn't increase her tip. The other girls followed suit. Mike and Wiley dug into their pockets to keep the party going.

The presentation of Bon Voyage gifts rounded out the celebration. As Al slumped on an improvised throne, with his wreath askew on his head, the party-goers showered him with presents. Among the offerings: a book on human sexuality and the prevention of disease, several porno magazines, a Bangkok travel book, a rubber dildo, and four boxes of condoms. Treating the gifts with great reverence, Al promised to use each one to its full potential.

The crowd declared the party a complete success. Mike and Wiley had to heave Al into the jeep for the ride home. Singing way off-key, the big man waved his wreath in the air during the entire trip. After they arrived at the hooch, he smothered them with hugs. The advanced state of his inebriation greatly enhanced this display of profound gratitude. Dropping him into bed, they left him to dream about his upcoming foray into the Bangkok fleshpots.

Although Lance had attended Al's party, he remained on the fringes of the action. Feeling out of place in the company of the raucous crowd, he much preferred seclusion. Tagged as a loner, Lance seemed to require little human interaction. Mike had known Lance for only two months, but the man's morale had undergone considerable deterioration during that period. Convoy duty served as the only respite from his troubles. He gravitated toward those assignments where he could focus his attention on each mission. Depression never emerged until he returned to the company.

Following Al's departure, Mike decided to visit him one evening. He found the sullen man sitting at his desk, holding his head in his hands. "Hey, Lance. Can I come in?"

Looking around with some apprehension, Lance waved Mike inside.

"I thought you could use a cold beer. I don't like to drink alone." Hardy offered him one of the cans.

Accepting it, Lance moved to his bunk to sit down.

"Thanks. I'm trying to write to my wife, but I can't find the right words."

"Give it a rest," Mike said. "Sometimes the words come easier if you don't work at it so hard."

"Maybe you're right." Lance shifted uncomfortably. "Sometimes I think if I say the right words or write the perfect letter, all my problems will be solved. I guess it really doesn't work that way. People don't change because of a few words on paper."

Sitting quietly, Mike stared deeply into his beer can. This could turn into a tough conversation. "I guess you're right."

"Have you ever been in love, Mike?"

Hardy hated that question. He hesitated before responding, "No, not really. I tried real hard to make it happen once, but the chemistry just wasn't right."

"What's the closest you ever got?"

After searching his memory, Mike attempted to lighten the mood. "There was a little girl in the third grade."

Lance reacted with a cold stare.

"Okay, I don't know. I guess the girl in San Francisco. Her name was Clara. Three days before leaving for Vietnam, I felt desperate for love. I thought I needed to have one meaningful experience before going to war. I really believed I was going to the bush and didn't expect to come home alive. I found Clara in a nude dancing joint. We hit it off right away. After we made love, I wanted to hold onto the relationship. It didn't happen. We had three days of passion before it ended. I knew it was over when I kissed her goodbye. The hardest part was accepting the reality of losing her. I still miss her, but I know I'll never see her again."

Hardy took a long drink of beer.

Lance stared at him before speaking. The first words emerged in a raspy whisper. "I met Laura in college. When I was going to school at Michigan I studied late every night. I didn't go to parties much and girls never showed any interest in me. It was easier to avoid everyone and study. My grades were outstanding, but I had no social life."

Fidgeting with the beer can, he rose from his bed.

"Anyway, I used to go to this all-night diner for coffee after midnight. A pretty waitress worked behind the counter and sometimes we'd talk. She acted real friendly and smiled a lot. If she didn't have any customers, we could talk for hours. She said she liked my company and after a while we became friends. We started sharing our hopes and dreams. She wanted to open her own restaurant. I was a business major and wanted to start my own business. We laughed about becoming partners."

He took several slugs of beer before sitting back down on his bunk.

"I wanted to ask her out, but it took a long time to work up my courage. When I finally invited her to dinner, I used the excuse that we could discuss restaurant ideas. She just patted my hand. She said she'd love to go, but she had this 'thing' with her boss, and couldn't date anyone. Since the jerk was a real jealous type, she could lose her job. She asked me to wait until she could work things out. I was in love with her, so I waited. I found out later that her boss was about forty and a real rough character. I couldn't believe she really cared about him. Anyway, one day the asshole beat her up and she came to me for help. She was afraid to return to her place. I only lived in a small apartment, but I invited her to stay with me anyway. She agreed. I offered her my bed, but she insisted on sleeping on the couch. We lived that way for a week. One night, she climbed into bed with me. She said she was frightened. As I held on to her I'd never felt happier in my entire life. She said she needed me." Tears started to flow from his eyes.

Not knowing how to respond, Mike moved to Al's refrigerator to grab two more beers. Stalling for several minutes, he returned to find Lance trying to pull himself together.

"Listen, Lance. You don't have to tell me this if you don't want to."

The distraught man accepted one of the cans of beer. "Thanks, but, if you don't mind, I need to go on."

"I don't mind. I'd like to help if I can."

"Thanks." Lance took a long drink from the beer can. "It took a while for her to break away from the guy. She had to get the police involved before he'd leave her alone. When he was out of the picture, Laura moved in with me. She said she loved me and we were happy. While I worked to complete my degree, Laura found another waitress job. The whole time we talked about going into the restaurant business. After graduation, I landed a job with a local restaurant chain. I started as a marketing associate before working my way up to assistant manager for development. Laura joined me in the company as an administrative assistant. We were married soon after. Things were going great until I got drafted. The army sent me to OCS because I had a college degree. I went to AG school because of my background in personnel."

Hardy had never heard Lance so deeply engrossed in conversation. The words seemed to erupt from his inner core as if trying to avoid further repression. His pent-up anguish had finally bubbled to the surface. Mike continued to listen attentively.

"Things went wrong soon after I went into the army. Laura worked hard for promotions. I'd call home late at night, but no one would answer. I wanted to believe she was working late. She got angry when I started asking questions. I stopped asking why she was never home. I didn't want to know. She wrote letters filled with news about her management contacts, and how she was moving up in the company. She missed my graduation from OCS. Later, she acted annoyed when I came home on leave. It looked like I was no longer part of her plans. I should have left her then. I knew what was going on, but I still loved her. I remembered the scared girl with bruises who said she needed me. I wanted that girl back. I wanted our life back together the way it was in college. I know it's stupid to think like that."

He paused to rub his face with his hands.

Mike considered his response. "It's not stupid, Lance. You love her and you just can't turn off your emotions. I also know that love doesn't always last and, once it's gone, you can't turn back the clock. I'll never be able to relive those three days in San Francisco with Clara. All I can do is hold onto the memory of those three days. If I ever find love again, it'll be with someone else. I've accepted that, but I'll always miss the girl who worked at Moe's."

Staring back at Mike, Lance shook his head sadly. "I know you're right. I need to let her go. She wants a divorce and has asked me to sign the papers. Why now? Why couldn't she wait until I get back? I keep hoping I can go home so we can work things out. I know it's hopeless, but she's all I have. There's nothing else I want to live for."

Mike felt stung by the despair in his voice. Lance looked like a man teetering on the edge of a precipice.

"You live for tomorrow, Lance. You live for the hope of new love and new relationships. You have a great deal to offer someone. There are lots of women who would kill to receive the same love you've given to Laura. Don't let her destroy you."

Lance smiled for the first time that night. "Thanks Mike, I've never shared my problems with anyone before. You've been a great help. I know what has to be done. Go back to your hooch. I'll be okay."

"Are you sure?" Hardy asked.

"Yes, I'm fine. I'll see you tomorrow. Thanks for the beer."

Satisfied that he looked better, Hardy patted Lance's shoulder before leaving the distraught man alone with his grief.

Mike spent restless hours trying to sleep. He continued to mentally review Lance's story, over and over. The woman in Michigan had claimed total possession of her husband's spirit. Unfortunately, she could use this advantage to destroy him at will. To Lance's detriment, she had decided to exert her control while he was alone and far away from home. Hardy couldn't comprehend how anyone could indulge in such cruelty. Coping with Vietnam required a soldier's undivided attention. Any GI having to deal with the war and personal turmoil at the same time suffered ungodly torment.

After dozing off, a loud CRACK jolted Mike out of his sleep. At first, he thought a rocket had caused the noise. In a panic, he remembered Lance. Running out of the hooch, he crossed the hill to the officer's quarters at full gallop. A light still burned in Lance's room when he rushed in. He found the broken man sitting on his bunk holding a pistol in his lap. Wiley stood in the doorway with a look of terror on his face.

Considering the circumstances, Lance appeared uncommonly serene. "It's all right, Mike. The thing just went off. Look, the bullet hit the wall over there. I couldn't do it.

Maybe, I'm a coward or maybe I just want to live. I really don't know. Here take this."

He handed Mike the pistol.

"It's time to move on. I'm not going to let her mess up my life. Let's get some sleep." Lance closed his eyes as he settled his head into the pillow.

Wiley stared at Hardy in confusion. Before turning off the light, Mike gestured for him to come outside. Under a brilliant full moon, Mike gave his friend an edited version of the circumstances leading up to the incident. Hardy promised to give him more details later. Digesting the information, Wiley shrugged before heading back to bed.

Five days later, Al returned from Bangkok.

CHAPTER 25
The Movie Star

Hardy loved mornings in Chu Lai. If the wind blew in from the east, it carried the scent of the South China Sea to the top of Sand Hill. As the sun rose with majestic splendor, it cast golden rays over the water in spectacular fashion. The morning light stretched across the glistening waves as it reached for the shore. Soaking in the energy moving toward him, Mike would stand transfixed until the solar rays warmed his face. Absorbing the power of the rising sun, he felt ready to start another day.

After the pistol shot jolted his sensibilities, Lance acted like a changed man. Although some vestiges of pain remained, he appeared to have conquered the bulk of his depression. A new spirit of hope had replaced the dark cloud of gloom. He no longer harbored any thoughts of reconciliation with his wife. Having accepted that the relationship was over, he now understood life contained an infinite number of possibilities. He might have difficulty making new adjustments, but Mike felt confident that the crisis had passed.

Mike made a point of watching Lance for danger signals. He saw none. After the momentous night in Lance's room, they never engaged in further conversations about the man's past. The two officers only spoke about the here and now. On one occasion, Lance thanked Mike for helping him cope with his problems. Sometime later, he announced that he'd signed the divorce papers. Otherwise, they only discussed the present and daily life in Chu Lai. Mike looked forward to the time when Lance would speak about his plans for the future.

Unfortunately, Lance had lots of company when it came to broken relationships. Thousands of men in Vietnam suffered the same fate. Every soldier clung desperately to the dream of loved ones waiting for him back home. They needed to maintain this essential link with family and girlfriends for emotional security. Too often, when wives or lovers couldn't endure the strain of separation—they'd find comfort elsewhere. Once the soldier lost this vital connection, he'd suffer the acute pain of loss. At times, Hardy felt grateful for not having a girlfriend waiting for him back home. He remembered a marching song from his days in basic training:

> *Ain't no use in goin' home,*
> *Jody's got your girl and gone.*

Jody ruined the trip home for too many GIs returning from Vietnam.

Al arrived from Bangkok late on a Sunday night. Hardy heard a jeep drive up several hours after he'd gone to bed. He recognized Al's voice thanking the driver for a lift back to Sand Hill. Mike briefly considered interrupting Al's homecoming, but discounted the notion as he drifted back to sleep. Convoy duty waited in the morning. He'd have lots of time to hear about Al's misadventures in the days ahead. It felt good to have the big guy back home.

The next morning, Mike checked in on the wayward voyager before heading to the mess hall. He found the travel-worn man snoring deeply on his bunk. Al appeared dead to the world. Mike and Wiley joked about Al's state of exhaustion as they walked down the hill.

"I know how he feels," Wiley laughed. "It'll take weeks for him to charge up his batteries again."

"I can't imagine a whole week of constant sex. I bet he established a new endurance record. Those poor Thai girls were probably grateful to see him leave," Hardy said.

"You can count on it. Al was so pumped up, he probably left a wake of female destruction behind him."

"We really need to bust his chops," Mike said. "He grilled you pretty hard after you got back. Let's take him to the club tonight and give him a taste of his own medicine."

"You bet," Wiley agreed. "I owe him big time. I'll make him spill his guts in public."

"Let's work up to it slowly. We'll take it real easy at first—like we're not really interested. We'll have a few drinks, talk about his flight and then...BAM! We'll give him both barrels. What do you think?"

"I think it sounds like a plan." They continued to refine this strategy all the way to the mess hall.

Hardy thought about the plot during the trip to Duc

Pho. The men loved scheming against each another. The victim usually knew something was up, but had difficulty unraveling the complexities of the plan. Accepting his status as an easy target, Al usually enjoyed his role as the focus of attention. As a master of giving grief to others, he also did well on the receiving end. Tonight was his turn to receive.

After returning from convoy duty, Mike found Wiley in Al's room. Both men held a beer as they engaged in casual conversation. Stretched out on his bunk in his underwear, Al looked like he hadn't bothered to get dressed all day. Mike reminded himself to maintain a nonchalant attitude.

"Welcome back, Al. Has Wiley filled you in on everything that happened while you were away?"

Al viewed Mike with suspicion. Dark circles puffed up under his eyes. It smelled like he needed a shower.

"Yeah, he did. So it was pretty quiet, except for the thing with Lance. Wiley told me the gun went off by accident. He's not going to have any more of those 'accidents,' is he?"

"No, he's in good shape," Mike replied. "Lance is tougher than he looks. He acts like a changed man."

Al regarded them both with wariness. He knew something was afoot. "Good. You two don't have anything else to report do you?"

"No. Everything is great," Wiley assured him. "We're just glad to have you back safe and sound. We thought we'd take you to the club tonight for a few drinks, if you feel up to it. How do you feel?"

"I feel fine you little snake. I'll be up and running long after you're under the table. I'll be right back after I take a shower."

Mike and Wiley agreed that a shower sounded like a great idea. Wiley gave a 'thumbs up' sign after Al left the room.

As usual, only a few customers graced the club on this Monday night. Not because the truck company had just finished a busy weekend—weekends in Vietnam didn't exist. Every day turned out exactly the same with weekends holding no special significance. Mondays ended up slow in the club, because—they were traditionally slow. No one could explain why.

Only a few people lounged at the bar playing dice as they entered. Jefferson held court with Mary at his usual table.

Waving them over, he handed Mike a piece of paper. "Look who's going to be doing a show here this Friday— Mimi Van Horn."

Hardy stared at the flyer in disbelief. Mimi Van Horn, a sexy movie star, had made a series of B-movies over ten years ago. Lately, her career had stalled, but her colorful lifestyle still earned attention by the tabloids. She worked hard to maintain a reputation for fast living with an inexhaustible supply of male lovers.

"Why is she coming here?" Wiley asked.

"Who knows—probably it's just a publicity stunt to recharge her sagging career," Jefferson said. "You know, the kinds of stunts that prompt headlines like, 'Movie Star Visits Troops on Front Line,' or 'Mimi Brings cheer to Lonely Boys in Vietnam.' This shit happens all the time. Marilyn Monroe tried to pull it off in Korea."

"She's not Marilyn Monroe, but she'll do in a pinch," Wiley said. "What movies did she make anyway?"

Al stood ready with the answer. "I've seen 'em all. There was *Hot Rod Queen*, *Co-ed Confidential*, *Jungle Princess*, *High School Lovers*, *College Weekend*, *The Passion Pit*—"

"Okay, okay, we've got the idea," Hardy laughed. "I wonder if Mimi knows her biggest fan is waiting for her in Chu Lai?"

"She was hot stuff on the big screen," Al declared. "She's packed on a few years, but I bet she still looks good."

Jefferson stood up to leave. "We'll definitely have to give her a warm welcome. Let's meet here early Friday night. Maybe, she likes to go down on men in uniform."

Mary gave him a dirty look. Smiling, he patted her bottom before she followed him obediently out of the club.

During the first round of drinks they avoided asking Al anything specific about Bangkok. Wiley inquired about his flight and arrival at the airport. Mike talked about Lance. He went on to explain how the dispirited man had managed to shake off dependency on his wife.

Al fidgeted during the entire conversation before finally exploding. "All right, you turds what's up? I keep waiting for all the questions." He glared at them from across the table.

"My, my, what questions do you mean?" Wiley asked.

Charging to his feet, Al attempted to grab him by the throat. Wiley pushed back in time to avoid the two hairy paws.

"Al, take it easy," Mike said in a soothing tone. "You act like you've been under great strain. Something seems to have drained all your energy and stamina."

Mike and Wiley burst out laughing. The trap had closed nicely. Strangely, Al didn't react or join in the merriment. He seemed distracted by issues outside their circle of friendship.

"Okay, okay, out with it. Give us every gory detail," Wiley demanded.

Hesitating, Al blinked back at both of them. "It was great, everything you said it would be."

"Come on, out with it," Mike said. "You're not going to spend a whole week in Bangkok without sharing the adventure with your friends."

"There's nothing to tell. Everything happened the way Wiley said it would. I had a great time."

"Wait a minute, something's up. This is payback, right?" Wiley asked.

"No, you guys got me real good. I'm just a little tired. I think I'll call it a night." Al stretched, stood up, and left the table. Mike and Wiley followed him out the door.

Al had changed since his return from Bangkok. He still

displayed good humor, but refrained from repeating his antics of the past. Outwardly, he seemed like the same fun-loving guy, but Mike and Wiley knew something wasn't right. He acted like he carried a secret burden from his R and R—something so secret he couldn't share it with his friends.

Friday arrived. Everyone eagerly anticipated seeing Mimi Van Horn in the flesh. Returning from convoy duty, Mike rushed back to his hooch for a quick shower and change of clothes. The Sand Hill gang planned to arrive several hours before the show to claim good seats. Jefferson had promised to save a block of tables for them in advance, but they decided to leave nothing to chance. Al fussed over his wardrobe like a teenager preparing for a big date. He kept asking Wiley for advice on what to wear. Even Lance joined in the excitement. Lately, he'd started spending more time with his fellow officers. His days of solitude and letter writing lived in the past. After a flurry of obscenities from Al, the four of them piled into the jeep three hours before show time.

True to his word, Jefferson waited with their reserved tables. Seeing them barge through the front door, he smiled and waved them over. Dressed to the teeth, the bargirls were in the process of hanging decorations. Two stagehands unrolled electrical cord and overhead lights. The technicians explained that Miss Van Horn required special lighting for all her shows.

"Can she sing?" Al asked one of the men. "I can't remember her singing in the movies."

The man rolled his eyes. "She can't sing worth a shit, but then again, she doesn't have to. Once you boys see her on stage, you won't care what comes out of her mouth." He let out a hearty laugh and poked his friend in the ribs.

"How old is she?" Wiley asked.

"She was in her thirties when she was makin' those college girl movies ten years ago. She's no spring chicken, but she still has enough stuff to make you cream in your jeans." It sounded like he really enjoyed his role as an authority on Miss Van Horn.

The club filled to capacity. News of Mimi Van Horn's visit had traveled rapidly throughout the compound. Mike observed a number of faces in the club he'd never seen before. He suspected some of those faces masqueraded as officers. Based on past experience, no one issued any challenges to the strangers. Instead, they turned their attention to the evening ahead.

The band took their place on stage. When the lights dimmed, a drum roll announced the entrance of the star. Mimi Van Horn appeared as advertised. She floated onto the stage in the glow of a single spotlight. Blonde hair, cascading to her shoulders, framed an aging face disguised with layers of make-up. Her costume, made of translucent gauze, screamed that Miss Van Horn wore no underwear. Exposed for all to see, her nipples and pubic hair strained against the transparent fabric. Every male in the club gasped in unison. No one had ever witnessed such a provocative entrance.

Enjoying the reception, Mimi posed for the crowd. Blowing kisses to the men in the back row, she knew that she'd captivated her audience without uttering a word. When the applause began to fade, she spoke into the microphone in a soft, husky voice. "Hi, is everyone comfortable?"

A groan of ecstasy surged from the masses.

She smiled playfully. "Good. I hope everyone can see all right. I don't want any of you to miss a thing."

With more posing, she rubbed her hips, and bent over at the waist to showcase her large breasts.

The audience went wild.

"We're going to have some fun tonight. I'll sing a few songs, and tell a few stories so we can get to know each other better. Before the show is over, I want every one of you to feel satisfied."

As the crowd roared with approval, the band introduced the opening musical number.

Mimi sang a collection of love ballads, along with some old Marilyn Monroe songs. Her voice had a raspy quality, but she knew how to work an audience. Laughing and teasing, she delighted in playing to the front row. At one point, she walked behind Al and leaned over him. Pushing her breasts firmly into the back of his head, she rubbed his chest with her fingers. He faked a swoon.

She targeted Lance as another one of her victims. Snuggling into his lap, she gyrated slowly. Watching Lance's face turn beet-red, she held up her hand for the band to stop the music. "Stop, it's getting too HARD to sing, and I thought the Rock of Gibraltar was big."

The audience howled with appreciation.

"OOOOOh lover, if I don't leave now, you and I will have to finish the show alone."

More cheers and whistles followed. After lifting herself from Lance's lap, she kissed him fully on the mouth. Turning a deep, dark crimson, he squirmed in his seat. Lance's friends slapped him on the back.

The show ended with her singing the Kate Smith standard, *God Bless America.* The song lacked the power of Kate's version, sounding more like a lament to lost love. The audience ate it up anyway. When she had finished singing, she blew her fans a big kiss and said, "I love you all. Come home safe real soon." The show was over.

When the lights came up, Mimi Van Horn had left the stage. Everyone sat stunned trying to prolong the sensation. The crowd attempted to bring her back with enthusiastic applause, but, except for the band, the stage remained empty. Eventually, the band stopped playing and left, too.

Leaping from his chair, Jefferson whispered in Mike's ear. "Come on, let's go outside."

Before Mike could respond, Jefferson grabbed his arm and urged him to follow. They left the club together.

Once outside, Mike asked, "What's up?"

"We're going to meet a movie star."

"You're crazy," Mike said. "She won't talk to us."

"Sure she will. I'm going to invite her to a party."

"You're nuts! She'll call the MPs."

"Calm down. Everything will be okay. Follow me."

Walking to the back of the club, they found a jeep waiting for Miss Van Horn to emerge from her dressing room. The driver advised the two men that she never spoke to anyone after a show. Jefferson said they'd wait anyway.

Mimi appeared thirty minutes later, with most of her stage make-up removed, tastefully dressed in slacks and a blouse. A large middle-aged woman served as her escort. The escort gestured for the two of them to move out of the way.

Jefferson stepped boldly forward. "Miss Van Horn, I know you must be tired, but I'd like to invite you to a little party."

"Miss Van Horn does not go to parties," her escort snapped.

"I think you'll like it," Jefferson insisted. "The music is low and I have some real smooth smoke. It's just what you need to relax and unwind."

Appearing amused, Mimi turned to Jefferson. "What makes you think you know what I need?"

Applying his most engaging smile, Jefferson moved closer to her. "Movie stars are just people. There are times when everyone needs relaxation, and the comfort of a little weed. Come on, I know you'll like it."

"Go away you pest!" barked the companion.

Smiling, Mimi patted her lightly on the arm. She leveled her gaze on Jefferson. "How do I know I can trust you?"

"Because ma'am, I'm a gentleman from Texas. If necessary, I will protect you with my life."

Mimi laughed gaily as he bowed. "I believe you would. I have never received a more gallant proposal. All right, I'll go with you and only with you. I can't handle a room full of GIs."

Jefferson gave Mike a helpless look. Shrugging, Mike signaled for him to go-ahead. Lt. Jefferson Swift walked off with Hollywood movie star Mimi Van Horn on his arm. Mike stared after them in astonishment.

The next day, Jefferson refused to comment about his tryst with the celebrity. He declined to provide any details, except that they'd smoked grass, listened to music, and enjoyed each other's company.

"She was a mighty fine lady," Jefferson said.

Jefferson's nerve impressed Hardy. He could never have approached anyone of Mimi's stature. By taking on the challenge, Jefferson had accomplished the impossible. He offered Mike a simple explanation. "You never know what the answer's going to be, unless you're willing to ask the question."

CHAPTER 26
The Korean Lady

Life slowly returned to normal after Al's homecoming from Bangkok. Assigned as the Commander of the 73d Transportation Company, his real function went deeper to the core. He served as their leader, their advocate, their judge, their mentor, but more importantly—he was their anchor. Al held them together with a mix of good humor and a dedication to duty. Believing in the essential worth of the convoys, he instilled everyone with a sense of purpose. Working side by side with his men, he participated in all the functions associated with road duty. Hardy had never seen morale at such a high level in the truck company.

Mike's relationship with Mama San entered a period of transition. Not due to any change of feeling on her part, the difference rested with him—he had changed. She remained warm and tender, while he felt restless and impatient. He never mentioned the girl in Quang Ngai to anyone, but that experience had left him craving greater delights. The girl at the bath had radiated an exotic and mysterious aura. Mama San, on the other hand, offered him sincerity and warmth. She revealed everything to him through honest emotion. In spite of her affection and loyalty, Hardy wanted more.

Mike limited his contacts with Mama San to his days off. Normally, he rode with the convoy while she cleaned the hooch. He made a habit of leaving little presents behind before reporting to duty. Sometimes these gifts consisted of candy, fruit, soap, perfume, or cigarettes. She could trade the cigarettes on the black market for food or clothing. Mike had designated a spot on his desk for her to receive these offerings. Frequently, he would return to find a small token waiting for him. Usually handmade, she offered him gifts like bracelets or handkerchiefs. At other times, she left postcards or small Vietnamese trinkets.

During Mike's days off, she'd enter the hooch in silence while he lay in bed. He always heard her arrive, but he took time before opening his eyes. She'd wait patiently for him to sit up and rub his face. At that point, she'd bring him a warm washcloth and a cold soda. After completing the ritual, they either made love or waited until after breakfast. Lately, he'd begun to avoid physical contact with her. On one occasion, he walked away without any show of affection. In spite of the hurt it caused her, he thought it necessary to escape the involvement. He needed to expand his horizons.

Jefferson played a key role in helping him discover new carnal opportunities. Immediately following the episode with Mimi Van Horn, Mike regarded Jefferson with new respect. He admired the man's spirit of adventure, and his willingness to take risks. Mike began to spend more time in his company. Although he still considered Wiley and Al his closest friends, Jefferson boldly pursued extraordinary pleasures. Avoiding the mundane interests of his peers, the man from Texas didn't seem content until he had blazed a new trail. Mike enjoyed the anticipation of waiting to discover Jefferson's next move.

One week after the Mimi show, Jefferson invited Mike to accompany him to Da Nang. Jefferson had an appointment with a friend up there in property disposal, but they would do more than just inspect junk.

"I'm going to introduce you to the most beautiful Korean woman you have ever seen," he promised.

Koreans surfaced everywhere in South Vietnam. Many of them ran concessions that sold goods to Americans. On the war front, Korean soldiers fought alongside the US Army. The two allies had signed a pact to stem the communist tide flowing down from the north.

"You have a gift for finding beautiful women," Mike said.

"Right you are, my friend." He put his arm around Mike's shoulder. "I promised you the best, and I will deliver."

"Who is she?"

"She is a former lady of pleasure who now claims my friend, Warrant Officer Dave Ballard, as her sole benefactor. We're going to visit Dave in Da Nang."

"I don't understand. If Dave is your friend, why do you want me to get hot for his girl?"

"She is a woman worthy of your attention, and you

never know what possibilities exist. Dave has an open mind, but I don't expect him to hand over the keys to her virtue. On the other hand, she has a mind of her own. I've wanted to explore her depths for some time. Maybe, we'll both get lucky."

"If she doesn't work out, I bet you have some other good prospects lined up for us."

Jefferson smiled slyly. "Da Nang is full of prospects. We might stumble onto a few."

Al had no problem granting Hardy two days off. Since Mike had never asked for much leave in the past, Al felt he needed a break from the road.

"Your damned dedication is driving me nuts!" Al slapped him on the back before wishing him well.

Sgt. Rodriguez heard about the trip to Da Nang. He stopped by Mike's hooch for a visit.

"Hey there, Lieutenant Miller told me he was kicking you out of here for a couple of days. He said you were going to Da Nang."

"That's right. I'm going with Lieutenant Swift."

"Great. Lieutenant Swift will show you a good time. What are your plans?"

The question sounded innocent enough, but Hardy knew a specific purpose waited behind the query. "Not much. We're going to the junk yard to visit his friend, Warrant Officer Ballard."

"Perfect. I know Mr. Ballard well. He makes deliveries for me. I hate to ask, but can you take him a box of stuff? I could send it with someone else, but if you're going there anyway, I'd appreciate the favor."

Groaning, Hardy wanted to avoid the entanglement.

"I don't know. I'm not driving. I'll have to ask Lieutenant Swift."

"That's okay, I understand. I'm sure you'll help me out if you can."

Smiling, Rodriguez waved goodbye. Hardy watched him walk down the hill. Since Sgt. Rodriguez had shown him so much generosity, Mike had no recourse but to cooperate—at least for now.

Without any hesitation, Jefferson agreed to transport the box from Sgt. Rodriguez to Da Nang. After making space in the back of the jeep, they stopped by the supply room.

Sgt. Rodriguez looked happy to see them drive up. "Thanks for coming by. Good to see you, Lieutenant Swift."

Mike should have realized they knew each other.

"You too, George, I hear you've got a little box for us to carry."

Rodriguez laughed. "It's not so little, but Mr. Ballard is expecting it."

"Okay, bring her out," Jefferson said.

Two of Sgt. Rodriguez's supply clerks carried out a large cardboard box meticulously taped shut. They placed it with great care into the rear of the jeep. Hardy recoiled at the sight of it. He had now progressed from delivering small packages to making major deliveries.

Sgt. Rodriguez took him aside. "I really appreciate this, Lieutenant."

Pulling a bulky envelope from his pocket, he handed it to Hardy. "I want you to take this money to buy yourself and Lieutenant Swift a nice dinner. You've really helped me out."

Hardy hesitated for a few seconds, but Rodriguez forced it into his hands. Mike stuffed it awkwardly into his pocket. "Thanks," he muttered.

"It's not much," Sgt. Rodriguez chuckled. "Have a nice trip." He waved goodbye to them.

Mike enjoyed the ride to Da Nang. It felt good to drive north for a change instead of making the daily trek south. During the trip, the two men discussed various attributes of oriental women. Although Mike had never made love to a Korean woman, he assumed no differences existed between Vietnamese and Korean bed partners.

"No way," Jefferson said. "They're larger and much more energetic in bed. Korean women are dedicated to pleasing their men. I think you'll appreciate having one attend to your needs."

"So far, I have no basis for comparison. I guess I've led a sheltered life."

Normally, Mike wouldn't have made such an admission, but he felt safe from ridicule in Jefferson's company.

"That may be," Jefferson said. "But you're about to become an experienced man of the world."

A short while later they arrived at the Da Nang PDO yard. Warrant Officer Ballard's hooch stood at the edge of the compound.

Dave greeted them at the front door. "Hey, Jefferson, it's great to see you, my man."

Wearing a cheerful smile, Ballard was a rugged, good-looking man in his early thirties, but his face bore scars from too many fights.

"Hi, Dave," Jefferson replied. "I brought along my friend for the ride. This is Mike Hardy."

"Welcome. It's good to meet you."

Grabbing Mike's hand, he pumped it vigorously. During the introductions, the most beautiful woman Mike had ever seen joined them. Viewing her distinctive features, no one could mistake her for being Vietnamese.

Dave introduced her. "This is my girl, Kim. She speaks good English, so don't use any fuckin' profanity."

After Kim punched Dave in the arm, they all laughed.

Bowing from the waist, she spoke to them in careful English. "You are both welcome to our home."

Not knowing how to respond, Mike awkwardly returned her bow.

Smiling at his discomfort, Jefferson turned to Dave. "We brought you a box from George Rodriguez. It's in the back of the jeep."

"Thanks, I've been expecting it. Once we get it unloaded I'll show you to your quarters. The hooch next to ours is empty, so you'll both have separate rooms. I thought you could use the privacy in case you get lucky." Kim smiled demurely as the men laughed.

They unloaded the box in Dave's warehouse. Jefferson's friend neglected to open it, or discuss its contents. After locking the box away, he escorted them to the guest hooch. Separated by a sturdy door, both rooms offered comfortable furnishings. The door had a lock on both sides. Throwing his travel bag down on the bed, Mike began to unpack. Remembering the envelope from Sgt. Rodriguez, he pulled it from his fatigues. After ripping the seal open, he discovered a stack of bills. Counting the money, he found a total of five hundred dollars in US bills and MPC (Military Payment Certificates). MPC was the only authorized currency for use by American servicemen. However, US dollars served as the currency of choice on the black market. Cursing, Mike changed into civilian attire. He stuffed the offending bills back into his pants pocket. Having already accepted the money, he couldn't very well give it back.

They shared dinner with Dave and Kim at a French restaurant. The cuisine and wine tasted extraordinary. When Mike attempted to pay the bill, Dave refused. He insisted on paying for his guests. Later, they toured the city in two pedi-cabs pulled by barefooted-Vietnamese men. During the excursion, Dave stopped by a jewelry store to purchase a gold necklace for Kim. He also bought solid gold cigarette lighters for Jefferson and Mike. He requested that they keep them as souvenirs of their visit.

The two visitors from Chu Lai returned to the hooch in high spirits. Before dropping them off, Dave said he had to make some important deliveries that evening. He didn't expect to return until noon the next day. Saying goodnight, he promised to join them for lunch the next day.

Jefferson and Mike talked until midnight. They discussed dinner, the cigarette lighters, and Kim. Mike admitted that Kim qualified as one of the most beautiful women he had ever seen.

"I knew you'd like her," Jefferson said.

"Dave's a great guy," Mike said. He felt self-conscious about his feelings for the Korean woman.

"He sure is," Jefferson replied. "He's just not as pretty as Kim." They both laughed at the comparison.

Crawling into bed, Mike felt happy and content. He enjoyed the experiences of leaving Chu Lai behind and being in the company of new friends. At the same time, Dave's generosity left him feeling unsettled. At no time in his life had Mike received such lavish gifts. Gift-giving seemed like a common practice in the world of Jefferson, Dave Ballard, Sgt. Rodriguez and Mr. Van. Having entered this new social circle, he realized members in the exclusive group had money to burn. Drifting off to sleep, he wondered if he could ever join them as a full-time associate.

During the night, a soft hand on his forehead interrupted his sleep. At first, he attributed the sensation to a dream. Opening his eyes, he realized the hand belonged to his beautiful Korean hostess. In the dim light, he could see Kim smiling beside the bed.

"Are you awake?" she whispered.

"Yes, I think so." His voice sounded hoarse.

"Do you want to make love to me?"

Stunned by her proposal, he sat up in bed. He experienced a greater shock at seeing her naked. Reaching out, she gently placed his hand on one of her breasts. As his heart pounded, he left it affixed to her warm flesh. Lifting the sheet, she crawled in beside him. At that moment he couldn't recall having answered her question.

Immediately, her hands went to work tearing off his underwear. His hands raced over her body as his fingers sought her softness. She moaned and writhed in his arms. Her lips and tongue traveled the length of his body. Responding in-kind, he tasted her musky flesh. Opening herself, she pulled him down on top of her. His entire body ached with desire. They joined in a desperate attempt to achieve the ultimate release.

After their internal fires had subsided, Kim snuggled beside him. He lightly teased her nipples.

"Yes," Mike whispered.

She looked at him curiously. "What do you mean?"

"Yes, I would like to make love to you."

Giggling, she pushed tighter against him.

"What are you doing here?" he asked.

"Shhhh," she replied. "I have to go now. Go back to sleep. I'll come back later."

Rising from the bed, Kim walked naked to the door leading to Jefferson's room. She moved like a dancer as threads of light illuminated her flawless body. Waving goodbye, she quietly closed the door behind her. Mike felt a strong sense of loss as she disappeared from view. For a while, he listened to the sounds of vigorous lovemaking in the next room. After a while, he fell into a deep sleep.

Kim returned the next morning. Light from the sun had begun to filter through the window. Wrapped in a sheet, she stood above Mike. "Do you want to make love to me?"

Still tingling from their earlier encounter, he didn't hesitate to offer a reply.

When she dropped the sheet, he fully appreciated her beauty in the morning light. She possessed a perfectly proportioned body that exuded the scent of sex. Although strong, the odor had a stimulating effect on him. Mike pulled her into bed to mingle his fluids with those left by Jefferson.

Dave returned later in the day as promised. The four of them enjoyed lunch in the city, followed by another tour of the markets. Making an earnest attempt to appear casual, Mike still caught himself staring at Kim. She didn't seem to notice, and Dave seemed oblivious to Mike's glances at his girl. Mike wondered if Dave knew what had happened. Maybe he'd arranged for Kim to visit them both. In retrospect, the entire episode seemed too neat and contrived. On the other hand, Dave could have fallen victim to a girlfriend with raging hormones. In any event, Kim didn't pay them a return visit on the second night.

After exchanging good-byes the following morning, Dave handed Mike the obligatory package for Sgt. Rodriguez. Thanking Kim for her hospitality, Mike shook her hand. Jefferson, on the other hand, kissed her cheek and gave her a big hug. Slapping Jefferson on the back, Dave urged them both to return soon.

Jefferson and Mike spoke about Kim during the return ride to Chu Lai. Mike agreed with Jefferson's assessment of Korean women.

"Korean women are much better at making love than the Vietnamese. At least, I know one that is."

Jefferson slapped him on the leg. "My friend, Kim is just the beginning of much better things to come."

Sgt. Bates had three weeks left in his tour of duty, but he never spoke about leaving. It fell to PFC Johnson to inform Hardy about Bates' upcoming return to the States. Although pleased to learn about Bates' departure, Hardy felt disappointed when he heard the news. Convoy duty wouldn't be the same without the *Bloody Mama* sergeant. Mike knew he'd regret the loss of his friend and mentor.

Bates gave no hint that his tour of duty had almost come to an end. In fact, his dedication to *Bloody Mama* intensified. He pushed his crew to new levels of achievement by barking orders with greater enthusiasm. In spite of the tirades, Pvt. Ames developed into a more efficient member of the team. Hardy knew that Ames had earned acceptance when the new crew member received the same amount of abuse as *Hit Man* and *Basher.* Almost able to meet Sgt. Bates' high expectations, Ames had turned into a different man.

Great speculation followed about who would assume control of *Bloody Mama.* Hardy knew of no one qualified to command the gun truck. Although some good NCOs remained in the company, none of them possessed Bates' leadership ability. At one point, Hardy asked the departing sergeant to suggest a replacement for himself. Shrugging,

Bates said he'd think about it. For his part, Hardy promised to keep the *Bloody Mama* crew together, and to find the best NCO possible for the job. This news seemed to make Bates feel better.

Wiley, Lance, and Mike rotated convoy runs to Duc Pho and Quang Ngai. In addition, each of them took turns at night duty. Now that Lance had evolved into a full-fledged participant in these assignments, Al had more time to handle administrative chores. Enjoying an occasional escape from the confines of his office, he still filled in when one of the officers needed a break. He much preferred the open air of the road to the restricted existence of a company commander. The role of commander never fit him with complete ease.

Several weeks after his return from Bangkok, Al had still not spoken about the experience. Mike and Wiley continued their speculation about the cause of this silence. They couldn't understand why he rejected the topic after exhibiting so much enthusiasm before making the trip. The mystery deepened when Al stopped lusting after bar girls and female entertainers. Mimi Van Horn had ignited a temporary spark of life in him, but he never spoke about her after the show. A week in Bangkok had diminished his thrill of the chase. This change in behavior puzzled everyone in the truck company.

Aside from worrying about Al, Mike found himself thinking about Joe Tice. He wondered how Joe had dealt with the Quang Ngai connection. Joe had probably fallen victim to the same ploys Van had used on Mike. It seemed likely that an attractive woman had helped seal Joe's association with the icehouse gang. Whatever the bait, Joe Tice had committed himself to Quang Ngai duty. With dogged determination, Mike refused to accept full participation in the enterprise. If he resisted Van's manipulation, he could always exercise the option of walking away at will.

During a visit to the supply room, Sgt. Rodriguez sensed his wavering resolve. "Hey Lieutenant, I'm a little worried about you. I hope I haven't asked too much? I know you wanted to keep things low-key."

"That's right." Mike agreed.

"You've been a great help to me and I appreciate all you've done. I want to make sure that I stick to our bargain."

Hardy had not prepared himself for such a direct approach. Sgt. Rodriguez's candor threw him off-balance. "No, No, things are fine. I just want to make sure I don't get too involved."

"Sure, sure, I understand. It was irresponsible of me not to check with you before now. I've been so busy I haven't asked if you needed anything. What can I do for you?"

Hardy considered the possibilities but avoided requesting anything. "Nothing thanks, I'm fine. I just need find a good replacement for Sergeant Bates." He spoke the last sentence as an afterthought.

Rodriguez regarded him seriously. "We've got some good NCOs in the company. Why not pick one of them?"

"None of them seems right. Bates is a tough gun truck commander. I want to find a suitable replacement."

Rodriguez appeared thoughtful. "Let me work on it. I think I can help you out. I've got some good contacts in troop assignments."

With mounting comprehension, Mike realized Rodriguez might come to his rescue again.

"Thanks," Hardy said.

"No problem. Are you going to Quang Ngai tomorrow?"

"I'm scheduled to."

"I know you've carried quite a few packages for me, but I need one more favor. Van needs a few essential items tomorrow. If you do this for me, we'll call things even."

By Hardy's account, the scales of obligation had already balanced. "You're right. I have made a lot of deliveries."

"I know you have. I really hate to ask, but I'm in a bind. I can't spare anyone for a special trip. If you help me out one more time I'd be very grateful."

Mike cursed his lack of resolve. "Okay, I'll do it."

Rodriguez grabbed hold his hand with appreciation. "Thanks, Lieutenant. I'll make it up to you." He hurried into the back room.

When Rodriguez returned with a wrapped shoebox, Mike thought he detected a gleam of satisfaction in the man's eyes. Masking his distaste for the chore, Hardy accepted the box before promptly leaving the supply room.

The next day, Van waited with open arms to receive the package from Sgt. Rodriguez. After extending a warm welcome, he ushered Mike into the reception room. The lovely girl from the bath waited for him.

He seated Mike beside her. "You have hard trip. You need to rest."

As Van patted his shoulder, Mike shot back a look of resentment. Van didn't seem to notice.

"I'm fine. I'll just wait here until the trucks are loaded."

When old woman brought in the food, the girl poured him a cup of tea. Mike ate without relish.

"Maybe, you like bath after you eat," Van suggested.

"I'm okay. It's not raining today."

The girl moved behind him to massage his shoulders.

"No bath, okay. This lady gives number one massage— she help you relax, Mike," Van said.

Mike resisted the probing fingers at first, but eventually relented to her insistent ministrations. As she kneaded his muscles, his anger and tension melted away. He wanted more. Forgetting Van, he concentrated fully on the pleasure she offered. Moving in front of him, she held out her hand. Taking it, Hardy followed her to the back room.

Time after time, Hardy attempted to resolve the conflict between his involvement in the black market and his quest for sexual fulfillment. He had no interest in reaping financial gain from the operation. Admittedly, Sgt. Rodriguez provided comforts he couldn't find elsewhere, but he cared little about the money. Drawn to encounters with exotic women, he couldn't resist the allure of a beautiful face or an open pair of arms.

He considered a number of reasons for this fascination. As a young, inexperienced and lonely soldier in a war zone, normal rules of propriety didn't apply. His current situation gave him the freedom to explore the erotic side of his nature. Each encounter served as another step in his sexual awakening. Craving more contacts, he realized that his association with Sgt. Rodriguez, Mr. Van, and Jefferson made it all possible. Whenever he experienced regret about his involvement in the organization, the benefits of female companionship overshadowed his guilt. Part of him wanted to shake off total connection with Sgt. Rodriguez. The other side of his nature longed for more sexual activity. The conflict raged on.

The next day Mike prepared for a routine run to Duc Pho. As usual, the convoy assembled in the staging area. The sun had not yet cleared the early-morning fog. The oppressive humidity saturated jungle fatigues; the fabric clung to the skin. Drivers milled around smoking cigarettes. Recognizing a number of new faces, Hardy realized that only a few veterans remained from his first days with the truck company. One of the familiar faces belonged to Tex Jackson. Although Tex still worked with the convoys, he was scheduled to return home soon. To improve his chances of survival, he had switched from tankers to driving flatbeds.

Tex greeted Mike with his usual good humor. "Good mornin', Lieutenant. What a great day to go out on the road."

"How do you do it, Tex? How do you manage to act so cheerful this early in the morning?"

"Mama told me if you start each mornin' with a big smile, it'll last you all day long."

"It's not that easy for me," Mike chuckled. "By the time I wake up, the day's half over."

"Shucks, it's not so hard. I drink hot coffee and listen to hot country. I'm awake in no time."

"Sounds like a good prescription. Are you ready to go home next month?"

"You bet! I've been with this posse long enough, so it's time to head back to the ranch. I miss Texas so much, it hurts."

Mike patted him on the arm. "Well, hang on partner. We'll have you out of this dump in no time."

"Ya-hoo, sounds good to me! I'm goin' home to the big rodeo."

Laughing, Hardy waved goodbye. He'd miss Tex's unique perspective on life.

By the time Mike arrived at the staging area, the crew of *Bloody Mama* was hard at work. He found Bates exhorting Ames to improve his performance.

"Damn it, *Thud,* stop acting like a clumsy ass. You'll fall out of the truck if you're not careful."

Surprised by the new nickname, Hardy approached Bates. "*Thud?* You call him, *Thud?*"

"Yeah, as long as that dumb shit keeps dropping things he'll keep the name."

Smiling with satisfaction, Mike watched Ames struggle with a load of ammunition. The young man had finally earned his nickname. In spite of the scolding, he thought Ames looked happy.

Departing on schedule, *Bloody Mama* took up her usual position in the rear of the convoy. In spite of limited VC activity in recent weeks, new intelligence reports warned the lull would not last. Enemy movement had increased from the north and along the Cambodian border. Military advisers warned convoys to expect sapper attacks as a possible diversion. Sgt. Bates added extra ammunition as a precaution. Hardy surveyed the countryside observing nothing unusual. He settled in for the ride south.

The sun rose high in the sky burning off the early-morning fog. The heat intensified the odors associated with village life. The smell of smoke, excrement, cooking food, decay, and rotting flesh grew stronger as the day wore on. The trucks passed through Quang Ngai without incident. However, some local residents still shook their fists in protest at losing loved ones to the convoy. Deeply saddened by their anger, Hardy wished those deaths could have been avoided.

Less than one hour away from Duc Pho, the convoy approached a small village consisting of no more than twelve huts. So obscure, the village barely appeared on any of their maps. Hardy usually ignored this point of the journey. Today, this village and the tragedy that followed would become a permanent fixture in his memory.

The incident began with a sharp CRACK and a loud BOOM! The noise sounded so close, it jolted Hardy off his perch.

He yelled at Sgt. Bates. "What the hell was that?"

Bates screamed back at him over the noise and confusion. "VC, they hit one of our trucks!"

Rushing to the radio, Hardy grabbed the handset. He made an urgent call to Sgt. Hayes. "Baby Bear, this is Mama, over!"

Sgt. Hayes responded immediately. "This is Baby Bear. What the hell—"

"Shut-up and listen—keep the convoy moving! We've been hit! Do not stop, I repeat, do not stop!"

"Roger that, Mama; We're out of here!"

Hardy turned his attention to notifying headquarters. "HQ, this is Mama. We've been hit—one truck down, damage unknown. Request assistance ASAP! Position is one Mike Sierra Charlie Papa sixteen. Do you read me, over?" He had just advised the command post they were located one mile south of checkpoint sixteen.

"Roger, I read you. One Mike Sierra Charlie Papa sixteen—assistance is on the way, over."

In a situation like this, Hardy knew to expect helicopter support in a matter of minutes.

Immediately following his radio transmissions, he heard Bates yell. "There he goes! He's runnin' through the rice paddy. Take him out, *Thud*!"

Ames hesitated for several seconds on the M-60 machine gun.

"Goddamn it, I said take him out!"

Ames began pumping out rounds in the direction of the running fugitive. Hardy watched in fascination as some of the rounds found their mark. The impact lifted the VC off his feet throwing him to the ground. Ames' finger remained fixed on the trigger after mowing down the target.

Bates had to restrain him. "Okay, okay, you got him. Stop firing!" Grabbing Ames' arm, he pulled him away from the gun. The young soldier stared numbly into space.

Hardy turned his attention to the damaged truck. "Let's go to the scene. Stay alert! There might be more VC around."

Bloody Mama roared down the roadside past six trucks blocked by the crippled vehicle. A flatbed, loaded with ammunition, had been the target of the attack. As the cab burned, black smoke from the crippled engine shot skyward. The front of the truck looked like it someone had pried it open with a giant can opener. Several drivers worked furiously to put out the flames with fire extinguishers and dirt.

Hardy yelled at Sgt. Bates. "We've got to separate the trailer from the cab! That ammo will blow if the fire spreads!"

Grabbing a pair of gloves, Bates ran to the rear of the burning cab. Furiously, he started to crank down the trailer legs. A reefer truck stood directly behind the disabled flatbed. Pulling the driver out of the cab, Hardy ordered him to help out. He shouted at the other trucks to move out of the way. After removing a tow chain from *Bloody Mama*, they attached it to the rear of the ammo trailer. The desperate crew members secured the other end to the front of the reefer. As soon as Bates had the trailer separated from the cab, the reefer pulled the flatbed about twenty feet away from the flames. The trailer legs chewed up the pavement during the dragging process, but no one worried about the damage. The prompt response had prevented a serious catastrophe.

Five minutes later, two helicopters arrived filled with GIs from Duc Pho. The troops formed a circle around the convoy as protection against further attacks. Shortly after their arrival, Hardy's men extinguished the fire. All that remained was a charred wreck with the driver burned beyond recognition.

"Who was it? Who was driving?" Hardy asked.

Covered with dirt and grease, one of the drivers turned to him. "It was Tex," he replied.

A dozen images of Tex's smiling face besieged him. He struggled to keep his voice steady. "What happened?"

"I was behind Tex. I saw this old Papa San standin' on the side of the road. He had one of those sticks over his shoulder with a basket on each end. I couldn't believe it when the old man stepped in front of Tex's truck. After Tex slowed down, the old guy turned and fired at him. He wasn't carryin' no stick! It was an RPG. He fired a rocket grenade right into the engine block. After he hit Tex, he took off runnin' through the rice paddy. It happened real fast," the driver explained.

It took a while to clear the road and clean up the damage. Hardy watched as two medics removed Tex's burned remains from the truck. The corpse had stiffened into a sitting position, so they couldn't put him in a body bag. The medics had to settle for covering him with a sheet after placing his remains on a stretcher. Hardy stayed behind with the body until a helicopter carried him away.

After they removed Tex from the scene, Mike sobbed in private. He had difficulty accepting the blackened mess on the stretcher as a former human being. How could Tex's life have come to such a grisly end? This wasn't the way he should return to his beloved Texas. As the convoy commander, Mike would write a letter to Tex's mother. At the moment, he could think of no way to express how much the young man had meant to everyone in the truck company. He hoped the words would come later.

The truck company grieved for weeks after the loss of Tex. Al seemed particularly hard-hit by his death. He organized a memorial service in the battalion chapel three days after the attack. Everyone in the unit attended. Mike arranged Tex's photograph, a pair of his boots, his cowboy hat and some of his country music tapes as a display in front of the altar. These images of Tex's life served as a fitting memorial. The army would return the personal effects to his family after the service.

The chapel filled to standing room only. Many of Tex's friends from outside the company also came to pay their respects. A hushed and somber atmosphere permeated the chapel. The mourners sang the old hymns, "Nearer My God To Thee" and "Amazing Grace." Tex would have liked those selections.

As the unit commander, Al gave the eulogy. After pausing to gather himself, he spoke in a somber tone. "Tex Jackson was a member of the 73d Transportation Company. I had the honor and privilege to be his Company Commander. Many men die during war, because that is the nature of this business. War does not discriminate. It takes away life without regard to religion, skin color, or economic circumstance. We feel the loss of every soldier who falls. Most of them we do not know, but all of them leave loved ones behind. Every death is a loss for someone. This soldier, whose death we mourn today, is a personal loss for all of us here. We feel the pain of his death and we will miss him."

Al paused to regain his composure. Looking visibly shaken, his voice sounded on the verge of cracking.

"As far as I know, Tex Jackson did not have an enemy in this company. He had a great sense of humor and was willing to help out whenever he was needed. Tex was a true Texan and loved to talk about his state. I know he came from a warm and loving family. We cannot feel this loss as deeply as his family. We did not grow up with him. We did not see him take his first steps, or climb on the bus for school. We did not live with him on the ranch, or go with him to church. We were only with him for a short time, but we were his comrades when he suffered an untimely death."

Al paused to reach for a drink of water.

"I am not going to remember Tex Jackson as a dead soldier in a coffin. I'm going to remember him behind the wheel of his truck, wearing a cowboy hat. I'm going to remember his love of music and his big smile. I'm going to remember Tex Jackson as a friend to everyone in this company. All of us here are better off for having known him. May he rest in peace."

When Al finished a total hush fell over the crowd. The only sounds heard—an occasional sniff or someone blowing his nose. Mike had never known Al to speak with such eloquence. He had no doubt that the words had come from the heart. The eulogy had not only touched Tex's spirit, it had captured the essence of his life. Tex would live on. Mike knew that most of those present would never forget Tex Jackson.

Pvt. Ames' demeanor changed after the rifle grenade attack. He seemed moody and distracted most of the time. Sgt. Bates feared that the young man might return to drugs. He shared his concerns with Lt. Hardy.

"He's fucked-up, Lieutenant. Shootin' that gook messed-up his head."

"Have you talked to him about it?"

"I've tried, but he clams-up. It's too bad. He was really startin' to come around."

Gratified to hear Ames had made progress, Hardy shared Bates' worries. "I know. We can't lose him now."

"I don't know what else to do. It's like he's gone inside a shell."

"I'll talk to him tomorrow," Mike said. "Maybe we can bring him back if we both work on him."

Hardy spent a restless night in bed. He kept thinking about the good people victimized by the war. He could see all their faces clearly: Richard, Tex, the dead Vietnamese boy in Quang Ngai, and the bleeding fireman. Although still among the living, Bobby Waters had also suffered. Lance, too, had come close to joining their ranks. By now, Mike had spent almost eight months in Vietnam. At this point, he felt the need to escape from the carnage. He wanted all the pain and suffering to stop.

A loud pounding on his door awakened him at 2 a.m.

Sgt. Bates yelled through the screen. "Lieutenant, get up! We've got trouble!"

Sitting up in bed, Hardy couldn't comprehend what had caused the disturbance. He rubbed his face in an attempt to clear his head. "What is it?"

"C'mon, get up. It's Ames. He's in trouble."

Hardy rushed outside after pulling on his shorts and a pair of boots.

"What happened?" he shouted.

"Let's go. I'll tell you on the way down!"

They ran down the hill in darkness. Bates moved so fast, Hardy could only catch a word or two of explanation.

"Drugs...OD...Puke...He's out of it!"

After entering the barracks, they rushed directly to Ames' room. They found the helpless soldier quivering on the floor in a pool of vomit. Several GIs stood by watching helplessly.

"Fuck!" Hardy yelled.

Bending over, Hardy grabbed Ames' head to turn his face upwards. The lifeless man's unfocused eyes rolled in their sockets. His skin felt cold and clammy.

"Get him out of here!" Hardy ordered. "Take him to the jeep."

The unit always left a jeep parked by the orderly room in case of an emergency. Grabbing hold of Ames, three

GIs carried him out of the room. Sgt. Bates and Hardy followed close behind.

After conveying Ames across the compound, the GIs deposited him in the rear seat of the jeep. Jumping into the passenger seat, Hardy told Bates to drive to the hospital. Turning to face Ames, he found him unresponsive. Hardy rubbed the man's arm in a desperate attempt to keep life flowing through his body. Unable to maintain his balance in the speeding jeep, Mike grabbed onto the seat with his free hand for stability. Sgt. Bates tore up the road in a desperate effort to hold off the grim reaper.

The jeep screeched to a halt in front of the emergency room. When Bates hit the horn, the blast brought two medics out the door. Taking one look at Ames, they yelled for a stretcher. After the medics rolled him inside on a gurney, they transferred him to a table. While one medic cut off his tee shirt, the other began to take his blood pressure. Without uttering a word, Sgt. Bates and Hardy observed the urgent struggle to save the young man's life.

"Blood pressure eighty over forty, respiration shallow," called out one of the medics.

During the commotion, a doctor appeared. He checked Ames' eyes and listened to his heartbeat. After completing the initial examination, he motioned to Hardy and Bates.

"What is it—drugs?"

"I think so," Bates replied.

"Smak?"

Hardy nodded in reply.

"Christ, not another one." The doctor turned his full attention back to the patient.

No one ordered them to leave, so Bates and Hardy remained in place. Hardy watched the lifesaving procedures with great interest. After hooking Ames to an IV, one of the medics injected something into one of the tubes. An oxygen mask covered the ailing man's face while a machine monitored his heart rate and vital signs. Since the medical team offered no signs of encouragement, Bates and Hardy had no way of knowing if Ames would win the battle.

The doctor and medics worked on him for nearly an hour without leaving his side. At one point, Ames' body began to spasm as he choked and vomited. After clearing his throat, the medics replaced the oxygen mask. Eventually, the frantic pace began to slow as the scene lost some of its urgency. Hardy could see the heart monitor working, but Ames still looked unconscious. He had no idea if the patient had won the fight, or if the medical team had run out of options.

The doctor made his way over to the two observers. "He's still with us. To tell the truth, I didn't think he was going to make it. He's not out of the woods yet, but I've got him stabilized. At this point, he could go either way. There might be brain damage. We'll watch him closely to see what happens. There's not much else I can do."

"Thanks for everything," Hardy said. "We'll check back on him tomorrow."

After the doctor gave them a tired nod the two men drove back to the company area.

Ames did make it. Hardy visited him in the hospital the next day. The young soldier looked terrible, but at least he'd regained consciousness.

"How are you feeling?" Hardy asked.

"Okay," Ames whispered.

"I was worried about you. We almost lost you."

"I know." Closing his eyes, Ames covered his face with his hands.

"Can I get you anything, Ames? Do you need anything?"

Wiping his mouth, he looked at Hardy. "No. I'm fine."

"Do you want me to write to your parents? I could say you're sick, but doing better."

"No, I'll do it. I need to tell them the truth. The doctor says I'm going home as soon as they clean me out."

"That's good. You need a fresh start. Once you get home, try to put all the crap over here behind you. Don't blame yourself for anything."

He stared at Hardy with a look of skepticism. "I'll try."

"Good. I hope everything works out." Hardy took his hand. Ames tried to prolong the connection.

"I'm sorry. Thanks for everything."

Removing his hand, Hardy walked out of the room. He never heard from Pvt. Ames again.

One week later, the truck company had to say farewell to Sgt. Bates. Hardy dreaded the arrival of this day, but took comfort in the fact that he'd follow the sergeant home in a few months. Although Bates never talked much about his family, Hardy knew the man looked forward to returning to the States. Bates' parents lived in a little town in Missouri. His father ran the only hardware store in town. From earlier discussions, Mike knew that Mr. Bates wanted his son to join the business after his release from the army. Undecided about his future, Bates hinted that he might stay in the military as long as he could work with trucks. Hardy knew the sergeant would never find another gun truck to take the place of *Bloody Mama*.

Basher and *Hit Man* planned to throw Sgt. Bates a farewell party he'd never forget. Bates, in all likelihood, probably preferred to depart without ceremony, but he dearly loved a party. *Basher* and *Hit Man* organized an outdoor cookout. The menu consisted of steak and lobster tails. *Basher* made sure that he located enough damaged boxes of the frozen delicacies. Sgt. Rodriguez delivered the beer with his compliments. The organizers planned the entertainment in great secrecy. All attendees were encouraged to bring a humorous gift.

When the big day arrived, Al declared a holiday for the entire company. In view of the recent tragedies, he felt that everyone in the unit needed a break. Earlier, he had made an arrangement with LtCol. Hollins to cancel the convoy runs for one day. If necessary, the trucks could carry extra supplies on the next trip south. The decks were cleared for an all-out bash.

They held the event at the top of Sand Hill. Someone had made a cardboard replica of *Bloody Mama* and placed it on a platform. Next to the gun truck stood a fabricated throne. Bates' crew had gone to a great deal of trouble making preparations for the party. The guests arrived dressed in a variety of attire. Some GIs wore black pajamas. Several revelers wore hula skirts and flak jackets. One trucker wore combat boots, shorts, and a padded bra. Another brave soul wore a Santa Claus suit, while another wore a bed sheet like a toga. Hardy loved the party atmosphere.

The guest of honor arrived on a stretcher. Carrying him to the platform, the stretcher-bearers deposited him on his throne. After feeding and pampering him, *Basher* signaled for the entertainment to begin. Two bar girls did a go-go dance in their bikinis. *Hit Man* dressed up like Shelley Winters to play a scene from the movie 'Bloody Mama.'

After *Hit Man* finished his skit, *Basher* entered dressed like Suzy from Duc Pho. He plopped down on the guest of honor's lap. "Oh, Sergeant Bates, you go home and I miss you so much!" When he pretended to give Bates a big kiss, he ended-up on the ground.

"Ouch! Sergeant Bates you hurt little Suzy." Picking himself up, *Basher* knelt by the throne.

"Sergeant Bates, I love you so much. You give me such good hickeys on my neck. You're my secret boyfriend!" *Basher* made grotesque kissing sounds.

Jumping off the throne, Bates chased him off the

platform. Applauding, the audience tried to rip-off *Basher's* dress.

Following the entertainment, the guests ate their fill. The party organizers forced Bates to eat his lobster sitting on the throne. After the meal, Al presented Sgt. Bates with a *Chu Lai Survival Certificate*. The departing sergeant also received gifts of toy trucks, tee shirts, Vietnamese bracelets, malaria pills, french tickler condoms, hand-carved water buffaloes, and other assorted souvenirs. Hardy presented him with an engraved plaque bearing a likeness of *Bloody Mama* with the words: *BEST WISHES FROM YOUR CREW*.

Bates stared at it for a moment in silence. Finally, with moist eyes, he thanked everyone for the farewell. Hardy considered the event a fitting tribute to an outstanding NCO.

The night before Bates' departure, Hardy met with him on the rear of *Bloody Mama*.

"Take care of her for me, Lieutenant."

"I will, I promise."

"I know you will. I think you're the only one who cares about her as much as I do."

"No one will ever care about her the way you do," Hardy replied.

"We had some good times back here. I was glad when you started ridin' with us on every trip."

"You taught me a lot. I needed a friend while Captain Adams was around."

"Everything goes so fast and now it's over. I'll miss the excitement, but I'm ready to go home. Hell, if the war goes on much longer they'll probably send me back here."

"If you come back, *Bloody Mama* will be here waiting for you."

Bates sniffed. "If not, I'll design another gun truck to look just like her. I'll call her *Bloody Mama II*."

They sat quietly, enjoying their last moments together. After a while, Bates asked the lieutenant to take a picture of him standing next to *Bloody Mama*. Mike snapped the last photo of the sergeant with his beloved gun truck.

The next day, Mike drove Bates to the departure point. He helped him load his gear on a helicopter. Shaking hands for the last time, Lt. Mike Hardy said goodbye to Sgt. Willard Bates. After the helicopter lifted off the ground, Mike watched as it disappeared over the horizon. The farewells had ended. Turning away, he drove back to his hooch. With Bates gone, he still needed to find another NCO to command *Bloody Mama*.

Sgt. Rodriguez came through with a replacement for Sgt. Bates. One week after Bates' departure, someone knocked on the door of Hardy's hooch. Rodriguez had arrived with a new soldier.

"Lieutenant, come outside. I want you to meet someone."

Dropping his paperback novel on the bunk, Hardy went outside to join them.

"Lieutenant Hardy, I want you to meet Staff Sergeant Burt Roche."

"It's good to meet you."

Hardy shook Sgt. Roche's hand as he regarded him with interest. The new man stood tall with an easy smile. He looked like a linebacker for the New York Giants. Hardy turned to Sgt. Rodriguez for further explanation.

"Sergeant Roche just came to us from the south. He heard that we needed a top-notch gun truck commander up here so he volunteered for the job. He's had lots of experience and comes highly recommended."

So far, Hardy liked what he heard, but he wanted to hear more.

"Great. Come on in and let's talk." He ushered them inside. "Can I get you a beer?"

They both accepted the offer. Hardy returned with the cold brews. After punching a hole in each can, he handed them out. They settled down to get acquainted.

"Where are you from in the States, Sergeant Roche?"

"Greenville, Mississippi. We live right on the Mississippi River. Best place in the world."

"Are you married?"

"Yes sir, five years. I've got two kids and we're lookin' to have more. My wife loves havin' babies. Me, I just like makin' babies." Enjoying a hearty laugh, he seemed completely at ease.

Smiling, Hardy took a drink of beer. "What did you do down south?"

"I was with the 22d Transportation Company in Nha Trang. I commanded the gun truck *Dr. Death*. We ran convoys to four different base camps."

"Why did you want to leave?"

Roche responded without hesitation. "I needed a change of scenery. I've been with the 22d for six months. My crew was really squared away and there wasn't much else to do. Besides, I hear ya'll got some shootin' up here." He hesitated and grinned. "The real reason was the mini-gun. I heard about the mini-gun. I'd give my left nut to ride on a truck with a mini-gun."

"Your wife might not appreciate you giving away important body parts," Hardy said.

"Shit, she wouldn't care as long as I keep one to do the job."

Mike liked the man's sense of humor. "Well, Sergeant

Roche, welcome to the 73d Transportation Company. Tell me, how did you hear about us?"

"It was funny. I got the word from my supply sergeant. So I checked with the orderly room. After they heard I was interested, things happened real fast. Ya'll must have a lot of pull up here."

Hardy glanced at Sgt. Rodriguez. Rodriguez responded with a look of amusement.

"Yeah, I guess we do," Hardy replied. "Let me tell you all about *Bloody Mama....*"

Hardy spent some time giving Sgt. Roche details about their experiences on the road. He also explained convoy operating procedures and how Sgt. Bates had worked the crew.

"Sounds like you have a good operation. We'll keep it that way," Roche promised.

Hardy advised the new man to use the rest of the day to get settled. He could start work in the morning.

Sgt. Roche took Hardy's hand in a vice-like grip. "I'm ready. Thanks for everything."

"Good luck and welcome."

Leaping off the top step, Roche jogged down the hill. Hardy watched with amazement at his energy and enthusiasm.

He turned to Sgt. Rodriguez. "He's a real firecracker!"

Laughing, Rodriguez grabbed Hardy's shoulder. "You wanted the best and that's what you got. My sources tell me he's the cream of the crop."

"Thanks, I really appreciate it."

"No problem at all. I'd do anything to help you out, Lieutenant. Stay in touch, okay?"

He left the hooch after giving Hardy a big wink.

Mike realized he had worked his way into debt again. Sgt. Rodriguez's chain of influence had reached hundreds of miles to find Sgt. Roche.His powers of acquisition seemed to have no limitations.

Hardy watched with interest as Roche took control of *Bloody Mama*. He didn't yell or chastise the crew like Sgt. Bates. Using the force of his presence, he employed a strong physical approach to relay his messages. Without any hesitation, he'd put *Basher* or *Hit Man* in a headlock to get their attention. It was like watching a circus performance, but it worked. Hardy had no doubt that *Bloody Mama* had landed in good hands.

Mike continued to have regular meetings with Jefferson at the club. Laughing about past adventures, they made plans for more excursions.

One evening, Jefferson offered an irresistible proposal. "My friend, we have been invited to spend an all-expense paid weekend in the beautiful city of Da Nang. We will stay at the best hotel, eat in the finest restaurants, purchase the most beautiful women, and buy the most expensive jewelry. This can all be yours for the small price of agreeing to go with me."

Mike felt overwhelmed by the generous offer. He couldn't believe his good fortune. "How can this be possible?"

"I have an associate who wishes to remain anonymous. He is grateful for the opportunity of doing business with the US Army. He shows his gratitude to me, because I help him support our war efforts," Jefferson replied.

"He sounds like a good friend to have." A flush of discomfort warmed the back of Mike's neck.

"He is. Do you want to go with me?"

Mike resisted the small voice urging caution. "Sure, I do. Let me work out my schedule at the company. When do you want to leave?"

"Next weekend, we have reservations at the *Paris Hotel*."

"I'll be ready."

Mike worked out his schedule with Wiley and Lance. They had no problem changing plans so he could have a two-day break. Approving the changes, Al told him to stay out of trouble. Mike promised to bring him a bottle of expensive French wine.

"Bullshit! I don't drink that grape piss. Bring me some German beer."

Mike promised to do his best.

Friday afternoon, Jefferson and Mike left for Da Nang after taking a detour to the company supply room. They made the stop after Sgt. Rodriguez asked them to deliver a package to Dave Ballard. A smaller box this time, but Rodriguez assured them it contained valuable contents. Hardy accepted the task without comment. He looked forward to getting another look at Kim. A quick look at best; Jefferson wanted to waste no time checking into the hotel. After Rodriguez thanked them, they embarked on their adventure.

Dave Ballard looked pleased when they pulled into the PDO yard. He invited them to stay for dinner, but Jefferson declined with regret. Undaunted, Dave insisted that they return for another overnight stay. He'd have the guesthouse waiting for them. He further insisted that they say goodbye to Kim before leaving. She'd feel disappointed if they didn't stop by. Claiming his package, he walked off toward the warehouse. Jefferson drove to the hooch.

Meeting them at the front door, Kim pulled the two men inside. Grabbing Mike, she kissed him full on the mouth while rubbing his crotch with her free hand. Turning to Jefferson, she gave him the same treatment.

"You both are bad. Why are you going away so fast?"

Laughing, Jefferson gave her a hug. "Kim, my dear, we would love to stay, but Mike and I have important business in Da Nang. We'll come back again soon, I promise."

"You better come soon. I'll give you a special surprise."

"We love your surprises, Kim. We'll be back."

Before returning to the jeep, Kim showered them with more sloppy kisses.

One of the most elegant buildings in Da Nang, the *Paris Hotel* stood in the heart of the city. It looked like it belonged in one of the capitals of Europe. Uniformed bellhops carried their bags into the plush reception area.

French-speaking desk clerks welcomed them in style. The staff presented each man with keys to adjoining suites. Mike felt as if he had stepped into another world.

While they settled into their rooms, Mike bounced on the king-size bed. Iced champagne and a bowl of fresh fruit welcomed them. Fresh flowers decorated the tables and original works of art adorned the walls. Mike had never experienced such luxury. Jefferson seemed to take it all in stride—obviously, not a new experience for him.

They ate dinner in an expensive French restaurant. Mike had begun to develop a great fondness for French cuisine. He especially loved the wines and the rich custard desserts. They both ate with relish. Mike had no doubt this weekend would qualify as the greatest of his life.

Returning to the hotel, Jefferson announced the time had arrived for an evening of entertainment. Calling a bellboy to his room, he wrote down some items on a piece of paper.

"Take this to a local drug store and buy these things for me. Get a good price and you keep the change. Do you understand?"

"Yes, sir, thank you."

"Good, and when you come back, I'll have something else important for you to do."

"Yes, sir." The bellboy turned and left.

Mike was awed by how well his friend operated in this environment. Jefferson popped open a bottle champagne. They had it nearly drained by the time the bellboy returned. Handing Jefferson a paper sack, he stood by for more instructions.

Looking inside the bag, Jefferson took out several bottles. "Ah yes, that's the stuff we need. Good job."

The bellboy smiled and bowed his head.

"Here is the next thing I want you to do. We would like some ladies to spend the night. Not ladies from the street but beautiful, first-class ladies. Bring some here, and we will choose. Do you understand?"

"Yes, sir."

"Okay, hurry back." Turning, the bellboy rushed off on his errand.

"Now, are you ready for a lesson in chemistry?" Jefferson asked.

Removing one of the small bottles, he broke the seal. Sniffing the contents, he gave Mike a look of satisfaction. He tipped the bottle into his mouth to drink some of the liquid.

"That should do it." He passed the bottle to Mike.

"What is it?"

"Supposedly, it's diet medicine to lose weight, but it's really pure *speed*. It'll pump you up so high you'll screw all night long. If it gives you too much of a rush, I have some *downers* here, or we can smoke a little grass. You can get as high as you want. Have you done *speed* before?"

"No," Mike admitted.

"No problem. Try a little. It won't make you crazy."

Grasping the bottle with caution, Mike let some of the bitter liquid slide down his throat. He felt no immediate reaction.

"Don't worry," Jefferson said. "It takes a while to work."

It took thirty minutes for the bellboy to return. By the time he arrived, Mike had begun to feel a tingling sensation in his body as his heart pounded in his chest. The bellboy ushered in a group of four ladies. Looking worn around the edges, they all appeared to have come right off the street.

Jefferson expressed his dissatisfaction with the selection. "No good. I said first-class ladies. Find me some fresh ones in a hurry, or I'll call another bellboy.

The bellboy almost fell over himself forcing the women out of the room.

The next batch of ladies looked much better. One young girl caught Mike's eye. She looked like a mischievous teenager. Flashing a cute smile, she gazed at him without any shyness. He selected her immediately. Jefferson chose a more mature and sedate partner. Satisfied with his purchases, Jefferson sent the bellboy on his way.

Before leaving for his bedroom, Jefferson offered a suggestion. "Let's switch off in the middle of the night. That way, we'll get more bang for our buck."

Reluctant at first, Mike remembered that they'd shared Kim during that fateful night at Dave Ballard's place. "Sure, just knock on the door when you're ready."

Taking his girl by the arm, Mike led her to the oversize bed. His heart pounded as the *speed* took hold of his nervous system. Sitting on the bed, he tried to relax. Waiting for instructions, the smiling girl stood in front of him. In an attempt to overcome his drug-induced condition, Mike told her to undress. Giggling, she unfastened the buttons on her dress. The garment fell away, leaving her in bra and panties. Her breasts looked remarkably full for someone so small. Mike gestured for her to take everything off. Naked, she stood before him proud and unafraid. His heart began to beat faster. Pulling her toward him, he caressed her soft skin. He massaged her breasts and rubbed the inside of her thighs. Encouraging this contact, she begged for more.

Unable to control his surging heartbeat, Mike decided to take a warm shower. After removing his clothes, he carried the naked girl into the bathroom. She watched him curiously as he turned on the water. Leading her under the spray, he rubbed her body with his soapy hands. Reacting playfully, she returned the favor by washing him in return. The shower had a calming effect on his over-heated system. Stepping out of the shower, they dried each other off. The girl's golden skin gave off the scent of perfume soap.

Carrying her back into the bedroom, Mike dropped her onto the huge bed. They played and chased each other like children. The wrestling continued until the bedcovers fell to the floor in a heap. The interplay had a stimulating effect on Mike's libido. The intimate contact primed him for more serious business. They tackled sex like an erotic extension of the wrestling game. The girl responded with insatiable enthusiasm. They made love twice more before a knock on the door interrupted the fun. Jefferson was ready to exchange partners. Reluctantly, Mike bid farewell to his little friend.

Jefferson's lady lacked the energy of Mike's young partner. All business, she applied a professional approach. The woman didn't seem to enjoy her work. It took a while for her to stimulate Mike into action. In order to fulfill her financial obligation, they made love once. Unimpressed by her technique, he had no need for a repeat performance.

The next morning, Jefferson couldn't stop raving about the young prostitute. "She was completely nuts! She couldn't get enough. I had to beg her to leave me alone. That's never happened to me before."

Enjoying lunch in the city, they later toured the shops. Announcing that he wanted to purchase a gold necklace, Jefferson insisted that they visit a jewelry store. He told Mike to pick one for himself. Mike selected a 24 carat gold coin with a chain attached. Choosing a similar combination, Jefferson insisted that they wear them immediately. He paid for the purchases with hard currency.

"Once you put it on, you'll never forget this weekend in Da Nang."

Thanking him, Mike attached it around his neck. The gold settled soft and heavy against his skin.

They ate dinner in another upscale restaurant. Mike had never enjoyed the luxury of ordering something off the menu without asking the price. Knowing that he could easily grow attached to this lifestyle, he still felt like a fraud. He didn't belong here; he viewed this foray into the world of luxury as a temporary excursion. Tomorrow, he'd return to reality and c-rations. Strangely enough, he didn't think he'd regret leaving the opulent life in Da Nang behind.

Jefferson orchestrated the evening's entertainment in the same manner as before. He sent the bellboy away to find more willing ladies for their pleasure and enjoyment. After taking hit of diet medicine, he offered the bottle to Mike.

Mike turned him down. "No thanks. The stuff made me too edgy last night. I think I'll smoke a joint instead."

Jefferson handed him a joint from his pocket. The smoke had a familiar, soothing effect.

"I'm going to pick a young one tonight," Jefferson vowed. "If she's anything like yours, I'll be a happy man."

Mike replied that he planned to keep his options open. They both agreed to switch partners again in the middle of the night.

This time, the bellboy brought in six ladies of good quality. Selecting first, Jefferson chose a slender, young girl with lovely features. Appearing more refined than her peers, she looked out-of-place in the company of the other women. Mike selected a buxom girl with a warm smile and friendly demeanor. He believed that sex worked much better if the participants brought a cheerful disposition to the union.

Mike enjoyed the lady he'd chosen. She possessed a warm, friendly, and loving manner. Forgoing gymnastics in the bedroom—she fit perfectly into his mellow mood. When he confessed to a little fatigue from the night before, she still seemed anxious to please him. He couldn't ignore her probing fingers or wandering lips. They made love twice with satisfying results.

The knock came earlier than expected. Mike met his friend at the door.

Jefferson's girl had turned into a total bust. "I hope you have better luck than I did. How's yours?"

"Great. We had a good time."

"That's good. I need a good time." Wishing Mike good luck, he headed toward the bed.

Mike found the girl in Jefferson's bed covered with a sheet. He slipped in beside her. As she stared straight at the ceiling, he removed the sheet to survey her delicate features. Small breasts not fully developed, narrow hips, but gracefully curved; her pubic hair had formed into a thin, narrow line. She didn't acknowledge his presence, and did nothing to encourage his advances. Mike couldn't believe she participated in the world's oldest profession.

Confused by her remote attitude, he attempted to approach her with gentle contact. He softly stroked her thick, silky hair, and caressed the smooth skin on her arms.

Moving slowly to her tight little belly, he advanced upward to her small breasts. His fingers lightly teased the nipples. She didn't react or move. Persisting, he continued his careful exploration. Curiously, her withdrawn demeanor had a stimulating effect on his body. He wanted to explore every inch of her.

Moving his hand from her breasts to her pubic hair, he explored the area above and below. His fingers searched through the soft tissue, until he found her opening. Her body jumped from the intrusion.

"I'm sorry. Did I hurt you?"

She offered no response.

Mike continued his exploration. His body ached with desire. When he climbed on top of her, she wouldn't open her legs to accommodate him. This wasn't an act or a ploy. Although he considered pulling away, he forced her legs open. Hearing her gasp, he felt her body tighten below him. When he encountered difficulty entering her, she did nothing to facilitate the process. She sobbed with each thrust. Increasing the pace of his exertions, he focused on reaching a climax. Spent, he collapsed on top of her.

Several minutes later, his breathing returned to normal. He looked down at his reluctant partner. Her lips quivered as tears streamed down her pretty face. He recoiled in horror. What had he done? What was she doing here? Why did he feel like a rapist? Mike experienced sharp pangs of remorse as the young girl continued to sob.

Jumping out of bed, he ran into the bathroom for a wet

washcloth and towel. Returning to her side, he washed her face with the damp cloth. Wiping away the tears, he spoke to her softly. His repeated apologies fell on deaf ears. Convinced that she didn't understand him, he washed her lower body. She didn't protest as he gently dried the area with the towel. He continued to tell her he was sorry, but the words had no effect. Since she made no attempt to run from the room, he covered her with a sheet. They remained side-by-side for the rest of the night. Neither of them went to sleep.

The next morning, she turned to him as the first rays of sunlight entered the room. "May I go home now, please?" She spoke the words in perfect English.

Mike felt dumbfounded. "You speak English?"

"Yes. May I go home now?"

"Of course, I just want you to know how sorry I am. I had no idea... I thought you were a... I feel terrible!"

"I know. You already told me."

"Can I make it up to you? Is there anything I can do?"

"No."

He watched her move around the room as she collected her clothes. She dressed in silence. After gathering her belongings, she glanced at him briefly before walking out the door. She departed without saying another word.

When the door closed, Mike pounded his fists on the mattress. He felt disgusted with his behavior. The young girl had too much education and class to work as a prostitute. Obviously, someone had forced her into the business. Maybe, she had a family to support. Maybe, someone had threatened her life. Whatever the circumstances, he had overlooked her distress in favor of satisfying his sexual curiosity. Without meaning to, he had taken advantage of an innocent victim from the turbulent Vietnamese culture. He viewed his expensive surroundings in search of an outlet from his shame. Finding nothing to give him solace, he felt compelled to escape from the *Paris Hotel* as soon as possible.

CHAPTER 30

The Snowy Mountains

The days seemed heavy after Hardy's return from Da Nang. He went about his duties without enthusiasm, speaking to no one unless necessary. He felt an urgent need to find the girl from the *Paris Hotel*. If he could locate her, he might have a chance to redeem himself. Clinging to this rescue fantasy, he dreamed about liberating her from bondage. His sketchy plan included paying off the pimps, or stealing her away and returning her to her family. Salvation from guilt required decisive measures on his part. In reality, he doubted his ability to change her predicament.

What are you going to do now, Lieutenant?

Still nursing his guilt, Mike returned to convoy duty.

Sgt. Roche took to *Bloody Mama* with zealous enthusiasm. He overwhelmed the crew with his dedication to perfection. The mini-gun received special attention, but nothing important escaped Roche's scrutiny. He ordered the crew to clean the gun daily, and order extra parts to expedite necessary repairs.

"This baby will always be prepared for action," Roche said. He had an intuitive sense that a VC attack on the convoy was imminent. "If they come, we'll be ready." Recent reports about enemy activity confirmed that his suspicions were well-founded.

Routine trips to Quang Ngai had turned into pure drudgery. Hardy not only hated to see Van's smiling face waiting for him, he resented his lack of resolve in dealing with the icehouse baron. To make matters worse, he lost his desire for the girl in Quang Ngai. Despite her best efforts, he brushed off her attentions. Mike still suffered from the *Paris Hotel* experience.

Van noticed this disinterest. "What's wrong, Mike? You want me find you different girl?"

"No," Hardy snapped. "I don't want a girlfriend."

Storming out of the reception room, he walked into the street. From that point on, he spent most of his time with the children, or waiting with the trucks until they finished loading. Van had no success in luring him back inside.

When Al noticed the change in Mike's disposition, he asked him for an explanation. Shrugging, Mike offered a lame excuse for his unsociable behavior. Accepting the response on the surface, Al let him off the hook without further interrogation. Al had changed, too. One month ago, he would have twisted Hardy's arm until he obtained a full confession. Like Mike, he had lost some of his exuberance for living.

One week after Mike's return to duty, Al summoned him to his office. "Hey Grunt, get in here."

"What's up?" Mike asked.

"It looks like your dream vacation has been approved. You're going to Australia on R and R."

"Great," Mike replied.

One month ago, he'd applied for R and R to Australia despite an intense curiosity to visit Bangkok. He dreamed about blue-eyed, blonde Australian girls running on the beaches. Needing a break from oriental culture, he considered a week in Australia as his best option. He later discovered that July in Vietnam meant winter in Sydney.

"I never figured you for Australia," Al said. "I thought Bangkok for sure, or at least, Taiwan or Hong Kong. What made you choose a trip to kangaroo land?"

"I don't know. I have a weakness for blondes and wanted to look at round-eyed girls for a change."

"I know what you mean." Al shook his head sadly.

"I'd like to go to Bangkok, but I need a change of scenery. Besides, you and Wiley have probably ruined all the real pretty girls."

Al stared at him blankly. "No, there are lots of them left. They're waiting to give you whatever pleasure you want."

An awkward silence followed between them. Mike couldn't summon a light-hearted retort to ease the tension. Instead, he chose to confront the mystery.

"What is it, Al? What happened?"

Al appeared ready to brush him off, but then changed his mind. He leaned back heavily in his chair.

"Everything happened—everything Wiley said would happen. The women were beautiful and willing. I screwed their socks off and found everything I wished for. My dream came true, but something happened I didn't expect.

On the plane ride home, I kept seeing my wife's face. I started to feel like shit. All this time I've been acting like a big stud, but I never did anything about it. It was just a game. Bangkok changed all that. The games stopped and things got real. I went crazy and lost control. My wife was home with her sick mother, and I'm humping everything in sight. I don't know how to deal with that."

Mike watched this man he admired so much struggle with his conscience. Holding his face in his hands, Al rubbed his eyes.

Mike attempted to soothe Al's anguish. "This place makes you crazy. I know you love your wife. You've got to put Bangkok behind you."

"Bangkok was a nightmare. It's so easy. Sex is for sale everywhere, and it's legal. All I could think about was getting laid. The only problem is—now it's over—I feel dirty."

"We've all done dirty things, Al. It's the war, it's the loneliness, it's the fear, it's...shit, I don't know. We do things here we'd never do back home. I know all about guilt. I think I raped a girl in Da Nang."

Al stared at him with interest, but didn't say a word.

Gulping several times, Mike continued. "I thought she was a whore, but she was just a scared girl. She was naked in bed, so I jumped on her. I never bothered to find out if she had feelings. I didn't treat her like a human being. I hurt her, Al. I can't forgive myself for that."

Rising out of his chair, Al walked behind him. He put

his big hands on Mike's shoulders. "You're right, we're all dirty. I know you feel bad Grunt, but you never raped anyone. I'm sure it was just a misunderstanding."

"I should've stopped but I didn't."

"I shouldn't have gone to Bangkok, but I did. We both fucked-up."

Al pulled Mike out of the chair.

"We can't let this place get to us. We used to have fun —remember? Go to Australia and have a great time. When you get back, we'll forget all this crap and get on with life."

"I've got a lot to forget."

"Well, forget it all. What happens here stays here. When we get home, we can start over. Is it a deal?"

Mike watched him smile for the first time in several weeks. Al grabbed his hand, and Mike returned the handshake. He walked out of the office wanting to believe Al's suggestion would work.

After leaving Al's office, he found a letter waiting for him in the orderly room. Addressed to: *1ˢᵗ Lt. Mike Hardy from the Department of the Army*, it looked official.

> *This is to inform you that your request for early release from active military duty to attend college has been approved. The effective date for this action is 3 September 1971.*

Two months. Mike would leave the army in two

months. Without any explanation, the army had approved a program to release soldiers up to 90 days early to return to college. Since these GIs had indicated no intention of extending their military careers, the army cast them off early.

Yelping with joy, Mike hugged PFC Johnson. Johnson looked at him like he'd lost his mind. Releasing the company clerk, Mike ran back into Al's office to give him the news.

"Good for you, Grunt. Two pieces of good news today —you'll still leave one month behind me, but two months ain't nothing. It'll go fast."

Al punched him on the arm. Mike grabbed Al's wrist, attempting to throw him off balance. Laughing at this futile effort, Al wrapped both arms around his chest. Mike gasped for air as Al lifted him off his feet. His boots banged into Al's desk knocking a coffee mug on the floor. They tipped over chairs, scattered papers, and ripped plaques of the wall. PFC Johnson rushed into the office to assess the situation. Al had Mike pinned on the floor.

Al yelled at the company clerk. "Get the hell outta here! Can't you see I'm counseling this lieutenant?"

With an abrupt about face, Johnson slammed the door on his way out.

Relaxing his grip, Al rolled off Mike. He started laughing. "God damn, I needed that. It sure is a good thing they didn't send you to the bush. You can't fight worth a shit!"

Hardy massaged his sore limbs. "Bullshit! You're five times the size of any gook. You're lucky I didn't use my secret, self-defense moves. You'd be begging for mercy."

Chuckling, Al helped Mike to his feet. He surveyed the damage to his office. "No big deal. The place needed a good cleaning, anyway." He put his arm around Mike. "Get out of here and have a great time in Australia."

Hardy waved at Johnson on his way out. Johnson stared after him in bewilderment.

Mike left for Australia on a commercial airliner. All through the long flight, the passengers on the plane celebrated their temporary release from duty. After all, Australia offered a temporary safe harbor from the hell of Vietnam. For one week, they could escape the jungle, the danger, and the threat of death. Many of these GIs had come straight from the bush. Australia beckoned with the promise of beer and the availability of beautiful women.

As they flew over Sydney harbor, Mike could see the famous arch bridge from the window. After the plane landed, he had to endure a long wait in customs. Once released, Mike stepped outside the terminal into the cool air. Wearing a short-sleeved shirt, he had not prepared himself for 58-degree temperatures. Riding in a city taxi, he asked the driver about the chilly climate.

"Don't you know its winter here, mate? I hope you didn't come down for a swim?"

Hardy introduced himself as an American soldier on temporary leave from Vietnam.

The driver nodded. "Right, mate. We get lots of you types down here. How's the war going? I bet it's rough."

"It's rough. I'm glad to be out of it."

Mike asked the man to take him to a good local hotel. The driver delivered him to a respectable looking accommodation in the downtown area. Before depositing his passenger on the curb, the Aussie driver put in a strong recommendation for Australian beer. Hardy promised to take him up on it.

Mike unpacked with haste in his modest hotel room. Anxious to take in the sights of Sydney, he first purchased a warm jacket for protection from the night air. Taking the taxi driver's suggestion, he visited several bars to sample the local beer. The beer tasted strong and robust. Working his way down the street, he found a club advertising *Nude Dancers*. The girls all looked beautiful, but he didn't experience the same thrill he'd felt in San Francisco. He observed the dancers trying to tantalize their customers as they worked for tips. All too familiar, the club scene dredged up painful memories. He retreated from the bar after finishing one beer.

He made his last stop of the night *The Texas Bar*. The bar featured a real Texas flavor. On one wall, someone had painted a picture of the Alamo. Steer horns, Indian blankets, and pictures of cacti contributed to the old west atmosphere. Films of old NFL football games served as the main attraction. Mike settled down to watch the distorted action despite the noisy and chaotic environment in the bar. Curiously, he watched as young Aussie women endured indifference from their male counterparts. The men seemed to prefer the company of other men. After discovering that an American GI from Vietnam drank in their midst, they dragged Mike into one their groups. Rewarding him with free beer, they besieged him with questions about the war. Later, feeling the need to escape for the second time that evening, he forced his way out the door.

The next day, Mike visited a travel office to register for a four-day ski trip to the Snowy Mountains. He had no idea that it snowed in Australia, but the agent assured him that plenty of the white stuff waited for him down south. Jumping on a small plane, with some other hearty souls, he began the flight south. Several of the passengers stared at him during the flight. He had no idea what attracted their notice until one of them inquired about his suntan. Mike explained that he'd acquired it during an extended stay at one of Vietnam's finest resorts. This admission generated more questions involving him in conversation for the rest of the trip.

The plane landed in the middle of nowhere. The thirsty landscape looked like an endless plain besieged by interminable drought. Except for small flags at each end of the runway, nothing indicated they had landed at an airport. Mike looked out both sides of the airplane but saw no buildings in view. A tour bus waited for them as they disembarked from the aircraft. Searching the horizon, he noticed some mountain peaks in the distance covered with clouds.

It took several hours to reach their final destination—the Snowy Mountains. The tall summits looked out of place in relation to the rest of the landscape. The god of the mountains must have dropped the snowy peaks in the middle of nowhere during an illogical fit of humor. No other reason for their evolution came to mind. It looked like they existed to break up the landscape, and to provide a change of scenery for the tourists.

Mike checked into a huge ski lodge made of logs and stone. After settling into his room, he observed only a light cover of snow at the base of the mountain. He wondered if he had made a mistake in coming. However, plenty of skiers wandered in and around the lodge. He left quickly to join them.

He purchased an entire ski wardrobe and rented the necessary equipment. It seemed like a surreal experience to clamp on a pair of skis after leaving the tropics of Vietnam. Mike had grown up in the snow, but it felt strange to return to the mountain slopes. It struck him as curious that his path through life had taken this turn. After some reflection, he reached the conclusion that everyone follows a different route through life. Sometimes a toll-keeper intervenes to extract a heavy tax during the journey. Having paid the right of passage at several critical junctures, his excursion through Vietnam would soon end. Whenever he was fortunate enough to return home, his life would take off in a new direction. In the meantime, he rode the chairlift up the mountain through the falling snow.

He met a girl on the chairlift named Melissa Gardner. A resident of Melbourne, Melissa had traveled to the Snowy Mountains with her mother. With curly blonde hair and pale green eyes, Melissa loved to laugh and enjoy lively conversation. Calling Mike *Yank,* she bombarded him with questions about Vietnam and New England. Although she attacked the ski slopes with youthful enthusiasm, Mike followed her with little effort.

Once Mrs. Gardner took a liking to the curious *Yank,* she gave her blessing for them to enjoy the nightlife. The young couple spent evenings dancing and drinking beer in the lounge. After forging a fast friendship, they made other friends. Melissa socialized with the same enthusiasm that she displayed on the ski slopes. Mike could not have asked for a better female companion. Everything between them seemed so normal.

They spent their final night together holding hands and making promises to stay in touch. She promised to write, and he promised to return to Australia—someday. Without making love, they had formed a bond of intimacy. Mike felt clean and refreshed. Their last lingering kiss, although filled with regret about parting, contained the promise of reunion. Mike wanted desperately to spend more time with her, but, in the end, they left the ski lodge in opposite directions.

Flying away from Sydney in a somber mood, Mike realized that his companions shared the same state of mind. As they headed back to Vietnam to face an uncertain future, the good life in Australia faded into history. Fortunately, he only had two months left in his tour of duty. Somewhere on the slopes of the Snowy Mountains in Australia, he'd found new strength to confront the remaining challenges.

CHAPTER 31

German Fest

After Mike returned to the company, Lance peppered him questions about Australia. Lance's whole attitude had changed since signing the divorce papers. Like Mike, his plans for the future included meeting new friends and traveling to Australia on R and R. After completing his tour in Vietnam, he hoped to start a new life in the restaurant business. Anxious to learn about Australia, he especially seemed interested in the dining habits of the Aussies.

"It sounds like you're thinking about opening a restaurant in Sydney," Mike said.

"You never know," Lance replied. "I need a new start and Australia might fit the bill. I hear they encourage new businesses and welcome Americans. Besides, I'll be out of reach of Laura."

Mike regarded him with concern. "What are you afraid of? Once you're divorced, she can't touch you."

"I know, but I need to make a clean break. She's very persuasive. If I'm too close, she can come after me. She knows my weaknesses. I don't think I could turn her away."

"What's the point? What could she want from you?"

"I can think of lots of things—money, contacts, ideas, references. She might just want to see if she can still control me."

"Do you think she can?"

"I don't know. That's why life in Australia looks really good right now." Crossing his arms, Lance leaned back in his chair. "Okay, tell me more about where you ate."

Mike spent an hour answering Lance's questions. One week in Australia hardly qualified him as an expert on the country. He'd spent most of the vacation on the ski slopes, but he did his best to satisfy Lance's curiosity. Convinced that Lance would benefit from visiting the country, Mike figured he might do well to settle there.

Sgt. Roche had not sat idle during Mike's absence. *Bloody Mama* had acquired a whole new look. In addition to a fresh coat of paint, someone had added new detail to the truck logo. Beneath the lettering, an artist had drawn a cartoon of an old woman smoking a cigar while firing a mini-gun. A new set of snarling teeth decorated the front hood and grill. Hardy expressed his admiration for the artistic quality of work.

"Sergeant. Roche, she looks great!"

"Thanks. I hired a Korean artist to do the job. We all chipped in."

"I thought she looked fierce before. The way she looks now, the Vietnamese will run even harder to get out of the way."

"My daddy always said: Make 'em respect you and they'll leave you alone. I want *Bloody Mama* to have lots of respect." He patted the gun truck.

"You know, Sergeant Bates would be proud. I'm going

to take a photo and send it to him. I've already written him about what a great job you're doing."

"Thanks. He did a great job finding the mini-gun before I got here. I hope we put her to work soon. Right now *Bloody Mama* only looks pretty, but I bet she can fight like hell."

"You bet she can."

Hardy told him the story about the attack on Tex and how Ames had shot down the sniper. Sgt. Roche had heard it before, but Hardy wanted to stress how they had taken the old Papa San for granted.

"A dozen trucks passed him without noticing a thing. We see these people all the time carrying baskets on sticks. They blend into the landscape. This time it cost a good man his life because we didn't take enough notice. Too much routine can be dangerous. We make the run every day and it's easy to get careless."

"I'll keep 'em tight," Roche pledged. "*Bloody Mama* don't like surprises. We'll be ready if something happens."

"Good." Complimenting him again on the great paint job, Hardy departed for his hooch.

Two days later, Hardy ran into Sgt. Rodriguez. Rodriguez invited him to stop by the supply room.

"Hi, Lieutenant, how was the trip to Australia?"

"Great. I had a good time."

"Glad to hear it. I've been a little worried about you. Mr. Van tells me you won't talk to him."

Hardy responded sharply. "That's right. I don't trust him. There's a lot more going on in Quang Ngai than meets the eye. I didn't fight it at first, but I'm a little wiser now. I'm not going to get sucked into his operation."

Sgt. Rodriguez shook his head sadly. "I'm sorry you feel that way. Mr. Van has done a whole lot to help us. He's been able to find things for me when no one else could."

"I'm sure he has. He's very good at getting what he wants, but there's always a high price to pay. I saw a man almost beaten to death in front of him. Later, I found out the man was killed. I'm not willing to pay such a high price to keep working with him."

Rodriguez shrugged his shoulders in resignation. "I understand. This is a violent country and people are getting killed. They make the rules. I'm just trying to make the best out of a bad situation. Sure, I'm making a profit, but I believe in helping those who help me. We can all live better over here by cooperating with each other."

"At first, I believed in that and I cooperated. You did a great job sharing the wealth. It looks good on the surface, but innocent people suffer. The Vietnamese are turning themselves into whores fighting for American dollars, and we're letting them do it."

"Anyone who lives in a sewer wants a better life. I don't blame them. They deserve more than they've got. Maybe, the war will settle things."

"I don't know," Hardy sighed. "I'm almost out of it, and I don't want to do any more damage while I'm still here. I've already hurt someone in Da Nang. I don't want to do it again."

Rodriguez regarded him with interest. "I didn't know."

"It's a long story, and I can't go into it. It's just over. I'm done running errands, and I'm out of the business. I appreciate all you've done, Sgt. Rodriguez. I hope you don't have any hard feelings."

When Hardy extended his hand, Rodriguez accepted it.

"No hard feelings, Lieutenant," the supply sergeant said. "I appreciate how you feel. Just remember, I'm still here to help. If you ever need anything just look me up."

"Thanks," Hardy replied. "I hope I won't need any more favors." He left the supply room with a wave of acknowledgment.

Mike had limited his contact with Jefferson since the *Paris Hotel* incident. When they had discussed their weekend activities in Da Nang, Mike didn't mention his experience with the Vietnamese girl. Jefferson asked about her, but he avoided discussing the encounter. It seemed easier to minimize the incident, rather than bringing the painful details to the surface. Unable to share his anguish about the occurrence with anyone except Al, he chose not to discuss the subject. Jefferson took note his friend's reticence but avoided asking too many questions. They parted company after Mike thanked him for a great weekend.

Still considering Jefferson a friend, Mike had difficulty justifying a break with him. After all, Jefferson had done nothing wrong to damage their relationship. On the other hand, Jefferson supported a system from which Mike needed to escape. Unable to continue his current level of involvement with the *Junk Man*, he hoped they could still remain friends. In spite of everything, Mike still admired the Texan's unique style.

Mike met Jefferson at the club shortly after his return from Sydney. He found him with Mary sitting on his lap.

"Hi, Mike. It's good to see you. How was Australia?"

"Great."

Mike told him all about the sights of Sydney and the Snowy Mountains' ski trip. He also revealed his romantic interest in Melissa, along with his eagerness to receive her first letter.

"Fantastic. I always thought it would be great to meet an Aussie girl. I love free-spirited women."

Mary poked him in the ribs. "You no meet other women. I give you everything free."

Jefferson squeezed her waist. "Mary, no one could give me what you do—not for a thousand dollars."

This seemed to placate her. "Good. I come see you tonight—no charge."

Jefferson kissed her on the neck. "I look forward to it. Now, go back to work. I need to talk to Mike."

"Talk, talk, talk. GI all talk, no action." Playfully pulling his mustache, she pranced off.

Mike took a moment to appreciate the view as she wiggled away. "I never get tired of watching her move," he confessed.

Jefferson leaned over to him. "She knows you're

watching. That's why she puts on her act. She wouldn't enjoy herself as much if she didn't have an audience."

"Well, I'm a loyal fan." Mike took a long drink of beer.

"I'm going back to Da Nang next weekend," Jefferson announced. "I'm taking some stuff to Dave Ballard. We could spend the night with Kim. Do you want to go?"

Mike hesitated. "I can't. I've got duty. I've been away so much I need to give the other guys a break."

"Too bad, Kim will be disappointed."

"Yeah, me, too. You'll just have to fill in for me. I know you can do double-duty in a pinch."

"True, true, but she's a very demanding woman. I won't be able to walk for a week."

"What we do for love. Give her my best."

"Okay, but it won't be the same without you. I'll tell her you'll try to come next time."

Mike offered a vague response. "We'll see."

Jefferson changed the subject. "Did you get an invitation to Lieutenant Colonel Hollins' German Fest?"

"Yeah, he invited all the officers in the company. He's calling it a late 4th of July celebration, an early October Fest, and a farewell to Chu Lai. He and Al are leaving about the same time."

"I got an invitation, too. I hear the guy is a real nut about Germany. He spent some time over there and can't wait to get back. I think I'll go for laughs. I could show up dressed as Pancho Villa."

"That would be appropriate. Maybe, you could bring Mimi Van Horn dressed as Lady Godiva?"

Jefferson slapped him on the back. "That's an idea. I'll have to check her schedule."

Mike had to admit that Jefferson possessed great energy and wit. The *Junk Man* seemed determined to preserve their friendship.

LtCol. Hollins pulled out all the stops preparing for his German Fest. The club had set up tables and chairs outside battalion headquarters. Hollins had hung banners on his hooch advertising:

OKTOBERFEST 1971

Authentic German beer steins occupied prominent positions on all the tables. A buffet table offered a variety of sausages, sauerkraut, and hot potato salad. The battalion commander even had bottles of genuine German beer available for the guests to sample. Out of necessity, most of the beer consisted of the less exotic American variety. Recordings of polkas and *Oom-pah* music rounded out the atmosphere. Hollins greeted all his guests dressed in lederhosen.

Decked out for the occasion, Mike arrived at the festival with Al, Wiley, and Lance. Although none of them owned German costumes, they'd done their best to improvise. Al suggested that they wear shorts with army-issued socks pulled up to their knees. Lance contributed red ribbon for garters. They made suspenders out of bright cloth and elastic. Mike wore his ski hat from Australia as the crowning touch. The result made them look like rejects from vaudeville. Undaunted, Al expressed his satisfaction with the costumes.

Over fifty people attended the fest. Many of the officers came from the battalion, while others guests arrived from the hospital and smaller units within the compound. The dozen or so nurses at the party took turns dancing with the men. It didn't take long for the atmosphere to turn loud and raucous. Al appeared to enjoy himself more than at any time since Bangkok. Jefferson arrived smoking a cigar and wearing a cowboy hat. He claimed the party needed an infusion of western culture. When he zeroed in on several nurses in his acquaintance, they gave him a warm greeting.

LtCol. Hollins celebrated like a man in his glory. Mike had never seen him operate in an informal setting. The elated man danced and drank with relish. As his last hurrah in Chu Lai, he looked determined to make this party a memorable event. Several hours into the German Fest, he quieted everyone down so he could make a speech. Thanking his guests for their support, he encouraged them to continue partying after a short ceremony. He called Al forward to receive special recognition.

"Lieutenant Miller has done an outstanding job as the Commander of the 73d Transportation Company. He had a difficult job pulling the company together at first, but he now leaves behind an outstanding unit. His convoys have experienced delays and an enemy attack, but they always got the job done. Lieutenant Miller will be hard to replace, but we'll do our best to find someone. In the meantime, I'm pleased to announce Lieutenant Miller will be awarded the Bronze Star Medal for meritorious service. I am proud to have had him as a member of this battalion."

After they shook hands, Al said a few words. "Thanks. It's been a real experience. I need to share the credit with my staff. You might have noticed the three clowns who arrived with me tonight. I know they look strange, but they're a mean bunch of road monsters. They did the job, so I could get the glory—my special thanks to them. Everyone here is invited to visit me back in the States. I'll buy the beer."

An inebriated voice called out from the crowd. "Where do you live?"

"Shit," Al replied. "If I told you, I'd have to move."

When Al rejoined the party, Hollins started a beer drinking song. Mike regarded Al with a degree of sadness. He'd miss him more than anyone else in Chu Lai. Serving as his mentor, Al had also functioned as a significant source of moral strength. The big man helped him pick up the pieces every time he stumbled. Al Miller would never fully understand his impact on Mike Hardy's life.

Later in the evening, LtCol Hollins walked over to put a big arm around Mike.

"Are you having a good time?"

"Yes sir, it's a great party."

"Good. I'm glad you're enjoying yourself. You've come a long way since our last chat together."

Mike vividly remembered that meeting and the battalion commander's words of encouragement. "Yes, sir, I have."

" Lieutenant Miller tells me you're an outstanding officer. I'm sorry to hear you're leaving the army."

"I have less than two months left. I need to return to college to finish my degree. I think I'd like to teach some day."

"Sounds like a good plan. I just hate to see the army lose good officers. You would do well if you decided to stay in. I think you're ready for command. In fact, I'd appoint you the acting company commander if you had more time left over here."

Surprised, Mike felt flattered. "Thank you, that means a lot, but I've already made my decision. I need to finish college before taking off in other directions. I appreciate your confidence in me."

"I knew you'd do well. Good luck and thanks for taking care of the convoys." After shaking Mike's hand, he left to join his guests.

Full of high spirits and beer, the truck company officers left the party after midnight. Mike felt remarkably sober for someone who'd engaged in drinking for the last five hours. Al sang off-key all the way home. The German Fest had turned into a huge success. Al had received well-deserved recognition, while Mike had received unexpected praise from the battalion commander. Although he'd miss Al and Chu Lai, Mike had charted a direct course to New England. Lt. Mike Hardy would not waiver from his plans to return to the sanity of the college campus.

CHAPTER 32
Goodbye Al

The days passed in a blur of motion. Mike felt overwhelmed by a myriad of details to complete before going home. Having finished college registration by mail, he needed to arrange payment for his tuition. The army had also inundated him with paperwork to begin out-processing. On top of all that, he still had regular duties to perform and truck convoys to command. Beginning to feel more restless with each passing day, he experienced increased concern about his mortality. He remembered a remark by Sgt. Hayes, "You think more about dying the closer you get to going home." Hayes had nailed it on the head. Mike felt more vulnerable than ever.

Hardy's relationship with Mama San had cooled during the past months. Due to his recent indiscretions, he felt guilty in her company. He invented excuses to leave the hooch whenever she arrived to clean. Unable to face her questioning eyes, he lacked the courage to explain his feelings. He knew his detachment caused her distress, but she continued to leave gifts. Whenever he took the time to notice, she offered a smile of encouragement. In addition to his feelings of guilt, Mike attributed this change in attitude to his preoccupation with leaving Vietnam. Now, he decided to alter all that.

Returning to his hooch one day after a run to Quang Ngai, he found Mama San sitting on the floor.

When she looked up at him, he smiled down to her. "Mama San, I haven't been very good to you lately. I'm sorry."

She didn't understand all his words, but Hardy knew she understood his apology. Reaching into his pocket, he brought out a thin, gold bracelet. He attached it to her slender wrist. After touching it lovingly, she threw her arms around his neck. She had accepted his apology.

Mike had no intention of resuming their physical relationship. It seemed more prudent to apologize without initiating personal contact. That was the plan, but he lingered too long in her arms. After she unbuttoned his fatigue shirt, he submitted to her touch. Moving behind him, she began to massage his neck and shoulders. The sensations generated by her hands created exquisite pleasure. The overall effect stimulated and relaxed him at the same time. Finishing with his upper torso, she removed his pants. When he stretched out on his bunk, she went to work on his lower extremities.

As soon as she finished the massage, he made room for her on the bed. Watching her remove her clothing, Mike stared longingly at her ample breasts. He had missed the comfort of her body. During the love-making that followed, they shared a mutual need for each other.

Mama San lingered beside him long after the fire had subsided. Touching her gently, he stroked her silky hair. "I wish I had done more for you. After I leave, I'll never know if you're safe or alive."

Pressing herself tightly against him, she seemed content to let him do all the talking.

"Okay, I won't get emotional. I can't control the future, but I'll never forget you, Mama San."

Reaching between his legs, she stroked him back to life. She seemed determined to cling to the present for as long as possible. They made love with the sadness of impending loss. Mama San remained with him until she had to leave.

Hardy still made runs to Duc Pho on a regular basis. He continued to command the convoys from the rear of the 'new and improved' *Bloody Mama*. Sgt. Roche had developed into an entertaining traveling companion. He loved to tell stories about life on the Mississippi. Mike pictured him as a young Huck Finn, building rafts, and fishing with his friends.

"Once you get the Mississippi mud between your toes, you never get it out." Roche loved to share quotes from his daddy, along with a unique brand of homespun wit. Mark Twain would have been proud.

Roche made some significant changes in the *Bloody Mama* operation. His biggest adjustment occurred by placing the gun truck in the middle of the convoy. "If Charlie starts shootin', I want to be in the middle of the action and not playin' catch-up from the rear."

He also rotated driving responsibilities to ensure someone

stood on watch at all times. He didn't want any surprise attacks. "It's better to use your eyes, than lose your ass."

Hardy appreciated this extra attention to security. Although fond of his posterior, he didn't want to sustain damage to any other part of his body. If at all possible, he planned on leaving Vietnam in one piece. The prospect of going home in four weeks prompted him to exercise extreme caution on the road.

Hardy had learned to respect Sgt. Roche's instincts. Roche seemed to have a sixth sense when it came to detecting danger. With uncanny perception, he once spotted an unusual group of civilians outside of Quang Ngai. Immediately, he put everyone on alert. Hardy waited nervously as they closed the distance between the villagers. When the civilians began to throw stones at the trucks, Roche's intuition had proven accurate. Although the encounter didn't involve guns, the protesters displayed hostile intent. American convoys had worn out their welcome in this part of the country.

Lately, Roche appeared more restless than usual. "It don't feel right. The gooks seem real edgy when we pass through their villages. It's not like they're afraid of us. They look like they're waitin' for us to blow-up. I don't like it."

"I know what you mean." Suddenly something dawned on Hardy. Earlier in the day, he recalled seeing children running away from the convoy. In the past, the kids would stand by the roadside begging for handouts. "I wonder if they know something we don't?"

"I don't know," Roche replied. "I don't like it at all. We'd better stay on our toes."

Hardy and Roche held a meeting with all of the drivers. Hardy reminded them of the past attack on the convoy and the need to stay alert. Roche told them to look for unusual signs: empty rice fields, suspicious groups of civilians, empty villages, or deserted areas usually full of activity. Barking dogs or running villagers could also indicate VC movements. After the incident with Tex, they already knew to watch for little old men carrying baskets. A long blast on a truck horn would signal potential danger.

It didn't take long for the readiness of the convoy to face a major test. Intelligence reports warned of increased enemy activity in the Chu Lai area and in the south. Saigon already stood at a high state of alert. The VC had taken bolder steps to demoralize the South Vietnamese government. Daylight attacks on official buildings and highly protected areas had become more commonplace. The enemy no longer seemed content to just rule the night. Their message left no doubt: *We can attack you anywhere, at anytime.* The VC wanted to appear invincible to the world.

Hardy dreaded facing this new offensive. He had hoped to leave the country without seeing any additional action. Focused on going home, it took real effort to concentrate on the tasks at hand. He worked hard to keep these concerns to himself, but Sgt. Roche sensed his distraction.

"Don't worry, Lieutenant. I know you're real short, but we'll get you home safe and sound."

"I'm not worried. The VC need to worry if they tangle with *Bloody Mama*."

Roche accepted Hardy's forced bravado. "You're right!" he laughed. "*Bloody Mama* is ready to kick some ass!"

"Don't get me wrong. I hope we don't have to fight. Maybe, *Mama's* new paint job will scare them away."

Roche slapped Hardy on the back and laughed."Don't worry. You just keep your head down, and we'll do the rest. I won't let Charlie put a wrinkle in your uniform."

"Thanks," Hardy replied. "If anything happens, I'll be in it with you. I'll do what's necessary."

"I know that. I just like to see you squirm."

Hardy pretended to take a swing at him, but Roche ducked neatly. He'd started to take a liking to Burt Roche.

The convoy assembled in the staging area in the early morning. The air felt heavy and damp. Now that Vietnam had entered the rainy season, typhoons posed an added threat. Rain hadn't yet started to fall, but the clouds couldn't hold onto their moisture much longer. With visibility already poor, rainfall would do more to obscure their vision. Watching Sgt. Roche pace with restless energy, Hardy's anxiety increased. Mike had never felt so uneasy about going on the road.

After the convoy passed through the gates of Chu Lai, rain began to drench the trucks. In spite of the deluge, *Basher* tested the mini-gun on the sand dunes as he drove by. Completing the exercise, he gave a 'thumbs-up' that everything worked well. The speed of the convoy slowed as a result of the bad weather. The trucks seemed to move at a snail's pace. Roche and Hardy took turns on watch. During his watch, Hardy tried to stay focused on the terrain, but rain blurred his vision. Finding it impossible to stay dry, he attempted to clear his eyes with a towel. It didn't take long for the rain to saturate the towel.

Sgt. Roche had covered the radio with a plastic sheet. Hardy had to crawl under it to call in the checkpoints. Although he appreciated the temporary respite from the deluge, he didn't linger by the radio. He wanted to be on his feet if the VC attacked. He hoped the radio would stay dry and operational. They couldn't afford to lose contact with the command post.

The heavy trucks passed by rice paddies that looked mostly deserted. Hardy attributed this to the heavy rain. The same held true of the small villages. Normally bustling with activity, today they appeared empty. Refusing to accept these observations as bad omens, Mike figured the rain must have forced everyone inside. Later, he recalled that the rain never stopped farmers from working in the rice fields. Gulping back his distress, he glanced nervously at Sgt. Roche. Roche's face looked rigid with tension.

The attack began with the firing of a command-detonated mine. It blew the front tires off one of the lead trucks leaving it crippled on the highway. Hearing the explosion, Hardy immediately called the MP jeep for a situation report.

The reply came shouted over the radio. "Mama, this is Point Man! We have one reefer disabled and partially blocking the road. The driver is not seriously hurt, over."

"Roger, Point Man. Push it out of the way and keep the convoy moving. Do you copy, over?"

"Roger, Mama. We'll get right on it!"

Hardy waited impatiently for the convoy to start moving. The minutes ticked by with no additional fire from the enemy. It didn't take a military tactician to understand that a halted convoy made a juicy target. Mike held his breath hoping that no more VC fire would rain on the trucks. Unfortunately, the enemy didn't cooperate.

Several minutes after the initial explosion, small arms fire erupted from the old church ruins. The convoy had passed the ruins hundreds of times in the past without giving them much notice. Today, the VC had set up an ambush inside the consecrated grounds.

Hardy called back to the MPs. "Point Man, get these vehicles moving! We'll be cut to pieces, if we don't get out of here. Mama will give you cover—Go, Go!"

"Roger, Mama. We're clear and moving."

Minutes later the trucks began to roll.

Sgt. Roche didn't wait for Hardy's command to begin firing. He knew what to do. He had *Basher* point the mini-gun at the church and open fire. The entire gun truck vibrated as hundreds of rounds pounded into the ruins in a matter of seconds. Moving to the fifty-caliber machine gun, Roche squeezed the butterfly trigger. The noise from both guns sounded deafening.

Hardy remained on the radio to maintain contact with the command post. "HQ, this is Mama. We're under attack! Enemy in old church ruins."

Hardy gave them the coordinates and waited for a response.

"Roger, Mama. I read you. There is no air support available due to bad weather. The best I can do is a fire mission. I think we can reach you. Give me the coordinates again, over."

Hardy recited the map coordinates one more time and waited.

The heavy fire from the mini-gun had silenced the VC attack, but Roche kept up the pressure. The convoy trucks drove past them as the guns continued to roar. Hardy held his hands over his communication helmet to block out the noise. The command post called back.

"Mama, we've got you locked on. Fire mission on the way—keep your heads down!"

Seconds later, artillery shells screamed into the old church and exploded. No one could have survived the devastation that followed. The barrage lasted for five minutes and suddenly—quiet. When the shelling ended nothing remained of the old church. Hardy called the command post to report the success of the mission, and to request a tow truck for the disabled reefer. After the *Bloody Mama* crew shared a cheer of celebration, they left to rejoin the convoy.

The convoy had sustained little damage thanks to the fast reaction of the mini-gun. Due to the devastating fire, the VC had little opportunity to cause much destruction. Several trucks sported bullet holes, but no one had suffered serious injury. The driver of the unlucky reefer survived with only a few bumps and bruises.

Sgt. Roche expressed his satisfaction with the outcome. "Those VC sure made *Bloody Mama* mad. They'll think twice before they tangle with her again."

"You're right. I think the mini-gun cleaned them out before the artillery attack began," Mike agreed.

After returning to Chu Lai, Al congratulated the truck crews on their response to the ambush. He wanted to leave Vietnam without any more injuries or deaths on his conscience.

Later, Al spoke with Hardy in his hooch. "You guys did real good today, Grunt."

Mike watched him as he packed up his gear. "Thanks. Roche and the mini-gun made the difference. Do you need any help, Al?"

"Yeah, I do. I need someone big and strong to go to the refrigerator and return with two cold beers. Do you think you can handle that?"

"Sure," Mike replied.

He left on his journey to the refrigerator. Returning with the beer, he hesitated before throwing one across the room in Al's direction. Al had to leap into the air to seize it in a huge paw.

"Nice catch!" Mike said. "Too bad we never had a football team. You promised I could play when I first got here."

"Oh, well—tough shit! I always lie to cherry lieutenants especially when they're dumb grunts!"

Foam exploded from the opening when Al popped the beer can top. Cursing, he inhaled the contents in a single motion. Beer dripped from his chin as he lowered the can. He wiped his mouth with his sleeve. "There, that was good. Next time pass it gently out of respect for your departing commanding officer."

"Next time, I will," Mike said. "I did owe you that one."

"Okay, we'll call things even. I guess I need to give you some advice. Old soldiers are supposed to share their wisdom with the young. What do you need to know?"

"How can you drink a whole beer in one gulp?"

He patted Mike on the shoulder. "Years of hard work and dedication, young man. You, too, can reach my heights of glory if you set your mind to it."

"Thanks, I'll work on it."

"Do me a favor, Grunt. Look after my dog while you're still here. He ain't much, but he deserves good care."

"Sure, I will. Before I leave, I'll make sure he's left in good hands," Mike promised.

"Thanks." Al grabbed Mike's hand. "You're a good man, Hardy. It's been a pleasure to know you."

"You, too," Mike said. "I couldn't have had a better

friend over here." He wanted to hug the big man but let the notion pass.

"Yeah, well...be safe and look me up when you get home. My wife and I would love to have you over for dinner," Al said.

"Great, I'll show her the photo of you and Mimi Van Horn."

"Hey, friends are supposed to keep secrets." He slapped Mike on the stomach. "Call me when you get home, Grunt."

They took Al to the club that night. Wiley, Lance, and Mike gave him a plaque engraved with 'Our Thanks to a Great Commander.' Mike presented him with a black baseball cap embroidered with the words *Bloody Mama* in red letters. Offering profuse thanks to the assembled crowd, Al picked up the tab for all the beer. Mary contributed to the celebration by giving him a farewell kiss. She even tolerated Al patting her bottom.

At the end of the party, Al's friends were forced to carry him back to his hooch. The three lieutenants had to endure his off-key singing all the way back to Sand Hill. Before escaping from Al's clutches, each man received an emotional farewell hug. Mike searched for a profound statement of gratitude, but could only manage a weak, "Thanks."

After hugging Mike one last time, Al turned, and wobbled toward his hooch singing a tortured version of, "We've got to get out of this place."

Al left for home the next morning. No words could express Mike's sense of loss over his departure. They shook hands and said 'Goodbye' one last time. After that, Al Miller disappeared into the sunset. The big man had left an indelible mark on Hardy's life. Al had proven himself a loyal friend by giving Mike the strength to deal with adversity. Grateful for Al's friendship, Mike made himself a promise to call the Miller residence after he returned to the States.

Time no longer hovered over his head like an enemy threat. As the hours rushed by, the number of days remaining in Hardy's tour of duty paled in comparison to the months he'd already served. Fatigue felt like less of a burden and the rigors of the road seemed easier to bear. Lately, VC activity had diminished to the point that the convoys completed each mission with relative ease. Excitement and anticipation increased with the completion of each trip. He wanted to shout with joy: THREE DAYS AND A WAKE-UP! Forget Hank the bartender's warning —I'm going home!

Mike thought about Joe Tice's reluctance to leave Chu Lai. Unable to relate to those feelings, he no longer craved the excitement of Vietnam. No fantasies remained unfulfilled. No illusions about the 'electric environment' plagued his curiosity. Experiencing the reality of the myth had left him tainted with guilt. Now, he only wanted to survive the turmoil. Although he harbored no regrets about leaving, regret would follow him home. Bad memories wouldn't stay buried in Vietnam. He had years to consider all the choices and mistakes he'd made, but that would come later. At this point, he concentrated on returning to the security of his former life as a civilian.

A new company commander and a new lieutenant arrived within a day of each other. Capt. Jack Pollard reported as Al's replacement. New in country, he wore the insignia of a transportation officer. The staff of the Da Nang Support Command considered him the obvious choice to take charge of the company. 2Lt. Aaron Wise also had a transportation background. They both took-up residence in the officer's hooch with Wiley and Lance.

Capt. Pollard didn't have Al's out-going manner. Looking intense, he spoke in short, clipped sentences. He had arrived to fight a war and lead a company of men on combat missions. The new company commander seemed to expect recognition as the ultimate soldier. It appeared to Mike that Pollard was convinced of his destiny to pin on the star of a general officer. Hardy thought the new CO would better serve the truck company by developing a sense of humor. Since he didn't have much time left in the unit, Mike chose to ignore the posturing of the new leader.

Lt. Wise, on the other hand, had no great career aspirations. Coming from Northern New Jersey, he resented the assignment in Vietnam. ROTC had helped pay his college bills, but he didn't like paying back his debt of obligatory military service. When Wise acted nervous and jumpy, Lance volunteered to take him under his wing. Once Lance took charge of his welfare, the newcomer appeared to calm down considerably.

Lance had matured during the past six months. Considering the amount of personal pain he had endured, the transformation appeared remarkable. He now spoke and moved with confidence. Lance assumed the role of a seasoned veteran and a trusted leader. Hardy wondered if he had changed just as visibly. He knew that he had developed new perspectives and self-confidence. Experience had taught him some difficult lessons, but he had no way of judging the extent of his own evolution.

Hardy spent his last two days packing and saying goodbye. Relieved from road duty to complete out-processing, he missed the camaraderie of the *Bloody Mama* crew. He still ate breakfast with them. They spoke of old times and past adventures on the road. Mike arranged for someone to take a photograph of the crew in front of *Bloody Mama*. He promised Burt Roche that he'd display it as one of his significant memories.

Mama San remained quiet during his last day with the truck company. She touched him often as he cleaned out his hooch. Setting aside a special bag for her to take home, he filled it with toiletries, towels, paper, pens, clothing and anything else he didn't need. He also gave her an envelope with some money to share with her son.

That left only one more thing to do. "Thank you, Mama San. I hope you survive all this. I promise to never forget you."

Clinging to him, she sobbed against his chest. He held her in silence for a long while.

"Come on, I'll drive you to the gate," he offered.

Mike drove her to the front gate after helping her load

her bag in the jeep. Before separating, she gave him a final hug. Moving away from the jeep, she turned around one last time to wave goodbye before disappearing inside the MP station. Suppressing a surge of emotion, Mike watched as another influential human being walked out of his life.

They held a big farewell party for him at the club that night. Jefferson, Wiley, and Lance had conspired to make it a memorable event. It was. They showered Mike with food and drink. The bar girls danced and snuggled against him. Wiley and Lance gave him an engraved plaque and a beer mug. Jefferson, true to form, presented him with a solid gold pen. Thanking them all, Mike kissed the bar girls good-bye. Mary's kiss proved the most passionate. It left him breathless. Laughing, Jefferson slapped him on the back.

Leaving the club after midnight in great spirits, they headed back to the jeep. It was gone. The jeep was gone! Prior to entering the club, Mike had wrapped a chain around the steering wheel and locked it to the floor. Someone had cut the chain and driven the jeep away.

Mike panicked. "Holy Shit, I'm signed for it! I'm supposed to go home tomorrow. They could hold me back for an investigation."

Desperate, he turned to Wiley and Lance. "This isn't a joke, is it?"

"No, I swear," Wiley said. "We might try to pull some weird shit but nothing like this."

"Fuck, what am I supposed to do? We'll never find it. I can't report it stolen to the MPs."

"There's only one thing to do. You've got to go see Sergeant Rodriguez," Wiley suggested.

Mike considered his options. "You're right," he conceded.

Hating the thought of asking Rodriguez for help, he could see no other alternative. After hitching a ride back to the company, Hardy went off in search of the supply sergeant. He found Rodriguez still awake in his quarters next to the supply room.

"Hey Lieutenant, I hear that you're going home tomorrow. It must feel great to be leaving."

"Not so great," Hardy replied. He explained his dilemma and the possible consequences.

"Tough luck, you're right. If you report it stolen, there will be an investigation. I think I might be able to figure something out."

Mike sighed with relief. "Thanks, Sergeant Rodriguez. I know you're the only one to help me out of this mess."

"I'll try," he said. "Remember, I told you that we have to help each other. Cooperation is the best way to stay out of trouble."

"I know. I tried, but things got out of hand."

"Don't worry about it. Go to your hooch and get some sleep. I'll take care of everything and you'll go home tomorrow."

After thanking him, Hardy trotted up the hill to his hooch. He had no idea what remedy Sgt. Rodriguez had in mind, but he knew the supply sergeant could perform miracles. Attempting to sleep, he couldn't shake off his anxiety about the stolen jeep. Tossing restlessly, he conjured up the faces of Richard Chang, Tex, Bobby Waters, Ames and others. They had suffered losses much worse than a stolen jeep. In spite of everything, he had ended up as one of the lucky ones.

Sgt. Rodriguez knocked on his door at daybreak. He invited Hardy to meet him outside. Jumping out of his bunk, Mike rushed from the hooch. A brand new jeep greeted him. The registration numbers matched those of the stolen jeep, but this one looked like a much newer model.

Rodriguez grinned with satisfaction. "It took me a while last night, but I found it. I know it looks a little different, but we cleaned it up for you."

Hardy reacted with stunned excitement. "It looks great. How can I ever thank you?"

"No problem. I told you before that I always take care of my people. I'm glad it worked out."

Mike shook his hand with gratitude. "I'm grateful. I owe you a lot."

"Don't mention it. Have a safe trip back to the States." Rodriguez headed back to his supply room.

Hardy watched him leave with gratitude. Although Rodriguez had actively dealt in the black market corruption he'd tried to avoid, the man had been unselfish in his dealings with him. Not only had the supply sergeant mastered how to manipulate the system, he had developed considerable skill in human relations. Rodriguez had refined the art of getting what he wanted without creating resentment or making enemies. Mike had learned much from his association with the sergeant and Rodriguez had earned his respect. In spite of that respect, he hoped to use those lessons for more reputable endeavors in the future.

When Mike said goodbye to Lance, the AG officer promised to write once he developed his plans in more detail. Wiley offered to drive him to the helicopter pad. They loaded his duffel bag in the new jeep. Mike took one last look at his hooch before saying farewell to Sand Hill. After driving down the dusty hill, they passed through the company area. At that moment, Lt. Mike Hardy said goodbye to the 73d Transportation Company.

While Wiley remained silent during the short ride, Mike used the time to take in all the familiar sights. Since this area had served as his home for over ten months, he wanted these last impressions to last a lifetime. Beginning to feel nostalgic about leaving, he thought about the great parties at the club. He remembered the times spent at the staging area in the early mornings. In the beginning, he had so much to learn. Now, he would leave the learning to others.

The helicopter stood ready for departure when they arrived at the landing pad. Travel plans called for Mike to fly to Da Nang on the first leg of his journey, and then to Cam Ranh Bay for the flight to the States. The army would separate him from active duty at Ft. Lewis,

Washington. If all went as scheduled, he could return home as a civilian in four days. The thought of these fast-moving events filled him with excitement.

"Take care of yourself, Mike."

"I will, Wiley. You take care, too. You're going home in a few weeks."

"Yeah, I can hardly wait. I still don't know how I let you beat me out of this dump."

"It's just dumb luck. The army screwed-up by putting me in a truck company. They're just trying to correct the mistake by sending me home early."

"You're a pretty good trucker—for a grunt. You can ride with me on convoy anytime."

"Thanks. You were the first person who welcomed me into the company. I'll never forget that. Adams treated me like shit."

"He never realized what a great guy you really are, not to mention a brave defender of naked ladies in distress. Not many men would jump on stage to protect a dancing girl."

"I just did it to help Al. Besides, you jumped up, too."

"Not on purpose. I was just afraid to be left alone."

The helicopter blades began to rotate. The time had come to leave.

"Goodbye, Wiley. Stop by for a beer when you get back."

"Sure, I will. Try to stay out of trouble."

Grabbing his duffel bag, Mike shook Wiley's hand.

Turning around, he waved one last time before climbing aboard the chopper. Smiling, Wiley waved back. The helicopter lifted slowly off the ground before gaining altitude. Chu Lai disappeared in the distance.

Cam Ranh Bay teemed with activity when Mike arrived. It served as a major dispatch point for GIs returning to the States, and for fallen warriors resting in metal boxes. It also gave the army one last opportunity to identify drug users. Every departing GI was screened for drug residue in his urine, along with an admonition not to carry drugs home in his baggage. Stiff jail terms waited for those who dared defy the warning. Under the watchful eyes of MPs, the staff herded home-bound troops into a latrine to collect urine samples. Hardy had heard stories about GIs borrowing urine from friends to avoid detection. The cagy culprits would tape IV bags under their armpits full of the borrowed fluid. At the appropriate time, they'd pull a plastic tube out of their pants to fill the bottle. This subterfuge served as a last-ditch attempt to beat the system.

Hardy, dutifully, completed all the out-processing requirements while waiting for his turn to depart. He spent hours filling out forms and receiving security briefings. The briefing officers warned him not to divulge any secrets about the war after he returned to the States. To do so, would put the lives of fighting men in mortal danger. Mike signed a paper promising to keep his mouth shut before re-checking his baggage thoroughly for contraband. He didn't want to risk any delays at customs.

Hardy received his flight assignment twenty-four hours after arriving at Cam Ranh Bay. He and his fellow passengers passed through customs in the early morning hours before landing in a holding area for six hours. Stranded on a wooden bench, Mike attempted to sleep with his head against the wall. As the minutes ticked by with sluggish precision, it reminded him of the long wait at Travis, Air Force Base. This time, his tedium was punctuated by the anticipation of going home. Following this interminable wait, an airplane would carry him home —and carry him home alive.

The detainees waited until noon before a military official escorted them to their aircraft. The sun burned high overhead as intense heat radiated from the tarmac. Everything smelled the same—smoke, exhaust, frying food, and decay. The heat and odors had an all too familiar impact on his senses. Mike recognized the passenger plane as a Pan Am 707. It looked similar to the one that had carried him from Travis. After climbing the long stairway to the passenger door, a smiling stewardess greeted him. Patting his shoulder, she acted pleased to see him. Taking a seat by a window, he took one last look at the Vietnamese outside the fences. Life continued on the streets as usual and everything looked normal. Based on this pretense of normality, an uninformed bystander would never know a war waged within and outside the city limits.

Great excitement built among the passengers as the plane began to taxi toward the runway. Although exhausted by the rigors of out-processing and the long hours of waiting, the escapees charged the air with anticipation. The low murmur of voices swelled to a deafening roar of celebration as the 707 began taking-off. When the aircraft freed itself from the runway, a great cheer erupted from the restless horde. After waiting hours and months for this moment, they had survived the war in Vietnam to return to the safety of their former lives.

Mike had entered an alien environment. The campus of the New England college seemed foreign to him. Students walked about in a daze between classes. They moved without drive or energy. After close examination, he concluded that most of these professed scholars exerted just enough motivation to attend a few classes and study only when necessary. At this point in their development, the undergraduates lived to escape the responsibilities of the adult world. Unraveling the mysteries of the opposite sex and testing the limits of their alcohol intake served as the chief sources of their inspiration. Mike found it difficult to believe that he had once existed among them.

Three days earlier, he had rushed to the campus after leaving Vietnam. Although classes had already started, the college administration permitted him to register late. He must have appeared a curious figure as he wandered among the long-haired students. Sporting short hair and a dark suntan, he drew stares from his peers. Unlike his counterparts, the cool September air had forced him to wear warmer clothing. He had yet to make the climatic adjustment to New England after living in the tropical heat of Vietnam. Occasionally, someone would question him about his appearance. Truthful most of the time, he invented different scenarios when it suited his purposes. Most returning Vietnam veterans didn't enjoy hero status among their classmates. Radicals considered them lackeys who had blindly done the bidding of their country. The current climate made it more fashionable to protest the war rather than support US involvement in the conflict. Mike avoided political discussions whenever possible.

He scanned the Student Union bulletin board to catch up on the campus news. A protest group had scheduled an anti-war rally on Saturday, followed by a march through the city. One of the Black Panthers was coming to lecture on racism. A group of students planned to mount a boycott of the dining hall to protest the poor quality of the food. Several fraternities offered open invitations for freshman women to attend weekend parties. He recalled Harry Clay's commentary about virgins sacrificing themselves on the fraternity altar. Upcoming college events included a student poetry reading contest, and a film series on the gay movement. So it went.

Walking away from the notices, he recognized his need to adjust to college culture. Although this required a major change in thinking, he had chosen to return and accept assimilation. He wondered what Al would have said about an anti-war rally. Stifling an outburst of laughter, he tried to visualize Al at a film series on the gay movement. These were, indeed, different times.

Too many memories crowded his brain to relive at the moment. Mike arranged his Vietnam photos in a scrapbook that he kept hidden from his guests. He wrote a letter to

Melissa begging her to come for a visit. Earlier, she had urged him to travel to Melbourne. It seemed impossible to find middle ground for a relationship. If they didn't resolve the quandary soon, he'd jump on an airplane to Australia. He didn't want to lose her.

He wrote to Al once or twice, but they lost contact after a few months. Lance wrote from Chu Lai to report that Capt. Pollard received little support as the company commander. Pushing much too hard, Pollard stood on the brink of driving his troops to mutiny. Mike felt fortunate to have escaped in time.

His tan faded and his hair grew longer. Compelled to succeed as a student, he attacked academia with an energy he didn't think possible. Finding it difficult to forge new friendships, he focused on distancing himself from the past. He still had episodes when he mentally returned to Vietnam, unable to forget the people who had impacted his life. At this moment, with thousands of memories to recall, he could only think of Joe Tice's parting words.

"This is the real world. People struggle to exist and stay alive over here. Vietnam has been the greatest adventure of my life."

Adjusting several textbooks under his arm, Mike walked toward his next class. Ten months in Vietnam had amounted to more than just an adventure. The time he'd spent in-country had tested his character, his friendships, and his courage. Having survived the experience, he now chose to move forward. The 'real world' still lay ahead.

ABOUT THE AUTHOR

Neil Howard was born in Bangor, Maine. After joining the Army and completing Officer Candidate School at Ft. Benning, Georgia, he was commissioned as a 2nd Lieutenant. Howard received a Bronze Star Medal for meritorious service in combat during his tour of duty in Vietnam.

Upon returning from Vietnam he earned his Bachelor of Arts degree from the University of New Hampshire. After earning his Master of Fine Arts degree from Smith College Mr. Howard joined the faculty of Mary Washington College as an Instructor in Dramatic Arts. The next year he founded the Fredericksburg Summer Theater and served as its Producing Director for four years.

Mr. Howard later left Mary Washington College for a position with the US Government and has held assignments in Germany, California, Massachusetts, and Florida. Owing to events arising out of Operation Desert Storm, he accepted a brief assignment in Saudi Arabia.

He now works with the Air Force at Hurlburt Field, Florida.

The Lighthouse Press, LLC, published the author's first two novels, *Student Body* and *Hunter's Prey,* under the imprint, The Lighthouse Press, Inc. Mr. Howard is now working on his fourth novel. In addition to his novels, he has penned fifteen children's stories, three plays, and numerous travel articles for the European *Stars And Stripes*.

Neil Howard resides in Gulf Breeze, Florida.